Alexandra Joel is a former editor of the Australian edition of *Harper's Bazaar* and of *Portfolio*, Australia's first magazine for working women. She has also contributed feature articles, interviews and reviews to many national and metropolitan publications.

Her first novel, the bestselling *The Paris Model*, was published around the world, including in the United States, Canada, Germany and Romania. Alexandra's memoir, *Rosetta: A Scandalous True Story* was optioned for the screen by a major US-owned production company. She is also the author of *Parade: The Story of Fashion in Australia* and *Best Dressed: 200 Years of Fashion in Australia*.

With an honours degree from the University of Sydney and a graduate diploma from the Australian College of Applied Psychology, she has been a practising counsellor and psychotherapist.

Alexandra has two children, lives in Sydney and regularly visits London with her British-born husband.

To connect with Alexandra, visit:

AlexandraJoel.com

 @AlexandraJoelAuthor

 @AlexandraJoelAuthor

The Paris Model

ALEXANDRA JOEL

HarperCollins*Publishers*

HarperCollins*Publishers*
Australia • Brazil • Canada • France • Germany • Holland • India
Italy • Japan • Mexico • New Zealand • Poland • Spain • Sweden
Switzerland • United Kingdom • United States of America

First published in Australia in 2020
This edition published in 2021
by HarperCollins*Publishers* Australia Pty Limited
ABN 36 009 913 517
harpercollins.com.au

A catalogue record for this book is available from
the National Library of Australia.

ISBN 978 1 4607 5815 1 (paperback)
ISBN 978 1 4607 1188 0 (ebook)
ISBN 978 1 4607 8134 0 (audio book)

Cover design by Hazel Lam, HarperCollins Design Studio
Cover image by © Ayal Ardon/Trevillion Images
Author photograph by Juli Balla
Typeset in Bembo Std by Kirby Jones

Printed and bound by CPI Group (UK) Ltd, Croydon, CR0 4YY

To Blair

On ne naît pas femme: on le devient
One is not born a woman, but becomes one

Simone de Beauvoir, *The Second Sex*

PROLOGUE

Sydney, 1 September 1922

If anyone had asked her who she was, the woman would have been unable to tell them. Nor could she have determined whether it was night or day. She existed in another realm, one in which identity had been extinguished and time itself was marked solely by the ebb and flow of relentless, inner waves.

She glimpsed faces stilled by concentration; they meant nothing to her. She was in a jurisdiction of her own. Her mind, her very being, was fixed upon a single resolution. No matter the hour, nor the exquisite agony, she would continue until her child was born — healthy, safe, whole.

At last, her body surrendered its possession. Only then did she experience a sweet release. Happiness was her narcotic; she felt intoxicated with pleasure and relief.

'It's a girl,' a voice said. 'What a pretty little thing.'

Then another voice, more urgent. 'My God, come quickly. I need help!'

That was when the woman raised her head. She saw that she was in a place of soft, tumbling snow and swansdown, for everything was white. It was the colour of the walls, the nurses' uniforms, the doctor's coat, the towels, the linen on the bed. But as she looked about her, this impression changed. Her bleached world had become a pale sky at sunrise, one that was now streaked with red.

The woman heard her baby cry then. Just once, but it was enough. She closed her eyes and whispered, 'Let all be well.' It was her most fervent hope.

BOOK ONE

La Débutante

The Beginner

CHAPTER ONE

Paris, December 1948

Grace Woods danced out of the Paris Metro with a buoyant step and visions of an enticing future whirling through her mind.

'Oh!' she gasped. Having been in Paris for just three days, she still found the icy air a shock — Grace had never felt its knife-like penetration in Australia.

Home signified heat and a pure, brilliant light; lofty cobalt skies; the sharp, sweet smell of eucalypts; the shrill cries of milky cockatoos, vibrant rosellas and rainbow-coloured lorikeets. Here, on wintry avenue Montaigne, everything she gazed upon — the charming townhouses, the bare trees, the boutiques and cafés — was veiled by a pearly luminescence as captivating as it was strange.

Even less familiar was the version of herself Grace spied in the glass of a shop window. As she moved backwards and forwards, her image blurred, then rippled into focus once again. She was satisfied that her dark curls remained swept into their neat chignon, her crimson lipstick was intact and her emerald eyes were clear, but still she felt a faint eddy of concern. Her navy-blue dress, with its long, pointed collar and cinched waist, was the product of a Sydney dressmaker's labours. Would it withstand the scrutiny of a connoisseur?

Drawing closer, Grace considered her appearance once again. Yes, she was certain. The frock bore sufficient resemblance to a Paris original so that with the addition of a new black hat — the azure feather had been added on a whim — it would surely pass as chic. She gave her reflection a happy nod and continued on her way.

Striding along the pavement, Grace passed a restaurant with a stand outside its door displaying succulent Belon oysters arrayed on frosty beds of ice, a florist with bunches of soft-pink anemones in the window, and a small art gallery exhibiting tender pastels of ballerinas. Then, quite suddenly, there before her eyes was an unobtrusive nameplate on a pale grey stone façade. At last she had arrived at her famous destination.

Grace yearned to know what marvels she might find inside. She peered up, blinking in the early morning light, but saw only the carved bust of an ancient goddess set above the entrance, rows of tall mullioned windows and a line of balconies encircled by delicate fronds of curling black wrought iron. Number 30 avenue Montaigne was an edifice that emanated discretion; it gave no secrets away.

Unwilling to wait a moment longer, Grace skipped towards the distinguished, frock-coated gentleman stationed outside the front door. He was a man of perhaps forty-five, with steel-grey hair, an aquiline nose and the dignity of a royal courtier.

'*Bonjour!*' she called out cheerfully. '*Je suis le nouveau mannequin d'Australie.*'

'*Oui?*' This brusque response was accompanied by a single raised eyebrow.

Undaunted by the man's hauteur, Grace snapped open her suede handbag and produced a printed card. 'I have an appointment with Madame Raymonde Zernacker. Could you take me to her, please?'

'Of course, mademoiselle. Follow me.'

Grace was led beneath a scalloped awning, through an archway and into a large room. Then she stopped.

'Is there a problem?' the doorman inquired with a slight frown.

'Not at all. It's just … Oh, monsieur, it's glorious.'

Grace stared with wide-eyed admiration at the crystal chandeliers above her, their arrows of glittering light falling on gilded mirrors and doors glazed with bevelled squares of glass. She took in the lush kentia palms that emerged from brass urns, curtains hanging in lustrous silvery folds, and a group of white-lacquer, medallion-backed Louis XVI chairs of such refined proportions Grace concluded they had surely been designed for the exclusive accommodation of that category of woman who could only be described as *soignée*.

Perhaps most appealing of all were the spectacular arrangements of flowers: an abundance of white roses, hyacinths and lilies of the valley spilled from cut-crystal vases artfully placed on marble-topped tables. The blooms' intoxicating fragrance accompanied Grace long after she had left the enchanting room behind.

She stayed close to the concierge's measured footsteps as he climbed a set of winding stairs then walked down a narrow corridor. When he reached a door painted a delicate grey, he knocked sharply with a white-gloved hand, inclined his head towards Grace and was gone.

'*Entrez.*' It was a woman's voice, firm and, from the sound of it, belonging to someone long accustomed to occupying a position of authority. Grace's heart skipped a beat. For the first time, her self-belief threatened to dissolve. She felt ridiculous, an impossibly foolish impostor with — what had her unhappy husband said? — a head filled with nonsense.

Willing her anxiety away, she told herself not to be absurd. There was too much at stake to succumb to doubt now. Grace straightened her shoulders, opened the door and stepped inside.

The woman who greeted her was impeccable. Dressed in a swirling, calf-length black skirt and fitted burgundy jacket, she walked briskly towards her and extended one manicured hand. 'You are Mademoiselle Grace Dubois, are you not?' Without waiting for a response she continued, 'Everyone in the *maison* calls me Madame Raymonde. I invite you to do the same.'

Grace was then instructed to stay where she was as the woman circled her. She felt acutely aware that madame's enigmatic blue eyes were scrutinising her shape, her hair, the cut of her dress (its modest provenance, Grace now realised, was impossible to hide), her hat with its feather (had it been the right decision after all?), her shoes, her gloves — in fact, every detail of her appearance.

At last, Madame Raymonde spoke. 'Yes, you are tall and slim. Your deportment is commendable and your face — it is certainly striking.' She stood back, regarding Grace from a different angle. 'Naturally, these attributes are essential, although if you did not possess a unique quality we would never have extended our invitation. No, you display a special vitality that makes you different to our French girls. Just the same, I wonder if you have sufficient ...'

'Élan?' asked Grace with a quick laugh. 'Sophistication? Panache? I can't blame you for wondering whether an Australian country girl has what it takes to become a Parisian mannequin,' she said. 'You're probably imagining me in a paddock, rounding up some sheep or out riding on a wild horse. But I promise you, madame, you will find that

I am just as comfortable — and as effective — when I'm modelling a ball gown.'

A wave of the older woman's hand indicated she had heard enough. 'Mademoiselle, what is under discussion is a challenging and difficult role. You must show off the most desirable clothes in the world to its richest, most glamorous and most demanding inhabitants. There are few young women, as lovely and poised as they might be, who can remain undaunted by such a task.'

Grace wondered whether her confidence had appeared excessive.

'Nevertheless,' Madame Raymonde smiled for the first time, 'now that I have had the opportunity to observe you, I am prepared to set aside these reservations.'

She kissed Grace lightly on both cheeks.

'Welcome to the House of Christian Dior,' she said.

CHAPTER TWO

Brookfield, NSW, August 1934

Sunset was Grace's favourite time of day. As she cantered on her chestnut pony, Illyria, across the wide paddocks of her parents' vast Australian property, the sky above looked as if it had been painted gold and red by an angel wielding an enormous brush. What made the experience even better was that her father, with his broad felt hat set firmly on his head and a gleaming rifle slung around his back, rode beside her on his black stallion.

'Tell me about great-grandfather George,' she called out to him, slowing her pony.

'What, again?' her father asked, pulling up his powerful horse so it matched Illyria's pace.

'Please!'

She listened avidly as Alfred Woods related the familiar tale of his intrepid forebear. Due to being a younger son, he'd been obliged to leave his father's flourishing Dorset farmland in England, board a sailing ship and cross the seas to seek his fortune in Australia.

'I'm going adventuring far away one day, just like Grandad,' Grace declared.

'Perhaps you will.' Alfred smiled. 'But I think George missed his home — that's why he named the farm Brookfield. After all, there aren't any bubbling streams or neat little fields here, are there?'

'No, we've got billabongs and a creek and heaps and heaps of wheat!' Grace giggled. She screwed her eyes up, focusing on the heavy yellow crop that grew all the way to the horizon, where the bright blue sky pressed down in an unforgiving line.

'And don't forget the sheep,' Alfred added. Over to the west, where the land was more undulating and the occasional clump of spindly eucalypts dotted the paddocks, grazed thousands of the woolly beasts. 'Speaking of which, I had better stop at the next waterhole. The foreman said there's a ewe we need to keep an eye on.'

'I'll race you,' Grace said with a grin.

With a touch of her heels to Illyria's flanks, the pony surged forward. Grace couldn't think of anything more exciting than galloping over Brookfield's paddocks with the wind streaming past her cheeks and the sound of hooves thudding in her ears.

'Beat you!' she cried triumphantly when they reached the edge of the waterhole. Sliding out of her saddle, she tied her pony to a solitary gum tree.

'So you did,' her father said indulgently. 'Now, just stay here a minute while I see to that sheep. She's due to give birth any day now and, by the look of her, it could be twins.'

Grace lay on her back, listening to the distant sound of birdsong as she inhaled the delicious aroma of fresh grass grown thick and lush after a recent bout of rain. Staring up at the sky, she decided the streaky pink clouds looked like great-grandfather George's sailing ship, before they changed into a shape more like a fairy castle.

She was contemplating ever more fanciful possibilities when she heard her father say sharply, 'Don't move!'

Grace felt something smooth and satiny slither slowly across her bare leg.

'Daddy! It's a —' The word stuck in her throat.

'Yes, it's a snake,' said Alfred, adopting a matter-of-fact tone. 'And you know what to do. Stay quite still until I say you can move.'

Grace fought the urge to jump to her feet, to grasp the deadly thing and fling it far away. She wished she'd worn jodhpurs instead of shorts that day. Her skin prickled as the creature gradually traversed her knee and made its way across her thigh. She knew that if it sank its fangs into her flesh she would die.

From the corner of her eye she glimpsed her father raising his rifle. 'Now, Dad, now?' she whimpered.

'No, child,' Alfred replied steadily. 'You wait until he is clear of you. Just a moment more … Now turn! Quick, Gracie, now!'

As she twisted away, Alfred swooped. He flicked the snake aside with the barrel of his gun, then killed it with a single shot.

Springing to her feet, Grace wrapped her arms around her father.

'You're a brave girl, Gracie.' He kissed the top of her head. 'I'm proud of you. Seeing as you're turning twelve next month —'

'We're all going to the city and I'm having a special tea with Siddy!'

'That's right,' Alfred said with a patient smile. 'It's been ages since you two have seen each other. But right now I have something else in mind.'

'What do you mean, Dad?'

'It's time to start teaching you to shoot. You've just seen how dangerous living out here can be; you need to know how to look after yourself. This is a serious matter, though, so do exactly as I tell you.' He handed Grace his rifle. 'Here, tuck this into your shoulder and support it with your hands like I do.'

Grace had never touched her father's gun before. It was far heavier than she'd imagined, hard and cold.

'Now, close one eye and look through the sight.'

Nervously, Grace focused on the deadly snake she saw lying on the ground.

'Press the trigger.'

Again, the bullet met its mark. But Grace wasn't expecting the rifle to kick back — it felt as if she was struggling to keep a wild, savage creature in her grasp.

'I'll take it now, sweetheart. I can tell you've had enough for one day.' Alfred strapped the gun across his shoulder. 'We had best get back to your mother,' he said, frowning. 'She'll be wondering where on earth we've got to.'

He helped Grace mount Illyria before swinging up onto his own horse. Taking the reins, he said, 'You know how much Mum worries about you, so maybe it's best to keep today's events just between us. All right?'

Grace nodded her head gravely. 'I know how to keep a secret, Dad.'

CHAPTER THREE

As she ambled into the front room the following Sunday afternoon, Grace caught sight of the half-finished jigsaw she'd left on a table. Flinging herself down onto the nearest sofa, she leant forward and began moving around the scattered pieces of the puzzle.

While Grace pondered whether one oddly shaped bit of scalloped blue cardboard fitted into either the sea, or perhaps the sky, she became aware that, outside on the jasmine-draped veranda, her parents were talking.

'It's simply impossible for me to spend as much time with Grace as I'd like, what with my rose garden and my committees.' That was her pretty, fair-haired mother. 'Then there's overseeing the kitchen staff and the maids — it takes a lot to keep such a big homestead running properly.'

'Isn't that why we have Pearl? She's always been very good with the child,' Alfred said mildly.

'Not any longer,' her mother retorted. 'She's become reckless.'

Grace looked up. This was unexpected.

'Pearl has started trooping all over the countryside with her — and the things they do! Tracking kangaroos out by the creek, chasing after goannas and what have you. It's not safe.'

Grace smiled to herself as she imagined what her mother would have to say if she found out about the hair-raising adventure she'd so recently shared with her father.

'Olive, dear, you really must stop mollycoddling our daughter.' Alfred's voice was accompanied by the distinctive rattle of a china cup being placed emphatically upon a saucer. 'It will end up doing more harm than good. In any case, Pearl's people know the land better than we ever will. I have every confidence in her.'

'Alfred, I —'

'No, Olive,' he insisted. 'That is my last word.'

Grace swung around the door the next morning, her shoes polished and her curls brushed until they gleamed. 'Mum, you don't look exactly ready.' She screwed up her eyes. 'Have you forgotten we're going into Parkes?'

Olive waved a sheaf of paper. 'The Country Women's Association has asked me to advise them on a new treasurer. I've been sorting through the candidates.'

She smiled. 'I'm sorry. I know you were hoping to meet up with Charlotte Fairweather, but we're leaving for your birthday trip to the city tomorrow and I've simply no time. Dad said something about showing you his new atlas — why don't you see if he's in his study?'

'First, I'll tell you something that will make you laugh.'

'Mmm?' Olive's eyes had drifted back to the applications.

'When I told Pearl we'd be seeing Siddy in Sydney, she called him the silliest thing.' Still chortling, Grace told her mother what Pearl had said.

The applications Olive had been clutching in her hand crashed to the floor. 'Honestly, that girl is the limit!' she fumed.

As Grace made her way to Alfred's study, she wondered why her mother was so upset. Anyone could get into a muddle. It didn't mean anything.

Sydney, September 1934

Curled up in a large armchair advantageously tucked away in a corner of the Hotel Australia's majestic granite foyer, Grace gazed around with delight. Well-dressed women swept by in clouds of perfume, their furs and silk scarves trailing behind them; foreign visitors arrived with label-adorned, stout leather trunks and beribboned hat-boxes, as staff in uniforms every bit as splendid as those worn by toy soldiers attended to each guest's requirements. Grace tingled with pleasure as she watched. They were like characters in a play, entering and exiting against a backdrop of sparkling chandeliers, ringing bells and the buzz of a dozen different conversations.

As her family never considered staying anywhere other than the opulent Hotel Australia, over time Grace had become as familiar with its out-of the-way nooks and crannies as she was with its grand public rooms. The only place she liked better than the foyer was the Winter Garden, with its deep-blue velvet curtains and dainty tables and chairs. Here, amid leafy aspidistras, she loved to observe ladies in remarkable hats and gentlemen wearing stiff white collars drinking tea while they engaged in polite discourse or enjoyed the occasional musical soirée. Her mouth watered as she contemplated her birthday treat, especially the delicious frosted cakes that waitresses in frilly white aprons would distribute from their silver trays.

Best of all, Siddy would be there. Although his real name was Reuben Wood, as she only ever saw him in the city and she hadn't been able to pronounce 'Sydney' properly when she was tiny, somehow Siddy had become her nickname for him.

He was a huge, strapping man with thick black hair, green eyes and a battered felt hat he liked to wear pushed to the back of his head. Grace knew Siddy was not only a good pal of her father's, he also supplied Brookfield with its horses. For her, though, Siddy was more like a giant in a fairy tale, although not the frightening sort of giant. He was like an oversized, burly hero with the power to make everything turn out right.

She had been told that Siddy was a kind of uncle, but Grace regarded him as her very own grown-up friend. He had a name for Grace too — Princess — and whenever he addressed her this way she felt a warm glow inside.

Last Christmas he had given her a music box. 'Come here, Princess,' he'd said, before slowly unfolding his enormous hands. And there it was: small, square and made of smoothly planed wood. When she'd opened the lid a miniature ballerina in a pale pink dress had twirled around and around as tinkling music played.

Siddy just loved music, which was another reason why Grace liked the Winter Garden so much. The room featured a magnificent grand piano and she knew if she asked him, Siddy would sit down and play.

Grace watched eagerly as Siddy, dressed in his usual old tweed coat, settled his immense frame upon the diminutive stool. He gave Grace a brief wave, then raised his hands, hands that looked more suited to buckling on a bridle than coaxing music from a row of shining keys.

After just a few bars, it seemed as if he had cast a spell. The gentle hum of conversation died away. Teapots were suspended in midair, glasses of sherry remained untouched, slices of airy sponge and tiny triangular sandwiches stayed on porcelain plates.

A lady at the next table remarked in an unfamiliar accent, 'That's Chopin's "Prelude No. 6 in B minor".'

Turning, Grace saw that this foreign music lover was wearing a fox fur around her neck, its pointed nose and whiskers still in evidence along with a pair of glassy eyes and a tail captured between the creature's sharp little teeth. The sight of it made Grace grimace, although she warmed to the unknown woman when she heard her declare 'Extraordinary!' to her much younger male companion.

'I have heard that piece played all over the world,' she pronounced, 'but never before like that. I must find out the pianist's name.'

Bursting with pride, Grace wanted to run over to let the lady know Siddy was her own special friend. Yet she knew that would be to act in a manner her mother, who was sitting right opposite, would consider 'forward', so she forced herself to remain seated. Only after Siddy had made his way back to the table did Grace leap up and embrace him, crying, 'That was brilliant! Did you see how much everybody loved it?'

'It's the composer who deserves the credit; wasn't much to do with me.' Despite Siddy's protests, the joyful expression on his face revealed how much her praise had meant to him.

'I'm sure we all enjoyed it very much,' Olive said quietly.

'I agree. Well done, old chap,' her father added, hailing a waiter.

'Yes, Mr Alfred?' the man inquired, then stiffened. 'Oh, I am sorry, sir.' He looked embarrassed. 'I know I should have addressed you as Mr Woods, but as I often see you and

Mr Wood together when you're visiting, and what with your surnames being so similar, I always think of you by your first names so I don't confuse the orders.'

'Very sensible of you,' Alfred said. 'Now, perhaps you could fetch my friend "Mr Reuben" a cup of tea. No, make it something stronger — a performance like that deserves at least a Scotch and soda!'

After deciding on their drinks, Alfred and Reuben began to deliberate the merits of a new foal. Wriggling in her seat with renewed impatience, Grace occupied herself with a vanilla slice until, hopeful that a brief silence meant the two men had at last finished their discussion, she blurted, 'Siddy, remember when you said you'd teach me piano?'

'I do seem to recall something of the sort,' he said, stroking his chin.

'Well, I was wondering if we could start while I'm here. I could practise on the old upright we have in the hall when I go home and then you could show me a bit more each time I see you, which will be lots once I'm going to The Ravenscroft School in Sydney next year. What do you think?'

'Of course, Princess.' He smiled. 'But only if it's all right with your parents.'

'As long as you're willing, Reuben, I believe it's a splendid idea,' said Alfred. 'And I'm sure Olive is of the same opinion, aren't you, dear?'

There was a pause. 'Perhaps,' she eventually conceded.

Grace was surprised to discover the door of her parents' hotel room had been left ajar. She'd just spent a happy half-hour enjoying a late afternoon stroll with her father beneath the towering Moreton Bay fig trees of Sydney's Botanic Gardens, but now he was meeting with a wool-broker in the bar and she was hoping her mother might be in the mood for a game of cards. When she heard raised voices coming from within the room, however, Grace hesitated. Something was wrong.

'You know it as well as I do, Olive, she should be with me!' That was Siddy's rumbling bass; she'd recognise it anywhere, although Grace had never known him to be angry like this.

'No, Reuben, it's out of the question!' It was her mother. Alarmingly, she sounded close to tears.

Grace was torn. She would be in terrible trouble if she was discovered standing in the carpeted corridor for no apparent reason other than to eavesdrop on what was clearly a serious, grown-up conversation, yet she found it impossible to wrench herself away.

'Have you forgotten what we agreed? You simply cannot provide her with what she needs,' Olive was saying.

'I know I'm not a wealthy man —'

'I'm not just talking about the things money can buy!' Olive burst out. 'I mean the kind of love and care only a woman can provide.'

Grace heard a sob that tore at her heart. Then her mother said, 'Please, I'm begging you, Reuben. Don't do this to her — or me.'

She sounded incredibly distressed. But who were she and Siddy arguing about? What did it mean?

Grace walked into the silent room, her footsteps echoing on the polished parquet floor. The Winter Garden was not open for custom in the early morning. Without either guests or staff, the sound of orders being taken or the subjects of the day being discussed, it made Grace think of an empty stage waiting for a performance to begin.

A beam of bright sunshine escaped from a gap in the heavy velvet curtains, dazzling her eyes so that, for a moment, her vision blurred.

'Princess! Come on over,' Siddy called.

'There you are.' Grace skipped between the tables. 'I couldn't see because of the light.'

He was already seated behind the grand piano. 'Why not hop up next to me?' he asked. 'It's very good of the hotel to let us use this fine instrument, but we'll have to scoot in half an hour.'

Grace took a seat. 'Where's the sheet music?'

'To tell you the truth,' Siddy said, 'I'm not really good at reading the notes.'

'Well how do you know what to play?'

'The thing about music is you have to feel it. Oh, there's scales and octaves and so on; I'm not saying they're not important, but you need to sense the notes, right inside you.'

'How would I do that?'

'Listen.'

Reuben showed her how to find middle C, then the way to play a simple arpeggio. 'Over to you, Princess. Just do the same.'

Grace picked out the keys slowly and carefully. Siddy was right; each note vibrated deep inside her belly.

'You've done well,' he said. 'No one would believe you were just a beginner.'

'What's next?'

'Well, seeing as we only have a few more days before you go back to Brookfield, I think I should teach you how to play a song — and sing it too, if you like.'

'What kind of song?'

'A French one. It's called "*Frère Jacques*".'

'Siddy!' Grace's eyes widened. 'I didn't know you could speak another language.'

'I picked up a bit when I was a much younger man, back in the Great War. Now, do you remember how to find middle C?'

After a moment spent staring in confusion at the keyboard, Grace pressed the first finger of her right hand down on a wedge of ivory.

'Good. Now, see if you can play the notes again and sing "la" at just the same pitch.'

Grace coloured, but gave it a try anyway.

'Not bad — with a voice like that I ... I'd say you were a natural,' Reuben said unsteadily.

Grace was as surprised to see his mouth tremble as she was to detect welling tears. 'Is there something the matter, Siddy?' she asked, slipping her small hand into his paw.

'Nothing to worry about, Princess.' He smiled. 'Must be the sun in my eyes.'

CHAPTER FOUR

Brookfield, September 1934

Her mother was unpacking when Grace walked into her bedroom the morning after the family's return. 'Have you sent Pearl on an errand, Mum?' she asked. 'I haven't seen her anywhere.'

'I was just going to tell you,' her mother said as she hung up a pile of new summer dresses in her wardrobe. 'Pearl's left.'

'What do you mean?'

'She has an auntie up in the Darling Downs she's gone to stay with. Your father's foreman, Bill Gleason, organised a lift for her with some of the young shearers who happened to be heading up that way.'

'She's coming back, though, isn't she?'

Olive shook her head.

'Why not?' Grace sank onto the bed. 'Is it because I'm going to Ravenscroft?'

'Darling, you're twelve now, almost a young lady — you have different needs.'

Her mother smiled brightly. 'As it happens, I have a friend in the Downs with two small boys; she has been searching for a girl to help her out. I thought it would be nice if I recommended Pearl. Then she'd have a new job waiting for her.'

Grace swallowed hard. Pearl had been much more than a nanny; more like a beloved friend who'd shared special knowledge, from where the sweetest honey could be found to the way that magical creatures from an ancient time of dreams had created the mountains, the rivers and the seas.

'I never even had a chance to say goodbye,' she said, blinking back tears.

'It's a shame, I know. But things don't always work out the way we'd like,' her mother replied.

November

A catchy new Cole Porter song called 'Anything Goes' had just finished playing on the wireless. Grace was concentrating on picking it out on the homestead's ageing upright piano when she heard two pairs of high-heeled shoes tripping down the hall.

'Sorry to interrupt, darling — that tune was sounding awfully good, by the way — but I'm just saying goodbye to Mrs Evans,' Olive said.

Marjorie Evans, a plump, ginger-haired woman who lived on the adjoining property, was her mother's best friend. 'Hello, dear,' she greeted Grace. 'I expect you're looking forward to starting at your new school.'

'I can't wait!'

'Your poor mum will miss you, though.' The women exchanged a look. 'Ah well, what can be done about it?'

Grace heard her mother showing Mrs Evans out. A moment later, she received a hug.

'My British and French *Vogues* finally came in the post.' Olive smiled. 'Would you like to see them?'

'I'd love to!' Grace sprang up from the piano stool. 'Let's sit together, Mum, so we can share.'

It was funny, Grace pondered, as she snuggled up to her mother on the sofa, that up until recently she hadn't given the subject of clothes any thought at all — they were simply garments you pulled on in the morning. Now, she was fascinated by every detail.

Grace adored the glamorous pictures in the magazines. It was true, they took months to reach Australia, but her mother had told her this didn't matter as the northern winter took place while they had their summer. By the time the copies arrived it was just the right season.

Her mother had wonderful taste; she was always far better turned out than any of the other graziers' wives. If she didn't have quite the same hard-edged chic the fashion models displayed, instead favouring feminine dresses, well-made suits and flattering hats, she still had her own appealing style. Even now, here on the farm with no one around but themselves, she was wearing a delicately ruffled white frock and antique sapphire earrings.

Reaching for a copy of *Vogue Paris*, Grace began to flip through the pages. 'This black dress with the bows made from ribbon is gorgeous!'

'You know, Gracie, you have a very good eye,' Olive remarked, looking over her daughter's shoulder. 'That dress is by Coco Chanel, one of Paris's greatest designers. She has always been famous for her simplicity, but lately she's created some quite intricate evening gowns.' There was an expression of longing on Olive's face. 'The one you have picked out is divine.'

Grace was thrilled. 'Are you taking the picture to Miss Louise to copy next time you're in Sydney?' she asked excitedly. 'Then it would be ready for when you go to the Jockey Club Ball with Dad.'

'I agree, it's a lovely idea,' her mother said, 'but the problem is I'd never be able to find the fabric — I'm sure it's Chantilly lace.'

Grace turned to a page that depicted two elegant women swathed in pale pink. 'How about these?' she asked.

'I'm afraid not.'

'No material again?'

'Oh, I think silk jersey is available.' Olive scrutinised the image. 'The difficulty is that although dear Lou Lou is talented, this style requires perfect technique. That,' she said, tapping the picture with her finger, 'has been created by Madame Grès. Unfortunately, there is no one in Australia — or possibly the world — who can drape fabric like her.'

'Gosh, there's a lot more to clothes than you'd think, isn't there?'

'You're right.' Her mother nodded. 'Personally, I believe a woman should always strive to look her best, no matter whether she's off to a garden party or baking a cake, so I suppose that, in a way, being well dressed is hard work.' She gave her daughter a conspiratorial smile. 'On the other hand, goodness me it's fun! It's a part of what makes it so special to be a girl.'

'But how do you work out what suits you?' Grace asked.

'Well, once a young man said my eyes were the colour of delphiniums, so that gave me a clue that perhaps I should favour blue.' Olive laughed. 'But mostly, it's just trial and error. I know — why don't you try on some of my new evening clothes? You have grown so much lately, we're practically the same size. We could start with my emerald satin cocktail dress — that would match your eyes beautifully — and then move on to the blue silk shantung.'

'You're the best mother ever!' Grace beamed.

She was about to jump to her feet when she heard a sharp intake of breath. 'What have you seen, Mum? It sounds like you've had an inspiration.'

'That is exactly what I've had,' Olive said with an unexpected grin.

Puzzled, Grace drew her dark brows together. Instead of a dress, her mother was staring at a page of indecipherable French.

Paris, December 1948

The formalities completed, Madame Raymonde announced with a sweeping gesture of her hand, 'In a short while, you will meet the man who made all this possible. But first, please be seated.' She indicated a cream sofa. 'I have a small matter to which I must attend; it shouldn't take long. In the meantime, would you like coffee?'

'I'm fine, thank you.' Grace was still becoming accustomed to the bitter black brew.

'In that case, *à bientôt*.'

As she waited in Madame Raymonde's tranquil office, Grace reflected on her recent giddy arrival in Paris three days before. Muffled up in her warmest winter coat, a pair of new knitted gloves and a red woollen scarf, she had stepped from the train she'd caught in Calais onto the crowded platform of the cavernous Gare du Nord. The past few months had been turbulent. Then, just when it had appeared that all was dark and hopeless, everything she'd wished for had miraculously fallen into place. As if to remind herself of her good fortune, she'd felt in her handbag and touched the letter — the wonderful letter! — that had arrived from the House of Christian Dior just ten weeks earlier.

Grace didn't know a soul in Paris, yet she'd not felt perturbed. Instead, as she'd gazed about the bustling station, the thought of her anonymity had filled her with glee. After a lifetime when so much of what she did had been prescribed by what it seemed would be her inevitable destiny, Grace's newfound liberty had made her tingle with exhilaration. She could assume whatever identity she wished, make choices she would never have dared at home in Australia. Tempted to burst into song or at least to execute a sudden pirouette, she'd settled instead on giving the delighted elderly porter who had carried her suitcase up the Gare du Nord's stairs an enthusiastic handshake and a large tip.

As her taxi had sped away from the terminal, Grace had prepared herself for the sight of a war-ravaged city. To her surprise, what she saw through the car window was undiminished beauty. She marvelled at the wide boulevards lined by elegant stone buildings, the formal parks displaying clipped hedges and groomed trees, the slim spire of Notre-Dame cathedral, a gilded bridge and, beneath it, the swirling water of the River Seine. This was not the Paris she had seen in photographs. What she saw was so much better, greater, grander.

Not until she alighted at 25 rue Dauphine did Grace become aware of the dilapidation that war had left behind. Yet, despite the flakes of peeling paint and the slats missing from the wooden shutters that stood, guardian-like, on either side of the long, narrow windows, she could see that it remained a fine old building. There was something determined about its solid masonry that suggested it would endure no matter what havoc existed in the world.

Having pushed open the heavy timber front door, Grace found she was standing in a small inner courtyard. Barring her way forward was a tiny woman.

'What do you want, mademoiselle?' she demanded in a high, querulous voice. 'If it's a room, you might as well go now because there isn't one to be had. I can't send you somewhere else, either, so don't ask.' The concierge shook her head vigorously. 'Paris is completely full. If it's not the poor souls returning from God knows where, it's hordes of foreigners pouring in.'

With that she turned her back on Grace, shuffled over to what appeared to be a small ground-floor apartment, slipped inside and firmly shut the door behind her.

Despite the woman's discouraging words, Grace knocked. *What else can I do?* she thought. It had grown even colder and the day's translucent light had begun to fade.

'Go away! I told you no,' was shouted at her from behind the door.

'But madame,' Grace cried. 'I have come all the way from Australia. I was told there would be a room here waiting for me. It's all been arranged.'

Silence. Then the sound of mewing. The door opened and a sleek black cat sauntered out, followed much more slowly by the tiny woman who, hands placed firmly on hips, stared at Grace with disbelief.

'You come from the land of the kangaroos?' Her tone had become wistful. 'Ah, I remember your soldiers and the way they helped us in the first war — my people are from the Somme,' she said. 'Even so, I'm sorry, I can do nothing for you.' The woman bent over and stroked her pet cat, whose purr was more like a rumble. 'There is one room left, and the young lady I am waiting for is French. Just a minute, I'll get the piece of paper.'

She made her way back into her apartment. Grace heard a drawer bang, an exclamation and then the woman once more shuffled out.

'You see, I am right. The only girl due to arrive today is a Mademoiselle Dubois.'

'But that is me!' said Grace.

The woman looked puzzled, then gave an exaggerated shrug. 'In that case, follow me.'

It was only when she had climbed six vertiginous flights of age-worn stairs that the wheezing concierge stopped, peered up at Grace and said, 'Dubois — what sort of name is that for an Australian?'

Brookfield, January 1935

'You must acquire a new identity,' Mademoiselle Elise insisted at the commencement of Grace's first French lesson.

'I — What did you say?' Grace was still recovering from her astonishing discovery that mademoiselle bore no resemblance to the image she'd had of a governess — old, ugly and mean. The woman who sat opposite was not at all old and, while not traditionally pretty like her mother, was undeniably attractive in a way Grace found difficult to explain.

At first, Grace had been bitterly disappointed by her mother's decision. 'But why can't I go away to school, Mummy?' she had wailed as she sat in one of the wicker chairs on the wide veranda. 'I've been dying to board at

Ravenscroft. Charlotte is starting next term. How come she can go and I can't? It isn't fair,' she said petulantly.

For the first time in Grace's life, Brookfield's isolation felt bleak and oppressive. 'Now there'll be no exciting life in the city, no new friends, no time with Siddy. There won't be a single thing to look forward to.'

Olive had insisted that she was only thinking of Grace's best interests. 'Having a governess means you will be able to speak perfect French, improve your piano and your drawing and learn, well, lots of other things,' she'd said. 'Just because we're closer to Parkes than Paris shouldn't stop you from being able to make soufflés, you know. You'll be far better off than all those other girls who have gone away to school in the city — and just think what an asset you will be to your future husband.'

'Mum, I don't care a fig about that sort of thing!' Grace cried.

Olive ignored this remark. 'Why on earth would you want to live in Sydney when everything you could possibly want will be right here on our own beautiful property, including your father and me? There's not a soul in the world who can keep you from harm the way that we can. Young girls can get mixed up in all sorts of trouble in the city,' she warned.

Grace rolled her eyes. Her mother was being ridiculously over-protective: they were talking about her attending school, not being let loose in nightclubs.

'And there are plenty of very nice young people staying on in the district,' her mother continued. 'The Osbournes' son, Jack, for instance. He's enrolled at Parkes High so he can learn to run that huge property of his father's while he goes to school. I hear he's a lovely boy.'

No matter what her mother said, Grace had felt thoroughly wretched, yet now she found herself intrigued by Brookfield's exotic new arrival. Mademoiselle Elise had dark blonde hair that she wore swept up in a sophisticated French roll, and lively brown eyes. Even though her clothes were simple, she had the knack of making them appear effortlessly smart — in fact, Grace thought, Mademoiselle Elise would not have looked out of place in the pages of one of her mother's *Vogue* magazines.

'Listen closely,' Elise instructed as she turned back the cuffs of her white piqué shirt. 'While studying the world's most beautiful language, you will no longer be a Miss Woods of Australia — *non, non, non.*' She clasped her hands together. '*Ma petite*, in order to speak French, you need to adopt a quite different identity. The first word I shall teach you is *bois*, which means "woods". *Voilà!* When you are with me, Mademoiselle Dubois you will be.'

Six weeks later, Grace sat behind her desk taking careful note, as she did every day, of the way mademoiselle was attired. Today, Elise had selected a dove-grey pencil skirt and a pink pleated blouse, the latter a perfect match for one of Olive's prize-winning roses that stood on the bureau in a narrow crystal vase. The former spare bedroom now contained a blackboard, two shelves of books, and a row of coloured maps depicting Paris, then France, followed by the patchwork that was Europe and, finally, the great island continent of Australia. There were also posters of the Arc de Triomphe and the Eiffel Tower.

'You are ready?' The governess opened a book. '*Bon.* We will continue our exploration of the incomparable French culture.'

As she spoke enthusiastically about the fabled art treasures in the famous Louvre museum, the beauty of the magnificent tree-lined boulevard known as the Champs-Élysées and the splendours of Notre-Dame, Grace yearned to see these sights for herself.

'The French capital is known as the City of Light, or *la Ville Lumière*,' said Elise. '*Vraiment*, I cannot think of a more appropriate way to describe it. In my opinion, Paris is the only place where a person can acquire true enlightenment.'

Pointing to the map of France, she said, 'However, the country also has many special regions, each with its own characteristics and cuisine. In fact, if you will wait *un moment*, you will be able to enjoy a *délicieuse* first-hand experience.'

Mademoiselle Elise disappeared, returning promptly with a steaming dish that did indeed look delicious. Grace inhaled its faintly spicy, delectably sweet aroma as Elise placed a slice of what appeared to be an upside-down tart onto a small plate.

'*Bon appétit!*' mademoiselle said gaily.

'*Merci beaucoup*,' Grace replied.

Never before had she tasted anything like the sticky, caramelised apples and buttery pastry. Savouring the syrupy, slightly burnt flavour, Grace imagined she was no longer on a sheep and wheat station in Australia's hot and dusty interior, but was instead in a pretty French farmhouse surrounded by fruit-laden orchards.

'The tart was first made by the Tatin sisters,' mademoiselle advised. 'They lived in the Loire Valley, a rich agricultural region that is also known for the many elaborate, fairy-tale castles we call *châteaux*. Ah, I do hope you will see them one day.'

Grace listened intently.

'Mademoiselles Stéphanie and Caroline were making a pie for the patrons of their little hotel, but they accidentally burnt the apples they were cooking in a mixture of butter and sugar. *Quel désastre!* What were they to do?' Elise paused theatrically.

'The sisters had no idea. All they knew was that they must act quickly, so they placed a fine layer of pastry on top of the apples and put it all in the oven to bake. When it was ready, the pie was turned over and — *voilà!* — out of disaster the sisters produced something splendid.'

The governess nodded meaningfully at her charge. 'It is a valuable lesson for us all.'

CHAPTER FIVE

Parkes, August 1939

Grace stood in the moonlight outside the corrugated-iron shed where a spirited version of *Twelfth Night*, performed by the Parkes District Amateur Players Society, had just concluded. As she waited for her boyfriend, Jack Osbourne, to return with their drinks, she considered a line from the play: *How does he love me?*

With fertile tears … and sighs of fire had been the reply. Although she'd never expect Jack to spout that sort of poetic language, as Grace watched him walk towards her through the crowd while juggling a couple of ginger ales, she had to admit he still had the same ardent look in his deep-set brown eyes as on the day they'd first met, years before, on Charlotte Fairweather's tennis court.

Ever since then, their lives had continued to intersect. They'd bumped into each other in Parkes, at the agricultural show, out riding. Aided by their approving parents, they'd started visiting each other. With her friend Lottie away at school, Jack helped fill the gap in her life. At first they were simply good mates and then, almost without realising it, their companionship turned into something more serious.

Now, whenever Grace was invited to a local dance, a bush picnic or a tennis party, it was presumed that Jack Osbourne, the good-looking son of the wealthiest grazier in the district, would be there too. The names of the striking pair were inextricably linked; everyone she knew in the area seemed to assume that a shared future was inevitable.

Only the previous week, when Grace had passed by the open door of the homestead kitchen, she'd overheard her mother's friend Marjorie remark, 'Heavens, that Osbourne boy is a good catch. It seems you did the right thing keeping Gracie at home after all.'

'They do say mothers know best,' Olive had responded with a tone of self-congratulation, before adding, 'That's why I've made quite certain that my daughter won't risk her future with him by letting herself get, you know, carried away.'

Grace could just picture Marjorie's raised eyebrows.

'Hey, come back to earth.' Jack grinned. 'You look as if you're miles off in space.' He passed her a glass of ginger ale. 'What did you think of the play?'

'Beautiful words, of course. And hilarious in places, although maybe not always in the bits Shakespeare had in mind.' Grace took a sip of her drink. 'Charlotte made a lovely Viola; I'm so glad she's home for the holidays. And Kev the postman — or should I say Sir Toby Belch — certainly revealed a few hidden talents.'

'I thought it was terrific,' Jack said. 'Except, with all that confusion about the lovers' identities, even I began to lose track of exactly who was who.' He glanced at his watch. 'Gee, time's getting on. It's a long drive back to Brookfield in the truck — we should get moving.'

Grace felt her stomach tighten. Jack was a great pal and

wonderful fun, but she hoped he wasn't expecting too much. So far they'd done nothing more intimate than exchange innocent kisses and hold hands, although it was obvious he wanted to go further. All night he'd taken every opportunity he could to stroke her hair or slip his arm around her waist.

After an hour of bumping along the dark, dusty road, Jack made a right turn onto a narrow bush track.

'Wait a minute. Where are you going?' Grace asked, biting her lip. Overhanging branches slapped against the windscreen as the truck plunged forward, its headlights casting ghostly shadows onto the smooth trunks of silvery eucalypts and patches of scrub.

'I know a spot on a rise up ahead that's the perfect place to see the full moon,' Jack said.

There was a crunch of gravel as he brought the truck to a stop. 'What a gorgeous sight,' he said. But Jack wasn't observing the cool white disk shining in the night sky. He was staring at Grace with hungry eyes.

Pulling her towards him, Jack eagerly pressed open her lips with his tongue. As they kissed in this new, more passionate way, Grace became vaguely aware he was unfastening her zip. Her dress fell from her shoulders, its flimsy fabric pooling around her waist.

Grace felt as if she were being carried along by a fast-flowing current. It wasn't that she desired Jack exactly, but at the same time she seemed unable to summon the will to stop him. Only when his fingers began probing the swelling softness inside the cups of her bra did she freeze. Each of her mother's repeated warnings tumbled, unbidden, through her mind.

Nice young ladies are not interested in sex.

If a girl sleeps with a man before marriage, she's nothing but used goods.

A baby born out of wedlock means just one thing — utter disgrace.

Grace pushed Jack away.

'Sweetheart, what's wrong?' he panted. 'You know how I feel about you.'

'It's not that,' Grace said, struggling back into her frock. 'There's too much risk, and —'

'I get it,' he sighed. 'You're saving yourself, isn't that what you girls call it?'

'Oh Jack, I'm sorry.'

'You're not to blame,' he said with a rueful smile, 'unless being way too pretty for your own good counts as a fault.' Jack reached for Grace's hand. 'Trust me,' he said, with an earnest expression she found so endearing it vanquished any lingering concerns she might have had about his intentions. 'I swear I won't ever make you do something you don't want to. Cross my heart, Gracie.'

December 1939

A fly was buzzing about in the simmering air. First it circled Grace's head, then landed on her arm, before settling briefly on some drawing paper. Annoyed, she flicked the insect away.

Grace was attempting to sketch Jack's portrait while he lounged against a paperbark tree on the grassy banks of the Lachlan River. As the dappled light played on his dark brown hair, olive skin and strongly delineated angular features, she thought she'd never seen him look more handsome.

'It's strange,' she said.

'What? Your picture of me?'

'Probably!' Grace laughed. 'No, I was just thinking about how we've both finished school, but what people call "real life" hasn't actually begun. It's as if we're neither kids nor adults, but instead we're just floating about, in a kind of no man's land in between.'

'I've been wanting to talk to you about that.' Jack looked unusually serious. 'You know that war has broken out ...'

Of course she knew. Nobody had talked of anything else for the past three months.

'But it's so far away,' she said, putting down her sketch pad and pencil.

'That doesn't mean we won't be called upon by Britain.' Jack leant forward. 'Gracie, I'm not waiting around. As soon as I turn eighteen, I'm going to sign up.'

'What do you mean?' She was shocked. 'You can't do that — your dad will expect you to stay on the farm.'

Jack shook his head. 'I've seen in the newspaper that there's plenty of blokes from around the Empire who are heading for England and joining the RAF. Seeing as the government has built an air base just a few miles out of Parkes, it's a perfect opportunity for me. I can start there, then ship out to Britain to finish my training. In no time at all, I'll be shooting down German planes over the English Channel.'

'You seem to have everything worked out.' She twisted a stray curl around her finger. 'Only, you waited long enough to tell me.'

'I'm sorry, Gracie.' Jack rose to his feet. 'I wasn't sure how you'd take it. As for Mum and Dad, I reckon they'll come round. The worst bit is that I'll be leaving you behind.'

Grace was still grappling with Jack's sudden announcement when he took a few paces towards her. He hesitated for only a moment, before abruptly dropping down onto one knee.

'There's something else I have to say, Gracie,' he declared. 'Will you marry me?'

'Jack!' This proposal had always been a distant prospect, a vague possibility, never quite real. She delighted in the easy familiarity of her and Jack's relationship. But did she love him? She wasn't sure she knew what that felt like. Though he could never get enough of kissing and caressing her, somehow she never felt swept away. Was liking Jack and having fun together really enough for her to want to spend a lifetime with him?

Sitting on the riverbank that day, she knew with a sense of claustrophobic certainty that if she said 'yes' her future would be a duplicate of her mother's life: she would live on a great country property, spending her spare time on bridge games, flower shows, gardening and charity committees, interspersed with the occasional visit to the dressmaker or the races in the city. Grace wanted more than that.

But she said none of this, merely protesting, 'Jack, we're still only kids …'

'Gracie, that's where you're wrong,' he retorted. He sprang to his feet, then reached down and pulled Grace up so she was facing him. 'This is what "real life" looks like,' he said. 'If I'm old enough to fight, I'm old enough to ask you to marry me.'

Grace had no idea what to say.

'We don't have to tie the knot anytime soon,' Jack added, hugging her to him. 'Anyway, it wouldn't be right, with me about to sign up and take off for the wild blue yonder. But will you wait? Wait until after I've done my bit for king and country?'

Grace escaped from his arms. Stumbling towards the tree, she scooped up her sketch from the ground. The pencil marks no longer had any coherence about them; she saw only a disconnected jumble of charcoal lines.

'Gracie,' she heard Jack say, 'I thought this was what you wanted, what you'd been, you know, waiting for …'

She tried to think. The boy she cared for so much, who'd been such an important part of her life, was going away to fight. Darling Jack was prepared to make the ultimate sacrifice. Ignoring her misgivings, she nodded. 'I'll wait.'

As soon as the words were out of Grace's mouth she experienced a wave of dizzying nausea. The ground seemed to shift beneath her feet.

Jack put out a hand to steady her. 'Hey! What's the matter?'

'It's just that it's all very sudden, and now you're going away.'

'If you ask me, I think it's this damn heat,' Jack said, swatting away another fly. 'Come on, Gracie, I'll take you home. You need a bit of shade.'

He put his arm around her, but again she broke free. 'Let's not tell anyone until after the war, when you come home,' she said. 'It will be our secret.'

'I can live with that,' Jack agreed.

Finally alone, Grace retired to her favourite retreat — her father's book-lined study, where he not only worked but, on occasion, still read her the Australian bush poems of Banjo Paterson and Henry Lawson as well as works by his favourite English Romantics, Wordsworth and Keats. She loved the smell of this special room; it was a mixture of leather bindings and old paper, with the faintest hint of whisky — her father kept a decanter of single-malt Glenfiddich together with some crystal glasses on a side table.

In the coolness of this quiet refuge, Grace drifted over to the brass-mounted globe that stood next to her father's desk. Rotating it slowly, she found Rome, Madrid, Vienna,

London and, best of all, Paris; the mere thought of this legendary city never failed to ignite her imagination. 'One day,' she murmured dreamily, 'one day …'

At least she hadn't said yes to Jack's proposal; surely a promise to wait was an entirely different matter. The war might take ages, and even if it lasted just six months or so, it gave her time to sort out her feelings. Grace admitted to herself, a little guiltily, that she was envious of Jack. If only it was as easy for her to pursue adventure on the other side of the world. Instead, she was sentenced to be left behind, in the isolation of vast inland Australia, with no apparent means of escape.

She recalled the map of Europe pinned on the schoolroom wall by Mademoiselle Elise, the fizz of excitement she had felt as she'd gazed at the way the countries fitted together, their borders marked by rivers and mountain ranges or by hand-drawn lines. For the longest time, she'd had the feeling that her destiny lay far away. But if she married Jack, it was unlikely to turn out that way.

CHAPTER SIX

Sydney, March 1940

Clutching a red umbrella, Grace huddled amid the sodden crowd that stood on the Sydney dock. She'd come to say goodbye to Jack. Any minute now, he'd board the ship that would take him to a war being waged far away. Waiting around in the pouring rain was a miserable experience.

The night before, she and Olive had met with Jack and his mother, Betty, in the Hotel Australia's plush dining room. During their meal, Grace had felt false and unnatural; this morning's breakfast had been even more stressful. Jack had eaten a huge helping of bacon, sausages, eggs and toast, while maintaining a near-febrile animation. He'd chattered away to the three of them about the fascinating ports he would visit during his voyage, what he imagined London was like and whether he would fly a Spitfire or a Hurricane.

Grace'd had no appetite and could think of little to say. 'There, there,' her mother had clucked sympathetically, while exchanging knowing glances with Betty.

Now, here she was, standing beneath leaden skies in the shadow of the great grey ship, surrounded by keen young men and their more subdued mothers and fathers. There was also a plethora of girls milling about, clad in their best dresses and coats, their mouths carefully coloured with lipstick, and a variety of damp berets or bonnets crammed onto their heads. Many of the soldiers' sweethearts were pale-faced, most wore strained smiles. There was the occasional sound of a sob, sometimes a peal of forced laughter.

Grace was certain that Olive and Betty interpreted her own silence as a sign that parting from Jack was weighing on her equally heavily. In fact, she was struggling to contain both her envy of him as well as an even more disturbing sense of shame. The truth was, although she'd hate for anything awful to happen to Jack, rather than longing for him to stay by her side she felt relieved — perhaps even a touch elated — he was going away.

A deafening hoot from the ship's mighty stack sounded three times.

'Time to be off, Gracie,' Jack said.

He wrapped his arms around her, then kissed her passionately in front of everyone, although she saw from the corner of her eye that both mothers had turned discreetly away.

'Just you remember that I'm coming back to marry you, Grace Woods,' he whispered in her ear. 'Then we'll be together until the end of time.'

She watched, dry-eyed, as the country boy she had promised to wait for hitched his kit bag onto a broad, muscled shoulder. He pecked Betty and Olive on their respective cheeks, turned around and, with the rain beating down, bounded up the gangplank.

Having declined Olive's offer to cheer her up by trying on hats at Henriette Lamotte's exclusive Rowe Street shop, Grace was instead sitting at a corner table of the Winter Garden. She fiddled distractedly with the bunch of artificial violets she had pinned to her jacket's lapel, while darting occasional glances at the entrance to the room.

At last she spotted Reuben over by the door, handing his shapeless hat and long overcoat — both appeared to be soaking — to a disgruntled attendant. After smoothing back his damp unruly hair, he strode across the room.

'Princess, my goodness, you do look grand!' Reuben said, greeting her with a wink. 'All the other blokes here will be jealous.'

'Siddy, please sit down. You mustn't say such ridiculous things. I'm not a twelve-year-old any longer,' Grace protested, laughing for the first time in days as she gave him a kiss on the cheek.

'Oh, I know that right enough,' Reuben replied. 'In fact, a little bird's told me it won't be long before a certain fellow proposes.'

Grace remained silent.

'Hmm … Now, let me guess. It's the young Osbourne boy, isn't it? Although I did hear from your father that he was due to ship out today. I'm guessing you went down to the wharf to say goodbye?'

Grace said it had been so depressing she didn't want to talk about it.

'That's fine by me. Actually, I have something pretty important to say to you.'

This was unnerving. She wasn't used to Siddy addressing her so seriously.

He ordered a pot of tea and some shortbread biscuits, then said with a sad smile, 'Your old mate has enlisted too. In fact, I'm leaving for England myself pretty soon.'

'Siddy, no!'

'There's nothing else for it, Princess,' he added despondently. 'Look, you didn't know my darling wife, Rae, though I wish to God you had.'

'You never talk about her,' Grace said.

'Ah, she was a real sweetheart. She had lovely red curls and she sang like a bird.' Reuben sighed. 'Anyway, she's been gone a long time now and I'm still a single man.' He shifted uncomfortably in his seat; it looked far too small to accommodate a man his size.

'At one stage I thought my life would be, oh I don't know, let's just say very different to the way it turned out. I wish I could explain it all, really I do, but the last thing I'd want is to take off knowing I'd messed everything up for you.'

'Siddy, you're not making a lot of sense,' Grace said anxiously.

'Well, I've never been very good at saying goodbye.' Reuben ran a hand through his shock of black hair. 'Princess, all I really want you to know before I go is that you've always been the apple of my eye. I couldn't be more fond of you than …' He paused, clearing his throat before continuing, '… than if you were my own. The fact is, I'm not doing anything important here. I've heard Great Britain needs men to help keep the Germans out of France. Christ knows why they might be interested in a horseman like me, but it seems the Frenchies have a plan. Anyway, I've signed up. Let's face it, I won't be leaving anyone behind.'

'How can you say that!' Grace said. 'What about me?'

Vivid images flashed into her mind of the special people who had already vanished from her life. First Pearl had disappeared, then Charlotte had gone off to school. Recently, Mademoiselle Elise had departed, amid mutual tears, for the safety of neutral Switzerland. Now Jack had left and soon it would be Siddy's turn.

With a pang, she thought about just how much Siddy meant to her. Ever since she could remember, he'd never failed to make the effort to come and see her when she was in Sydney. He was always keen to hear what she'd been up to, and though he loved to joke and tease, he couldn't be kinder. The outbreak of war meant that so much was changing, but she'd never imagined that one day she would visit the city and find Siddy missing.

'Princess, I tell you what,' he said. 'I hate to see you looking so down in the dumps. How about we both take a stroll over to the piano and do that new Vera Lynn tune, "We'll Meet Again". You know it, don't you?'

'Yes, but ...' Grace wished Reuben hadn't put her on the spot.

'Come on, then. It's just the thing to raise your spirits.'

Siddy caught the eye of the silver-haired maître d', then pointed at the piano. After the man gave a regal nod of assent, Grace reluctantly allowed herself to be steered towards the gleaming instrument.

'I'd better play and you do the warbling, Princess,' Reuben said. 'You've developed a lovely tone.'

Almost as soon as Grace began to sing in her clear soprano, a hush fell over the busy room. A moment later she was surprised to hear the first voice join in — it belonged to a young woman she recognised from the dock that morning. Next, from across the crowded salon, a confident baritone was added to the girl's hesitant quaver, and then there was another voice, and still another, until it seemed that not only every guest, but every waiter and waitress in the Winter Garden was on their feet singing in spellbinding, heartfelt unison.

Rousing applause rang through the room when the last bitter-sweet note died away. Then a gentleman in a pin-striped suit raised his glass high in the air and cried out loudly, 'A toast to our brave boys who have gone to fight for the Motherland.'

'To our brave boys!' As one, the crowded room's occupants — old and young, men and women, city dwellers and countysiders — replied.

The sight of so many proud, smiling faces induced a fierce mixture of emotions in Grace. All Europe was under Germany's vicious heel; countless souls would surely succumb to the carnage. If only she, too, could help combat the Nazi terror. If only there was a way to make sure Jack and Siddy would be safe.

She shivered violently.

'You haven't caught a chill, have you?' Reuben said, looking concerned. 'It must have been awful weather down at the wharf.'

Grace shook her head. 'I'm not ill. Siddy, I'm afraid, afraid this might be the last time I ever see you.'

Reuben put a large comforting arm around Grace's shoulders. 'Where, I'm not sure, and I can't tell you when,' he said with a catch in his voice, 'but I know that one day we'll meet again.'

CHAPTER SEVEN

Brookfield, November 1942

On a fine spring morning, Grace's mother was demonstrating the proper technique required for the application of royal icing onto a rich fruitcake, when she said, 'I do hope all this baking helps cheer up those poor boys who keep arriving at the air base. Most of them are miles from home, and who knows where they'll end up?' Olive stirred a small bowl of the thick, snowy paste with an uneasy expression. 'Probably somewhere dreadful like North Africa or the Middle East, I wouldn't wonder.'

'I'm sure the airmen love the treats you send, Mum.' Grace smiled. 'Especially when they're accompanied by your famous pineapple rum punch — a glass of that would put a smile on anyone's face.' She looked down. 'But I wish I could do more — to help the war effort, I mean.'

'What sort of thing are you thinking about?'

'Well, like Lottie,' Grace said. 'You know how she's found herself a job working in Sydney for a colonel in Victoria Barracks.'

Olive shifted her gaze to her daughter. 'Gracie, Charlotte might be employed by the army, but it's as a secretary —

she's not exactly on the front line. Anyway, you're needed here.'

Using the flat side of a knife, she returned to her task, expertly spreading more icing onto the side of the cake. 'Aside from old Bill Gleason and a couple of the youngest lads, all Brookfield's farmhands are away at the war. Your father has been doing the work of three.'

Grace sighed. 'Poor Daddy.'

'He simply couldn't manage without you,' her mother continued. 'Honestly, Gracie, I think you're amazing. I don't know any other girl of barely twenty who spends her days either up on a tractor harvesting wheat or out on a horse mustering sheep,' she said, 'especially one as beautiful as you.'

'Mummy, don't be silly!'

'Well, you are — beautiful, I mean, despite those ghastly farm clothes you get around in these days. And then, after all that, you coop yourself up in the study at night and help Dad with the books. If that's not putting in an effort, I don't know what is.'

Grace frowned. 'It's just that it doesn't feel like I'm doing something that matters.'

'Of course you are!' Olive protested.

'Well, not anything that compares with what Jack or Siddy are going through.'

'Oh, darling, once the men are home you won't need to worry about any of that — or farming, for that matter. You can put it all behind you.' She pointed in the direction of the half-iced cake. 'You will be doing proper women's work instead.'

'I know, Mum,' Grace said with exasperation.

She picked up a spatula and dipped it in the bowl of sticky icing, yet when she tried to copy her mother's example, she found that instead of a faultlessly smooth surface she had created only a ragged white trail.

The sheep woke her the next morning. Not just their gentle baaing, but the shuffling noise their little cloven hoofs made on the hard-packed ground. Grace opened her eyes and saw that light was already streaming across her bedroom's blue and white striped wallpaper. Yawning, she pushed back a tumble of dark curls from her forehead.

Grace ambled over to the window and looked out. As usual, the sun was shining brightly in an endless blue sky, the crops were the colour of spun gold, and the animals had gathered, as they always did, around a shallow trough of water, stuttering softly as they jostled and nudged each other out of the way. Nothing ever seemed to change.

In a fit of sudden annoyance, Grace grabbed a pillow from her bed and sent it sailing across the room. She'd had enough of wheat and sheep. She pulled on yesterday's moleskin trousers with a fresh shirt, then marched downstairs. It wasn't early, although the homestead was uncharacteristically quiet. She checked each room and found no one. When Grace came to her father's study she pushed open the door and, seeing that it, too, was empty, on a whim she sat down on his high-backed chair. The silent space, with its leather-bound books, had always been a good place to think.

After fumbling for a moment, Grace located the letter from Jack she had slipped inside her pocket the day before. There had been so much to do she'd only had time to skim its pages. Now, she held it up to the light.

Darling Gracie,

I'm sorry I haven't been a very good correspondent lately. The fact is, I got myself into a spot of bother. I was flying back from the last mission (as you know, we can't say where we go), feeling pretty pleased with myself, when a blasted Jerry in a Messerschmitt opened fire.

There's nothing to worry about, although I did make a crash landing — just as well it was in good old England. Actually, it was pretty exciting! Only, somehow, I managed to get myself tangled up with my joy stick, which wasn't the worst thing in the world — it got me a nice rest at some lord's stately home that's been made available for pilots who need a bit of time out.

You should have seen the place — it was a huge brick pile with towers and whacking great stables. They had cows grazing on rich pasture, plus plenty of fields sown with barley and oats. It was an impressive set-up, but for all that, I'd take our big, dusty property out in Australia any day. To tell you the truth, I'd be bloody happy (excuse the French) if I never left home again.

Anyway, I'm fine now — I've still got two arms and two legs, which means after this is over I won't have any problems carrying you over the threshold!

Much love, your Jack

Grace smiled. Yesterday, she had been concerned by news of the crash, but now she'd had time to read the letter properly, it was clear that Jack considered the experience to be more like something from a *Boys' Own* adventure story.

Yet, still something niggled. She looked at the creased pages again, then stopped, when she reached one particular line: *I'd be bloody happy ... if I never left home again.*

Grace put the letter down. Her eyes flickered around the room, coming to rest on the brass-mounted globe that stood, as always, next to her father's desk. She reached out and gave it a twirl for old time's sake and, as she watched the earth spin, Mademoiselle Elise's words came back to her as clearly as on the day she'd departed for Switzerland.

'*Ma petite,*' she had said, holding Grace's hand, 'it is very beautiful here, yes, and very safe. Your young man is nice. But do not forget, the world is large and full of fascinating people, extraordinary things, wonderful places. Imagine what — or even who — might be there, waiting for you.'

Grace slowly folded the letter and put it back into her pocket. It had been three years since her governess's departure and the war was still raging. Who knew what the world would be like once it had finally ended? Anyway, everyone said how lucky she was to have a man like Jack in her life — especially her mother. Elise had meant well, but perhaps it was time for the fanciful 'Mademoiselle Dubois' to put her foolish dreams of far-flung, foreign escapades aside.

The sudden rap of the door knocker sounded as loud as a rifle shot in the silent homestead. When Grace went to see who was there, she was surprised to find the district's ageing postman. Usually he passed by on his rounds in the afternoon, and never came up to the house. Brookfield's mail was always placed inside the corrugated-iron cylinder that stood next to the property's main gates.

'Hello, Kev,' she said. 'What brings you way out here in the morning?'

'I've a registered letter for Mr Woods,' he announced, his weathered face stern. 'It's from the war office.'

'That's odd. Well, just hand it over and I'll leave it for him. Want something to drink?'

'I'm right, thanks.'

Grace watched the postman hoist himself into his red van and waved him goodbye. Then she propped the buff envelope on the dining-room table against a vase of pink everlasting daisies. Her father would be sure to notice it there.

But Alfred didn't return until the sky had a vivid red bloom and the sun had begun to slip beneath the horizon.

'I rode out with Bill Gleason,' he explained, when he trudged in wearily through the open door. 'We had to check the feed in the far paddocks.'

Before Grace had time to mention the letter, Alfred said that he was off to wash and get changed. 'Then I need an uninterrupted half-hour to look over some crop estimates,' he added.

Only when her father joined them at the dining-room table did she have the opportunity to point out the envelope.

'I wonder what this can be about?' he said, tearing it open.

Seeing him pale, Grace whispered, 'Don't tell me something has happened to Jack.'

'Not Jack, no,' Alfred responded in a leaden tone. 'At least we can be grateful for that.' Yet still, his expression was grave.

'Grace, Olive,' he looked at each in turn, 'I'm so sorry. It's Reuben.'

'Siddy! What's happened?' Grace began to tremble.

'I'm not sure exactly. It seems his brigade was completely overrun by German tanks. Those poor souls stuck up near the border trying to defend France didn't stand a chance. I don't know what the generals were thinking, sending them into battle like that — it's blindingly obvious they were ill-equipped and undermanned.'

Alfred laid the letter on the table. 'We must prepare ourselves for the worst,' he said. 'Apparently, Reuben has been missing, presumed dead, for some time. The news was delayed as there was a fair amount of confusion over whether he might have escaped. However, the authorities have now concluded that it is most likely …' His voice broke. 'Most likely that Reuben has passed away.'

'No!' Grace screamed. Then, as the grandfather clock in the hall dolefully chimed the hour, she fell silent. Could it be true? A wave of desolation swept through her. She and Siddy had always had a special connection. She could not believe that her dear, knockabout friend, who knew horses better than anyone and yet played piano with the touch of an angel, could have died. Surely she would have known, surely there would have been some sort of sign? Yet everything had seemed just the same.

Finally, after several minutes, she shook her head with a new self-possession. 'Siddy isn't dead,' she said.

'Now, dear, of course it's terribly hard to accept that Reuben will never return,' Olive began, before Grace interrupted.

'Please, at least let me hope just a little. You can tell from the letter that the people in charge aren't sure what happened. If there isn't a body' — she shuddered — 'then maybe Siddy is still out there somewhere.'

CHAPTER EIGHT

January 1944

They were such a great distance from the turmoil and strife, from the bombs and the bloodshed and the terrible battles. Here at Brookfield, there was peace, tranquillity and good fortune. The wheat crop was bountiful and the wool clip had fetched record prices. Demand for the farm's produce from the Allies' vast military forces was insatiable.

'Food to eat, and uniforms to put on men's backs, that's what we're here for, Gracie.' Her father said it so often that it had become like a mantra. It seemed as if, by working day and night, he was somehow waging his own personal war against the enemies of the British Empire.

Grace glanced at him as he rode by her side, just as he used to when she was a child. Alfred had looked so tired and drawn of late, she and Olive had begged him to slow down. Never a heavy man, he had grown thin. His shirt hung from his shoulders and, beneath the straight brim of his hat, his hair was now more grey than brown.

'Everything all right, Gracie?' her father called as they cantered over the plains.

'Good as gold,' she shouted back.

And it was. For once, Grace had seen her father eat a hearty breakfast that morning; in fact, he seemed more robust than he had for days. Relieved, she was able to enjoy riding in the late-afternoon sun across the wide brown acres that he loved.

'Ah, I can see the problem — Bill mentioned it yesterday,' Alfred said as a distant dam came into view, its surface glittering in the sunlight. 'It will be tricky, but between the two of us, we should be able to set things right.'

The bank that bordered the dark water had grown soft and slippery after a sudden summer storm. As Grace slowed her horse, she could see that one of the sheep had strayed into a patch of deep mud and become trapped. It was struggling and making low, piteous sounds.

'Righto,' Alfred said as he swung down from his mount. 'Let's tether the horses to those red gums and get at it.'

Grace was grateful for the shade the trees cast. Now they had stopped riding, she realised how fierce the heat was.

'It would be a lot easier if we had a shovel.' Alfred frowned. 'Ah well, can't be helped. Sorry, Gracie, but I'm finding it hard to get down on my knees these days, so it's up to you. If you don't get rid of some of that bog, we'll never get her out.'

'Great! I get all the best jobs.'

Grace rolled up her sleeves, then crouched down in front of the sheep that, clearly exhausted, was now barely moving. Using a sturdy stick and her bare hands, she cleared away the worst of the clinging mud. A hearty laugh made her look up.

'What?'

'It's just that my sweet little green-eyed girl is practically covered in muck.' Alfred chuckled. 'You'd better clean yourself up before your mother catches sight of you!'

Grace pushed a muddy curl under her hat and grinned.

'Well, I'd better see what I can do about this poor beast.' Her father's boots made squelching sounds as he came closer. 'You support the ewe's rear so she doesn't damage herself, and I'll lift her front legs clear.'

'Are you sure, Dad? That's heavy work.'

'I've never felt better in my life,' he said.

Grace held the animal's hindquarters while Alfred, breathing heavily as his muscles strained, gently eased the ewe out.

'We've done it!' Grace shouted.

As she watched the creature wobble away, a piercing cry rang out, immediately followed by a thud. Grace wheeled around. Alfred was lying sprawled and still on the muddy bank.

'Dad!' She rushed forward and pressed her ear to his chest. His heart was beating, but it sounded weak. She quickly scanned her surroundings, her eyes wild with fear. If only a farmhand were about, or a drover, someone who could help. But there was not a living soul to be seen, just the flocks of heedless sheep nibbling at the stubbly grass, a remorseless sun in a cloudless sky and thousands of acres of emptiness.

Groaning with effort, Grace heaved her father's prone body out of the quagmire and into the shade of one of the red gums. Watched by a pair of black cockatoos, she folded his hat, placed it gently under his head, then tried to arrange his arms and legs as comfortably as she could.

Tears spilled onto her cheeks as she whispered, 'Hang on, Dad, just for a bit. I'll tell Bill; we'll come back and sort you out.'

Grace gently kissed her father's forehead. Then she flung herself onto her horse and began to ride across the plains like the wind.

Bill Gleason alerted Joe and Marjorie Evans — the road that snaked through the Evanses's property ran close to the boundary where Alfred had fallen. Grace called the doctor.

'What should I do next?' she asked the foreman with a tremor in her voice. It broke her heart to think of her father alone and untended. And what if he regained consciousness and found she'd deserted him?

'Your mother needs you,' Gleason said as he saddled his horse. 'I'm setting off straightaway with the young lads. We'll take care of your dad.'

Despite Bill's reassurances, Grace felt sick as she watched him and the two boys thunder out of the yard. She was torn, wanting desperately to return to her father yet, at the same time, knowing she couldn't leave her poor mother by herself.

The two anguished women waited tensely on the veranda. Her mother had screamed when Grace, her face filthy and tear-streaked, told her what had happened. Now Olive sat stiffly on one of the old wicker chairs, her lips pressed tightly together as she stared straight ahead. Grace's gaze, too, was locked on the horizon, searching for movement — a shape, a shadow, anything that might give her hope.

Inside the homestead, the telephone rang. Olive sprang up. Grace quickly followed.

'Yes, yes. I see. Right. I see. Thank you.' Her mother slowly put down the phone and sank into a chair.

'The men bypassed Brookfield,' she said tonelessly. 'They took your father by horse to the road, then on to the hospital in the Evanses's truck. He's had a heart attack.'

'Don't worry, Mum,' Grace said, kneeling beside her. 'We'll go straight there now.'

Olive didn't move.

'Mum, why are you still sitting down? Dad needs us!'

'Oh darling, he doesn't need any of us now.' Olive gave a wrenching sob. 'Your father has passed away.'

Dead. Grace was numb. Surely this couldn't be true. It was Jack who was away fighting, Siddy who was missing. Alfred had been on the farm, safe on his land, protected from misadventure. He was that rare man who, though engaged by the mind's inner landscapes, dearly loved the earth and its seasons. Now she had been told that her father was no more. It was incomprehensible.

Grace pressed her knees into her horse's smooth brown flanks, urging him onwards. She was riding hard, her heart thudding, the wind stinging her ears. It was what she craved, something tangible, a harsh, physical connection. Yet, without Alfred beside her, the wild beauty of the landscape offered little solace.

Her father's funeral was over and, finally, so was the wake. She had listened to Father Bartholomew's service, but the words of the sermon, the prayers and the lesson had slid past her, every utterance as insubstantial as a cloud of dust motes that, having been briefly illuminated by the light, just as quickly faded.

During the long wake that followed at Brookfield, Grace had felt only a hollow detachment. It was as if she had escaped from her own body and was gazing down while another Grace Woods thanked the mourners for their attendance, offering them sherry while agreeing, 'Yes, it's a great loss.'

Once she had left the cleared paddocks behind her, Grace slowed the sweating horse's pace to a walk in order to negotiate a path between the black pines and the paper-barked melaleuca trees. The creek was close by.

She heard the water before she saw it, the soft, swirling noise it made as it idled past reeds and stones. Grace dismounted and led her horse forward so that he could dip his head and drink. Then, cupping handfuls of water, Grace drank too, before tethering the horse to a branch. Save for the sound of the creek as it meandered by, the low buzz of insects and the occasional currawong's mournful cry, it was silent.

This was how it had always been, she thought, nothing had changed. The place belonged to a happier, long-ago time in her life, before Jack and Siddy had left for the war, before death had brought sorrow to Brookfield.

Grace sat down on a flat rock by the water's edge, her back against a tree stump. She thought of the many rides she and her father had shared, their mutual delight in bringing in a good harvest, even the pleasure they'd taken in each other's company as they went through the accounts late at night in his study.

Her heart ached when she contemplated a future without him. He had always been wise and dependable — so balanced, so certain. He had been devoted to Grace, yet she'd been miles away at the moment of his death. If only she could have told him how much he meant to her, smoothed his brow or held his dear hand while he drew his final breath. Overwhelmed by sadness and guilt, Grace hung her head and wept.

A soft, dry wind rustled the leaves at her feet. She felt immensely tired; the day seemed to have lasted an eternity. As her eyes began to close she murmured, 'I loved you so much, Daddy. Why did you have to go?'

Grace was almost asleep when she thought she heard her father's voice on the breeze whispering, 'In the end, we all do.'

When she woke up — she was sure she could only have drifted off for a few minutes — the wind had died down. Other than the gentle movement of the creek sliding by, it was perfectly still.

She untethered her horse and led him out of the scrub, past thickets of flaming red bottlebrush and spiky banksia. When they were clear, Grace hoisted herself onto the saddle and began to ride slowly back to Brookfield.

CHAPTER NINE

Sydney, March 1945

With her eyes fixed on the screen of the elaborately gilded Mayfair cinema, Grace watched intently as the flickering, black and white newsreel unspooled frame after frame of victorious images. Her breath caught as the camera panned across a group of pilots leaping jubilantly out of a row of Spitfire bombers, their faces wreathed in triumphant smiles.

'They look so handsome, like film stars,' Charlotte whispered.

'And do you know something?' Grace whispered back. 'To me, every one of them is Jack.'

Sitting in the darkened picture palace, she realised how much her feelings about him had changed. Once she'd thought of Jack as just a sweet local boy who'd always had a crush on her. Now, she cared for him on a deeper level, especially as his letters left her with no doubt about just how important she was to him. Grace had received a postcard depicting Big Ben only the day before; she still recalled the two simple sentences he had hurriedly scrawled: *Each night I dream that you're back in my arms. That's all I want.*

At the start of the war, Grace had found the overly bright tone of Jack's letters confusing. His words were too cheerful; they didn't ring true. While each day she steeled herself before reading the newspaper's growing lists of the dead and the wounded, Jack never referred to the heavy loss of life his squadron was suffering during its raids over Europe. Only when he stopped mentioning the name of a particular mate did she have an inkling that another of Jack's friends had met his fate.

Over time, this breezy tone altered, becoming increasingly grim until in his latest letter, he'd written:

Had a really bad day. We were out doing reconnaissance when one of the boys' planes copped heavy fire. The cockpit went up in flames and the poor bugger got trapped inside. I saw him struggling to get out, but there wasn't a bloody thing I could do about it.

If I didn't have you, Gracie, waiting back home, I don't know what would become of me. When I'm so damned sick and tired of it all that I just want to crawl into a deep black hole and never come out again, I tell myself that it's our future happiness I'm fighting for. That's what keeps me going.

Grace tried to imagine how desperate Jack's life had been. No doubt he'd had his share of horrifying narrow escapes, yet she'd only received that one letter where he referred to a crash landing, and even then he'd never disclosed exactly what had happened.

She told herself there was one thing she did know. After the years of hell Jack had endured, she couldn't let him down.

'Imagine what he has achieved, what he's done,' she said to Charlotte, ignoring the irritated 'Shhh' that came from the middle-aged couple sitting in the row behind. 'Jack Osbourne is not a boy anymore. He is a hero.'

Brookfield, December

It was nearly Christmas. The last three months had been bone dry. Formerly lush paddocks were the colour of parchment and the wheat crop was struggling to survive.

A sigh escaped Grace's lips as she dribbled a jug of water over her mother's wilting roses. She had been expecting Jack for days now. The war had been over for months, but it had taken him an age to be officially discharged. Even then, she'd had no idea when he would be able to board a ship for Australia.

Jack had been away for more than five years, she thought disconsolately, and during that time he'd covered himself in glory. But what had she achieved? It felt like very little. Yes, she'd laboured hard on the farm, even harder since her father's death the year before. She dropped into bed at night, her fingers blistered and her back aching. But mustering sheep or harvesting wheat was not dangerous; it wasn't as if she had risked her life.

Lending a hand at the charitable functions held in aid of the war effort had been an even less onerous undertaking. There had been dances in the district and more sophisticated balls and receptions she'd whirled off to during trips to Sydney. Grace smiled. She had to admit, these glamorous events had provided a pleasant distraction from the long, hard days spent working on the property.

The city had been filled with military men — at first only Australians, but then the Americans had arrived. Fresh-faced admirers had doffed their hats and called her 'ma'am'. Whenever she'd accepted one of their invitations — perhaps for dinner at the elegant Prince's restaurant or to go dancing at the Trocadero — a box of chocolates or a dewy orchid corsage would be sure to turn up before their arrival. Grace had even received a couple of sudden marriage proposals, although she'd never offered the ardent young men who pursued her anything more than a mildly flirtatious relationship.

Once she'd met a dashing officer at a party at the Parkes Air Base. They'd had fun, dancing energetic foxtrots and even some American swing, until she'd made the mistake of inviting him to enjoy the cool air outside. He'd wanted to make love to her, but when she'd turned him down, the fellow had accused her of being a tease. Had she led him on? He was very good-looking, and Grace had to admit, for a moment she'd wondered if, just this once, she might let herself go. Then an unnerving chill had come over her, and the temptation had passed. The fact was, no matter how appealing a man seemed, she had never felt the thrilling attraction other girls described. Grace had told herself that only went to prove how much she loved her childhood sweetheart. She'd be sure to find Jack irresistible when he finally came back.

As Grace upended the jug, sprinkling the last drops of water over the parched flower bed, she heard the faint sound of hooves in the distance. Looking up, she saw the blurred outline of a horse and rider through a cloud of reddish dust. Probably one of the station hands returning after checking the boundary fences, she thought. But something about the angle of the rider, the way he sat tall in the saddle, sent a quiver down her spine. Blinking, she tried to dispel the heat haze. A moment later, she was almost certain. A couple of minutes more and she was sure.

Grace Woods ran out of the homestead's open gate just as Squadron Leader Jack Osbourne leapt from his horse and into her waiting arms.

Sydney, May 1946

Wearing a cream, square-shouldered day dress made by Miss Louise, a small Lamotte cocktail hat with a veil and her mother's gift of a cultured pearl necklace and earrings, Grace entered the mellow, brick church of Saint James on the day of her wedding. She had been moved when Mr Fairweather had offered to walk her down the aisle, yet as she stood poised with her arm in his, she could not help but yearn for her own father's touch. Tears misted her eyes when she thought of Alfred, and Siddy too. Though she steadfastly nurtured a small flicker of hope, as the years went by she'd been forced to admit that the survival of the special man who had always meant so much to her seemed less and less likely.

The wedding was a modest affair, with perhaps fifty guests, for neither she nor Jack had wanted a fuss. In any case, butter, sugar and even fabric were still strictly rationed by the government — it was easier for everyone this way. Lottie, charmingly dressed in blush pink with a circlet of rosebuds in her fair hair, was her sole attendant; John Finch, a pilot mate of Jack's from Sydney whose eye-patch and walking stick indicated a narrowly averted disaster, was his best man.

Grace was neither nervous nor was she elated, not even when, to the rousing strains of the traditional Bridal Chorus, she arrived at the side of her delighted future husband. Instead, she had the impression that, ever since she'd first met Jack at the age of twelve, she had been travelling on a slow-moving conveyor belt. Now it had simply arrived at a predetermined destination.

As Grace handed Lottie her bouquet of red roses, she glimpsed her mother's pretty face, filled with a joy she had rarely seen since Alfred had passed away. If ever Grace had a doubt about marrying Jack, one look at Olive's transcendent expression was enough to reassure her that she had made the right decision.

The fragments of jewel-coloured light that spilled through the church's stained-glass windows seemed to dim momentarily. The final throaty notes of the pipe organ faded away. Then Grace heard Father Edwin clear his throat, and the wedding service began.

There was a bible reading, hymns were sung and an earnest homily on the sanctity of the matrimonial state was delivered. She and Jack repeated their responses, then exchanged solemn vows to honour, love and cherish each other for ever and ever. The best man limped forward and handed over the platinum ring. Jack smiled broadly as he placed the tight little band onto the third finger of Grace's left hand.

When the minister announced, 'You may now kiss the bride,' the groom obliged so enthusiastically he almost swept Grace off her feet. She felt herself blush as several of the younger male congregants cheered.

Once the register was signed, the two of them made their way outside the church. Grace stood arm in arm with her husband beneath a grey sky, receiving congratulations amid shouts of 'Good luck!' and flying clouds of confetti. Only then did it strike her that from this day on she would be Mrs Jack Osbourne. Somewhere inside the church, Grace Woods had slipped away.

'Crikey!' Jack exclaimed when Grace met him that night in the foyer of the Hotel Australia. 'You look like a movie star, sweetheart.'

The wedding reception had been held in the hotel's famous Emerald Room. Grace knew she should have felt on top of the world, but the cloying effect of the airless room's heavy Italian chandeliers, white marble statues and bubbling fountains combined with the noise of their guests talking, eating, laughing and drinking had made her head spin. Afterwards, feeling overcome with exhaustion, Grace had pleaded with Jack for an hour or two to herself. Thank heavens he'd agreed, going off to spend the time in the bar with John.

Once she had removed her formal hat and dress, Grace had sunk gratefully into a luxurious bath scented with rose oil. As the fragrant water had rippled around her, she'd hoped her wedding-night nerves would not be too obvious. Perhaps the daring, low-cut, red satin cocktail frock and the teetering platform shoes she planned to change into would bestow a veneer of worldliness she didn't feel.

'Would you be upset if we changed our plans and didn't dine at Romano's?' Jack asked, eyeing Grace appreciatively. 'I've been sharing my gorgeous bride with other people all day and I'm dying to have you all to myself. How about I organise to have dinner sent up to our suite instead?'

The naked desire in Jack's eyes made Grace's stomach flutter. 'I think that dining alone with my new husband might be a very good idea, indeed.' She smiled.

A few minutes after they returned to the luxurious bridal suite, a bow-tied waiter arrived bearing an ice bucket containing two bottles of champagne — 'So we don't run out,' Jack confided with a grin. Then another waiter glided in with a trolley on which were arrayed a dozen rock oysters and, under a silver dome, grilled fillets of flounder. There were also strawberries and cream and mint chocolate slices.

'I hope you like it,' Jack said. 'I know we cut back on the reception, but you only have one wedding night, don't you? I figured we should go all out.'

As soon as they were alone, he poured two glasses of the fizzing champagne.

'To you, my beautiful girl,' he said thickly, before taking a gulp.

They sat opposite each other at a small table, eating their oysters, laughing over the best man's unexpectedly funny speech and the three punch bowls that had featured among their wedding presents.

'I hate to tell you,' Grace giggled, 'but we've also been given three toasters.'

'Well, I think what we need right now is more champagne,' Jack announced. Grace tried not to worry about the number of times he had already refilled his glass.

'The thing is,' he said with a rasp in his voice. 'I seem to have lost my appetite. Sweetheart, why don't we lie on the bed? It looks awfully comfortable.'

Grace kicked off her shoes and, still fully dressed, turned back the counterpane before reclining on top of the crisp cotton sheet. To her relief, she felt few of her usual inhibitions. Instead, a lick of heat curled through her body. Tonight, she would give herself for the first time to a man; it was the precious gift she had been saving for her husband. As he lay down next to her, she anticipated a romantic, slow induction into the art of lovemaking.

Jack seemed to have other ideas. He gave her only a perfunctory kiss before she felt his fingers fumble with the small covered buttons that ran down the front of her red dress.

'Dammit, Gracie, give me a hand,' he grumbled.

Grace hurried to unfasten her frock; she couldn't bear to annoy Jack now. Then, somehow, the dress was on the floor, her brassiere was off and his fingers were bruising her nipples.

She'd hardly had time to grow used to this new sensation before he tore off her briefs and plunged his hand between her legs. Everything was happening too quickly.

'Jack, stop!' she said, thrusting his hand away.

'What the hell is the matter?' he groaned.

'You're ... you're taking things too fast.'

'God, I'm sorry, Gracie, but I've waited so long,' he panted. 'You looked so damned sexy in that dress and, well ...' His hands were roving over her thighs and pawing her breasts. 'Just try to relax, okay? Trust me, everything will be great.'

But it wasn't. What Jack was doing only made her feel tense — and it all seemed horribly rushed. Perhaps this was the way such things always transpired between a husband and wife, Grace thought uncertainly. If that was so, then she had to at least seem enthusiastic. Pasting a smile onto her face, she wrapped her arms around him.

'You see?' Jack said. 'I knew you'd like it.'

She waited while his body bore down upon her own, tried not to scream as she felt his crushing weight, a penetrating insistence and then a final, searing pain.

Breathing heavily, Jack grunted, 'Christ, that was good.' He rolled onto his back and was asleep within seconds.

Grace couldn't understand it. Olive had always claimed that sex was for men to enjoy, yet several of her married friends had hinted at nights of shared bliss. Why hadn't she, too, been swept away by passion?

Stiff, sore and disappointed, she wondered if there was something wrong with her. Perhaps she was — what had those girls called it? — frigid. Grace had heard them talk knowingly about women like that. They said it was the reason why men strayed.

As she listened to Jack snoring, Grace told herself that when it came to such things, she was, after all, a novice. She would just have to learn to perform and — who knows? — even enjoy those physical intimacies that husbands expected from wives. Surely their lovemaking would improve. It was only a matter of time.

CHAPTER TEN

Paris, December 1948

Grace stayed close behind Madame Raymonde's narrow, burgundy-clad back as she led her through a labyrinth of rooms and passageways. Then, just as she rounded a corner, the stylish woman stopped abruptly.

'Jeanne,' she said, gesturing impatiently to a passing assistant dressed in an understated charcoal suit. 'Why are these gardenias in the corridor? I am quite sure that *le patron* wanted them in the salon. The Viscountess de Noailles is due for her fitting today and they are her favourite flowers. Please take them there at once.'

Intrigued, Grace was about to inquire whether the floral preferences of the house's other clients were indulged in this way, but Madame Raymonde had not finished.

'And what is this doing here? So careless!' she said, picking a strand of white cotton from the plush grey carpet. She turned to Grace. 'I see you are looking at me with a curious expression. You are asking yourself, "What exactly is Madame Raymonde's role?"' She chuckled quietly. 'Monsieur Dior has been known to refer to me as his "other self".

In fact, what I do is eliminate problems.' She paused, seeming to contemplate her position's endless responsibilities.

'I organise *le patron*'s very busy schedule, employ staff, oversee production, order fabrics and ensure that every department knows exactly what is expected of it,' Madame Raymonde said, ticking off each duty on one of her long fingers. 'Yes, I do many things. Some of them — such as worrying about a client's favourite flower or a stray thread — may appear to you to be of little consequence. But, Mademoiselle Dubois, you will soon discover that in this particular couture house everyone, no matter what their job may be, seeks perfection. If you are incapable of delivering it, you will not be with us for very long.'

This sobering remark prompted Grace to declare, 'I promise to do my absolute best; that is the very least a genius like Christian Dior can expect.'

'Monsieur Dior is not *just* a genius,' Madame Raymonde corrected her. 'And for that matter, he is not simply the couturier who invented the New Look. He is the man who saved Paris fashion.'

Both fell silent.

'Now, where was I?' Madame Raymonde said with a small frown. 'That's right.' She nodded. 'I was about to explain that while we are en route to your rendezvous with *le patron*, I will have the opportunity to bring several remarkable women to your attention. Each, in her different way, strives to ensure that the *maison* continues to run with the smoothness of — how shall I put this?' She nodded again. 'Yes, with the smoothness of the finest silk mousseline.

'First of all, over there in the red suit with that little man from *Vogue* is Madame Luling, our public relations director,' Madame Raymonde advised, as she began conducting Grace briskly around the atelier. 'Whether it is the press or our clients, Suzanne has an uncanny ability to meet even the most unreasonable requests.

'And in that room on the right is Madame Beguin, the *maison*'s *première vendeuse*,' she continued, while lingering at the entrance to the salon. 'We had to woo her away from Mainbocher, you know.'

Grace glimpsed Dior's chief saleswoman in close conversation with a rail-thin, smartly dressed lady.

In a hushed voice, her elegant guide said, 'We knew that if she came to us, then the Duchess of Windsor would follow. As you may have noticed' — she inclined her head — 'that is exactly what happened.'

Next, they were acknowledged by a striking creature who nodded to them as she stalked down the corridor. The woman looked the way Grace imagined Cleopatra might have done, had the Queen of the Nile been partial to attiring herself in an exceptionally chic, close-fitting black dress, ropes of gleaming pearls and a leopard-print turban.

'Heavens, who was that?'

'Madame Bricard. She provides her eye.'

'Her eye?'

'Why yes, it is unerring. La Bricard is one of the very few women who have perfect taste. I would go so far as to say that for *le patron*, she is indispensable.'

Finally, Madame Raymonde led Grace up a set of stairs. 'We will now visit the workroom, where you will meet our *directrice de technique*. We refer to her as *la première*, for you see, as far as this *maison* is concerned, she is incomparable.'

Grace entered a large, light-filled room containing bolts of fabric, tailor's dummies, cotton reels, scissors and ribbons. There were wide cutting tables and small desks at which sat numerous women, all clad uniformly in white smocks, sewing by hand with intense concentration. Among their ranks Grace saw an apple-cheeked, buxom lady who might have stepped out of a Renoir painting.

'May I introduce you to Madame Carré,' Madame Raymonde said. 'Marguerite not only oversees the workroom, she also bears the great responsibility of bringing Monsieur Dior's sketches to life. It is her magic that transforms a few black lines on a page into a debutante's dinner dress, a suit for the wife of an ambassador, or an evening gown fit for a queen.'

The *première* looked up from her worktable. 'And the outcome must always be the same — flawless!'

Madame Raymonde smiled. 'Mademoiselle Dubois, I shall leave you in Marguerite's very capable hands. By the time she has finished with you, *le patron* should be available.'

Once Dior's manager had swished out of the room, Grace said, 'I have been wondering how long it actually takes to make a dress.'

'For something simple, perhaps eighty hours,' the *première* replied airily.

'*Eighty!*'

'Why yes, mademoiselle. Although when I say "simple" I mean, of course, that it only *appears* to be simple.' She picked up a plain black silk bodice and turned it inside out. 'Do you see the padding that creates the shape? And all the tiny stitches securing the taffeta lining? Rather like life itself,' she added philosophically, 'it takes a very great deal of time and effort to disguise the complexity that lies beneath a perfect exterior.'

Madame Carré gestured for Grace to step closer. 'Most important of all,' she insisted, brandishing a small green volume, 'is this little book. It contains each mannequin's vital statistics. Everything we produce in the atelier is based on these numbers, so it is essential that they are accurate. Now, it is your turn to be measured, *s'il vous plaît.*'

Madame Carré bustled about, noting down the size of Grace's hips, waist and bust; the distance between each shoulder; the width of her back; the length of her arms; the circumference of her wrists, and the precise dimensions of a dozen other places.

As the tape measure flew about, Grace reflected on how fortunate she was that an immense stroke of luck had brought her to the one city in the world where she most wished to live. With the previous certainties of her life banished forever, Grace prayed that the answers she sought might be revealed in this legendary city.

'*Tournez, Mademoiselle Dubois!*'

Preoccupied by her thoughts, Grace had not been paying sufficient attention. She would clearly have to do a better job of keeping her wits about her if she had any hope of securing a permanent position as a house mannequin for the unusually gifted man who, it was universally acknowledged, was the most important couturier alive today.

Christian Dior: She cast her mind back to the moment, not quite two years before and half a world away, when she had first seen his name. It was near the end of an oppressive summer's day and, hoping for a breeze, she had left the homestead's front door open at Merindah, the sheep station Jack's parents had bestowed on him as a wedding present. She remembered that when she'd picked up the newspaper from the hall table her ears had rung with the screeching of the pink and grey galahs that were roosting in the old eucalyptus tree over by the gate.

Closing the door behind her, she'd walked through the shuttered house to the kitchen and spread the newspaper out on the scrubbed pine table. To her surprise there was a fashion story, not, as was usual, buried in the modest women's section towards the back, but enjoying pride of place, right on the front page. With a bold headline proclaiming 'New Look Stuns Paris', the article described the first collection created by a daring French couturier, of whom, it seemed, no one had ever heard. Once the Germans had marched into Paris there hadn't been a word printed about French fashion, and even after the war ended it appeared there'd been little to report on. But now the paper claimed that Monsieur Christian Dior's clothes were 'revolutionary', and that even the world's most sophisticated women had cried out and swooned over his lavish dresses and gowns.

As Grace read on about the ecstatic American fashion editors who'd attended the show perched on tiny gilt chairs and the marvellous mannequins who'd sent ashtrays flying with a flick of their fabulous flared skirts, she longed to have been there.

'Grace!' Jack stormed into the room, his face streaked with dust and sweat. 'What on earth are you dreaming about now? I've been out in the bloody shearing sheds all day. The least you could do is put down the paper and say hello to your husband.'

But so fascinated was Grace by the description of the unknown Frenchman and his radically different, glorious creations that she barely heard him. According to the article, Christian Dior's clothes were nothing like the uninspiring, meagre garments that Grace and everyone else she knew had been forced to wear ever since rationing had been imposed five years earlier. Annoyingly, since then there'd been no change, even though the war had been over for ages. But Dior's daring confections broke all the government's rules: sweeping from tiny, cinched waists were voluminous skirts made of thirty or forty, even fifty sinful yards of sumptuous fabric — fine wools, silk taffeta, velvets and satins.

Grace could see herself in the station's kitchen — the image still vivid — tugging at her skimpy checked frock. It had seemed somehow mean. And she remembered the words she'd repeated for days afterwards whenever she wondered what a woman dressed by Christian Dior would be like. 'Simply extraordinary,' she had murmured.

The memory now made Grace smile. For here she was, improbable as it seemed, at the epicentre of the world of high fashion, with the trusted *première* of Dior herself making careful preparations to ensure that, at least during her hours of work, Mademoiselle Dubois would wear nothing but the great couturier's fabled creations.

CHAPTER ELEVEN

Merindah, May 1948

Silence reigned. It was broken only by the trickling sound of tea being poured from a pot, the jarring of cups as they were set down on the table and the jagged crunch of toast being cut with a knife.

Here it was, their second wedding anniversary, and there had been another terrible row the night before. Once again, Jack had drunk too much; Grace had rebuffed his whisky-scented, amorous advances. He'd been furious when she'd blurted out that since he had come back from the war, he wasn't the same man.

Jack had grabbed her and, well, he was her husband, so she couldn't say he'd forced himself on her. But when Grace had made it plain that she didn't want him, he'd gone ahead just the same. It had been degrading.

The sweet boy who'd once sworn he would never make her do anything against her will was long gone. Now they weren't talking to each other, and Grace was damned if she would be the first to speak.

Finally, Jack growled, 'Why do you always have to do that?'

'Do what?' Grace answered coldly.

'Humiliate me.'

'It's hard to get in the mood for making love when you're stinking of drink.'

'Bloody hell!' Jack exploded. 'What's wrong with you? Whether I'm drunk or sober, you're always the same. It's like being married to a frigging block of ice.'

Jack's barb hit home. Grace was only too aware that when it came to sex, she was an utter failure.

'And another thing. You think you're little Miss Perfect, that you know better than me!' He was shouting now. 'Well, I'll tell you something for nothing. There isn't a bloke worth his salt that would tolerate a woman interfering with his business.'

'Jack, all I've ever done is try to be useful. What I said yesterday — I just think that seeing we're verging on drought again, it might make sense if you sold off some of the sheep.' At least managing a farm *was* something she was good at.

'You can't help yourself, can you?' Jack slammed his fist onto the table, sending the cups flying. 'I won't have you poking your nose in where it doesn't belong. Stick to women's work. I thought I made that clear.'

'I was trying to help, to be a good wife,' Grace said.

'If you were a good wife you'd show that in the bedroom for a change, instead of meddling in something that's none of your concern.' His eyes flashed angrily. 'Are you trying to make me feel less of a man — is that what you want? Because if it is, sweetheart, you're going the right way about it.'

'But I've lived and worked on a farm all my life!' she protested. 'After Dad died I ran Brookfield practically single-handed.'

'It's high time you forgot all that.' Jack glared at her. 'It wasn't a bloody business partner I was fighting for in the war! I dreamt about coming home to a real wife, one who showed me a bit of love and affection — only you're not even capable of it.'

'Well, if you didn't treat me as if I was a fool —'

'That's it!' Jack said. 'I've had enough.' He flung his napkin down, jumped to his feet and stamped out of the house.

Quite alone, with only the wreckage of the half-eaten breakfast before her, Grace said in a small voice, 'Me too.'

Anxious to leave Merindah behind her, Grace leapt on one of the farm's new motorbikes, determined to ride over to the Fairweather property, Oakhill, and see Charlotte. Now the war was over, her friend had taken on a part-time job working for a doctor in Parkes. Fortunately, this was her day off.

Dear Lottie, I'm so lucky to have her, Grace thought as she started the engine. Gripping the handlebars, she revved the accelerator as she bumped her way along the uneven clay road. She reminded herself to be careful of the rocks and potholes; at least the long dry spell meant she wouldn't sink into a treacherous bog.

'What's up?' Charlotte asked after Grace removed her dusk-caked helmet and goggles. The two of them were standing in the shade cast by the spreading branches of an angophora. 'When you rang you said it was something important.'

'I really need to talk. Everything is just so complicated, and …' Grace took a moment to gaze at the arid paddocks before turning back to her friend. 'I can't help wondering, who the hell am I?'

'Hang on, where did that come from? What's all this about?' Charlotte frowned.

'Nothing seems right anymore, Lottie.' Grace bent to brush the clinging ochre dust from her jodhpurs, then straightened up. 'Look at me: I'm twenty-five, I've never had a real job, never earned my own money. Plus my marriage has been a huge mistake.'

'Gracie, it can't be as bad as all that,' said Charlotte. 'Come inside and we'll talk. I'll get us a cool drink.'

While Charlotte went to fetch some chilled barley water, Grace paced restlessly around the Fairweathers' sitting room. *Is it me*, she wondered. *Have I brought all this on myself?*

'Gracie, let's sit on the settee.' Charlotte handed her a long glass. 'All right, out with it. What's going on?'

'It's just that I was so terribly young when I told Jack I'd wait,' Grace confessed in a rush. 'Then the war dragged on and on. Afterwards, everyone was so — what's that expression the Americans use? So gung ho about us getting married, and I'd somehow built up all these ridiculous romantic notions about him. Jack had such an amazing life when he was flying, full of purpose, even though he had a terrible crash. I've seen his scars, but he still won't discuss it — and he doesn't say a word about how awful it was to lose so many mates.'

She set her glass down on a table. 'He's changed, Lottie. When Jack came back from the war he seemed so much older and bitter somehow. He started drinking quite a bit and now, when he isn't stomping around, roaring like an angry bull, he's just at a loss. One thing's for sure — I can't make him happy.'

'But Jack's lovely whenever I see him.'

'Oh, he can be charming if he wants to,' Grace said, 'but you don't know him the way I do. Look, maybe we're just not a good match. I'm not like my mother. Even without Dad, she still loves playing the country hostess, throwing herself into all the local activities. I've always wanted to travel, see the world, be something … not more, I don't mean that — but different.'

Grace swallowed the last of her drink. 'The worst thing is — it's embarrassing just to talk about it — I loathe having sex. Even if it starts off all right, it always ends badly. Now I simply make excuses — headaches, anything I can think of. It doesn't matter anyway. These days, Jack rarely bothers me. I wouldn't be surprised if he's got someone else.'

'Grace, surely not! You know Jack's always been crazy about you.'

'Well, whatever's been going on, we can't continue like this. We're both miserable.'

'I'm sure that lots of people have problems with their marriages,' Charlotte said soothingly, 'but then, after a bit, it all gets sorted out. You can't honestly be thinking of leaving him.'

Grace realised that Charlotte did not understand the depth of her unhappiness. *But then*, she thought, *I barely understand it myself.* She knew she had an abundance of all the things from which a woman was meant to derive fulfilment: a husband who, despite everything, she was fairly certain still loved her; more than sufficient income for a bulging wardrobe of clothes; her own car; and a beautiful home.

She did not have a baby, it was true, though considering their increasing physical estrangement, that wasn't surprising. *It's just as well*, Grace reflected, *because if I did have a child with Jack then I really would be trapped. I'd be tied to him forever.*

'Actually, I think we would both be better off apart,' she said.

'What? Where would you go — back to Brookfield?'

'No, I couldn't bear to live with Mum's disappointment. She and her friends always thought Jack was the catch of the century. Anyway, I want to move to Sydney.'

'And do what?' Charlotte asked cautiously.

'Good question. The fact is, I'm not trained for anything. Can I nurse or teach, let alone type or do shorthand like you can? No. It's hopeless, Lottie. I appear to be completely unemployable.' Grace clasped her hands together and placed them primly in her lap.

Charlotte laughed. 'Now you're just being silly.'

'Really? Well, let's see what I do well. I can sow crops and harvest them, drive a truck or a tractor practically blindfolded, ride just about any horse, muster as many sheep as you like and, at the end of the day, manage the farm's paperwork — only, there's not a lot of bosses in the city looking for that particular set of skills. On the other side of the ledger, I know a good dress when I see one, I can speak French, play the piano and sing a bit, plus I'm not bad at painting and drawing.'

She shook her head. 'It looks like the only occupations I'm suited for are either an eighteenth-century lady of leisure, which is not exactly a going profession, or running a property — and there is certainly no one I know who wants me to do that, least of all Jack.'

'Gracie, darling, I think you just have a bad case of the blues.' Charlotte smiled at her friend sympathetically. 'But don't worry, I have the solution.'

'Really? I'd love to know what it is.'

'Well, what always works when a girl is feeling gloomy. For goodness sake, pop down on the train to Sydney for a few days and buy a dress — or two! You'll see: you will feel better, things with Jack will settle down and life will go back to normal.'

CHAPTER TWELVE

Sydney, May 1948

Angling her slender body in front of Miss Louise's long, black-edged mirror, Grace considered the fit of the dressmaker's creation. 'Darling Lou Lou, you're so clever!' she said.

The navy blue dress with its unusual collar and full skirt did look good on her, flattering her narrow shoulders and slim waist. Of course, it wasn't quite as stylish as the latest Paris fashions but, on balance, it was a close enough approximation.

'You have a model's figure, you know,' said Louise. She removed her large horn-rimmed spectacles and took a couple of steps back.

Grace laughed. 'Lou Lou, now you are just flattering me.'

'I'm not!' she protested. 'Everything I make looks better on you than on any of my other ladies, and that's the truth. It's a wonder you're not a mannequin. As a matter of fact, I've heard something from my sister — you know, the one who's a salesgirl in the Exclusive Dresses department at David Jones?'

'I think so.'

Louise assumed a confidential air. 'Apparently, the higher-ups at the store are searching for beautiful young women —

as long as they're able to wear clothes really well. It's so they can model in a special parade. Would you consider it?'

Grace laughed again. 'I don't know what my husband would say. Anyway, why would I be interested?'

Louise's face bore the unmistakeable expression of someone with a trump card to play. 'Strictly between us' — she lowered her voice — 'my sister told me that their head buyer, Mrs Shiell, has had something of a victory. She travelled all the way to Paris and, well, to cut a long story short, you know how you're mad about the New Look?'

'Along with every other woman in the world,' Grace said. 'But what's that got to do with anything?'

'Just this: Mrs Shiell has convinced none other than Christian Dior *himself* to send his collection here, to Sydney. Imagine — the very first time the New Look will be seen outside Paris, and it's not going to London or New York, but Sydney!' Miss Louise beamed triumphantly. 'That's the reason why David Jones wants Australia's loveliest women to be the mannequins, and that's why I thought of you.'

Despite Grace's remonstrations, Louise wrote down Mrs Shiell's telephone number. 'You never know, you might change your mind,' she said, slipping the piece of paper into her client's black patent-leather handbag.

Grace had arranged to catch up with friends at the venerable women-only Queen's Club for afternoon tea, but found herself incapable of concentrating on the gossip they were exchanging amid the plump, chintz-covered sofas and the portraits of the British royal family. Instead, she sat fidgeting on one of the floral armchairs, fighting what, to her surprise, had become a near-irresistible urge to examine the piece of paper Miss Louise had insisted she take with her. Finally, when the last cup of tea had been drunk and promises to meet again soon exchanged, Grace said her goodbyes and swiftly climbed the carpeted stairs to her room.

Once she had turned the key and walked inside, however, she felt foolish. Telling herself that — no matter how spectacular the clothes undoubtedly were — the very idea of modelling in a fashion parade was absurd, Grace tried to read her new Hercule Poirot mystery. She found she wasn't in the right mood. Looking around for something else to divert her attention, she reached for an ageing copy of *The Home* that had been left on the bedside table.

Grace turned a few pages. Suddenly, she threw the magazine down, picked up her handbag and upended its contents onto the bed. There, among an assortment of hair pins, lipsticks and half a dozen other sundry items, was the slip of paper. She immediately placed it by the telephone, lifted the receiver and said, 'Operator? This is Mrs Osbourne. I wonder if you could connect me with David Jones.'

Sydney, 1 August

'Oh, wasn't it fabulous?' Grace said to Olive, her green eyes sparkling.

She felt as if only one half of her was eating breakfast with her mother in their sunny hotel room. The other half was still whirling through the previous night's Christian Dior fashion parade in the packed David Jones ballroom. Beneath the glass lanterns suspended from its soaring ceiling, she had swept past the glamorous audience, glimpsing the rapt expressions on their faces as she felt the thrill of taking part in a show that had, for one magical night, brought the enchantment of Paris couture to the distant harbour city.

She thought back to how nervous she'd been on her way to her audition at the store, concerned that she might appear idiotic. But as soon as she had slipped into the satin ball dress Mrs Shiell had handed to her, walked across the fashion department's polished floorboards and executed an experimental turn, she'd felt completely confident. Mrs Shiell had said, 'Again, please,' giving her a look of approval. Then, after a brief word with an assistant, she'd declared, 'Grace Osbourne, the job is yours.'

On the way home, Grace's anticipation of Jack's angry response to her news had dampened her excitement, yet when she'd told him about the show he'd simply shaken his head before growling, 'If you want to make a spectacle of yourself, go right ahead. I really couldn't care less.'

Fortunately, her mother had been delighted. 'As the gala parade is in aid of the Food for Britain Appeal, I think I can safely say that your participation is more than justified,' she'd said. Grace suspected that, altruism aside, Olive simply couldn't wait to see her own daughter wearing the fabulous French fashions. And, just as Grace had anticipated, last night she'd evidently had the time of her life.

As if on cue, her mother looked at her and smiled. 'I was so proud of you, darling,' she said. 'You took to the catwalk as if you were born for it. I only wish your father could have been there to see his beautiful daughter.' She tapped the side of her boiled egg. 'Marjorie agreed with me — you received far more applause than any of the other girls.'

'Well, I don't know about that,' Grace laughed, 'but I do know that I feel as if I'm floating on air. I've never seen, let alone worn such glorious clothes. Dior's colours, the fabrics, those huge wonderful skirts, the yards of velvet and satin and tulle …'

She stretched like a languorous cat. 'Do you remember that amazing flat hat and the red wool coat with the sable cuffs?' Grace could still see the opulent ensemble dancing in front of her eyes. 'And what about at the end, when we all came out and I wore that chartreuse silk gown with the diamanté necklace,' she said dreamily. 'It was just like being a fairy princess for the night, only I'm going to be doing it all over again — during the day, at least. I can't wait for the rest of the shows.'

'You're lucky you have such an understanding husband,' Olive observed.

'I think he was probably pleased to have me off his hands for a while,' Grace replied without thinking. She had forgotten she'd chosen not to reveal Jack's surly reaction.

'I certainly hope that you're joking,' her mother said tartly. 'You know perfectly well where your first duty lies. It's lovely that you've been able to have so much fun, and of course the event raised a great deal of money for the poor British people. But it wouldn't do for you to get carried away and forget that you are, first and foremost, Mrs Jack Osbourne of Merindah sheep station.'

Grace's ebullient mood suddenly evaporated.

'In any case, it's high time you started a family,' Olive added. 'I don't know what's taking you so long.'

CHAPTER THIRTEEN

Merindah, September 1948

Grace walked listlessly along the gravel road that stretched from the homestead to the property's white-painted gates, where the mailbox stood. Since returning to Merindah, her days had seemed less fulfilling than ever. Life might have been different if she'd been involved in managing the farm, but Jack still wouldn't hear of it. They had returned to a state of simmering tension, punctuated by the eruption of flaming arguments. *Something has to change*, she thought. *But what? And how?*

Preoccupied by her reflections, she stopped at the mailbox, flipped up the steel lid and reached inside. She was stuffing the usual collection of bills and letters into the hessian bag she'd brought with her when a thick, cream envelope caught her eye.

As soon as she saw the French stamps it bore, and her name, written with a flourish above the address, Grace felt a thrill of anticipation. *It must be from Dior*, she thought. No doubt it was just a polite note of thanks, but perhaps they wanted to tell her about their plans for another Australian show — that would be wonderful. Grace hurriedly tore open the envelope and removed a single sheet of heavy paper.

Mentally translating the French into English, she read the brief letter with rapidly mounting excitement until she arrived at two astonishing lines: *Therefore, as a consequence of your unique presence, we are delighted to extend an invitation to you to join Christian Dior in Paris as one of our elite house mannequins.*

'Paris! I can't believe it!' she shouted, before sashaying forward on the gravel road and performing several exuberant, catwalk-worthy twirls. Startled, a pair of bright-eyed wallabies that had been grazing nearby raised their heads with a jerk and shot off across the paddocks.

By that afternoon, Grace's carefree jubilation had begun to wane. She moved restlessly from one room to another, at first straightening a stack of books, then adjusting a silver picture frame, before picking up and winding the brass carriage clock that stood on the mantelpiece and putting it down again. *This is hopeless*, she decided. The only thing for it was to telephone Charlotte.

She hurriedly told Lottie about Dior's invitation before pleading, 'What do you think? Is it all too good to be true?'

'What on earth are you saying — you can't possibly be thinking of accepting! Imagine what your mother would say, let alone Jack,' Lottie cautioned. 'Gracie, darling, running off to the other side of the world is hardly the solution to any problems you imagine exist in your marriage. It was one thing to model in those shows in Sydney and Melbourne. I know how much fun you had, but surely you can see that to take up this offer is completely out of the question. You must say no.'

Grace sighed. 'You're right, of course. The whole venture sounds precarious and so, well, unlikely. In any case, it would mean leaving behind everyone I know.'

'Most particularly, your husband,' Charlotte said pointedly.

As she sped towards the Parkes post office in her blue Vauxhall, Grace reflected that if it had not been for the extraordinary determination of Mrs Mary Alice Shiell, Christian Dior would never have agreed to stage his first international parade in — of all places — Sydney, Australia. At the same time, had Miss Louise not strongly recommended her to be selected as a mannequin for the show, and had she herself not subsequently met with such widespread acclaim, she would never have been invited to model in Paris. Furthermore, if her marriage had been at all successful she would not be giving a moment's consideration to Dior's astounding offer. It was these random acts and decisions alone, she knew, that had opened a door to a new and glorious life. But would she walk through? She still wasn't certain.

Grace frowned. She couldn't even be sure whether she would be permitted to travel abroad. She'd been shocked to discover that a husband's permission was required before the Australian Government would issue a passport to a married woman. The regulation was positively archaic, but there was no way around it. Jack would hit the roof if she asked for his consent, which was especially infuriating, as the more she thought about it, the more tempted she was to accept Dior's invitation.

For years now she'd tried to live the sort of life that others expected of her, until she'd begun to feel as if she was turning into one of the Ugly Sisters — only instead of trying to cram her foot into a shoe that didn't fit, she'd been forcing herself to become someone she was never meant to be. The letter from Dior had rekindled all her dreams of travel and adventure.

Now she yearned to inhabit an enchanting world, one that would fit her as perfectly as Cinderella's glass slipper.

There was something else, too, that drew Grace towards France. It was the last place dear Siddy had been seen alive. At last, she might be able to find out what had happened to him during that terrible battle.

After a long, restless night spent wondering how she would ever be able to leave Australia, just as dawn broke, a simple, if potentially hazardous, solution occurred to her. How would anyone in the Department of External Affairs know she was married? All she had to do was to apply using the name Woods rather than Osbourne, tick the box on the application marked 'single' and post it together with her birth certificate.

The problem was, the plan entailed lying to the government. Grace felt her throat constrict. What if her ruse was exposed? At the very least, the Department would decline to issue a passport. Even worse, they might alert Jack, who would undoubtedly be fusious and refuse to cooperate. Most alarming of all, she could well be prosecuted — wasn't fraud a criminal act?

There was no alternative. She would simply have to take the risk.

Two weeks later, Grace held the official response from the Department of External Affairs in her clammy hands. Had her plan worked? Was the passport on its way, or had all her efforts failed? She took a moment to steady herself, breathed deeply, then began reading the letter.

'Thank goodness.' She heaved a sigh of relief. There was not a single mention of her marital status. However, matters didn't seem to be nearly as straightforward as she'd hoped. To her surprise, a completely different issue had been raised.

2 October 1948

Dear Madam,

We note that you have made an application to the Government of the Commonwealth of Australia for a passport.

Having closely examined your Birth Certificate, we further note that it would appear the letter 's' may have been added to your surname by a person or persons unknown.

This is a routine inquiry and should not unduly impede the issuing of a passport. However, the department does require clarification as to the spelling of your name for the purpose of correct documentation. Accordingly, we request your advice as to whether you are a Miss Grace Woods, or Wood.

Yours faithfully,

Miss E. Grieves, Junior Clerk, on behalf of Mr C. Redmond, Section Manager

It was as if an unseen hand had slapped her hard across the face. Familiar objects around her — a chair, a small table, a bright blue velvet footstool — became unmoored. The room spun like a fairground carousel.

Grace closed her eyes. Though her thoughts were racing, she willed herself to be still. What did the letter mean? It was there, pricking at the edge of her consciousness, yet, in her disoriented state, its significance remained elusive. She did not know for how long she sat, her mind wrestling with unthinkable possibilities. As she reflected on her life, on the questions left unexplained, she felt as if hours passed by.

Grace glanced at her wristwatch. It had been ten minutes at most since she'd read the letter, yet in that brief space of time her world had tilted on its axis. Just one small, serpentine mark had caused her life's easy certainties to be overturned.

Vague, half-recalled comments, odd similarities — and differences — assumed a new meaning. There could be only one devastating explanation. She was not the person she had always believed herself to be.

Grace grabbed her car keys, determined to drive to Brookfield at once and confront her mother. Furious, she gripped the Vauxhall's steering wheel and slammed her foot on the pedals, sending clouds of ochre dust flying.

When she arrived she raced across Brookfield's wide veranda and burst through the front door, calling her mother's name. She found Olive alone in the dining room, studying a scattering of seed catalogues spread before her on the table.

'Grace, is that you? Sorry it's all such a mess. I'm just thinking about planting some new perennials and …' Olive looked up. 'Why, whatever is the matter, what's happened? You don't look at all like yourself.'

'Really, Mother? Exactly who do you think I look like?' Grace spat the words out. 'Not your late husband, that's certain.'

'Grace!' Olive gripped the edge of the table, her knuckles white. 'What in God's name are you talking about?'

'Simply this. All my life you have been lying to me. But that's all over now. You see, I know the truth.'

'Know, know what?' Olive asked in a trembling voice.

'My real name is not Woods,' Grace said angrily to her mother. 'I only worked it out this morning after I received a letter from the passport office. I was born Grace Wood. *Wood!* The government queried my birth certificate.' She threw the document onto the table. 'I've never really looked at it before, but now I can see exactly what they mean. Someone added the "s" to my last name — it's obvious that the ink is not the same, and neither is the handwriting.'

Grace's expression was anguished. 'Reuben Wood is my father, isn't he?'

Olive paled.

'All this time you drummed your version of morality into my head, twisting my ideas,' Grace said. 'You told me nice girls weren't interested in sex, that I should keep myself pure for my husband. What a hypocrite you are.'

'Gracie, you're wrong!' Olive jumped up.

'I don't think so,' Grace said sadly. 'All things considered, I should have realised a long time ago. I never resembled Alfred. My eyes are green and my hair is black, just like Reuben's. I can even play the piano by ear like he does.'

'Darling, you can't hope to comprehend.'

'But that's just it — at long last, I do.' Grace folded her arms. 'I overheard you arguing with Reuben in the Hotel Australia when I was a child, but I couldn't understand what it was about. Now, I know he wanted me back but you wouldn't hear of it. And Pearl wasn't sent away because she was too reckless or I was too old. Her only crime was that she'd worked out who Siddy really was — you must have let something slip.'

Grace paused. 'Which brings us to Mademoiselle Elise, who was engaged because of your so-called concern for my welfare — but that wasn't true either, was it?' She glared at Olive. 'Reuben Wood was the reason you wouldn't let me go away to school — you hated the way we were so close. I suppose you were terrified that he'd eventually tell me who I really was. I called Reuben "Siddy" because the only time I was allowed to see him was in the city. It turns out, he's been exactly what Pearl called him — my "Sydney Daddy" — all along.'

'Wait, please, just for a moment,' Olive begged as Grace ran out of the room. 'I've been keeping something for you.'

She returned with a dark wooden box. 'I should have given this to you much earlier, Grace, I realise that now. There are things that took place years ago that you know nothing about —'

'So it seems.'

Olive winced. 'If I'd told you, it would only have made you upset, confused.'

She placed the box on the table, but Grace was not finished yet. 'How could you, Mother, how could you and Reuben have a child together and all this time pretend it was poor Daddy's — I mean, Alfred's? You betrayed us both.'

'All right, yes it's true! Reuben Wood was your father, but —'

'So, you finally admit it.' Suddenly, Grace felt completely deflated. 'For all the big house and the grand estate, not to mention my fancy French governess, I finally realise what I really am,' she said. 'Nothing but a little bastard.'

'Don't use that word.'

'I can't see why not,' Grace said. 'We both know what people call someone like me. Just as we are well aware of the reception we'll get when, sooner or later, the real story is revealed. Imagine, all those doors that will slam shut in our faces.'

'No!'

'No? You think you'll continue to get away with it? Avoid the sniggers, the snide remarks, the exclusion, the condemnation? Well, I can see there's no point continuing this conversation.' Grace was nearly at the door before she stopped and turned round. 'Goodbye, Mother,' she said with a leaden finality.

'Grace, let me explain!' Olive pleaded.

'There's no point. It's too late.'

It was only when she reached her car that Grace realised she was holding the box in her hands.

She drove back to Merindah, possessed by a new clarity. The decision she had wrestled with for so long now seemed very easy to make.

Her marriage was over, that was a fact. Yet, even as Grace had confronted her mother, a part of her had still clung to the thought that perhaps she had misunderstood the situation. That was until Olive herself had confessed that Reuben was her real father. She might have said that Grace didn't know the whole story, but it sounded straightforward enough to her. If Olive intended to plead that she had succumbed to a moment of madness, that her affair with Reuben had just been a fling or, worse, didn't 'mean anything', then Grace couldn't bear to hear it.

Thank God for Christian Dior's fortuitous invitation. Alfred had left her a small legacy; she would use some of it to travel to Paris. Then she could establish a new life for herself and, most important of all, try to locate Reuben.

She had never given up hope of finding him. True, tracking Siddy down would not be easy, but she had to at least try. It was the sole chance she had of discovering the reason he had walked away from his only child and why, with the war over, he had never returned — unless the unthinkable really had happened, and he had perished on a foreign field of battle. She tapped her fingers on the steering wheel. Alive or dead, she had to know.

Grace pulled up in front of the homestead and hurried inside. If she was quick, she could be out of Merindah and on her way to Parkes railway station before Jack came home.

Throwing a large suitcase onto the bed, she started hauling a jumble of clothes out of her wardrobe. What did she need to start a new life? Not very much else, she decided. Just a few keepsakes — among them some childhood books and the music box, that long-ago Christmas present from the man she called Siddy.

Somewhere, a dog barked, a door banged. The sounds should have alerted her, yet Grace was shocked when Jack appeared in the doorway.

'Where do you think you're going now?' He glowered. 'I thought all that fashion parade carry-on that's been filling your head with nonsense was over and done with.'

'I'm leaving you, Jack,' Grace said evenly.

'Like hell you are!' Fists clenched, he came towards her.

She stood her ground. 'Can't you see that being married doesn't work for us? We were friends once, good friends. That's the way we should have stayed.' Her voice remained steady. 'For the longest time I've been following a path that was not of my making. Now I want to live my own life. I need to find out who I am.'

Jack grabbed her by the shoulders, his dark eyes flashing. 'You're my *wife*, remember? Grace Osbourne. Doesn't that mean anything?'

'Let go of me, Jack,' Grace said quietly. 'I am walking out of this house and I am never coming back.'

Perhaps it was her icy tone that made him drop his hands, although he clearly wasn't finished. 'Oh, you'll be back all right,' he sneered. 'You've never had to stand on your own two feet in your life — just how far do you think you'll get by yourself?'

'A long way from here, that's for sure,' Grace replied as she picked up her suitcase and pushed past him. 'I'm going to Paris.'

CHAPTER FOURTEEN

The golden landscape rushed by. After passing the familiar fields of wheat and the paddocks dotted with sheep, the train rattled over a bridge spanning a slow-moving river before continuing to make its way across the wide western plains. Grace watched from her seat, an impassive spectator.

Hours later, the appearance of brick bungalows with red-tiled roofs and neat little gardens revealed that the train had reached the outer suburbs of Sydney. Only then did Grace turn her attention to the dark wooden box sitting next to her.

She had planned to open it earlier, had even gone so far as turning the key in its lock, but her apprehension about what she might discover within had stopped her. Like Pandora, she too might release malevolent spirits. Now, pulling herself up a little straighter in her seat, she reminded herself Hope also lay inside that mythical box. Perhaps the contents would yield something — a diary, a personal note or even a message — that would provide her with hope too.

She would wait no longer. Grace raised the lid.

The box contained only three items. The first was a photograph. It was of her parents with Siddy and a woman Grace assumed had been his wife, Rae. It looked to have been taken at the races; in the background she could see the track and people leaning over the rails. The two couples were dressed in a style that was popular well over twenty years ago. Her mother wore a straight, loose dress and a close-fitting hat, as did Reuben's wife. Rae's ensemble was not quite as stylish as Olive's, although she was carrying a gay parasol. It was nearly impossible to make out Reuben; he was standing in a deep shadow cast by a nearby stand.

Grace turned the photograph over to see if there was anything written on the back, but there was no message and no date, just their names: *Alfred, Olive, Reuben, Rae.*

The next item — a carefully folded rose-pink shawl — was even more difficult to fathom. Grace picked it up and touched the delicate fabric to her cheek. Although the shawl's velvety softness was strangely comforting, she could not imagine what its significance might be.

Grace then turned her attention to the last article remaining in the box: an envelope addressed to Olive. Judging by the dirty marks and creases, it had been through many hands and travelled a great distance. Inside was a brief letter. At last, here was something that might help her to arrive at the truth.

26 May 1940
Dear Mrs Woods,
Please excuse the hurried nature of this letter. I am in danger, so will write only to say that Reuben Wood was my friend and comrade.

While in the Ardennes, we came under heavy fire. Reuben fought courageously — he saved my life. I am currently on the coast of France with a vast crowd of troops from where I hope to be evacuated to England. No matter what my fate might be, I will do my best to see that this letter reaches you.

All I know about Reuben's whereabouts is that he headed south; perhaps he thought he might have a better chance of escaping via a Mediterranean port. As you might be aware, Reuben speaks some French. Fortunately, he is also enterprising and knows how to live off the land. I believe these attributes will stand him in good stead in the difficult journey that lies ahead.

I found your name and address in the pocket of a coat he gave to me. He said he wouldn't need it as he was going somewhere warm and sunny.

I assume Reuben is a friend of the family, or that perhaps you are related. I am not sure, as your names are not spelt quite the same way. Whatever the case may be, it is my sincere hope that there will come a time in the future when you will once again be united.

My best wishes,

Frederick Carruthers, Second Lieutenant, 51st (Highland) Infantry Division, British Expeditionary Force

Grace stared at the letter's date. Even if it had taken twelve months to reach Australia, that still meant it must have lain hidden in the box for at least seven years. Seven years!

No matter what anyone said to the contrary, ever since the notification from the war office had arrived, Grace had clung to the belief that somewhere, somehow, Siddy was still alive. At first, she had worried terribly that he'd been captured; later, that he was lost or ill or hurt somewhere in France. Yet Olive, who could easily have alleviated her daughter's distress, had chosen not to.

Now Grace knew why. It was so much more convenient for her mother if Grace believed Reuben was dead. In fact, she thought with horror, it was possible that Olive might well have welcomed his demise. Then the secrets of their shared past would be buried with him forever beneath the soil of a far-off, foreign land.

A sudden jolt made Grace look up. The train had come to a halt at Sydney's main railway terminal, Central Station. After gathering her possessions she stepped from the carriage, only to find herself swept up in a surge of rushing commuters, porters hauling bags, straggling families and harassed office workers. Looping her handbag over her left wrist and carrying her suitcase in the same hand, Grace was propelled towards the turnstile by the heaving stream of people.

She made certain the wooden box remained safe, however, by holding it in the crook of her strong right arm as if it were an infant.

Grace gave a sigh of relief as she entered the sanctuary of her room at the Queen's Club. She set down her suitcase, threw her handbag, coat and fedora onto a chair, placed the box on the dressing table and, grateful to be unencumbered at last, walked over to the window. As she gazed out across the green tops of Hyde Park's weeping fig trees, she caught sight of an errant spray of water arcing above the Archibald Fountain, and the square, unfinished spires of St Mary's Cathedral. She had seen this view many times before, yet today it appeared strange to her. *Nothing is as it was*, she thought sadly. Would it ever be the same again?

Turning away, Grace pulled off her high-heeled shoes and let them clatter to the floor. Finally, she stretched out on the bed, engulfed by confusion. The letter contained at least some information, but the other items in the box had not helped her at all. 'What on earth do they mean?' she said to the unresponsive picture of Queen Mary that hung on the opposite wall.

A soft knock interrupted her anguished introspection. Grace opened the door to one of the maids, carrying a tray. 'Mrs Osbourne, Cook said you'd had a long journey,' the girl murmured shyly. 'She thought you might like some tea and toast.'

'Please thank Cook. That's very good of her — and you,' Grace said, taking the tray with unsteady hands. This simple act of kindness almost reduced her to tears.

Reminding herself that she had a plan and was determined to follow it, she poured a cup of tea and returned to her earlier post at the window. Yet regarding the familiar scene did nothing to soothe her unruly emotions. Despite her show of bravado during her confrontation with Jack, the prospect of leaving Australia was utterly daunting. As for finding Siddy — she'd been deluding herself. After being protected all her life, having never been out of the country let alone worked for a living, how could a girl from the bush possibly expect to make her way in Europe's most glamorous, cultivated city?

Grace put her cup down. Of course she could. Ironically, thanks to her mother's intervention and the subsequent ministrations of Mademoiselle Elise, she had both excellent French and the ability to pinpoint the precise location of practically every landmark in Paris.

It might have been simple good luck, sheer coincidence or, as she preferred to think of it, fate, but the truth was that without ever knowing it, she had spent years preparing to discover her past — and forge a new future — in the City of Light.

BOOK TWO

Le Mannequin

The Model

CHAPTER FIFTEEN

Paris, December 1948

'Ah, Mademoiselle Dubois,' Christian Dior said, turning away from the length of midnight-blue velvet he had been examining. 'The young lady who has come to us all the way from Australia. What a pleasure it is to meet you at last.'

Despite Grace's awe at meeting such a famous and talented man, so courtly was his manner she felt completely disarmed. She put Dior's age at mid-forties; he was dressed in a conservative dark suit over which he wore a white smock, although neither garment successfully disguised his rounded silhouette.

'The pleasure is mine, monsieur,' Grace said, before adding, 'I can't tell you how exciting it is to meet the man responsible for creating the most beautiful clothes in the world. You might not believe it, but the first time I read your name, I was on a sheep station in the middle of nowhere.' Her hand flew to her mouth. 'Goodness, I hope that doesn't make me sound unsuitable.'

'*Au contraire.*' Dior smiled. 'You will be a refreshing addition to the *maison*. When you showed the New Look in Australia our people were very taken with your lively manner — it is a quality I have noticed in others who inhabit the New World.' He shrugged. 'Europe is tired, its inhabitants dwell so much in the past. But you Australians have a cleaner, brighter outlook.'

A thoughtful expression appeared on his face. 'Each of my *jeunes filles* provides me with a different source of inspiration,' he said. 'And you, Mademoiselle Dubois, what will you bring?' He paused. 'Something quite original, I think. *Alors*, we will see, we will see.'

Grace had barely time to murmur her thanks before Dior, lost in thought, took up a sketch pad and began to draw.

February 1949

Grace hurried into the crowded dressing room known by the mannequins as the *cabine*, delighted that she was about to take part in what was by now a well-established ritual.

As she hastily dispensed with her black felt hat and matching alpaca coat, she was greeted by several other fresh-faced girls with cries of, *'Bonjour, chérie, bonjour!'* Grace removed her new red dress with its calf-length flared skirt then, wearing only a nude brassiere, briefs, corselet and stockings, she donned a plain white cotton wrapper and slid behind one of the dressing tables that were set out in rows. Then it began — the assiduous process that would transform her unadorned, everyday self into a supremely svelte, high fashion goddess.

Each of the models had her favourite position: Victoire, a fiery brunette from Bordeaux, liked to face the door; Thérèse, with her platinum-blonde waves and heart-shaped face, preferred to be near the window; Grace's was somewhere in between the two. The dressing tables held not only make-up, brushes, combs and all the other accoutrements necessary for the serious business of a professional beauty, but also a few more personal items — perhaps a small teddy bear or a posy of flowers tied with satin ribbon. Grace had chosen Siddy's gift of the little wooden music box with its pink-clad dancer.

She inspected herself in the mirror. So much had happened to her so quickly and there'd been so many challenges, she was surprised she couldn't detect any evidence of strain. Apart from her work in the *maison* where the demanding days could easily stretch to eight o'clock at night — and during the recent frantic preparations for the new collection, until two in the morning — there'd been so much to get used to in her daily life.

She'd had to learn everything, from where to buy a ticket for the Metro to how to surmount the infamous French bureaucracy. As a supposedly single woman, merely opening a bank account had taken hours of negotiation with an uncooperative manager. Fortunately, the Dior mannequins had proved to be an invaluable source of advice.

'If you want to impress the bank manager, next time you go to see him simply wear pearls and as much beige cashmere as you can,' Victoire had recommended. 'As they are the mark of every good bourgeois woman, he will assume you are a person of indisputable respectability.' Another mannequin had explained the way to adjust her hemlines fractionally higher or lower each season (if combined with the single addition of a new, witty trim on a hat, this might be all that was needed to render an ensemble *au courant* rather than unthinkably *démodée*); and a third had explained how to judge the precise worth of shoes and handbags, it being a grave offence to invest in such items should they fail to be of the first order of quality. When it came to her new profession, however, the most important — indeed, vital — knowledge that she'd acquired was the proper application of what the girls referred to with the utmost seriousness as *le maquillage*.

Grace took up a stick of pancake foundation and smoothed it expertly over her skin. Next, she liberally applied loose powder with a swansdown powder puff, ensuring the flawless matt finish would last throughout the morning. Grace then shifted her concentration to the creation of a luscious vermilion pout, before considering her eyebrows. Although they were already dark and well defined, she nonetheless extended each one with a soft pencil in order to provide an additional degree of drama.

Her eyes were further emphasised by outlining them with a small brush dipped in black liquid; Grace made sure to create just the right upward flick at their outer corners so their kittenish quality would be accentuated. The application of several layers of sooty mascara provided the finishing touch. All that was required now was to twist her lustrous curls up into a chic chignon and pin them securely in place. Grace studied herself in the mirror once more. The woman she saw was worldly, sophisticated and possessed of an unassailable *sang-froid*.

Grace waited for her dresser to finish adjusting the first ensemble she would wear in that morning's show, with both patience and a sense of relief. At least she was now far less likely to make the sort of blunder that had occurred during her first fitting for the smart black and white houndstooth suit, one of Dior's signature looks.

'But Madame Carré, this cream fabric is so cheap and plain!' she'd had the temerity to remark, only to be met by a gale of laughter. Grace blushed when madame pointed out that the garment was merely a *toile*.

'The initial attempt at interpreting one of *le patron*'s sketches is always made of unbleached muslin or calico,' she had explained. 'Our materials are precious. No one would dream of putting a pair of scissors near the cloth until there was absolute certainty about exactly what is required.'

Grace had realised that, as far as the creation of haute couture was concerned, she still had a great deal to learn.

'All is ready, mademoiselle,' the dresser announced.

But am I? she wondered as she took her place with the other mannequins. Yes, she was beginning to master the complex world of the *maison*. But as for her plans to find Reuben, she'd been in Paris for more than six weeks, and she hadn't even managed to take the first step.

CHAPTER SIXTEEN

'*Voilà, c'est la petite Australienne!*'

Ferdinand Derel waved energetically from his table in the corner of the bustling Café Bertrand.

Grace raised her hand in return; the ebullience of the greeting from the House of Dior's imperious concierge still surprised her.

'I knew you were not an established client of the House,' Ferdinand had explained after seeking her out in the *cabine* on the day of her first parade. 'Yet there you were, with your dark curls and big green eyes and that open way you have — are all Australians like this? You know, greeting a person they have never met before with the same degree of familiarity as if he were an old friend?' Ferdinand had chuckled. 'I was shocked.'

'If only I had known.'

'Would you have done anything differently?'

Grace had laughed. 'Probably not.'

From then on, she'd become one of Ferdinand's favourites, meeting him at the Café Bertrand most mornings for coffee laced with a liberal helping of gossip. Over time she had discovered that, due to his unique position, he was able to acquire all manner of information.

For Dior's clients, Ferdinand was but an immaculate, white-gloved being who would help them into their taxis or private cars, assist with the management of small packages, or perhaps keep a watchful eye over one of their pet poodles. Yet, ironically, by maintaining this discreet presence he had acquired a cloak of near invisibility, so that a veritable torrent of incautious conversation took place in front of him.

Ferdinand knew when a mistress was about to reject her current lover almost before the woman in question had made up her mind to do so. He was aware of which client had dismissed her maid, whose chauffeur was considered to be the most handsome, and whose personal wealth had plummeted after an unfortunate run of losses at Monte Carlo's casino.

'*Ça va*? All goes well?' Ferdinand inquired when Grace sat down at the table.

'I suppose,' she responded.

'Hmm. I'm not so sure,' the doorman replied. 'Your usual high spirits appear to be absent. I hope one of your suitors is not causing trouble. If that is the case, he will have Ferdinand to contend with!'

Grace stirred her steaming *café au lait*. 'Romance is the very last thing I'm seeking,' she glumly insisted.

'Well, I can see that something is on your mind.'

The avuncular Ferdinand appeared so concerned that Grace felt sorely tempted to unburden herself. However, she wasn't about to alienate his affection by revealing either her married state, or the real reason she was in Paris. On the other hand, she knew she had to tell someone at least part of the truth or she would never make any progress. And who better than Ferdinand — the man who knew everyone — to go to for help?

'Actually, I'm looking for someone,' she said.

'And who is this someone?'

'He's …' Grace searched for a way to describe Siddy. 'He's an old family friend named Reuben Wood.'

'Tell me about Monsieur Wood,' Ferdinand prompted.

'Reuben volunteered to fight in the war on behalf of the Allies,' Grace explained. 'But during the Fall of France, he went missing. I have a feeling that he's still alive, although for some reason he has chosen to remain here and not make contact with anyone in Australia.'

'Such things do happen.' Ferdinand nodded as he bit into a croissant. 'What with all the turmoil and chaos, war can provide many opportunities for a man to disappear and begin a new life. Would you like my assistance?'

'That would be wonderful. When I was still at home I knew that finding him would be a challenge, but now I'm in Paris I've realised I have no idea where to start.'

'Tracking down old soldiers is not exactly my area of expertise,' he said, smiling. 'Nevertheless, I will do what I can.' Leaning forward, he spoke in a serious tone. 'But I must warn you, *ma petite*, disturbing secrets is a risky affair. It is a little like turning over a rock that has been lying in a shady place for a long time — you do not know what you will find.'

Grace perched anxiously on the edge of a hard-backed chair.

'Yes,' the officious bureaucrat said crisply from behind his desk. 'The name, Reuben Wood — there it is.' He pointed with a bony finger at a long list. 'He is certainly the same person you are looking for. However, since he was reported to be missing, presumed dead' — the man peered at her over his wire spectacles — 'there has been no further trace of him.'

'Nothing?'

'*Rien.*'

'You mean to say, in all these dusty filing cabinets,' Grace cast her eyes despairingly around the vast, overcrowded repository, 'there is not one other word about this man?'

'That is correct.' The official's manner became a little milder. 'I owe your colleague Monsieur Derel a favour and, in any case, I do not enjoy seeing the distress of those friends and relatives who are attempting to locate their loved ones. If there was something more I could do, I would oblige. Unfortunately,' he said, turning the palms of his hands up as if surrendering to the weight of impossible circumstances, 'in this instance, I can be of no further assistance. Goodbye, mademoiselle.'

As Grace left the depressing government offices with their millions of files, not one of any use to her, she felt utterly dejected. On Ferdinand's advice, she had first contacted the British War Office, but to her great disappointment she had learnt that Lieutenant Carruthers, the author of the letter that contained the only clues to Reuben's whereabouts, had tragically not survived the evacuation of Dunkirk.

Next, she had knocked on the doors of numerous French officials, including that of Ferdinand's nephew at the Police Missing Persons Department; his landlady's sister in the bureau responsible for those displaced by war; and an elegant, silver-haired Dior client who was a senior Red Cross volunteer. The National Archives had been Grace's last hope. Perhaps it would be wiser to simply give up?

Sighing, she buttoned her overcoat, crossed the road and entered a small park. Although the weather was still cold, a dusting of early narcissus had thrust its way through the hard earth. The fresh green stalks and white petals seemed to herald renewal, to point to a future that still promised hope; surely, she thought, they were a sign that she should continue her quest.

What did it matter if her efforts to use official channels had failed? There must be other ways to tackle the problem. She might not have found him yet, but this didn't rule out the distinct, tantalising possibility that somewhere in France, Reuben Wood was still alive.

CHAPTER SEVENTEEN

March 1949

Grace flinched. She took a quick, involuntary breath, then forced herself to be still. Just another pin. She should be used to the sharp pricks and scratches by now. It was best to simply detach one's mind, to ignore the murmur of voices: '*Où, patron? Là, ou là? Ah, oui!*' They would start, and stop, then start again as, under the direction of the serious, pink-cheeked designer, drifts of creamy fabric were swathed about her and pins inserted, only to be removed and tried in a different position.

The toile she was draped in would form the pattern for an extravagant ice-white ball gown with a tightly fitted satin bodice, a tiny waist and a skirt composed of an unheard-of quantity of silk organza and tulle. Mother of pearl petals, rhinestone beads, and sequins, each one painstakingly sewn on by hand, would add to the spectacular effect.

Grace had already decided how she would show the gown when the time came to model it for one of the *maison*'s most famous clients, the way she would spin so that shards of light from the salon's chandeliers would play across its shimmering folds.

She tried to suppress a shiver as the cold hands of an assistant reached around her waist, smoothing and flattening the toile.

'Yes, that is much better,' *le patron* said approvingly. 'And now we regard the correct width of the skirt, my dear Marguerite.'

Marguerite Carré scanned Monsieur Dior's face for an indication as to what his verdict might be. 'Does *le patron* believe I have achieved his vision?' she asked nervously, pulling at the tape measure that hung about her neck with the ubiquity of a doctor's stethoscope.

'No, you have not, Madame Carré. I require far more volume.' The *directrice* looked stricken as Dior grasped his gold-topped cane and pointed, saying tersely, 'Please be so kind as to place the fabric so that it extends from the waist, not the hips.'

So it continued. The business of pinning and draping, cutting and folding went on and on until Grace jumped. She'd felt the sharp jab of yet another of Madame Carré's pins.

'*Mademoiselle Dubois!*' Marguerite tut-tutted.

'Sorry,' Grace said. After all, what was a scratch or two, the sore feet or aching back that were the inevitable outcome of standing still in high-heeled shoes for hours at a time, when the world's most acclaimed fashion designer was creating one of his fabulous masterpieces?

It was a modest inconvenience. And she was in Paris, after all. The place where she had always longed to be.

At one o'clock, Grace joined Brigitte and Marie-Hélène — of the twelve house mannequins at Christian Dior, they were her closest friends — for a hurried meal of smoked salmon and baguette.

'All week, the one subject the girls in the *cabine* have been talking about is which client will be the fortunate owner of that incredible ball dress,' Marie-Hélène said as she nibbled a crust.

'Argentina's first lady, Eva Perón — I'm certain of it,' Brigitte broke in. 'You know the way she likes to put on a show. Anything that will sparkle for the cameras, that's what's important to her. You'll see, she'll want it the minute she sees it on you. I heard her confess to our dear *première vendeuse*, Madame Beguin, "My biggest fear in life is to be forgotten." Imagine! Well, she won't be if she's photographed wearing that dress. I wouldn't be surprised if it turns up on the front page of *Le Monde*.'

What marked Brigitte out from the other mannequins, apart from her honey-blonde hair and creamy complexion, was her reticence about disclosing any personal details. Two of the girls — Victoire and Corinne — said that they had heard she was the daughter of a count who lived in a grand château somewhere in the Loire Valley, but when they braved Brigitte's reserve to inquire if the story were true she merely responded with a laugh, 'How delightful that sounds. I wonder what I am doing here, working all hours, don't you?'

There was no mystery about Marie-Hélène's origins: everyone knew she was a Parisienne through and through. Her mother, a much sought-after actress in her youth, had passed on both her auburn-haired beauty and a flair for the dramatic.

'No, Brigitte! You are quite wrong.' Marie-Hélène tossed her abundant, reddish-gold locks, temporarily released from their usual plaited coil. 'That gown is going to Wallis, the Duchess of Windsor. She has something of your colouring, Grace, but unlike you, she is no beauty.'

With an arch expression, she added, 'Actually, I think she looks rather like a frog, although, I must admit, one who has been kissed by a king, and has a king's ransom of jewels.'

Grace assumed a sphinx-like smile. She knew exactly who the dress had been designed for: the young Princess Margaret of Great Britain. Apparently, the first sketches had already been revealed to the blue-eyed princess during a visit by Her Royal Highness to the French Embassy in London.

'Naturally, I was present to provide guidance,' Madame Beguin had confided in Grace. However, as the *vendeuse* had elicited a promise of absolute secrecy, Grace continued to maintain she had no idea who the gown was being made for.

'Ah, that's what you say,' Marie-Hélène remarked. 'But all the same, I have a feeling that you know.' She regarded Grace with narrowed eyes. 'You are clearly practised in the art of keeping secrets,' she said. 'In fact, I believe there is something else you haven't told us about — a hidden lover, perhaps, or is there a handsome man you have left behind?'

Grace struggled to maintain her composure. 'Why would you say that?'

'Because despite everything Paris has to offer, for the past three months you have stayed alone in your little room every night.'

Marie-Hélène couldn't possibly have guessed the truth, although Grace was unnerved by the accuracy of the vivacious redhead's suspicions.

'Never mind, Brigitte and I intend to change all that,' Marie-Hélène said.

'I can't believe that Le Chat Noir nightclub is so close to you and yet you have never even seen it.' Brigitte shook her blonde head. 'You are such fun, Grace — I simply do not understand.'

'And neither do I,' Marie-Hélène added. 'You certainly don't seem the shy type to me, nor do you have the tormented appearance of someone recovering from a broken heart.' She looked at Grace sceptically. 'Well, whatever it is that has been keeping you inside, that must end. You have until Friday to acquire a pretty dress, because that's when you are coming out to Le Chat Noir with us. And we're not listening to any excuses!'

That night, Grace looked around her airy attic room with its white-washed beams and smiled. She liked the way the walls were covered with rose-strewn paper of ancient provenance, just as she liked the capacious green velvet armchair, despite it being so worn in places that the plush pile had disappeared. There were few other features. A small, round wooden table and a chair had been provided, together with two shelves on which she had placed a couple of her favourite childhood books, including a volume of Alfred's beloved Australian bush poetry and the copy of Charles Perrault's French fairy tales that had been one of the first texts she'd studied with Mademoiselle Elise. On an impulse, she had also propped up the photograph from the mysterious box.

In one wall was a diminutive fireplace and, in the corner, a lone gas ring, sink and cold water tap served for a kitchen. At the other end of the room, a faded pink damask curtain shielded an alcove that accommodated a large bed with a twisting iron bedhead painted white, an old chest of drawers, a long mirror and a wardrobe.

Although her new home had all Grace needed, she would still have regarded it as pleasant, rather than exceptional, were it not for the view from the single, unusually large dormer window. From there she could see a vista she never tired of —

the slanting, slate-covered rooftops of Paris and its slender church spires. If Grace held her head at just the right angle, she could even catch a glimpse of the soaring Eiffel Tower.

Each week, Grace paid the rent to the tiny concierge with great pleasure. As she handed over her crumpled bundle of francs to Madame Guérin, she inwardly congratulated herself on at last becoming independent. After the tumultuous events of her recent life and the hectic days at the *maison*, the long, silent evenings she spent alone reading, sketching or simply dreaming brought her peace and contentment. Grace had savoured her solitude, yet now she found herself contemplating her new friends' insistent invitation.

Suddenly weary, she threw herself on the bed. So far, all her efforts to locate Reuben had come to nothing — shouldn't she be spending her spare time trying to find him? Even though she now realised that, contrary to her first hasty reaction, when it came to the affair he was just as guilty as her mother, Grace still found it painfully hard to accept that the man she'd known all her life was the same man who'd been willing to betray Alfred, his good friend. Had he ever suffered guilt, shame or remorse? She'd never seen any sign of it.

Curiously, she still cared for him deeply. No matter what he'd done in the past, it was impossible to forget either his kindness or their years of shared affection.

Chastising herself for having allowed another twenty-four hours to go by without any progress, Grace rose to her feet, walked over to the window and pushed open the shutters. As she looked out into the star-filled Paris night she called out softly, 'Siddy, where are you?'

The next morning, Grace was woken early by the bright spring sunshine pouring into her room. *Of course, I never closed the shutters*, she thought, as she pushed her blankets aside. She felt revitalised, as if the sun's energy itself was coursing through her veins. Jumping out of bed, Grace held her arms out wide, embracing the light. Her need to find Reuben was not the only reason she had come to Paris — she'd also wanted to discover a new way of life. *At least that's something I can throw myself into*, she told herself. Then she began to ponder how she might persuade Madame Raymonde to lend her a dress before Friday night.

CHAPTER EIGHTEEN

Brigitte and Marie-Hélène met Grace outside her building. The two women inspected her with critical gazes, before pronouncing her appearance to be '*ravissante*'.

'Victoire wore that design in the last spring collection,' observed Marie-Hélène. 'But with your green eyes, it suits you much better.'

The exquisite jade net dress Grace had successfully borrowed (Madame Raymonde had insisted that it be for one night only and that it had to be returned promptly the next morning) hugged her breasts and waist, then pooled into a frothy skirt.

Brigitte nodded her approval. 'You will be a sensation.'

'That's quite enough,' Grace said, waving her compliment away. 'In any case, isn't it time we went to this club you're so keen for me to see?'

The girls walked for just a few minutes before leading her to the end of a tiny cul-de-sac.

'I have wandered down this little street at least twice while I've been out exploring,' she said with surprise, 'but I didn't imagine there was anything much behind that black door.'

Now that night had fallen, a strategically placed light illuminated a sign attached to what had at first appeared to be nothing but a shadowy recess. On the coal-coloured board the name of the club, together with the outline of a cat, was picked out in white paint.

'No wonder I missed it,' Grace said, her eyes dancing with anticipation.

She walked through the door, descended a set of black-carpeted stairs, and found herself in a striking subterranean cavern. The dramatic decor was entirely monochromatic. Against the back of the dimly lit room, a long, black-lacquered bar was crowded with patrons. The walls were also black, while the wooden floorboards were painted in alternating bands of black and white that reminded her of piano keys. The tables and chairs were white, as was the stage on which sat an upright piano, a set of black drums and a gleaming double bass.

'This looks amazing,' Grace exclaimed, 'and so do the people. Who on earth are they?'

'Ah, I suppose you have noticed that Le Chat Noir's clientele is considerably more colourful than its style of decoration,' Marie-Hélène remarked drily. 'This is where you will find the grander type of bohemian. There are famous artists' models, fashion mannequins from all the best *maisons*, photographers, actors, painters, philosophers and writers, with the addition of a sprinkling of the more outré members of the old French aristocracy and the well-off bourgeoisie — at least, the ones that fancy themselves as intellectuals. Can you see Pablo Picasso over there in the corner holding court?' She tilted her head in the direction of a stocky, balding man who was gesticulating energetically. 'And look — there is the existential philosopher Jean-Paul Sartre, the one with the pipe and the thick glasses. He is usually to be found drinking martinis at the Pont Royal with Albert Camus, but his lover Simone de Beauvoir likes it here so she must have talked him round.'

Grace couldn't help staring — the patrons were as exotic as creatures in a zoo. 'Who is that tiny woman at the bar, the one talking with such animation?'

'Ah, we call her The Little Sparrow. Her name is Édith Piaf — she's a chanteuse. If we are lucky, she might sing "La vie en rose" tonight.'

'And what about that girl further down, the one with the interesting face?'

Brigitte peered across the room. 'She looks familiar, but I cannot place her.'

'Well, well,' Marie-Hélène broke in, 'I see that Baron Édouard de Gide is coming our way. He is known to escort only Paris's most gorgeous women, which means I'm sure he wants to meet Dior's enchanting new mannequin.'

'In that case, I had better make myself scarce.' Grace laughed.

'Too late!' Brigitte whispered as de Gide appeared by her side.

Grace was introduced to the eager baron, but having no wish to spend time with such a seemingly shallow man — or, for that matter, any man — she informed him that sadly, a girlfriend was waiting for her at the bar. With that, she plunged into the crowd, then wriggled her way onto a seat that luckily had just become free next to the girl she had noticed earlier.

'*Bonsoir*,' Grace said. 'I'm awfully sorry, but I just told a man I wanted to escape from that you're a friend. Do you mind if we chat for a few minutes? My name's Grace Dubois, by the way.'

'Hi, Jacqueline Bouvier — and I'm happy to help you out. But you're not French, are you?'

'Is my accent that bad?' Grace said in English, with a smile.

'It sounds perfect to me. No, it's just that most French women are way more reserved. Believe me, I know. I'm an American, and sometimes I feel like their etiquette is stifling. Speaking of which, please call me Jackie — all my friends do.'

The two rapidly engaged in conversation about the challenges young women from the New World faced while living in Paris. As they spoke, Grace decided that although the girl was not a classic beauty — her face was wide and her dark eyes were set just a little too far apart — the combined effect of her features was beguiling.

'I'd really love to talk more,' Jackie said in the breathy coo of a child, 'only I promised the grand French lady I'm staying with that we would have dinner together tonight. I know — tomorrow is Saturday. How about coffee at the Café de Flore, around half-past two? Do say you'll come.'

'That sounds like fun. À *demain*!'

The famous café was only a few streets away from Grace's home. According to Madame Guérin, a host of Left Bank identities — including Sartre, Camus, de Beauvoir, Giacometti and Cocteau — had for years crowded around the café's tiny tables, smoking Gauloises, drinking cheap wine, laughing and arguing until all hours.

'Those clever people have all moved on now, though,' she said, stroking Tartuffe, her cat, 'despite what the foolish tourists think. These days it is *les Americaines* who flock there in search of *la vie française*. They remind me of the hungry pigeons hunting for breadcrumbs in front of Notre-Dame.'

As Grace took a seat in the café, she thought about the wave of Americans pouring into Paris. Madame de Turckheim — or Tutu as the girls called the baroness in charge of the *cabine* — had informed them that most of the twenty-five thousand people — an astonishing figure in itself — who had attended Dior's parades during the past twelve months were from the United States. Tutu had added, 'At least two hundred thousand more are expected to arrive in France during this coming year. *Mes filles*, I ask myself, where will it end?'

A distinctive soft voice cut short Grace's reflections. '*Bonjour*! I hope you haven't been waiting long.'

'Not at all.' Grace smiled at Jackie. 'I was just thinking how at home you would feel in Paris these days — so many of your fellow citizens are here.'

'I know just what you mean,' Jackie said with a sardonic expression. 'My mother grumbles that with Paris being this popular and the franc so cheap, she and her friends are finding it impossible to book a room at the Ritz!'

'It *is* rather funny,' Grace agreed. 'Do you see, at that table over there, the college boys in black turtlenecks drinking their Picon citron? It's obvious they're desperately trying to be more French than the French.'

'And at the next table there's a group of young Frenchmen who are wearing US-style check shirts and downing Coca-Colas,' Jackie added. 'How absurd it all is!'

The two women looked at these impostors, then at each other, before both broke into peals of shared laughter.

'But what about you?' asked Grace. 'Your name is French.'

'Yes, but my family has been in the United States forever. Anyway, you have a French name as well.'

'Dubois?' Grace smiled. 'I'll tell you a secret. It's assumed. My real name is Grace, um, Woods.'

'You don't sound very sure.'

'It's a long story.'

'Well, one thing I do know,' said Jackie, 'we have something in common. We might have French names and speak the language, but we are both outsiders. That gives one quite a different perspective, don't you think?'

Grace laughed. 'You're right about that.'

'And as for our families ...' Jackie continued, 'I don't know what yours is like, but mine's definitely problematic. My father — everyone calls him Black Jack — is divine, even though he's a terrible drinker and simply wild for the ladies. My parents divorced when I was a child. Now Mum is married to a very rich but extremely dull banker called Hugh Auchincloss. I hardly ever see Black Jack these days. I do know that he didn't want me to come here, though.' Jackie bit her lip, before saying wistfully, 'Fathers and mothers — why is it all so complicated?'

'Believe me, I've often asked myself the same question,' Grace replied.

CHAPTER NINETEEN

17 March 1949

Dear Lottie,

I do wish you were with me so we could experience this wonderful city together. I also long to hear more of your news! Unfortunately, as you're not here, and I can't exactly pop over to Oakhill, this letter will have to do.

I wanted to tell you that thanks to two new friends, I had my first real night out in Paris just a couple of weeks ago. Suddenly, I'm like Sleeping Beauty. There has certainly not been a handsome prince — that's definitely not on the agenda — but I do feel as if I have woken from years of slumber.

Having spent most of my life in the bush (unlike lucky you!), being surrounded by so many stimulating people, challenging ideas and a wildly different way of living has taken some getting used to. Post-war Paris is simply abuzz with activity, filled with amazing art, books, fashion, music — and especially people! So, now that I'm more settled, I have decided not to seclude myself in my little attic anymore. That means I've been out to restaurants and gallery openings, and visited some jazz clubs and cabarets, including the famous Lido and the Folies Bergère (where the stunning girls wear hardly anything but some very immodest sparkly bits and pieces, false eyelashes and a few feathers).

It's all been a bit frantic, but I don't want to stop. It's as if each new experience is like one's first taste of chocolate ice cream — a delectable treat!

As you can imagine, Dior's mannequins command the interest of quite a few gentlemen — there are always flowers and love letters arriving at the atelier for them. Of course, all the models are extremely attractive and have amazing style, so it's understandable. The funny thing is, despite their sophistication, the girls are fascinated by the fact that I come from Australia.

In fact, practically all the French people I've met seem to find this immensely exotic, only they do have some bizarre views about life at home. You would laugh if you heard what they say — it sounds as if they think we're all quite wild! And I've lost count of the number of times I've been asked whether it's true that there are koalas ambling down the main streets of Melbourne and kangaroos bounding along the Sydney Harbour Bridge.

Grace put down her pen. She had kept her tone bright, but the mere act of writing a letter home had induced an intense melancholy. It made her think about Olive. Charlotte knew Grace and her mother had argued, but Grace had given her friend the impression that the reason was her decision to leave Jack and escape to Paris.

The truth was, despite Olive's shocking revelation, Grace missed her mother terribly. If only she would reach out, apologise for what was past, then perhaps they could find some way to heal their rift. Yet, in the long months since

Grace had arrived in Paris, she hadn't received so much as a line from her mother.

'*Bonjour,* Mademoiselle Dubois,' a voice interrupted her sombre thoughts.

Grace looked up. 'Pierre! Would you like to join me?'

'Well, if I am not disturbing you ...'

The tall, gangly Pierre du Plessis, scion of one of France's wealthiest banking families, was a self-described poet and a new beau of Brigitte's.

'Not at all. As you can see, I am all alone. And anyway, if one chooses to be at the famous Café de Flore one should expect to be disturbed,' she said, putting away her half-finished letter. 'Do take a seat — but only if you call me Grace.' She smiled.

'What can I say? We French are a formal people.' After ordering them both a chilled Dubonnet, he grinned good-naturedly.

Grace laughed. 'So I have noticed.'

'Yes, I know it is ridiculous; even among the bohemians who inhabit this quarter there are always rules.' Pierre tasted his drink. 'They might aim to break these rules — I do myself — yet still we know they exist. But you? I don't think you are bound by rules at all. You are friendly to everyone, have no sense of formality, and a manner that some — in my parents' circle, at least — would call shockingly straightforward.'

'And what does all this mean?' Grace asked.

'It means simply that you are what we must all strive to be.'

'Good heavens, Pierre. What is that?'

'Yourself, *ma chère.* Yourself.'

The next day, Grace received a dozen long-stemmed red roses from the Baron de Gide together with his latest invitation, this time to attend the premiere of a new production of *La Bohème*.

'What do you think — should I agree to go?' she asked Marie-Hélène.

To date, Grace had been unwilling to accept Édouard de Gide's entreaties, notwithstanding the fact that, with his combination of tanned skin, chiselled features and blond hair, he was undeniably good-looking. But there was something about him, a smooth over-confidence, she found off-putting.

'I certainly would,' urged her friend, 'were I in your Roger Vivier shoes.'

'Well, the roses are lovely … and I do like Puccini. Perhaps I will.'

As Grace alighted from de Gide's sleek, chauffeur-driven Hispano-Suiza in front of Paris's famously lavish Palais Garnier, he regarded her with open admiration.

'How fortunate that I reserved a box,' he said.

Startled, Grace said politely, 'Does that mean the sightlines will be very good?'

'No, not particularly. But think what a wonderful view the audience will have of my exquisite companion.'

Grace stifled the urge to laugh — really, the man's flowery compliments, not to mention his vanity, approached what could only be termed ludicrous. Composing herself, she entered the busy foyer, then swept up the grand staircase in a deep-red taffeta gown that provided a striking contrast to her porcelain skin and upswept raven hair. Around her throat she wore a paste Dior choker that sparkled as it caught the light cast by an enormous chandelier.

'This decor is magnificent!' she exclaimed.

'Ah yes, but not as magnificent as you,' the baron said smoothly.

As Grace took in the opulent gilding, pillars, domes, arches and elaborate ceilings, she wondered whether, rather like Édouard's fulsome praise, it might all be more than a little *de trop*. She decided, however, at least in Édouard's case, the benefit of the doubt was called for. Honestly, she told herself, how tiresome could an excess of compliments from a handsome French aristocrat really be?

When the baron suggested supper at La Tour d'Argent after the opera, Grace readily agreed.

'I'm not sure if you know it,' he said, 'being rather new to the pleasures of Paris. La Tour is famous, as much for its view of Notre-Dame as for the chef's way with pressed duck. Everyone who is anyone goes there: Europe's high society, film stars, French cabinet ministers — even the President of the Republic himself, on occasion.'

As the evening progressed, the combined effects of a delightful supper of foie gras accompanied by Dom Pérignon, the baron's flattering conversation and the captivating sight of the great cathedral's glowing stained-glass windows, produced in Grace a thoroughly delicious sense of indulgence. She wondered what it would be like to be the Baron de Gide. It was impossible to ignore the deference of the waiters, the way they hurried to bring him whatever he desired.

They were finishing their bowls of the tiny wild strawberries known as *fraises des bois* when he introduced the subject of his art collection.

'The works are quite well known,' he said, casually inserting the names of several Renaissance masters. 'Would you like me to show them to you?' Édouard's fervent expression left Grace in no doubt that the inspection of his paintings was not the only pastime he had in mind.

'What a tempting idea,' she said with as much sincerity as she could muster. 'But, sadly, I must work tomorrow — there is a very early showing.'

'Really?'

'Really.'

'Well, I … I am extremely disappointed,' Édouard responded, evidently nonplussed.

It took only the briefest of pauses for the baron to collect himself. With his usual savoir-faire once more intact, he reached across the table and trailed a finger down Grace's bare arm, an intimacy she found vaguely distasteful.

'I think you know how much I would like to share the experience with you,' he said.

The following day, Grace was kept busy modelling for a glamorous redheaded American film star named Rita Hayworth. Much taken with the New Look, Miss Hayworth — who was engaged to the fantastically wealthy Prince Aly Khan — had explained in her distinctive drawl, 'I'm after a few knockout outfits for my trousseau.'

When finally Grace had concluded the private showing and changed back into her own clothes, she saw Ferdinand coming towards her from the direction of the studio. He was carrying a small parcel in one hand.

'I believe this is for you, Mademoiselle Dubois,' he said, handing it to Grace with a stiff bow.

'Why so formal, Ferdinand?' Grace asked. 'Anyway, you must be mistaken. Who would be sending me something like that?'

'As I am familiar with the chauffeur who delivered it, I believe I know exactly who it is from,' he frowned, 'and, much to my regret, the reason why. Mademoiselle Dubois, I trust you have not entered into an unwise liaison?'

Grace was mystified, as much by the doorman's unusual manner as by the parcel's arrival. 'Dear Ferdinand, I have absolutely no idea what you are talking about.'

She quickly tore off the wrapping paper, revealing a slim red leather case embossed with gold lettering that picked out a single word: Cartier.

'Ah yes, that is to be expected. It is his usual choice,' Ferdinand observed with a disapproving sniff.

Grace opened the case, then gasped. Inside was a superb ruby and diamond choker. A note was enclosed, written in a flowing hand on a stiff white card adorned with an ornate crest: *For your red dress. When you decide you would like to view my art collection, please do me the favour of wearing this token of my esteem.*

'Good heavens!' Grace said. 'It's fabulous, isn't it?'

She was met with silence.

'Oh, now I see.' She chortled. 'You obviously think I have fallen into the baron's clutches.'

'Haven't you?' said Ferdinand. 'He is a notorious ladies' man, and it is well known that he gives all his mistresses an expensive bauble from Cartier after each new conquest. But, Mademoiselle Dubois, you barely know him, and to succumb to him so quickly, like … like some little chorus girl!'

'Do listen, dear Ferdinand,' Grace said. 'I have not begun an affair with Édouard de Gide. We simply went to the opera, had a very pleasant supper, and then I went home.'

'But that is unheard of! Believe me, I know. It is only after a woman has, shall we say, made herself available that he bestows a gift like this upon her.' Ferdinand looked puzzled. 'I wonder why he has broken with the habit of a lifetime and given you such a lavish present now?'

'Obviously, he felt I might require additional inducement,' Grace responded airily. 'Well, I'm afraid he has no hope of success.' She picked up the necklace. 'It is lovely, though. Ah, well. Would you mind wrapping it up and sending it back for me? I am more than happy to accompany Baron Édouard de Gide to the ballet or the opera or dinner, but to go up and see his Old Masters?' She giggled. 'It is quite out of the question.'

Now it was Ferdinand's turn to laugh. 'Oh, what a wonderful tale. Never before has the baron been rebuffed in such a way. *Le tout-Paris* will be talking about this remarkable event!'

'Well, I am very happy for *le tout-Paris* to be made aware that I have no interest in that kind of liaison.'

'Looking as alluring as you do? They will never believe it. Everyone will simply assume you are ... what is that excellent English expression? Yes — playing hard to get.'

Ferdinand gave Grace another of his formal bows, although this time he was chuckling. She watched as he made his way back down the corridor, his grey-clad figure shadowy against the pearly walls, the only flash of colour coming from the red leather case he held in his hand.

CHAPTER TWENTY

Wearing a new, full-skirted black dress that sported wide pockets, a tightly belted waist and a deep V-neckline that revealed a hint of décolletage, Grace was sitting on one of the high stools at Le Chat Noir's bar with her best friends, regaling them with the story of the hapless baron and his ruby and diamond Cartier necklace. Both were in agreement that she had done exactly the right thing.

'Though I would not blame you if you were tempted to keep it,' Marie-Hélène observed. 'In fact, I think few girls could resist.'

Brigitte spoke in a more serious tone. 'Grace, I am glad you are having a good time, really I am. But aren't you interested in love?'

'Absolutely not! Let's just say that I know what a relationship with a man can lead to. I don't want to become entangled — and I won't.'

Grace's stomach lurched as she reminded herself that, to date, she had done nothing about seeking a divorce. Somehow, the entire subject was overwhelming; every time she thought about writing to Jack she found a reason to put it off.

'Well then, you must meet Philippe Boyer,' said Brigitte. 'He can be a little mysterious and he's not always diplomatic, but I like him, as does Picasso, so you will probably think he is quite nice.'

'Brigitte, you haven't listened to a word I've been saying. I'm not interested,' Grace admonished her friend.

'I don't expect you to be. In fact, I can't see Philippe as your type. That's why he would make such a perfect casual acquaintance — there would be absolutely no risk at all of you getting involved.'

'What's he like?'

Brigitte put her head to one side. 'He is extremely good-looking in an intense sort of way, and he's clever, if a bit too political for my liking. It might be interesting for you to spend a little time with him.'

'I very much doubt it.'

Ignoring Grace's marked lack of enthusiasm, Brigitte stood and scanned the crowded room, then waved at the man she was seeking.

'Really, Brigitte, did you have to do that?' Grace laughed. 'You're incorrigible!'

A moment later, a tall, lean man with vivid blue eyes was by her side.

Brigitte immediately took charge. 'Philippe Boyer, I want you to meet a new friend of mine from Dior. You probably haven't come across an Australian before, so this will be a new experience.' She smiled. 'May I present my colleague, the very beautiful Grace Dubois.'

She gave Grace a barely perceptible wink, took Marie-Hélène's hand, and promptly melted away.

Philippe Boyer *was* good-looking. In contrast to Édouard de Gide's smooth blond elegance, he possessed a moody, tensile quality that Grace found, to her surprise, immensely appealing. Philippe's dark brown hair was a little long, brushing the frayed collar of his white shirt, which he wore with a black leather jacket, slim black trousers and black boots.

Grace felt confused. Here was a man who just a minute ago she'd not even wanted to meet, yet after setting eyes on him for the first time her heart had begun to beat unnervingly quickly.

'Well, Mademoiselle Dubois from Australia, what is your view of Le Chat Noir?' Philippe asked with a wry smile that only made him appear more attractive.

'I like it very much.'

'I thought you would — all the mannequins do. And the rest of the so-called smart bohemian set. By the way, would you like a drink?'

'I'm still on this martini,' Grace said, lifting her glass to her lips before adding, 'It doesn't sound as if you approve of the bohemian set.'

'Oh, they act as if they are so very free, so modern, so French,' Philippe said sarcastically. 'Yet for many it is all just a game of make-believe.'

'Monsieur Boyer, if you don't care for the club or its patrons, what are you doing here?' Grace inquired. 'I wouldn't think you'd want to darken its doors.'

'I'm here for work, not pleasure,' he responded, leaning against the bar as he ordered a Calvados. Seeing Grace's puzzled expression, he added, 'Brigitte did not tell you? I am a journalist. As it happens, I'm writing a profile on Sartre and his circle.'

'I see. And for whom do you write?'

'L'Humanité. But as it represents the views of the Communist Party of France, I doubt it is a newspaper you would have read.'

'What makes you say that?' Philippe Boyer might possess an undeniable magnetism, Grace reflected, but he could certainly be abrupt.

'A woman like you?' he asked with a return of that irresistible wry smile. 'In my experience, high fashion mannequins are not interested in politics.'

'Obviously that's because you have never met one who comes from Australia before,' Grace said breezily.

'*Touché*.' Philippe bowed his head in acknowledgement. 'All the same,' he continued, 'aren't Dior's models besieged by wealthy suitors? With all that lavish attention, I cannot imagine the Communist Party would enthral you.'

Grace found it difficult to know if he was serious or simply intent on teasing her; the man was as infuriating as he was intriguing.

'Is there anything else about me that you can or cannot imagine, Monsieur Boyer?' Now she was flirting. What better invitation could there be for a man to murmur any number of comments, ripe with flattery and innuendo? Grace wondered what had come over her.

'There is, as a matter of fact,' Philippe said. 'As you are from such a very safe, faraway land and as your manner is so delightfully carefree, I cannot imagine you have ever been burdened by significant worries.'

That was not the response Grace had expected.

'For that matter,' he added, 'I cannot imagine you would be accustomed to what the party's members would deem hard manual labour. Shall I continue?'

'Honestly!' Attractive or not, Boyer had an excess of cheek.

'Call me Philippe.' Grace could swear he was trying to stifle a grin. 'I prefer to discuss politics on a first-name basis.'

'Philippe, then — and you weren't talking about politics, you were talking about me. Are you always in the habit of leaping to conclusions?'

'Tell me if I am wrong.' His blue eyes twinkled in a way that would make her forgive him for almost anything.

'Absolutely, one hundred per cent wrong,' she said. 'Just for that, you will have to guess what I did in a previous life.'

'A previous life?' Philippe raised his eyebrows. 'Let's see — I really will have to use my imagination this time. Isn't there an English nursery rhyme that starts off with, "Butcher, baker, candlestick-maker ..." Am I getting close?'

Grace couldn't help laughing. 'I was a farmer. Sheep and wheat.'

To her great satisfaction, Philippe was astounded. 'Surely not!'

'Actually, I had to work really hard, for years, especially after my ...' She felt a sudden ache in her heart. 'After my father died.'

Philippe's insouciance disappeared. 'I am so sorry. Brigitte is always telling me I am too blunt, that I take everything too far.' He shrugged. 'She is right, although in my defence, I don't think many men could easily imagine an haute couture mannequin like you spending her days working in the fields.' He placed his hand briefly on her bare arm, where, in contrast to the baron's unwelcome touch, it left a trace of tantalising heat. 'Allow me to make it up to you. Why don't we leave this place?'

'Leave — with you? Why on earth would I do that?'

'Let me show you another side of Paris, one you haven't seen before. Perhaps then you will understand what has made me so insufferable.' He finished his Calvados and placed it on the counter. 'So, shall we go?'

'I don't think so.' Grace had no intention of going anywhere with this impudent Frenchman to whom she was curiously drawn — in itself an excellent reason to decline his invitation. Despite Brigitte's assurances, Grace had the strongest feeling that Philippe Boyer was not a man with whom she was destined to have a casual acquaintance. It would be far better — and safer — if their encounter ended straightaway. But ...

'What do you have to lose by saying yes?' he asked with a winning look Grace found difficult to resist.

She had spent most of her life attempting to be a good daughter, a good wife, to do the right thing, and where had it got her? Suddenly, she felt rebellious, excited at the prospect of a night that offered new discoveries in the company of this arresting man.

Outside the club was a powerful motorcycle attached by a chain to a steel railing. 'I don't suppose you have been on one of these before?' Philippe said.

'Goodness, you make a great many assumptions,' Grace responded with mock indignation.

'Well, if you have,' he said as he took his keys from his pocket, 'and quite frankly, Mademoiselle Dubois, I have reached the point where very little about you would surprise me, you will know that if you don't want to be flung off at the first corner, I am afraid you will be forced to wrap your arms around me.'

Grace knew Philippe was teasing her again but, to her surprise, she realised she didn't care. Her sole concern was that the dress she was wearing would still be in pristine condition when she returned it to Madame Raymonde on Monday morning.

All the same, Grace had no intention of allowing Philippe to think she was intimidated. Gathering up her skirts as well as she was able, she promptly straddled the bike, tucking herself in behind him. She gingerly held on to his waist, only to find any lingering reluctance she'd had about being in his company melting away. He was certainly completely different to Édouard de Gide, and nothing at all like Jack. Philippe seemed entirely unimpressed by her looks, or by her status as an elite Dior model. She found that she was unusually curious about him.

As the motorcycle sped through the night, Grace silently chided herself. No matter what her initial interest in a man might be, a point would inevitably arrive when she felt cold and distant. Every date she'd been on during the war had ended the same way. Her thoughts travelled back to the time she'd stepped outside with the good-looking officer during the party at the Parkes Air Base. Despite his appeal, she had frozen. She hadn't even been able to respond to her own husband.

Fortunately, her shortcomings were unlikely to become an issue tonight, as so far it appeared that Philippe was more interested in verbal jousting than anything else.

She became pensive as she thought over his remarks about the smart world of Paris. It was true that, apart from working at the *maison*, her recent weeks had been spent in a whirl of hedonistic pursuits. Dancing, dining, drinking cocktails, visiting the opera — it had all been fun, she supposed, but what did such a life add up to?

Perhaps this frenzy of activity had just been a way of putting off her search. Might it really be that, deep down, she feared that discovering Reuben's whereabouts would prove too distressing for her to bear? She was, after all, nothing but the illegitimate offspring of a man who clearly had no desire to claim her as his daughter. Wasn't her wish to avoid the painful confirmation of these facts the real reason she had done so little to find him since arriving in Paris?

As the chill air whipped her hair against her face, she told herself she would have to develop a little more backbone. She was reasonably well established in Paris now, her three-month trial at Christian Dior was over and Madame Raymonde had given her a permanent position at the *maison*. The time had come to renew her quest.

Perhaps this handsome man who'd had such an unexpected effect upon her knew something or someone that could help her. He was a journalist, after all. He must have contacts, ways of locating information, even missing people. On the other hand, she wasn't at all sure she wished to place herself in the debt of Monsieur Boyer.

CHAPTER TWENTY-ONE

Grace was so preoccupied by her thoughts she hadn't noticed the neighbourhood they had been passing through. Now, as Philippe brought the motorcycle to a stop, she saw that they were surrounded by decrepit buildings, some under-provisioned shops and a few run-down cafés.

'Up ahead it's just cobblestoned alleyways,' Philippe said, 'and as the drains in this part of town are virtually antique, there's likely to be a fair bit of water on the ground. We'd better walk from here.' He looked at her, although without a suggestion of admiration. 'That dress you're wearing is not exactly suited to a bumpy landing, is it?'

Grace had never before felt self-conscious in Paris in her chic clothes. Now she felt unpleasantly conspicuous. Thin, shabbily dressed people brushed past, casting disparaging glances in her direction. The new post-war prosperity on show in the heady world of smart nightclubs had clearly eluded them.

'We're in eastern Paris now,' Philippe said. 'Those who live here are mostly poor artisans — cobblers, garment workers or watchmakers. Some are masons who earn their miserable incomes carving the gravestones for Père Lachaise cemetery.'

Grace followed Philippe into the disorienting maze of alleys, so unlike the discipline and elegance of the *quartiers* she knew. The buildings here were low, cramped and dirty. She was relieved when they stopped in front of a café.

They entered a room which, although poorly lit, still revealed stains on the red-checked tablecloths and patches of dust on the furniture. A few burly types wearing cloth caps and blue overalls who were drinking pastis at the bar turned around and stared at her, but, after seeing Philippe, they nodded at him and turned back to their muttered conversation.

'Friends of yours?' Grace asked.

'Let's just say they're comrades,' Philippe replied. 'Welcome to the working man's quarter. We're in Belleville. A little different to the avenue Montaigne, isn't it?'

Philippe's light, bantering tone had been abandoned.

After they took their seats at a small corner table, he gestured towards the menu. 'There's always the same thing on each night — *pot au feu*, a green salad and then cheese. If you're lucky, there might be some chocolate or even coffee, though they'll both be from the black market.'

'At least that makes ordering straightforward.'

Philippe hailed the sole waiter. '*Pour deux*,' he said.

Grace was surprised to find that the stew, with its rich, robust flavours, was delicious. 'Mmm ... This is really good.'

'You can thank our generous American buddies and their Marshall Plan for that,' Philippe said with a frown. 'They continue to fly in planeloads of food every day.'

'Well then, why do you look so disapproving?'

'Because they are intent on turning us into a colony! You know what the comrades and I think of the Marshall Plan?'

'I have a feeling you're going to tell me.'

'It's a subversive way for the United States to exert influence and bring France under the Yankee yoke. The plan is a Trojan Horse and we are all to be subjugated.'

'But that's ridiculous!'

'Is it?' Philippe shrugged. 'You know, we French welcomed the Americans. But even that journalist Malcolm Muggeridge — who, by the way, I'm sure is an agent of the British secret service — says that everybody ends up hating their liberators. He's right. That is exactly how we feel.'

'I still don't see why,' Grace said.

'Because France has become nothing but a poor relation.' Philippe drained his glass of red wine. 'Suddenly, everyone wants chewing gum and Coca-Cola, to distract themselves with stupid, inane pleasures. We are turning into a little United States of America. You have seen some of the fashionable bars, I suppose, the ones with names like New York, or worse, The Sunny Side of the Street.'

Grace smiled. 'Actually, that one's rather good. They serve delicious Tom Collinses and Manhattans.'

'But that's the point!' he exclaimed. 'What the Americans have brought with them — like those cocktails — it has proven irresistible. Films, clothes, jazz musicians like Duke Ellington and Charlie Parker ...'

'I'm afraid to say, I like them too,' Grace admitted.

'As do I ...' Seeing her confusion, Philippe explained, 'I am not immune to these pleasures. But that does not mean we should embrace American capitalism, American values. That is not the right path.'

It struck Grace that there was something mechanical about Philippe's response, as if he were repeating words and phrases he had learnt by rote. 'Well, what is the correct path, as you call it?'

'The Communist Party, of course. Thousands of others think so too, but we are facing problems.'

'Which are?'

He raked his hair with his fingers in a manner that Grace found unexpectedly distracting. 'When rumours about the Red Army's disgraceful behaviour began to circulate, our members left the party in droves. Now we have to compete with the bounty showered on us by the blessed Marshall Plan, courtesy of Saint Harry Truman.'

Grace was intrigued. Philippe Boyer might veer between the recitation of party dogma and outbursts of spontaneous passion, but he didn't flatter her. It was a novelty to be treated as an intelligent individual, but still …

Philippe broke into her thoughts. 'My apologies. I thought you were interested, but you look so distracted, I must have been mistaken.'

She smiled encouragingly. 'I was actually wondering what your next step might be.'

'As we've had no luck gaining power in France via the ballot box, I believe that purer, more revolutionary measures are called for.'

Grace started as their waiter thumped down mugs of coffee on the table. 'That sounds frightening.'

'Grace, open your eyes! Look around you at the inequality. How many people buy their dresses at Christian Dior?'

Her temper flared. 'Just because only a few ladies can afford couture doesn't mean that most wouldn't love to. I may not be French, but even I can see that people are sick of years of doing without.' She leant forward. 'You said yourself they want pleasure. Well, for plenty of women that means something as simple as the dream of owning a wonderful new dress. Who are you to deny them?'

Unexpectedly, Philippe grinned. 'Perhaps you are right,' he said. 'Although I fear that if you have been seeking a little of that pleasure this evening, then I have done a very poor job at providing it.'

It was only when Grace had returned to the rue Dauphine, wished Madame Guérin and Tartuffe a quick *bonsoir*, trekked up the six flights of stairs, undressed and dropped into her bed that she was at last able to think about Philippe Boyer.

The man both attracted and puzzled her. Yes, he was a political radical, yet his behaviour revealed a curious duality. Perhaps there was more to him than the outspoken firebrand he seemed so anxious to be taken for. She wondered what he might be hiding.

CHAPTER TWENTY-TWO

'Quick! Did you see that woman, the one who just stopped in front of the window?' Brigitte said excitedly.

'Of course — she was dressed head to toe in Chanel,' Grace replied. 'The tweed suit with the camellia pinned just so, the little boater, and all the faux-pearl necklaces. I'm not such a hayseed that I can't recognise her designs when I see them.'

'Yes, but what you have failed to recognise is *her*!'

'What? Don't tell me that was actually the famous —'

'Coco Chanel herself. Well, this *is* a surprise.'

Grace and Brigitte were strolling down the charming rue du Faubourg Saint-Honoré, a narrow street lined with fashionable boutiques. Brigitte had been insisting for days that if Grace had any aspiration at all to be a truly chic Parisienne, an investment in one of Hermès's distinctive, hand-finished silk scarves was essential.

'I used to love looking at pictures in *Vogue* of Chanel's clothes with my mother,' Grace said wistfully. She felt a sudden yearning for the closeness she'd shared with Olive during those uncomplicated, happy moments. 'Nobody mentions Chanel anymore. What's she been up to, I wonder?'

'I can't really talk about it inside the boutique,' Brigitte said. 'It's a shocking story.'

'That sounds intriguing,' Grace replied. 'Let's stop at that sweet little place up ahead with the flowers in the window; you can tell me about it over a glass of wine. Anyway, I probably need fortification — otherwise, I might faint when I see Hermès's prices.'

The two women sat down at a banquette in the quiet bistro.

'So tell me,' Grace said, sipping chablis. 'Was it an affair? I thought the French were broad-minded about such things.'

'That is true,' Brigitte said, 'and Chanel has certainly taken many lovers to her bed.'

'Well then, what happened?'

'This was different. As soon as the Occupation began, she shut down her business and sacked hundreds of workers. But, far worse, she continued to live at the Ritz —'

'What was wrong with staying at a hotel?'

'Grace, she lived there with her lover, Baron Hans Günther von Dincklage, a German intelligence officer.'

'No!'

'Ah, I can see you don't know anything about what we French call *la collaboration horizontale*. Chanel was far from the only one, but in her case she was quite blatant.' Brigitte grimaced. 'Whether Chanel was a spy, I don't know. But she was lucky not to suffer *l'épuration sauvage*.'

Grace thought for a moment. 'I don't think I know that expression either.'

'It's the term given to the punishment meted out to anyone — but most particularly to women — who was believed to have collaborated with the Nazis.'

'You mean such a thing was common?'

'It was more complicated than you think. Let us say there were many grey areas.'

'How were they punished?' Grace asked.

'In the worst ways you could imagine. Women, some hardly more than girls, were publicly stripped of their clothes and paraded through the streets before being beaten by mobs. Thousands were seized all over the country and had their hair shaved off. They became known as *les tondues*.'

Grace shuddered. 'I had no idea.'

'*Ma chère*, you seem a little faint,' Brigitte said, frowning. 'Why don't we have something to eat?' It took only a slight incline of her lovely blonde head for her to attract the attention of a waiter in a long white apron. After omelettes and a green salad were ordered, the man scurried away.

Grace swallowed hard. 'But you said nothing happened to Chanel?'

'Oh, she was arrested, but quickly released. Apparently, she had friends in high places. Chanel has always been a great survivor.' Brigitte laughed bitterly. 'She put a notice in her rue Cambon window announcing she would give a bottle of Chanel No. 5 free to any GI who asked for it. After that, no one was willing to touch so much as a hair on her head.'

'What happened next?' Grace asked, her eyes wide.

'Our great survivor managed to slip out of France just before liberation. Now she is living freely in Switzerland, still with her kept German lover and, it is rumoured, both a Swiss bank account and a steady supply of morphine. Anyway,' Brigitte pursed her crimson lips with disapproval, 'she loathes current fashions — particularly the New Look. *Le patron*'s designs make women look like women, whereas Coco would rather they dress like boys.'

Brigitte paused as the eager waiter returned bearing their meal.

'Where was I?' she said. 'Ah, yes. I have noticed of late that people's memories can be surprisingly short. In fact, I would not be at all surprised if Coco returns permanently to Paris at some point in the future. When she does, no doubt the *beau monde* will once again beat a path to her shiny black door.' Brigitte looked at Grace. 'I can see you're not eating.'

'I've been thinking about something you mentioned earlier,' Grace said.

'What was that?'

'About the women who collaborated. You said there were many grey areas …'

'Grace, how can I explain what it was like here during the war?' Brigitte said. 'People froze to death in winter, there was so little fuel. And often it was impossible to find food.' She frowned. 'Not every woman who faced *l'épuration sauvage* was a collaborator. Some were unjustly accused, although, yes, many slept with German soldiers. In return, these women's lives sometimes became a little easier. Just think,' Brigitte said quietly. 'If your children were starving, what choice would you make?'

Grace shook her head; she had no reply. Unlike so many French women, she had never had to make a life and death decision. She wondered if she would have the courage to do what was right, when knowing what was right was itself so uncertain. Brigitte had opened her eyes to a sobering melange of moral complexities.

'I'm so sorry,' Grace said, as she reached for her friend's hand, 'but somehow I don't feel like shopping anymore. Would you mind very much if we left it for another time?'

CHAPTER TWENTY-THREE

Having assumed an expression of magnificent disdain, Grace positioned herself at the entrance to the salon.

'*Numéro cent vingt-trois*: Philadelphia,' announced Jeanne. She then repeated it in English: 'Number one hundred and twenty-three.'

Grace held her pose for just a moment longer, so that her audience would have time to admire the low-cut, daffodil-yellow evening gown and elaborate gold and crystal necklace before she began to glide across the room. Ladies in neat suits and pearls leant forward on their tiny gilt chairs murmuring, 'Simply darling' and 'Just divine'.

Grace paused again, one black-gloved hand positioned on her hip, before turning with just sufficient momentum to ensure the two black velvet panels attached at the waist of her full-length, pencil-slim skirt flew out, creating a striking effect.

Several members of the audience gasped. Grace was silently thankful for the long, albeit cunningly disguised slit — the famous 'Dior Pleat' — at the rear of her skirt. Then she continued her sinuous progress until she arrived back at her starting place. Once there, she posed again, gave a quick, dazzling smile and slipped behind a screen.

The private showing of Christian Dior's spring 1949 collection, held especially for the wives and friends of the diplomats from the United States Embassy, was almost over. Now, only the bridal gown, the grand finale, remained.

'*On y va, chérie*,' Grace whispered to Claire, a blonde mannequin who, despite being passionately in love with her new husband, had nonetheless retained her uniquely virginal radiance and thus continued to be, as she had for several seasons, Dior's preferred bride. Grace watched from behind the screen as Claire entered the salon, sublime in white guipure lace, her silk-chiffon veil billowing cloud-like behind her.

Grace had been delighted when she'd discovered that the seamstresses placed a sprig of lily of the valley, *le patron*'s favourite flower, into the hems of each new garment, but she'd been especially touched to learn that the unmarried girls in the workroom sewed locks of their hair into the wedding dresses. 'It's to make sure we'll find our own husbands soon,' one of the apprentices confided.

'Be careful what you wish for,' Grace had said, though when the girl had asked her what she meant, she had chosen to remain silent.

The mannequins had all returned to the *cabine*, and their hard-working dressers were standing ready to relieve them of their precious gowns, when Tutu clapped her hands three times and made an announcement.

'*Mes filles*,' she said, 'as the applause no doubt indicated to you, our American guests were very taken with Monsieur Dior's collection. Bravo to everyone for showing it to such advantage. I know it is not usual, but Madame Luling has informed me that the esteemed visitors would like to meet some of you.'

A scattering of disaffected murmurs followed.

'Yes, I know, it has been a long week. But you are under no obligation. Those who do not wish to participate may wait in the *cabine* for the usual hour, in case one of our guests wishes to review a particular gown.' Tutu paused, continuing in a more confidential tone. 'The fact is, already several other couturiers are fighting for the Americans' patronage, particularly that of the ambassadress, who is well known for her style. And by the way, although she speaks fluent French, many of the other ladies do not, so please volunteer only if you are able to converse well in English.'

A few of the girls who met this requirement — Victoire, Thérèse, Brigitte, Marie-Hélène and Grace — indicated they would oblige.

'Good. Remain in your dresses — but do not eat a scrap of food,' Tutu warned, before adding to general relief, 'although you will be permitted a little champagne.'

Collapsing into a chair, Grace kicked off her shoes and began massaging her feet. As the shows were two hours long, and she had been taking part in them twice a day for weeks now, the thought of standing about conversing for any length of time had little appeal.

On the other hand, the House of Christian Dior had been good to her. Her eyes welled with tears when she reflected upon the way that Ferdinand, Marguerite and the others had showed her so much kindness — and she had to admit, patience too. The least she could do was to help when it was needed. She slipped her shoes back on, powdered her nose and adjusted the black net veiling on her tiny feathered headpiece before joining the American ladies in the salon.

Grace was just in time to hear a very slender, elegant woman with striking hooded eyes begin to speak.

'My name is Evangeline Bruce,' she said, 'and I am the wife of the new United States Ambassador to France, David Bruce. On behalf of everyone present, I would like to thank you for this beautiful show.'

Grace was surprised by the ambassadress's youth — although thoroughly assured, she looked only a few years older than Grace herself.

'Having the chance to observe these marvellous creations reminds us all that France has not only survived, she has triumphed over the very worst adversity. I know I can speak confidently on behalf of us all when I say we are delighted to have this opportunity to congratulate you on your achievements.'

During the applause a waiter began to thread his way through the crush of women, distributing crystal glasses of Pol Roger. It was then Madame Luling's turn to glide around the room, where she gave a superb demonstration of her effective brand of charm.

'It will not be difficult at all to have this dress made in your size,' Grace heard her say encouragingly to a stout matron, and to a thin, pallid woman, 'Yes, I am quite sure that a different colour would not present the *maison* with a problem.'

Next, Madame Luling introduced Grace to Evangeline Bruce. 'I worked in England during the war,' the ambassadress said, taking Grace's hand. 'There were people in our office from all over the British Empire, so I became quite good at recognising accents. You're Australian, aren't you?'

Grace smiled. 'Indeed I am.'

'I thought so! But how on earth did you end up here? You're an awfully long way from home.'

Grace was saved from responding by the appearance of Madame Beguin at Mrs Bruce's elbow.

'Madame,' she said, 'do let me assist you. Which of Monsieur Dior's designs would you like me to reserve? I would hate to think you might miss out on something you admired.'

'I fear I have already,' the ambassadress replied. 'I saw the Duchess of Windsor at dinner only last week in that exquisite blue silk-velvet gown with the pearl embroidery — I think its name was Lahore. I would certainly have been interested in that.'

The *vendeuse* did not miss a beat. 'I am so sorry, Madame Bruce,' she said. 'This collection — Monsieur Dior calls it his *trompe l'oeil* — has been our most popular yet. But that dress, no, I would not have recommended it for you. Please come this way — I have something no less chic, but softer and more feminine that would be perfect, I think.'

The ambassadress's place was almost immediately taken by an extremely tall woman with a cheerful demeanour who, pointing at the morsel in her hand, remarked in a booming voice, 'Aren't these absolutely delicious? I've had plenty of cocktail food on the diplomatic circuit, I can tell you, but these little chicken canapés are in a class of their own. It must be that special way the French have with mayonnaise. By the way, my name is Julia Child,' she announced.

'I'm Grace Dubois, and yes, they look delicious,' Grace said, wishing Tutu hadn't warned her against eating anything.

'My husband, Paul, works in the embassy, but I'm spending practically all of my time learning how to make this wonderful food!' Mrs Child took another canapé from a passing tray. 'Of course, it has its challenges,' she continued. 'Apart from the fact that I'm only beginning to learn French, I've found that olive oil is almost impossible to get, and I have taken to raiding the embassy supplies for sugar and coffee. Oh, and there are no refrigerators here — I have to keep my milk on a window ledge!'

Grace confessed that she did the same.

Mrs Child chuckled. 'But it's all worth it, isn't it? I'll never forget my first *sole meunière* — it just captured my spirit. And don't even get me started on *boeuf bourguignon* ... Now, my dear, don't let me monopolise you. Paul says I have a habit of cornering people.' She peered over the crowd. 'You must meet a young woman — she's here somewhere. Anyway, she's a college girl from Vassar, or possibly Smith, who's been staying with the Countess Germaine de Renty while she attends classes at the Sorbonne. Germaine takes her everywhere; I think she's making it her mission to baste that girl in French culture — like a duck! Ah, good, they are coming our way.'

'It's you!' Jackie Bouvier embraced Grace.

'I see you two have already met,' Mrs Child said. 'I like eating French food far too much to fit into any of your Monsieur Dior's dresses, but I'm keen to have a closer look all the same. Countess, would you like to join me? We'll leave these young things alone.'

Jackie turned to Grace and said in a voice as soft and breathy as Mrs Child's had been raucous, 'I'm so glad you stayed behind for this soirée. I thought you were wonderful, but you know what I liked about you best?'

Grace shook her head.

'It was that smile! Right at the end, before you disappeared. Everyone else was so aloof throughout the show. You were the only one who dared to appear approachable.'

'I'm not sure the *maison* would share your opinion,' Grace responded. 'Monsieur Dior says our duty is to "conquer and convince" — we're really supposed to maintain our hauteur at all times. As you have seen, this does not come naturally to me.' She chortled. 'Appearing remote is something I had to learn. It's a useful trick, though, a little like putting on armour. If ever you are contemplating a life in the public eye, it's something I would recommend.'

Jackie laughed and said that should such an unlikely event occur, she would be sure to remember. 'In the meantime, I will practise!' she added, although the American girl appeared to have little need for lessons in the cultivation of a mysterious remove. There was something in her face, Grace thought, a quick mobility that could change in an instant from an engaging, full-throttle grin to an inward repose. It was near impossible to discern what emotional currents might be hidden beneath that enigmatic façade.

CHAPTER TWENTY-FOUR

April 1949

'I'm not late, am I?' Brigitte called out to Madame de Turckheim, her scarf flying and her umbrella clattering to the floor.

Tutu raised her eyebrows but said nothing. A few minutes' tardiness was permissible; any more and an intervention by Madame Raymonde might be required.

Brigitte undressed quickly, donned a white coverall and took her seat next to Grace. 'Darling,' she said, fishing in the pocket of her wrapper, 'this is for you.'

While Brigitte hastily began applying her make-up, Grace looked at the note. 'I can see it's not from the baron,' she observed drily.

Rather than one of Édouard de Gide's stiff crested cards, which had continued to arrive at regular intervals, Grace unfolded a piece of paper that seemed to have been torn from a school exercise book. Brigitte, now busy with her eye-shadow, regarded her friend in the mirror.

'Listen to this,' Grace said, bemused. She proceeded to read the letter aloud.

Dear Grace,
Now that I have shown you the other side of Paris, the time has come to venture further.
   I will collect you at 11.00 on Sunday morning.
   There is no need to reply. If you are not in front of your building at that time, I will continue on my way.
   My best wishes,
   Philippe
   PS It would be advisable to wear more suitable clothing.

'Good manners are not exactly his strong suit, are they?' Grace crumpled the piece of paper in her hand. 'He probably wants to give me another lecture on the indulgent life of an haute couture mannequin. If I'm really lucky he might move on to the decadence of the Americans.'

'Will you go?' Brigitte asked.

'Certainly not! For one thing, I have no idea where Philippe is planning on taking me. And for another, apart from his frankly radical political beliefs, I barely know a thing about him.' *And, for my own good, it would be best for it to stay that way,* she thought.

Grace turned to her friend. 'Come to that, how is it you're acquainted with Monsieur Boyer?'

'Actually, we're related.'

'Oh God, I haven't been saying awful things about your brother, have I?'

'No.' Brigitte laughed. 'He's a second cousin. There was a sort of scandal attached to his side of the family, so growing up I never saw him. In fact, I only came to know Philippe recently. He's not been part of my life.'

'A life about which you have always been very mysterious.'

'Only because there is nothing interesting to discover.'

'It's all right — we're all entitled to our secrets.' Grace smiled. 'But at least you can tell me, is Philippe always like this? You know, sounding off about politics.'

'Ah, Grace, the war changed so many things, especially people. I am not absolutely sure what Philippe did; he doesn't talk about it. But his experience with the Nazis, what he saw, or rather had to do … he told me he wasn't the same afterwards.'

Grace immediately thought of Jack. The war had changed him too.

'I think Philippe lost so many people that he cared about, the Communist Party became like a family.'

'Well, I'm still not going out with him,' Grace said as she beckoned to a dresser. 'Much as I adore you, Brigitte, my feelings most certainly do not extend to your cousin. In fact, I doubt I will give him another thought.'

But she did. One moment she would be strolling past the tall poplars that lined the banks of the Seine, admiring their mist of new green leaves, while the next she'd find herself contemplating his smile. During a show, as she was modelling a particularly grand taffeta opera coat, she struggled to maintain her equilibrium when, for no reason at all, she suddenly recalled the way her hair had whipped her cheeks as she held on to Philippe's waist on the motorbike. On Friday morning, when travelling in the crowded Metro, she was sure she'd seen his face, but when she looked again it was a different man whose eyes, unlike Philippe's, were an unremarkable shade.

Grace tried to take herself in hand. Each time this singular man's image insinuated itself into her mind, she pushed it away. At least this madness was temporary — it would all be over by Sunday. She would not be waiting for Philippe in front of her building at eleven o'clock. He would leave. She would never hear from him again.

Sunday arrived. Grace made coffee and gnawed at a corner of yesterday's now-stale croissant. She returned to bed. At nine o'clock she tried to read, but when she discovered she'd read the same paragraph three times she flung the book down instead. At ten o'clock she washed her face and dabbed a little cream on her cheeks before pulling on an old jersey and the pair of Levi's jeans Jackie had given her. Next, she scraped her hair back into a ponytail. There was no point making an effort. She wasn't planning on seeing anyone.

The minutes ticked by. She laced up a pair of plimsolls, then stared once more at the clock beside her bed. Eleven. Eleven-ten. Eleven-twenty. Slowly, she exhaled. She was free.

Grace jumped when she heard the knock at the door. What could Madame Guérin want? It occurred to Grace that due to her recent distracted state, she was likely to be behind in the rent.

'Coming!' she shouted, rummaging in her handbag for her purse. She didn't want to make trouble for madame with the building's owner; the gruff little concierge had done her many kindnesses.

Finally, purse in hand, she flung open the door, saying, 'Please, forgive me ...'

'Forgive you, Mademoiselle Dubois? I'm not sure that I should.'

Philippe Boyer stood in front of Grace, his hands resting nonchalantly on his hips.

'You!'

'Who else?'

'But you said that if I wasn't in front of the building you would leave,' Grace said with what she hoped was a withering look.

'That is true. But I thought as I had come all this way, going a little further would be of no consequence. *Bof.*' Philippe shrugged. 'Of course, I didn't know then that I would have to climb quite so many stairs.'

'Well, you can climb back down them. I'm not going anywhere with you.' Grace's heart was beating as quickly as it did the first time she had seen Philippe. She knew she should be cross, yet curiously, she felt nothing but an intensely pleasurable sense of expectation.

'Mademoiselle Dubois, that would be such a shame. I have packed food for the two of us. In this time of shortages, how can I let it go to waste?'

Grace made herself frown.

'You know,' he said, ignoring her forbidding expression, 'you look very nice like this. Without make-up, wearing simple clothes — I like it.'

She found her resistance crumbling.

'Perhaps we can make what our new American so-called friends call a deal,' Philippe suggested. 'I will take you on a picnic — it is such a beautiful spring day, the birds are singing and even the lilac trees have begun to flower. While we are together I will try very hard not to be rude or offensive and, most particularly, not to speak about politics. If you still think I am horrible then, I promise, you won't ever see me again.'

Grace couldn't help herself. She began to laugh. Philippe was being ridiculous, but perhaps she was too. What was there to be alarmed about?

'All right, all right,' she said. 'I'll go. But no lectures, and especially no comments on what you imagine is the way I lead my life. Otherwise it won't be just a matter of not seeing you again. I'll take your motorbike and ride back to Paris — alone!'

CHAPTER TWENTY-FIVE

Philippe handed Grace a leather jacket. 'Put this on,' he said. 'You won't feel it now, but it becomes cold when you're riding. We have a way to go.'

They followed the River Seine until they left behind both the glories of central Paris and the oppressive shabbiness of the *banlieues*, its impoverished outer suburbs. Only a few kilometres later they entered a very different landscape, fresh and verdant, burgeoning with new life. Grace marvelled at the pastures of lush grass, fields thick with the still-green heads of sunflowers and, next to the stone farmhouses with their pitched roofs and pale blue shutters, vegetable plots sewn with aubergines, courgettes and *haricots verts*.

'The beauty of the French countryside,' Philippe yelled over his shoulder as he stopped to let a farmer lead a small herd of black and white cows safely across the road. 'There is nothing else like it.'

With the cold air on her face, the sun warming her back and her arms once more around Philippe, Grace allowed herself to enjoy the journey. *Don't think*, she told herself. *And*, despite an overwhelming desire to kiss the back of his neck that shocked her, *don't imagine that a simple day in the country with this unusually attractive man will lead to anything.*

An hour and a half after they'd left Paris, Philippe slowed down before turning into a small dirt lane. He proceeded carefully, dodging potholes and stones, as the path wound its way beside the tranquil waters of one of the Seine's smaller tributaries.

'We're nearly there,' he announced as he brought the motorcycle to a stop.

They had drawn up next to a row of weeping willows, their leaves swaying gently in the breeze.

'You're being very secretive,' said Grace. 'Where are we going?'

'Come with me and you will see.' Philippe led her over a grassy mound. 'There! Do you like it?'

'Oh, yes!' Grace stared with surprise at the tangled remains of what must once have been a glorious garden. In front of a charming if dilapidated pink house with rickety front steps and bright green shutters grew a vast riot of rose bushes and twisted strands of clematis, delicate pansies, golden daffodils and deep-red tulips, all jostling for space amid a snarl of weeds.

'What is this extraordinary place?'

'The artist Claude Monet used to live here,' Philippe explained. 'It's known as Giverny. The garden was his life's work, more important to him I think than even his paintings.'

'But now it's such a ruin.'

'Monet died more than twenty years ago. Some of his largest works went to a museum in Paris called l'Orangerie and other smaller pieces to the Jeu de Paume, but as for his garden — it's been completely neglected. Do you see that building just to the side of the house?' He pointed to a tall, lopsided structure. 'That was his studio.'

'You mean the place with the tree growing through the roof?'

'I'm afraid so. What is worse, those parts that nature has not engulfed, the war has ravaged. Have you seen the big holes in the ground? Look, there's one over there, with brambles covering its sides — they're craters made by German bombs.'

Grace followed Philippe as he led her beneath rows of flowering apple and almond trees, their branches thick with pink and white blossom. 'To think this wonderful place has been left like this — it's a tragedy,' she sighed.

'A bit like France, don't you think? Despite everything, she is still magnificent, but with no discipline, no proper stewardship, the country could well be facing the same fate.'

'What I think is that you are drawing dangerously close to the subject of politics,' Grace warned, wagging her finger.

'I won't say another word,' Philippe said with a grin. 'Anyway, there is more to see.'

They retraced their steps, then Philippe guided Grace between the low-hanging boughs of one of the larger willows until they came to a clearing.

'*Voilà!*' he exclaimed.

'I've never seen anything so beautiful in my life,' Grace murmured.

A large pool of shimmering water, on which floated drifts of lily pads, drew her forward. Carefully, she picked her way around the irises that grew in purple and white thickets on the mossy bank until she reached a vivid green, Japanese-style wooden bridge that, from the look of it, had long since collapsed. Vines of wisteria now coiled around its remains, their mauve petals floating gently to the ground, while, overhead, dragonflies with iridescent wings buzzed and hovered.

'I hope this is where you planned to have our picnic,' Grace called out as she turned around, 'because I can't imagine anywhere more perfect.'

'You must have read my mind.' Philippe took a checked rug out of the bike's panniers, spread it in the shade and then produced two mugs, linen napkins and a knife from the other. Next came a baguette, some luscious-looking tomatoes, a piece of cheese wrapped in muslin, a small container of raspberries and a bottle of wine.

'Mademoiselle, your feast awaits you,' he said with a mock flourish.

Grace smiled. Everything pleased her: the sunlight that fell in stippled patches from between the willows, the fragrance of the flowers, the simple rustic food and, most particularly, Philippe's company. She couldn't help but make a comparison with her night out with the baron. That had been undeniably glamorous, and Édouard himself, with his compliments, roses and champagne, more than attentive. Yet it had all been tainted by artifice. With Baron Édouard de Gide, Grace knew she was on show, whereas with Philippe, maddening as he could be, she felt … what? What did she feel? To her surprise, Grace realised she felt at home.

They ate and talked, drank wine, and then drank more. By the time she had eaten the last delectable raspberry, Grace had begun to believe Giverny had cast a spell.

'It's so good to be in the country again,' she said, 'even if it's completely different to what I'm used to. I haven't felt this relaxed for, oh, I don't know — ages.'

'What's it like, this faraway place of yours?' Philippe asked.

'Australia — the part I grew up in, anyway — isn't gentle like France.'

'What do you mean?'

Grace lay down on her back and thought for a moment. 'For a start, the light is different,' she said, gazing around. 'In

Australia it's incredibly bright — almost luminous. The land itself is magnificent, but it can be rugged, even harsh. Then there's the sky. Look at that soft blue up above us; I feel as if I could almost touch it.' Grace stretched out an arm before dropping it back by her side. 'Australia's sky is miles higher. It's like a sort of vast, brilliant canopy of the bluest blue you can imagine. All the same, there's something about the peace out here, or perhaps it's the purity of the air, that reminds me of home.'

Her serene state of mind was disturbed when Philippe lay down next to her. When his hand brushed her own, she felt as if she'd come into contact with an electrical current. She wondered nervously what might happen next. Would he embrace her?

But Philippe did not move. 'It is very sad that Monet has fallen out of favour,' he said instead. 'Picasso and I get on well and, it goes without saying, he has been immensely generous to the party. Pablo's gifts are unique — he is not alone in considering himself a genius. For me, though, Monet's paintings are more precious. This is not an avant garde view, I know. I suppose I am simply susceptible to beauty.'

Well, he certainly doesn't seem susceptible to me, Grace thought. Philippe might be unsuitable in more ways than she could count, yet she found herself craving his attention. When, finally, he turned to her, it was only to observe that the shadows were lengthening.

'I suppose I should take you home,' he said.

CHAPTER TWENTY-SIX

Philippe brought his motorcycle to a stop in front of 25 rue Dauphine. After padlocking it to a railing, he said politely, 'I'll see you to your door.'

'*Bonsoir*, Madame Guérin,' Grace called when she passed the little concierge who was busily sweeping the courtyard in the fading light. Grace turned to Philippe. 'I'd like to thank you. I have to admit, it's been a wonderful day.' She smiled. 'Actually, I've got hold of some quite good coffee — the *maison*'s doorman gave it to me. It seems that one of the US Embassy ladies sent around an enormous tin. Despite your suspicions about the Americans' dastardly ulterior motives, would you like a cup?'

'Well, I don't know. That would mean not only compromising my principles, I'd be forced to climb those horrible stairs all over again.'

Grace laughed. 'Take it or leave it.'

'All right. Count me in.'

What was she doing, Grace asked herself as she started the ascent to her attic. This was folly. How would she feel if he made advances? How would she feel if he didn't?

Then there was the discomforting fact that she was still married — never before had she so much as contemplated being unfaithful. No, Grace told herself firmly, that wasn't an issue. She might not be divorced, but her relationship with Jack was well and truly finished. The far bigger problem was that should she succumb to her strange yearning to be wrapped in Philippe's arms, she was certain her incapacity to feel, let alone do, whatever it was that she should would ruin everything.

After they reached the apartment, Grace attempted to distract herself by concentrating on boiling water, setting two cups out on the table, straining the coffee grains and finally pouring. Philippe simply stood, staring silently out of the dormer window. She walked over to him, intending to make a casual remark about the view, but when she arrived at his side she discovered she was lost for words.

Philippe touched her cheek. 'Brigitte told me you don't want to become involved with anyone, especially me,' he said softly. 'Do you think I might be able to change your mind?'

Then Grace realised she did have something to say to this unusual blue-eyed man, after all.

'Yes,' she said.

Philippe took her in his arms and kissed her, slowly exploring her ready mouth in a way that was at once so delightful and yet so unexpectedy arousing, she felt she might swoon.

'I really don't know how I've managed to show such restraint,' he said with one of his irresistible wry smiles. 'I've wanted to do that since the first moment I saw you in that ridiculous club.' Then he led her by the hand over to the bed.

The setting could not have been more romantic. The attic was dark, lit by a single lamp that, due to the pink damask curtain, cast rose-tinted shadows. She was alone with a handsome man. In Paris.

Yet a horribly familiar awkwardness had enveloped her. This was sure to end badly; she should never have allowed herself to get into such an alarming situation. Jack had accused her of being a 'block of ice', incapable of showing love and affection. He'd been right. Already she felt sickeningly tense, her nerves as taut as piano wires.

'Something is the matter?' Philippe frowned. 'You look as if you would rather I left.'

'I'm not sure what you think,' Grace blurted out, certain that she was about to make a fool of herself. 'But — God, I'll just say it — I've only ever made love with one man.'

'Ah. And it wasn't good, is that it?'

She blushed. 'A disaster, actually.'

'Well, let us see if we can improve upon that,' he said. 'But first, I think you might find you are more comfortable if you lie down.'

When she'd lowered herself uncertainly onto the bed, Philippe unlaced her plimsolls and let them drop to the floor.

'Did anyone ever tell you that you have exceptionally pretty toes?' he asked in such a serious voice that Grace couldn't help smile.

Next, he undid the zipper on her jeans. 'My apologies,' he said, 'but do you think you could help me to take these off, and perhaps your jersey as well?'

She did as he asked.

'Thank you — I think I can probably manage the rest.' Very gently, he pulled down the straps of Grace's lace bra and began to lightly kiss her shoulders and neck. 'Mmm, what a delectable fragrance,' he whispered. 'Your skin has the same scent as the flowers of Giverny.'

Grace felt her tension begin to ease and soften. Then Philippe's mouth was on hers once more, kissing her fervently, reawakening that same glorious sense of abandonment. When at last he broke away, he gave her a long, lingering look that was more like a caress, moving his gaze from the slenderness of her legs and the curve of her hips to the swelling smoothness of her chest, the delicate bones of her shoulders, the pulse point at her neck and her full, parted lips.

Their eyes met. 'You really are incredibly beautiful,' he said. 'In fact, it's a great pity you are wearing anything at all.'

He reached behind her back and unfastened her bra, pausing to slowly trail the tips of his fingers across her breasts before sliding down her silky briefs. Grace moaned as he brushed her nipples with his lips. He stroked her hips and her thighs, the smooth plane of her belly, the softness between her legs.

'Just a moment,' he whispered.

As Philippe quickly discarded his own clothing, her eyes moved across his lean torso and broad, muscled chest. He lay down very close to her and looked into her eyes. 'A woman like you deserves to be given pleasure,' he murmured.

After taking his time to expertly touch and tease each sensitive part of Grace's body, Philippe devoted himself to her most tender places until she was engulfed by almost unbearable, blissful sensations. She felt a spiral of heat, then a fierce yearning and, with it, a deep, inner awareness. This was desire, this was how it was when a woman wanted a man.

Only then did Philippe join with her. As they moved together, Grace felt herself transform. Her shape and contours altered, became amorphous, filled with light, until, with an urgency that was at last unbound, she soared towards a brilliant, limitless sky.

The following day, Grace arrived at the *maison* in a rapturous state. She'd barely slept, but even Victoire, who was not known to be generous, complimented her on her appearance.

'I have never seen your complexion look better. Are you using a new preparation?' she inquired.

'If you ask me,' Madame de Turckheim remarked, 'what you see are the effects of romance. I can always tell when one of my girls has been struck by Cupid's arrow.'

Although Grace's thoughts kept straying back to Philippe, somehow she managed to take part in the usual two parades, a photographic session for *Paris Match* and then a private showing for a nineteen-year-old beauty who had recently married the Viscount de Ribes. It was only when Grace had returned to the *cabine*, changed into her clothes and was arranging her forest-green silk foulard that Brigitte approached her.

'What is it?' Grace asked her friend. 'You seem concerned about something.'

'Not exactly concerned, no,' Brigitte replied. 'It's just that, oh, it's probably nothing.'

'Now you simply have to tell me,' Grace insisted.

'Remember how you were so adamant about not wanting to get entangled with a man,' Brigitte said, putting on her hat and gloves. 'I thought you might enjoy my cousin's company — he's clever and quick-witted, as you know. But now I'm just a little anxious that I have landed you in some sort of situation in which you might, well, not want to be.'

'Whatever do you mean?'

'I don't know exactly, I just have a feeling that Philippe's life is more complicated than he lets on.' Brigitte smiled

uncertainly. 'I'm probably being silly and over-protective —
forget I said anything. Goodnight, *chérie!*'

Grace was puzzled. Her well-meaning friend was
very sweet, but Grace was convinced Philippe Boyer was
just what he seemed. The small inconsistencies in what
he'd said on the night they met, the vague feeling he was
concealing something, had been a ridiculous product of
her own overwrought imagination. Philippe was simply a
divine Frenchman who had some quirky ideas about politics.
She'd never known anyone like him before — intelligent,
thoughtful, sometimes droll but always utterly intoxicating.
As for last night — it had been like a dream, an experience so
tender and yet so exciting that its mere recollection made her
blush, even as she ached with longing.

With her mind occupied by thoughts of her lover, Grace
left the *maison*, dreamily contemplating the moment when,
later that evening, she would be with him again.

'Hi!' Wearing a chic navy-blue coat trimmed with gold
buttons, Jackie Bouvier was standing in front of the *maison*,
swinging her calfskin handbag.

'Why, what are you — oh, of course!' Grace exclaimed.
'What an idiot I am — we were going to meet for a drink
after work. My head has been in the clouds all day.'

'It's not due to a guy, by any chance?' Jackie's eyes lit up.

'You're right. But it's early days yet — I'm afraid if I say
anything I might jinx the whole thing.'

'That's okay by me but, as it happens, romance is precisely
the subject I want to talk to you about. Let's cross over the
avenue and head for the Plaza Athénée's bar.'

'I just love this hotel,' Jackie said as she took a sip of her cocktail.
'All the red awnings at the front and the red geraniums, not to

mention the fact that' — she raised her glass — 'they mix an excellent martini.'

'Monsieur Dior feels just the same way.' Grace laughed. 'In fact, he often requests the new collections are photographed here. Lots of people wonder why he named the most famous ensemble from his New Look show — the one with the very full, pleated black skirt and the ivory silk shantung jacket — *Bar*.'

'Beats me.'

'Because he was so fond of this … bar!'

The two women giggled as a waiter passed by and left a dish of roasted peanuts on their table.

'Well?' Grace asked. 'What's on your mind?'

'Actually, I've fallen for someone,' Jackie said, with a faraway look in her eyes. 'In fact, I'm mad about him — I won't say his name, but he's the son of someone quite well known.'

'And the problem is?'

'It's that I've done practically everything else with him but I haven't let him, you know' — Jackie's breathy voice dropped — 'go all the way.'

'Do you want to?'

'I don't know! What makes it so confusing is that my mother's from the old "save yourself for marriage" brigade — she'd be horrified if she knew I was even thinking about sleeping with a man. I thought as you're a little older than me and, what with you being a model here in Paris … well, you'd know what I should do. Should I? Save myself for marriage, I mean.'

The irony of this particular question being addressed to her, of all people, was not lost on Grace. Still, she had the feeling she was only being told half of the truth. Jackie and her beau might already be lovers; perhaps what she really wanted was to ease her conscience by securing approval.

Grace loosened her scarf. 'Despite what you say, I'm not at all sure I'm the right person to advise you about making love — before or after marriage. Although I can tell you what I have discovered — and it goes for everything, really, not just affairs of the heart. If you don't take a gamble, you're less likely to make a mistake. A world without risk is small and safe. But is that the life you want to live?'

CHAPTER TWENTY-SEVEN

It was in a lazy mood of pleasurable distraction that Grace sat happily beside Philippe on a low wooden bench beside the Seine. Although still only late April, the day was warm; she was glad she'd tied her hair back in a yellow scarf and chosen to wear a light sleeveless dress and espadrilles.

The past three weeks had been the most heavenly Grace had ever experienced. Her former life seemed insubstantial; only since she'd met Philippe had she become fully alive. She felt suffused with joy as she contemplated his azure eyes and the shape of his wonderful mouth; the way he took her seriously when it mattered, yet could still tease her wickedly.

Most of all, she marvelled at the way he made love, how exquisitely he ignited her desire. Philippe had changed her. No, he had *freed* her. Intimacy no longer rendered Grace shy or inhibited or cold. Since Philippe had become her lover she'd grown confident, even bold; every day her senses grew more acute. Even now, the sun's rays on her bare arms felt like a caress.

Philippe took her hand. 'There is something I'd like to talk to you about,' he said.

'Is it the *bouquinistes*?' she asked distractedly. 'I was wondering earlier if we should visit that little man with the moustache who has the stand down near the Quai de la Tournelle — you know, the one who sells those funny French translations of the Sherlock Holmes novels. Or do you think we should try a bookseller at the other end?'

'It's about something important,' Philippe added, his face stern.

Despite the warm weather, Grace shivered. He'd never looked at her in this way before. Perhaps Philippe had decided their relationship was a mistake, that she was hopelessly bourgeois and could never fit into his world. Perhaps his feelings had changed or he'd simply grown bored — one awful possibility after another flew through her mind.

'First of all, I have fallen in love with you.'

'What a relief!' she burst out. 'The way you looked, I thought you were about to give me an awful piece of news.'

Yet something wasn't right. Philippe's expression remained grim. He certainly didn't seem like a man who'd just made an ardent declaration to his sweetheart. Somehow he must have discovered she was married or, worse, illegitimate. She waited nervously to hear what he had to say.

'There is a great deal you don't know about me,' he began.

'I could say the same thing myself,' she said, biting her lip.

'What you choose to tell me is up to you. But because I feel so strongly about you, because I'm quite hopelessly in love with you, I have to reveal who I really am — even if it comes at a cost.'

Grace knew then with a leaden certainty that the first of her secrets must be the very same one with which Philippe was burdened. He was married. All the time he'd been making passionate love to her, he had a wife, perhaps even children, tucked away somewhere.

It was all she could do not to groan. She remembered Brigitte's words of concern — clearly, her friend had been trying to warn her. Instead of listening, she'd rushed into this mad affair, and look just how stupid, how naive, she had turned out to be! Everyone knew about Frenchmen and their mistresses. Yet she could have sworn that Philippe was different.

'I am not a communist.'

'What? You mean, you're not married?' Her spirits soared.

'*Chérie*, I have no idea what you are talking about.'

'It's just that, when you were so serious, I thought ...' Her voice trailed away.

'Let me assure you, I am not that sort of man.' Philippe's eyes flashed. 'How could you think such a thing? Don't you know me at all?'

'Perhaps I don't. You have been talking about your marvellous membership of the party ever since I met you. Now you say you're not a communist. I don't know what to think.'

'That is my fault,' he said. 'I know we haven't been together long, but you must believe me — I love you and no one else. That is why I want to be completely honest.'

Grace felt assailed by guilt, by the knowledge that she'd kept so much from him. She knew she must also disclose the truth. 'Why don't you start at the beginning?' she asked instead.

He fixed his gaze on the light dancing across the surface of the river. 'When the war broke out I joined the party. I was only twenty years old and communism seemed to me the best way, the only way to fight the evils of fascism. As soon as I could, I entered the Resistance,' he continued. 'We had some success at sabotaging the Nazis, but during one attempt, things went badly wrong. As a result,' Philippe's voice quavered, 'my mother died.'

'I'm so sorry.' Grace felt a hollow dismay. 'When I told you my father had passed away I never imagined you had endured something even worse. To lose your mother in those circumstances must have been horrifying.'

'Let's just say I didn't cope very well.' Philippe sighed. 'What with my grief, the constant fighting, forever running, always hiding, a sort of madness came over me. That's when my dedication to communism turned into an obsession.'

'And where is your father?'

'Gone. Gaston, the man I call my father, has buried himself away on a farm deep in Burgundy. I hardly see him.'

Grace silently berated herself. She should have asked Philippe about his family much earlier. Instead, she'd been relieved he never mentioned them — it had saved her from having to mislead him about her own situation.

'Anyway,' he shrugged, 'after the war I came to my senses.'

'That's what I don't understand,' Grace said, confused. 'I thought you were still committed to the communist movement. You work for their paper — and you had all those plans for the future.'

'I did once. I thought Stalin was building a workers' paradise — until I discovered his responsibility for cold-blooded crimes, for terrible purges. Then came the Prague coup, and I realised he was every bit as bad as Hitler.' Philippe paused. 'Grace, there's so much I need to explain. Shall we walk for a while?'

As they meandered hand in hand along the peaceful riverbank, he said, 'I'm sure you are aware that Berlin is like an island, completely surrounded by Soviet-controlled territory?'

Grace nodded vaguely, wondering what possible reason Philippe might have for mentioning this curious situation.

'But I am not certain if you know that last year Stalin cut off all rail, road and canal access; his intention was that no food or fuel would be able to reach the city. The great hero of the people was only too delighted to see thousands of men, women and children freeze to death or die of starvation in order to further his aggressive ambitions.'

Philippe paused in front of a man in a striped Breton jersey playing an out-of-tune accordion, then placed a few coins in the upturned beret on the ground in front of him.

'That was the first time I saw how America, France and Great Britain could work together, not to punish their former German enemies, but to save them,' he said. 'Only their constant airlift of supplies stopped Stalin's conquest.'

It seemed to Grace that the tranquil summer day had assumed a surreal dimension. While carefree Parisian families strolled by, their children licking ice creams, the people of Berlin were recovering from a threat to their very existence.

'I love France. I am a patriot. It is a very hard thing to admit you have been wrong, but I was utterly deluded.' Philippe shook his head.

'Well then, why haven't you left the Communist Party?'

'Because I cannot.'

'I don't understand.'

Philippe lowered his voice. 'I work for the French security service,' he said.

Grace gulped. 'What are you talking about?'

'I am what is called a double agent.' He stood very still. 'That means I have passed myself off as someone else, not only to the communist cell I have infiltrated, but to you.'

'So, everything you told me — it was all an act?' It was hard to grasp what Philippe was saying.

'Not everything, of course not. Just what I said about my job and the way I carried on about my supposed political beliefs. Believe me, there is nothing false about anything else, especially the way I feel about you.'

Grace placed her hand on his arm. 'Why are you telling me this now?'

'I shouldn't be telling you at all. There is a whole page of undertakings I have made to the French state that I'm breaking.' Philippe pushed a lock of his hair away from his brow. 'But I couldn't stand deceiving you.'

Grace felt guiltier than ever. This was the moment to disclose her own secrets. Mustering every bit of her courage, she said, 'There is something —'

'*Chérie*, I'm sorry to interrupt you but I must finish,' Philippe insisted. 'There's one more reason I had for telling you the truth. You have the right to know that your relationship with me could place you in danger.'

She felt as if, one by one, Philippe was destroying every comfortable assumption she'd made about their life together.

'I can see I have shocked you. If you want to end what we have between us, I will be completely broken-hearted. But I will understand.'

'I don't want to leave you!' Grace said in a rush. 'I'm just … taken aback. You told me you were a journalist — I never imagined you inhabited a completely different world.' Her mind reeling, she wondered just how many other people there might be in her life who were not what they seemed.

'You wanted to tell me something before,' Philippe said. 'I'd like to hear what it was.'

She couldn't launch into her own revelations now, not with everything she was trying to grapple with. 'Another time,' she replied, shaking her head.

Philippe sat on the grass in the shade of a sycamore tree and pulled Grace down beside him. As he kissed her she felt her anxiety begin to dissolve. Surely the two of them would be able to carry on just as they had before? But when the kiss ended, Philippe looked at her with a sombre expression on his handsome face.

'You must promise me you will not tell anyone what I have said today,' he said gravely. 'I mean it — not a soul. If the members of the communist cell discovered that I was an agent of the French state … well, you could imagine what they would do to me.'

Then he kissed her again. '*Mon amour*,' he murmured, 'I have placed my life in your hands.'

CHAPTER TWENTY-EIGHT

The Jeu de Paume museum was filled with exquisite treasures. Grace wanted to linger, to spend hours in front of the glowing paintings by Manet, Renoir, Degas and — especially since her visit to Giverny — Monet. Due to foolishly signing up for a guided tour, however, it seemed this would not be possible. Grace couldn't help feeling annoyed. The bespectacled guide instructed, 'Keep up, keep together!' as she rushed her straggling group past one fabulous canvas after another.

Philippe had made a startling revelation. Now she needed time by herself to consider his hidden life and what it might mean for them. First, however, she had to decide whether to share her own secrets. Only, she had ruined any possibility of solitary reflection by impetuously joining this maddening tour.

'*Mesdames et messieurs, arrêtez maintenant, s'il vous plaît.*' The guide, waving vigorously, brought the group to an abrupt halt.

'Some history is called for,' she announced. 'The museum is located in the Jardin des Tuileries, the formal park that lies between the Louvre and the Place de la Concorde. Le Jardin was created by Catherine de' Medici in the sixteenth century, although it did not become a public park until after the French Revolution.'

Grace's mind kept drifting back to Philippe. How much should she tell him, and when? Answers continued to prove elusive. The dogged recitation made it impossible to think.

'The museum measures eighty metres long by thirteen metres wide and approximately ten metres high. You have no doubt noticed it is an unusually elongated rectangular building. This is because it was not originally an art gallery, but a place where Napoleon III could play indoor tennis, sometimes called real, or in England, royal tennis. *Jeu de paume* is the French name for the game.'

Muttered remarks were made by several of the more restless members of the group. After glaring at the culprits, the guide commanded, 'Quiet, please! During the Occupation the museum was used by the Nazis to store, sort and ship stolen art. More than twenty-two thousand items passed through this building, among them some of the world's greatest artistic treasures. Today it houses France's most spectacular collection of French Impressionist and Post-Impressionist masterpieces. Among them are renowned works such as ...'

But Grace had stopped listening. *I don't want to hear any more about the building and its history or even its art*, she thought, *or at least, not yet. Not until I have been able to spend some time alone with the paintings — and my thoughts.*

When the guide indicated that the group should move to the next point of interest, Grace dawdled behind, then turned quickly into the first promising room.

As soon as she saw it, she stood still. Although surrounded by an array of superb works, Grace was drawn to just one image. She walked closer, admiring the delicacy of the brushstrokes and the soft harmony of its pastel palette. The painting depicted a dark-haired young woman, her chin resting on her hand, gazing intently at an infant who rested in a filmy, gauze-draped crib. *Berthe Morisot, Le Berceau, 1872*, read the small plaque beside the painting. 'The Cradle,' Grace whispered.

The name of the artist meant nothing to her, though she noted with interest that, unusually, it belonged to a woman. Grace wasn't certain she had ever seen a painting by a female artist hung in a museum.

At first glance, the picture appeared to be a straightforward depiction of maternal devotion, but as Grace examined it more closely, she became aware of more subtle nuances. There was a marked ambiguity in the woman's expression; this was no Madonna, but a multi-faceted human being. What was she feeling? There was love, yes, but there was also loneliness, anxiety — even a measure of irritation. Perhaps, Grace reflected, like life itself, there was room for more than one interpretation.

The translucent white netting Morisot had painted served to protect the sleeping infant from the viewer's gaze but, at the same time, it separated the mother from the child. Was this a metaphor, she wondered, perhaps the artist's way of conveying that the truth of their relationship was veiled?

While Grace was contemplating this question a vivid image flew into her mind. It was of another mother, this one fair-haired with delphinium-blue eyes. How well Grace remembered that same gaze, the devotion, but also the anxiety it contained. A sob escaped from her lips; she turned her head away.

'Are you well, mademoiselle?' a greying attendant inquired gently. 'You seem a little unsteady on your feet. Quite a few of our visitors find themselves overcome — these masterpieces can have a powerful effect. Perhaps you would like to sit down?'

Feeling shaky and weak, Grace sank gratefully onto one of the strategically placed padded-leather benches. She realised with a profound conviction that whatever Olive had done, whatever sins she had committed, she had always loved her daughter. Grace recalled the fun they'd had looking at fashion magazines and trying on clothes. Most of all, she recollected her mother's unwavering concern.

Then those final, dreadful moments in the dining room at Brookfield came back to her; the accusations she'd flung at her mother, the pain on her face. Grace hadn't understood how things could be between a man and a woman, what it was like to be overcome by passion.

On the other hand, Olive had betrayed Alfred. She'd lied to Grace all her life and kept her separated from Reuben.

Grace's mind went back and forth, veering between compassion and condemnation. Might it be that the truth lay somewhere in between? She realised how much the experience of living in Paris had changed her. Her relationship with Philippe had also played a part. She only had to look about her, to 'open her eyes', as Philippe had insisted, to realise how complex life could be.

She recalled her conversation with Brigitte, the outrage she'd felt when she discovered that many French women had formed liaisons with enemy soldiers. She was wiser now, more familiar with what Brigitte had termed life's 'grey areas'. Perhaps it was the only way such women could survive. Who knew, maybe some fell in love. Who was she to judge?

In the absence of even a single letter from her mother, Grace wanted desperately to write to her. She also knew she could not. *First, I must find Reuben*, she told herself. *Olive and I can never mend what has been broken until I know what took place between them.*

'Ah, good, you are feeling better now, mademoiselle,' the attendant remarked as Grace rose to her feet. When she thanked the man and assured him she was now quite recovered, he responded, 'You must return. You know, I have looked at these pictures for many years, and yet each time I see them they disclose more of their secrets to me.'

As Grace left *The Cradle* behind and began to walk slowly through the other galleries, she considered the guard's observation. A painting might take years to give up its secrets, but life was not a static piece of art. It was dynamic, constantly changing. Life demanded action.

She would not tell Philippe about her marriage.

She'd seen his offended expression when she'd asked if he was married. Grace cringed when she tried to imagine what Philippe would say, how he would feel, if he discovered she was guilty of the same sin of which she had wrongly accused him.

Finding she had arrived at the exit, she made her way through the turnstile and strolled into the Jardin des Tuileries. The fine day had brought out throngs of people, some admiring the gay rose gardens, others reading newspapers while they sat on small wrought-iron chairs, still more enjoying the simple pleasure of sauntering along the white gravel pathways in the sunshine. Grace resolved to continue to the rue Dauphine on foot — the walk would help her to collect her thoughts.

She decided she would tell Philippe only about her mother's relationship with Reuben, and the letter, although she was well aware that even divulging this much would be a risk. It was entirely possible that Philippe's view of her would change once he knew she was illegitimate. The French might appear free and easy, but she was not one of them. She was just a foreign mannequin, another Mademoiselle Nobody from Nowhere, without the protection of that realm of French society that might view the product of an illicit union with an accommodating sophistication.

Grace only knew that just as Philippe had trusted her, she had to trust him in return. Despite Ferdinand's help, she'd failed to find Reuben Wood. Now she must seek help again, but this time she would reveal that the man she was seeking was her father.

CHAPTER TWENTY-NINE

May 1949

'Grace, I think you should sit down.'

Leaning forward in the threadbare armchair she asked excitedly. 'What is it? Have you found him?'

It hadn't been easy to admit to Philippe that her birth was the result of an affair, that she was what his countrymen — should they discover her shame — would disparagingly call *une bâtarde*. Yet, after agonising for so long over his possible reaction, when at last she'd confessed he had merely shrugged. Although this muted response had left her uncertain about the way he felt, at least he hadn't displayed any obvious distaste. Even more heartening, when she'd asked him if he could try to find Reuben, he'd promised to do what he could. Ever since then, Grace had been impatient for news.

He knelt in front of her and took her hands in his own. 'I know this must be very difficult to hear,' he said gently, 'but, in my opinion, Reuben Wood is dead.'

'No, Philippe, that's not true!' This couldn't be right; she was certain Reuben was alive. 'What you mean is you couldn't find him.'

'That is another way of putting it, perhaps a kinder way, but it won't bring him back.'

Grace didn't answer. She couldn't, she wouldn't believe him.

Philippe rose to his feet and leant against one of the attic's patterned walls. 'Do you honestly think I haven't explored every possible avenue available to me?'

'But have you? Really?'

He held up one hand. 'Grace, if I could, I would move heaven and earth for you. I can only assure you I've done the next best thing. There is not a lead I haven't followed. Now, very sadly, I can do no more.'

'You must!'

Philippe shook his head. 'Let us start at the beginning. You gave me the photograph of your father, but it was useless — it could have been a picture of any big man standing in a shadow. Yes, I had Reuben's rank, the name of his unit and Lieutenant Carruthers' letter, but the only clue to his whereabouts was that he "headed south". Believe me, there is no sign of him in the south or anywhere else in France. Reuben Wood has disappeared from the face of the earth.'

'So you're just going to give up?'

Crossing the room, Philippe pulled the wooden chair away from the table so that it was facing her. 'I don't know what I can do or say that will satisfy you,' he said, sitting down. 'These are the steps I have taken. First, I revisited official channels. As you had already discovered, there was nothing more to be learnt. So I cast my net wider. I reached out to my old Resistance network — and drew another blank. Finally, I approached the demimonde: professional informers, black marketeers, even the blatantly criminal. If there had been a trace of the man,' Philippe said with an edge of frustration, 'I would have found it.'

'I haven't made myself clear.' Grace couldn't let go of her dream. It would mean losing Siddy forever, together with any chance of solving her own mysteries. 'It's not that I don't believe you've tried to find Reuben,' she said with rising desperation. 'I was hoping you would keep on searching.' She went to the sink, poured a glass of water and gulped it down. 'He must be out there somewhere.'

'After all this time?' Philippe asked. 'Grace, I hate to be brutal, but eventually you must face the facts. It would be unkind to let you keep living under this illusion.'

'What are you talking about?'

'Just this: it is eight years since you received any proof that your father was alive. And you have not received a word from him during all that time.' Philippe shook his head. 'There is only one other possibility, which I for one do not believe. Anyway, it seems cruel even to bring it up.'

'What do you mean, cruel?' Grace couldn't imagine feeling worse than she did already.

'Well, if Reuben is alive, and you haven't heard from him for nearly a decade, I'm sorry, but don't you think he sounds very much like a man who doesn't wish to be found?'

Grace's hand went to her mouth. Ferdinand had been right all along. The tumult of war had provided Siddy with the perfect opportunity to disappear. He'd never had any intention of returning to Australia, or to her. She had been clinging on to nothing but a fantasy. She slumped back into the armchair.

'Darling, if only there was something I could do,' Philippe said.

Grace's shoulders sagged. 'I can see now that for ever so long, I've been deceiving myself. It is perfectly clear that if Reuben isn't dead — and, after all, his body was never found — then he came to the conclusion he was better off without me.'

She felt as if an essential part of herself had been extinguished. 'All this time I've believed in a fairy tale,' she said slowly. 'Only, there are no fairy tales, are there? It's silly, really. When I was a little girl I thought Reuben was like a storybook giant with the power to make everything turn out right.'

'You were young.'

'Well, I'm not anymore. But the thing is, I've been acting as if I was still a child. It's high time I grew up.'

They both fell silent. Finally Grace said, 'Thank you for all you have done, Philippe. But are you sure you really don't care about my being illegitimate?'

'Grace, stand up.'

'Why?'

'Because I am hoping I can reassure you in the only way I know how.' Philippe wrapped his arms tightly around her, kissed her lips and stroked her hair. 'Is that better?'

Grace nodded.

'Even if I thought your parents not being married to each other was important — which I can assure you I do not — it is through no fault of your own.' He kissed her again.

Grace sighed as she looked into Philippe's eyes.

'Do you want me to stay?' he asked. 'Tell me now, because otherwise I don't think I'll be able to tear myself away.'

'Would you mind awfully if you didn't?' Grace said sadly. 'I just need a little time to myself to come to terms with everything.'

Philippe paused at the door. 'I came here this evening to tell you that, regrettably, my search for your father had been unsuccessful. But I also wanted to ask you something of great significance. That was stupid of me — the timing was all wrong.' He looked back at Grace. 'Let's meet tomorrow outside the Jardin du Luxembourg. We can talk about it then,' he said. 'Is six o'clock all right?

'Yes.'

'Well then, sweet dreams, *chérie*.'

'You are remarkably subdued today,' Ferdinand Derel said as he and Grace met over their customary morning coffee at Café Bertrand. 'I trust our friend Baron de Gide is not making a nuisance of himself?'

'He hasn't given up, if that's what you mean,' Grace smiled wanly, 'even though I've told him repeatedly that I am otherwise engaged. In a way, it's rather sweet, although I suspect dear Édouard has far too high an opinion of himself to actually believe it is possible for a woman to prefer someone else.'

'And what about this "someone else"? Does all go well with that young man you have been seeing?'

Ignoring the *pain au chocolat* Ferdinand had placed by her cup of café crème, Grace confided, 'He's a … well, he's a complicated man.'

'Is he indeed? Well, perhaps I can distract you. Do you remember modelling some clothes for Rita Hayworth, the ones she took on her honeymoon with Prince Aly Khan?' he asked brightly.

'I do.'

'The wedding reception took place at the Prince's Riviera mansion, the Château de l'Horizon, only last weekend. Between you and me, I was told by an impeccable source that forty lobsters and six hundred bottles of champagne were consumed.'

Grace nodded vaguely.

'My dear,' he continued, 'it appears you are not impressed. But perhaps you will be when I tell you that ten gallons of eau de cologne were emptied into the château's swimming pool! Even for those two, this was a little extreme.' Ferdinand chuckled. 'In fact, my trusted informant overheard the prince's father, the Aga Khan — no stranger to the high life himself — muttering to his new daughter-in-law, "Too much caviar, Rita, too much caviar". Apparently, even he felt that fifty pounds of the finest Beluga was a trifle excessive.'

Grace was only half listening to Ferdinand's account, for it had done nothing but remind her of her own married state. Although she feared Jack would be furious and likely to refuse, she couldn't put off asking him for a divorce much longer. Each day she delayed only provided more opportunity for the man she adored to discover the truth.

Grace felt like a small nocturnal bush animal, frozen to the spot in the glare of the headlights of a car that was speeding inexorably towards her. It wasn't just that she'd failed to approach Jack — she still hadn't told Philippe she was married. She simply couldn't decide whether she should carry out these actions — or not. Either way, the consequences could prove devastating.

She wondered miserably if her relationship with Philippe — so tender, so precious — was destined to end in discord and pain, just like her marriage.

Ferdinand interrupted Grace's unhappy deliberations. 'I see that my little attempt at diversion has not met with success. It is quite clear that you are preoccupied and, if I am not very much mistaken, the subject is love. Ah, I wish there was something I could say to make you feel better,' he remarked with a sympathetic smile. '*L'amour* is rarely easy, yet without it, what point is there to life?'

CHAPTER THIRTY

As soon as Grace returned to the *cabine* after the day's final show, she quickly changed into a green cotton frock with a Chinese collar, reached for her straw hat and, with barely a farewell to the other mannequins, hurried away from the *maison*. Philippe had said he planned to ask her something of great significance. Whatever it was, Grace wanted to hear it as quickly as possible.

She'd had a largely sleepless night. Grieving for the loss of Reuben — not just the man, but the man she thought she'd known — she had curled up in her lonely bed and wept. It seemed that having abandoned Grace once, he had welcomed the opportunity to do so again. Only this time, his intention was that the separation would be lasting. It was the bitterest of blows.

Grace was worried about Philippe, too. She'd virtually accused him of making only a paltry attempt to find her father, when he'd gone out of his way to help her. There was absolutely no reason why he should expend any more effort.

On edge and fatigued, she stood waiting for him to arrive in front of the Jardin du Luxembourg's elaborate wrought-iron gates. The long summer night meant a steady flow of Parisians from all walks of life passed her on their way to the famous fountains and gardens inside. She did her best to ignore the men among them who made muttered comments or cast overly appreciative glances in her direction.

Grace was thankful when at last Philippe appeared. He greeted her affectionately enough, but seemed unusually ill at ease.

'Let's go in and find a place to sit,' he said. 'Somewhere private.'

Philippe took her arm and for a few minutes they walked beneath the manicured rows of lime trees.

'I think over there would be good,' he said, pointing to a bench that stood in a secluded corner next to a white marble statue of a former Bourbon queen. As soon as they were seated he announced, 'I know I have no right, but I want to ask you …'

Grace felt as if she had been struck by a thunderbolt. It sounded very much as if Philippe was intent on proposing. If circumstances had been different, she would have been overjoyed, but as it was, she was so unnerved that she clenched her hands with such force the nails bit into her palms. He must not ask her that. If he did, she would be forced to reveal she was married. Then Philippe would know that all the time they'd been together she'd been lying to him. True, he had never asked about her marital status, but it was only natural that he'd made assumptions. If omission was indeed a sin, then she was unquestionably guilty.

'… to spy for France.'

'To … What did you just say?' Grace asked, dumbfounded.

'I want to know if you will agree to spy for France.'

She felt simultaneously overwhelmed by enormous relief and crushing disappointment, although both emotions were rapidly replaced by shock. 'For goodness sake, Philippe, I'm not exactly Mata Hari!' she said. 'It has struck you, I suppose, that I'm a fashion mannequin?'

'I know, I know,' Philippe held out his hands, 'and I've dreaded asking this of you. I feel even worse now that I have utterly failed to find Reuben, the one thing you begged me to do.' He put an arm around her shoulders and gently drew her to him. 'Darling, what I just asked you … I have to be honest. If you agree, it could mean putting your life at risk.'

'My … life?' Grace choked on the word.

'Yes. Believe me, I wish there was another way. Regrettably, there is not. Many lives — perhaps even the future of Europe — depend on your successful acquisition of a single piece of information.'

'But why me?' Grace pulled away. 'Why would you ask me to do something for which I'm so obviously ill-equipped?'

'Before I explain that, I'd better tell you the whole story.'

They were interrupted by the shouts of two small, fair-haired boys who'd begun energetically chasing each other around the marble statue.

Philippe frowned. 'Let's find somewhere we can talk in peace.' As he led Grace towards the park's famous baroque gardens, he asked, 'Remember that day, by the Seine, when I revealed I was a double agent?'

'It would be hard to forget, *chéri*,' Grace said drily. 'Not every girl is told something like that by her sweetheart while she's enjoying a romantic Sunday stroll.'

'I suppose not.' Philippe gave her a bashful smile. 'Anyway, since then things have moved on rapidly. I promised the communist cell I infiltrated that I'd swing the newspaper's support behind them, and as a result, its members have disclosed their plans.'

'So now you know what they're up to?'

'Exactly. Following his failure to bring Berlin to heel, Stalin has made up his mind that a major, very public act of terror is required here in France. Only in this way can he create the chaotic conditions he needs in order to assert Soviet power over Europe.' Philippe stopped in front of a tumbling fountain. 'The local cell is to carry out a political assassination that will make the greatest possible impact.'

Grace stared at him. 'You mean, General de Gaulle?'

'Fortunately, the general is safe — at least for now. The Soviets have chosen a target who will better serve their current objectives.' Philippe lowered his voice. 'They intend to murder the United States Ambassador David Bruce at the Bastille Day parade.'

'No!' Grace's thoughts flew to his wife, Evangeline. The poor woman would be terrified if she knew.

'Ambassador Bruce is not only very close to President Truman, he is also one of the key architects of the despised Marshall Plan. But more important to Comrade Stalin is his desire to spark severe American reprisals against France.' Although Philippe spoke in an even, almost expressionless manner, his set jaw betrayed his inner tension.

'The communists will use these measures as an excuse to incite the French people to rise up against the current pro-American regime,' he continued. 'They are already training cell members in the art of terror and mass agitation.'

Grace was stunned. 'But what exactly is their aim?' she asked.

'To install a communist government in France — one that will do Moscow's bidding.'

Lost for words, Grace clutched Philippe's arm.

'If they succeed, Stalin will grasp Europe in a pincer. He already controls the east; it is trapped behind what Mr

Churchill so aptly calls the Iron Curtain. If France falls into Stalin's hands, he will have a vital stronghold in the west.'

'What happens then?'

'The very worst outcome imaginable.' Philippe frowned. 'The only way to contain the Soviet Union's ambitions would be for the United States to unleash its formidable military. The Soviets would be certain to retaliate so ... Let me put this as simply as possible. If the plot to kill Ambassador Bruce is not stopped, it could very well lead to another world war.' Philippe placed his hands into his coat pockets and fell silent.

As they walked on, Grace became conscious of the clang made by *pétanque* balls, the happy cries of children running past with toy sailing boats tucked under their arms, the crunch of gravel beneath the feet of promenading Parisians. These were the sounds made by ordinary people enjoying a way of life that had only recently been restored, yet once more was in peril.

She followed Philippe past cascading jets of sparkling water and the palatial Senate building, until they reached a small stand of trees. Hidden behind was a stone bench from where it was impossible to be seen.

'The French Interior Minister, Giscard Orly, is the key,' Philippe said, sitting down.

Grace raised her eyebrows. 'Really? I'm surprised. Isn't he rather a *bon vivant*? I've seen his photograph in the odd magazine. He's quite attractive in a reptilian sort of way.'

'Our Minister Orly does not only enjoy the high life, he is also secretly in the pay of the Soviet state. As minister for the interior, he is well aware of David Bruce's security arrangements. Orly has been passing on all the information he has about the ambassador's schedule to Moscow.'

Philippe's expression was bleak. 'We know the attempt on Bruce's life is to take place on Bastille Day, but only the minister and a Soviet Embassy attaché — in reality, a KGB agent — have the precise details of where and when the hit will be made. Orly keeps the details of the plot in a small safe in his office. If disaster is to be avoided, it is vital the French secret service acquires this information — which is where you come in.'

'Darling, have you taken leave of your senses?'

'Perhaps I have.' He looked uncertain as to how to continue. 'How can I put this? During the war it was common practice for civilians from Allied nations to carry out specialist secret missions on behalf of France. Even today, if the appropriate skills cannot be found among our own ranks, it still happens.'

'Go on.'

'Orly has one weakness, and that is for extremely beautiful women of a particular type: tall, glamorous brunettes. In this regard you are, objectively speaking, abundantly well qualified. What is more, you have already come to his attention.'

'How? Where?'

'We have been following Orly for some time,' Philippe said. 'One evening at the Tour d'Argent, an agent overheard him remark to his male companion that he would do anything to meet, and I quote, "the ravishing woman at the next table". Our man made inquiries. It turned out the woman was you.'

It was difficult for Grace to comprehend that while she had been blithely dining on foie gras and sipping champagne with the baron, an undercover operation had been taking place in the same exclusive room.

'I swear I knew none of this when we began seeing each

other; the information has only recently been passed on to me,' Philippe said earnestly.

'But what is it you actually want me to *do*?'

'God knows, I'm sorry to put you in this position.' He placed his head in his hands. 'We need you to befriend Orly. The reason he has a duplicate of the assassin's instructions is so that, in the remote chance anything does go wrong at the Soviet end, he can take over. If this occurrs, they will send him a coded message. If no message is received, there should be no need for him to open the safe. You, however, must. It's the only way we can discover where, when and by whom the assassination will be carried out.'

'You can't be serious!' Grace's eyes widened. 'How would I even know where to start?'

'The combination is changed frequently,' Philippe continued, 'and Orly always carries the code somewhere on him.'

'But I suppose if you arrest him now, the Soviets will be tipped off,' Grace said.

'Exactly — the timing is vital. If the security service moves against the minister any sooner than the eve of Bastille Day, or gives any indication that we are aware of what is going on, the plan will simply be altered and the new details left with someone unknown to us — the KGB is never without a fallback.' Philippe's voice took on a new urgency. 'If that happens, we will have no idea which of their operatives has the duplicate information. Any chance of recovering it will be lost.'

Grace slowly nodded. 'So it's all down to me. That's quite a responsibility.'

'It is also a very great risk. It would be best to consider your answer overnight.'

She watched as two pigeons landed near her feet. Finding no food, they soon fluttered their wings and flew off in search of more promising territory. How fortunate these birds were, she reflected. For them, borders, power and politics meant nothing.

'I'll do it,' she said.

'Grace, you're being impetuous! This is a big decision. Are you sure?'

'Quite sure.' She felt very calm. Throughout the long years of war she had yearned to do something that mattered, to be like the men risking their lives on the frontline. Here, at last, was her call to action.

'There is just one problem, though,' she said, frowning. 'I don't know Giscard Orly. How will I meet him?'

'Actually, that is the easiest aspect of the entire operation.' Philippe's face broke into a sly grin. 'I happen to know where he will be in ten days time.'

'And where is that?'

'Minister Orly will be attending Count Étienne de Beaumont's first post-war *folie* — the grand masked Ball of the Kings and Queens. And so will we.'

CHAPTER THIRTY-ONE

'*Ma chère*, I am delighted to hear you are off to the good count's *grande fête*,' Ferdinand said while visiting the *cabine* during that brief desertion of the *maison*'s front door that sufficed for his lunch break. 'I can assure you,' he added, carefully unwrapping some thinly sliced ham, an oozing piece of camembert and a hunk of bread, 'it will be an unforgettable experience.'

Madame de Turckheim wrinkled her nose. '*Mon Dieu*, that cheese certainly has a presence,' she remarked before turning away from Ferdinand's pungent repast. 'Grace, you should be aware that the Count de Beaumont is a close friend of Monsieur Dior — he even designs some of our jewellery — so naturally *le patron* will be attending. Indeed, I believe he has already paid a visit to Cardin's atelier. Pierre used to work with us, you know, before he became a theatrical *costumier*.'

'The count has been entertaining the *beau monde* in his mansion at 11 rue Masseran for decades,' Ferdinand explained. 'And, not only does he host the crème de la crème of international society, almost alone among his fellow aristocrats, he also invites avant garde artists, writers, painters and performers.'

Ferdinand sipped from a glass of Perrier while he continued Grace's instruction. 'Between the wars, de

Beaumont became renowned for his masked balls. Let me
see if I can remember … ah, yes. There was the spectacular
Louis XIV Ball, the Fairy-tale Ball and the Ball of Famous
Paintings, although my personal favourite was the Ball
of the Sea — who could forget the delicious Maharani
of Kapurthala's remarkable entrance disguised as caviar
while being borne aloft on a tray by four men dressed as
waiters from the famous fish restaurant Prunier? Or, for that
matter, the host's own appearance in the guise of a horned
manta ray? *Monsieur le Compte* has been described as many
things — eccentric, even bizarre — but one cannot fault
his dedication.'

Saturday 21 May

At the appointed hour, Grace and Philippe waited in Count
de Beaumont's white and gold entrance hall, as a servant —
wearing a pale blue satin tailcoat and breeches, a ruffled
shirt, buckled shoes and a grey powdered wig — formally
announced his employer's masked guests, using only the
names of the characters whose likenesses they had assumed
for the night.

'*Mesdames et messieurs*, the Empress Josephine,' he boomed,
as a woman in a filmy, high-waisted pink gown, long white
gloves and a magnificent antique diamond tiara floated down
the marble staircase.

'If I'm not mistaken,' Grace whispered to Philippe, 'that
is the Countess de Ganay. *Le patron* engaged her only recently
to oversee his boutique. It seems that these days it has become
fashionable for French aristocrats to earn a living.'

The 'King of the Roses' was announced next.

'*Zut!* It's Count Sforza,' Philippe said, stifling a laugh. 'Imagine — the man is Rome's foreign minister and yet he has the appearance of a flower bed. But then, he is Italian ...'

'Shhh,' Grace chided. 'We're next.'

'King Solomon and the Queen of Sheba.'

When Grace arrived at the top of the stairs the waiting throng below fell momentarily silent, then burst into applause. She conducted her descent with the majestic bearing befitting a biblical queen, although she was attired in a manner that, as she overheard a man dressed as Pope Julius II remark, 'would have successfully tempted Saint Augustine'.

She had elected to wear nothing but a long gold brocade skirt that sat very low on her slim hips, a skimpy jewelled brassiere that barely covered her breasts, heavy gold necklaces, gold earrings and a pair of matching gold cuffs. Encircling her hair, which flowed in dark waves around her shoulders, was the *pièce de résistance*: a glittering, emerald-studded diadem that served to keep a brace of long white ostrich plumes in place. In contrast to her revealing ensemble, a golden mask concealed her face.

Arm in arm with Grace, Philippe wore black silk robes and a large turquoise turban. Dusky make-up, a full beard and a black mask completed his disguise.

'You look gorgeous, darling,' he murmured.

Grace replied with a smile, 'You don't look entirely unattractive yourself, considering you're three thousand years old.'

As soon as the pair entered the glittering salon, they were offered a glass of Cristal champagne by a bare-chested waiter sporting the elaborate headdress of an Aztec princeling. As Grace sipped her drink, she took in the opulent scene: over by the bar, an exotic King of the Gypsies with a bandolier slung across his chest was deep in conversation with Alexander the Great and a redheaded Virgin Queen; in a corner, three Napoleons were laughing at their own lack of originality; and at one of the windows, Hamlet, Prince of Denmark, was attempting to disentangle his cloak from the wings of a spangled Fairy Queen.

Philippe observed wryly, 'It is all very well to celebrate the end of austerity, but just look at these people — they seem entirely oblivious to the world around them. Here they are, dancing on the edge of a precipice. It is not difficult to understand why the communists despise the *ancien régime*.'

'Speaking of which,' Grace remarked, 'that exquisite Marie Antoinette in the pink crinoline is coming our way, and I think that the woman behind the silver mask is Jacqueline Bouvier, my American friend.'

'It is you, isn't it?' Jackie asked when she reached Grace's side. 'Thank heavens I've found you! I've been fending off the advances of that Emperor of Letters, Monsieur Voltaire, only it turns out that he is a she and her name is Vita Sackville-West!'

'In that case, it sounds like it's a good time for a stroll under the stars,' Philippe said, before escorting them through a pair of doors to the garden.

'How enchanting!' Jackie exclaimed.

Out of the darkness emerged trees festooned with sparkling lights, clusters of flickering candles on small alabaster-topped tables, and flaming tapers held aloft by towering candelabras. Among the lush foliage were beds of fragrant, all-white flowers — full-blown roses, gardenias, and a profusion of star-shaped oriental lilies.

'I think this must be what heaven looks like,' Grace said with a sigh.

'Parties like these are genuine works of art,' observed a rotund gentleman whose costume featured a golden mane. Upon closer inspection, Grace realised that it was none other than Christian Dior himself.

'Monsieur,' she said, dropping into a graceful curtsy, 'I believe I have the pleasure of addressing the King of the Jungle.'

Dior laughed. They spoke for a few minutes, until Philippe murmured to Grace, 'Let us leave Jackie in the capable hands of her favourite couturier. It is high time we commenced our little charade.'

As Grace and Philippe entered the ballroom, the orchestra began playing romantic Strauss music. 'And so it begins,' Philippe said, taking her in his arms.

All eyes soon turned towards the alluring spectacle of the scantily clad Queen of Sheba, her white ostrich plumes gently waving as she began to waltz around the ballroom with her tall, turquoise-turbaned king.

Many guests gossiped about the nature of the *petit scandale* that occurred next. One of the Napoleons said he felt sure the man masquerading as King Solomon had made a comment of an unforgivably salacious nature. An elderly Helen of Troy was quick to agree, reporting she had seen the fellow whispering in the Queen of Sheba's ear.

'And then,' she recounted, 'the woman stopped dancing, drew herself up with great dignity and slapped him on his cheek. I would have done just the same!'

Some were amused, others appalled, but worse was to come. Turning to leave, King Solomon inelegantly shouldered Sheba out of the way. The glorious creature staggered, indeed, might have fallen, if not for the deft intervention of a striking man in front of whom, as if by chance, the entire incident had taken place.

'My dear, are you all right?' the gentleman inquired. His black hair was swept back from his forehead and he wore an immaculate white uniform adorned with gold braid, a blue sash and a variety of imperial orders. 'What a terrible thing! Let me escort you outside.'

Ordering one of the liveried servants to bring some champagne, he led Grace towards two gilt chairs conveniently shielded from inquisitive eyes by a cloud of profuse white azaleas.

'I wish I knew who your dancing partner was,' Grace's self-appointed protector said. 'I would have been delighted to call the scoundrel out.'

'That's terribly sweet of you,' she purred. 'However, although you do bear a striking resemblance to the last Tsar of Russia, I'm afraid we haven't been introduced. I can hardly expect a man whose name I don't know to be dashing off defending my honour, can I?'

'Giscard Orly, Minister of the French Republic, at your service. And, do you know, despite the mask you are wearing on your lovely face, I believe I have seen you before — if I'm not mistaken, at the Tour d'Argent. You are …?'

'Why, the Queen of Sheba, of course.' Grace smiled.

'So you prefer to maintain your mystery?'

'I do. Why don't you tell me all about yourself instead?'

Grace spent the rest of the evening in Orly's company. She laughed at his stories. She admired his achievements. She allowed Orly to partner her in a foxtrot, a quickstep, several uneventful waltzes, and even a rumba. But she refused to tell him her name.

'It is of no concern,' Orly said. 'The only problem is that I have the greatest desire to see you again. How shall I find you?'

Grace gave him her most seductive smile. 'For a man as intelligent and powerful as you, that should not present too great a challenge. Think of it as a little test,' she said playfully. 'First you must discover who I am, then if I consider it worth my while, I might consider offering you my … friendship.'

'So, I gather you would not do me the honour of allowing me to escort you home?' Orly asked, his black eyes glittering.

'Certainly not.' Grace laughed. 'As a matter of fact, I have a car and a driver waiting. *Au revoir, Ministre Orly. Au revoir.*'

CHAPTER THIRTY-TWO

Monday 23 May 1949

'Who are all those extraordinary white roses for? There must be dozens of them!' exclaimed Brigitte.

'I'm more interested in who they're from,' said Victoire.

'Whoever he is, he's obviously been overcome by a *coup de foudre*,' Claire chipped in.

'He's lovestruck, all right.' Corinne grinned.

The mannequins clustered around Ferdinand as he staggered into the *cabine* on Monday morning, weighed down by an enormous box of dewy blooms.

'The card is addressed to Mademoiselle Dubois,' he announced. 'As to who they're from ... she will have to tell you.'

Grace jumped up from her dressing table, relieved Ferdinand of the huge box and dumped it on a chair. Having glanced at the accompanying card, she crumpled it in her hand before saying nonchalantly, 'Oh, it's just from some man I met at last Saturday night's masked ball — I barely remember him.'

'Well, you clearly made an impression,' Marie-Hélène said, arching her brows.

Grace gathered up some of the flowers. 'Would you like these?'

'Darling, of course. They're beautiful.'

'Anyone else?' she asked. 'Do help yourselves. I couldn't possibly lug them up to my attic.'

On Tuesday morning, an almost identical scene took place. Ferdinand's face was nearly obscured by the vast bouquet of white tulips he clutched to his chest. Once more, the mannequins were fascinated. Once more, the flowers had been sent to Grace from the same man although, this time, he included a flattering note that contained an entreaty to join him for an evening *tête-à-tête*.

Again, she distributed the lavish flowers among the other girls, brushing off their questions about her mysterious suitor with a light-hearted remark. 'Ah, men,' she said. 'If only some of them knew how absurd they appeared, they'd never do such ridiculous things.'

By Wednesday, when Ferdinand appeared for the third morning in a row, this time burdened by numerous oversized sprays of white orchids, the novelty had begun to wear off.

'Not again!' Brigitte cried. '*Chérie*, if this admirer of yours doesn't stop soon, Paris will be denuded of flowers.' Everyone but Ferdinand began laughing.

'*Ma petite*, I know this is none of my business,' he said to Grace quietly.

She smiled. 'Goodness, that's never stopped you before.'

'Well, it's different this time,' he said, frowning. 'You see, I know perfectly well who is sending you all these flowers. Giscard Orly might be an important government minister, but are you aware of his reputation? The baron — *bof*, he's simply a spoilt boy … Orly, despite the charming veneer he adopts, is a hard, cold man who will stop at nothing to get what he wants.'

'It's sweet of you to be concerned, Ferdinand, but honestly, there's no need to worry.' Grace patted his arm. 'I know what I'm doing.'

On the same day the minister's orchids were delivered to the *cabine*, Grace received a telegram. After first bestowing the flowers upon Madame Carré's appreciative seamstresses — the girls in the *cabine* having informed her their own vases were already overflowing — she had left the *maison* earlier than usual.

She was in the courtyard of 25 rue Dauphine, happily anticipating a quiet evening at home, when Madame Guérin called out to Grace as she passed her window.

'I'm not keen on telegrams,' she muttered as she handed Grace an envelope with as much suspicion as if it had been a live grenade.

Grace, too, was unnerved. Her thoughts moved quickly to Olive. *Please don't let anything have happened to her,* she prayed, *especially now, when our relationship is so badly frayed.* Filled with a sense of dread, as soon as Grace reached her room she opened the envelope. 'Thank heavens,' she murmured. Her mother was not the telegram's subject. Nevertheless, its contents were alarming.

JACK IN PARIS STOP WANTS MEET YOU 25 MAY
LE CARROUSEL 7PM STOP LOVE LOTTIE

But that was today, and in two hours, Grace realised. Telling herself not to panic, she tried to ignore her pounding heart and the sick feeling she had in her stomach.

Should she agree to see him? It took Grace no more than a minute to decide that she must. She had left Australia in such a hurry there had been no time to sort out anything. At least now, with Jack here in Paris, there was an opportunity for resolution.

Grace wondered what he wanted. Surely he wouldn't ask her to return to him? On the other hand, she thought hopefully, perhaps he was seeking a divorce. It could only be one of the two. What else would tear Jack away from his beloved Merindah and bring him halfway across the world?

'So, it's divorce then,' Grace said with relief.

'It's not what I want, Gracie,' Jack said wearily. 'You've always been the love of my life, you know that. But I have to face facts. You're not coming back to me, are you? We both need to move on.'

They were sitting at Le Carrousel's zinc-topped bar. Jack was drinking his third whisky while Grace nursed a single Manhattan. Despite his steady consumption of liquor, she was surprised at her husband's composure. *He's really behaving very decently*, Grace thought, *especially considering I took off to Paris without so much as a proper goodbye.*

Jack was still speaking. 'The grounds are desertion — that's right, isn't it? I mean, there's not been anyone else? Because I don't think I could stand the humiliation.'

'No, of course not,' Grace protested, experiencing a quick stab of guilt. It was the first of the lies she would tell that evening.

'I'm relieved to hear it, Gracie,' Jack said. 'If I thought you'd been with another man, well, I'd feel very differently about the split between us. I know that probably sounds irrational to you, but I can't help it. That's just the way I am.'

Grace produced a smile she hoped gave the appearance of innocence rather than guile.

'Actually, I have the papers here in my bag,' Jack continued. 'I'd like to go through them with you. There's a financial settlement too.'

'That won't be necessary,' Grace said quickly. 'I'm able to support myself.'

'I still think we should talk about it.' Jack downed the last of his drink. 'Charlotte wouldn't give me your address. She just said you'd mentioned this bar in one of your letters — she had the impression it was in the same neighbourhood. Would it be all right, do you think, if we went to your place, so we can go over the documents somewhere a bit more private?'

They were laughing and joking as they climbed the many stairs that led to Grace's attic. *It's almost like old times*, she reflected, *when we were still at school and each other's best friend.*

'No wonder you're in such good shape, Gracie,' Jack said when they finally reached her room. Eyeing her appreciatively, he declared, 'You're still the best-looking girl I've ever seen.'

'Thanks. But shouldn't we be getting on with things?'

'What's the rush? I've come all this way; we should catch up. I know, how about a drink?' Jack suggested. 'I bought a bottle of brandy at Calais; it's in this valise along with the legal papers.'

'I'm not sure a drink's such a good idea …'

'What are you talking about?' Jack said with a trace of irritation. 'Surely an occasion like this deserves to be marked.'

'I suppose so,' Grace said warily.

After she brought over tumblers and set them down on the table, Jack poured two large measures. 'Happy days, Gracie,' he said, then swallowed his brandy. She remained standing while he sat in the armchair, eyeing her up and down.

'Like I was saying,' he went on, a slight slur softening his voice, 'by Christ, you're a beautiful woman. I bet you get a lot of attention from those oversexed Frenchmen.' With that, he walked over and put a hand on her back.

'Come on, Jack. I really think we should sort out these papers.'

'We have all the time in the world.' He began stroking her shoulder.

'This isn't helping.' Grace tried to push his hand away.

'Well, here's an idea that might move things along. Go to bed with me.'

'What?'

'Why not? You're my wife.'

Grace laughed contemptuously. 'Out of the question!'

Jack's caress had become a firm grip. 'So, when it comes to the bedroom, you're still just the same — bloody frigid. But I still have my rights. Anyway, you invited me up here, remember?'

Grace was appalled. How had she allowed herself to get into this hideous position?

'I'm not changing my mind, sweetheart,' Jack said. 'If you don't give me what's mine, then I won't sign, simple as that.'

Grace looked at her husband. She'd seen this stubborn belligerence before. When he was in this kind of mood he wouldn't be moved. She knew that agreeing to Jack's outrageous proposition meant betraying Philippe. But if she didn't, she'd never be free. This impossible situation was just one more example of life's grey areas. It seemed there was no black or white anymore, just a series of moral compromises, all of which demanded dishonourable decisions.

'All right,' she said coldly.

In a voice thick with drink and desire, Jack replied, 'Good girl.'

CHAPTER THIRTY-THREE

Lying still, tension and hurt radiating through every part of her, Grace tried not to focus on Jack's cruel violation, but instead on her impending liberation. She told herself that what she was enduring was nothing more than a transaction, a price she had to pay. During the war, plenty of French women had no choice but to do the same thing. And, after all, this was hardly the first time her husband had forced himself on her. Yet she knew it wasn't the same as before.

Now that Grace had experienced the bliss of being made love to by a wonderfully skilled, adoring man intent on her pleasure, Jack's selfish attentions were even harder to bear than she remembered. At least, she reflected as she clenched her teeth, this would soon be over. Then, somehow, she would make herself forget it ever happened.

Afterwards, the two of them washed and put on their clothes in strained silence. Grace straightened her rumpled bed; Jack sat at the table and spread out the papers. He signed several times, stood up and said awkwardly, 'It's your turn.'

Grace signed. Each time she wrote 'Grace Osbourne' she felt a little less burdened. After tonight, at least that name would cease to exist.

'Hang on,' Jack said. 'You haven't done these.'

'I told you, I don't want your money.'

'I should have known. You've always been strong on doing the right thing. Much better at it than me, I'm afraid,' Jack said, colouring. 'I'm really sorry, Grace. I'm sorry about so many things, but tonight most of all. I don't know what came over me.'

Grace said nothing.

'No, really, I'm ashamed.' Jack took up the bottle of brandy. 'I shouldn't have drunk so much. It's a poor sort of an excuse, but bloody hell, I've never been able to resist you, whatever state I've been in. Here's a copy of the papers,' he said, returning his own set to his bag. 'When I'm back in Sydney, I'll finalise everything. I don't foresee any problems.'

'Goodbye, Jack.'

'Let's not leave each other on this note.' He smiled ruefully. 'We should at least shake ha—' There was the sound of two quick knocks on the door, followed by a key turning in the lock. 'What the blazes …?'

To Grace's horror, Philippe walked into the room.

'Who's this, some fancy French boyfriend?' Jack sneered.

Angry and bewildered, Philippe stepped forward. 'Monsieur, I —'

'Don't *monsieur* me!' Jack glared at Grace. 'I can't believe it was me doing the apologising, when all the time you've been acting like a little trollop.'

He swung a drunken punch that went wide and glanced off Philippe's cheek. A split second later, Philippe's fist thudded into his jaw.

Teetering back, Jack shouted at Grace, 'Looks like I'm well rid of you, after all.' He grabbed his bag and lurched out of the room, slamming the door behind him.

'Are you all right, darling?' Philippe rushed to Grace's side. 'Tell me, what can I do?'

'Don't do anything,' she pleaded.

'What are you talking about? I'm going after that man. Do you know who he is?'

'His name is Jack Osbourne,' Grace said slowly. 'He's my husband.'

Philippe's eyes had become very dark. 'I think you had better tell me what's going on,' he said curtly as he folded his arms.

Grace told him. She explained that she and Jack had been childhood sweethearts, that they had wed after the war but that the marriage had been a terrible mistake. She spoke of the telegram she'd received only that day announcing his arrival in Paris.

'Jack was here to sign the divorce papers,' she insisted. 'It's the sole reason he came.'

'Well then, why was he so furious?'

'Because I assured him I wasn't seeing anyone else, that even though we had separated I had remained faithful. If he thought I'd broken my marriage vows, he wouldn't have signed.'

'And then I walked in.'

'Yes.'

'I seem to recall you once accused me of being married. Now I discover that you have a husband.' Philippe began to pace angrily back and forth across the room. 'Doesn't that strike you as hypocritical?'

'I'm desperately sorry!' Grace cried. 'I was convinced that if you knew the truth, you would finish our relationship. It was stupid and wrong of me to hide my marriage from you, but I just hoped it would all be sorted out quietly and then go away.'

Philippe grasped her by the shoulders. 'Do you understand how shocked I am that only now you tell me about your marriage to this Jack Osbourne?' He paused. 'You knew full well that by revealing my identity to you I was willing to place my life in your hands. You, by contrast, could not find it within you to trust me. How do you think that makes me feel?'

Grace hung her head. 'Not very good.'

Tilting her face up in his hands, Philippe looked searchingly into her emerald eyes. 'You have told me everything now? There is nothing else that has taken place you should share with me?'

'Nothing.'

It was the second lie Grace had told that night. But how could she reveal to Philippe that she had just had sex with Jack?

'All right. We must put this behind us — otherwise everything we have together will be ruined by suspicion, and that is the last thing I want. Whatever has happened between you and that man will stay in the past, where it belongs.' He touched his cheek distractedly, then winced. 'As for not trusting me — you have agreed to risk your life. There can't be a much greater demonstration of your trust in me than that.'

Grace sighed. Her shameful deceit had very nearly spoilt everything, yet it seemed she had been given a reprieve. 'Let me fetch you something for your poor face,' she said.

'There is a reason I came here tonight, quite apart from the fact I would gladly see you every night.' Philippe tried to smile as he held the cold cloth Grace had given him to his swollen cheek. 'I need to explain exactly what steps must be taken to ensure the success of your mission. But, considering what's just gone on' — he winced again — 'I'm sure that is the last thing you want to do. We'd better leave it.'

Grace realised the evening's events had been so tumultuous, the subject of Giscard Orly had entirely escaped her mind.

'No, tell me,' she said. 'I'd rather think about how to entrap the minister than dwell on that scene with Jack.'

'You're sure?'

'Yes. As long as you feel up to it.'

Philippe pointed to his cheek. 'You mean this? It's just a bruise.' He pulled the armchair over to the table, saying, 'Sit down, Grace. I need to show you something.'

He withdrew a tiny vial of colourless liquid from his pocket. 'Inside is a drug that will knock Orly out for hours. It's fast acting, especially if mixed with alcohol. You should have plenty of time to get the job done.' He lay the vial on the table. 'Whatever you do,' Philippe cautioned, 'once you have opened the safe you must bring the information straight to the US Ambassador's residence. I will give you an official, top-level accreditation from the French security service that will guarantee automatic entry to the residence. This will be essential, because unless David Bruce is personally presented with proof of the plot, he won't countenance cancelling his Bastille Day appearance. The Americans don't want a show of weakness.'

'What if I can't reach the ambassador in time?'

'Bring the information directly to me. I will leave my motorcycle chained to a railing in a street around the corner from the ministry. What with the crowds and the security in place for the parade, it will be difficult for you to cross Paris. Ride the bike — it's your best chance.'

'Where will I find you?'

'In the Place de la Concorde, just to the left of l'Orangerie. Ambassador Bruce will be an easy target; he'll be on the official podium between the museum and the Jeu de Paume. It is an excellent place to see the parade, but unfortunately it also affords a man intent on murder many places from where he can fire.'

Philippe tapped the vial. 'You will be assigned an experienced, female agent, a specialist, who will help you devise a plan to get into Orly's office. She will also make arrangements so you can practise opening the same make of safe and anything else you need to rehearse.'

'Like what?'

'Like your interactions with the minister. It would be best if you don't discuss this aspect of the operation with me — we can't allow our emotions to get the better of us and, certainly in my case, that won't be easy.'

'I understand,' Grace said.

'Good. You will also be provided with a diagram of the room and a map of the route you should take, both to the embassy residence and from there to the Place de la Concorde. By the evening of the thirteenth of July, each detail should be so familiar to you that you would be able to carry it out with your eyes closed.'

Grace attempted to mask her nerves. 'That's still seven weeks away,' she said flippantly, though her mouth was dry. 'What a long time to put up with Monsieur Orly's floral tributes.'

Philippe turned to her. 'Just in case those bouquets have led you to think the minister is harmless — perhaps even ridiculous — make no mistake. Orly is a cold-blooded killer,' he said sombrely. 'Have I frightened you now?'

'Not at all,' Grace replied. It was her third lie.

CHAPTER THIRTY-FOUR

Tuesday 21 June 1949

The flowers stopped arriving.

'Looks like your beau has turned his attentions elsewhere,' Victoire observed. 'That's what happens when you play too hard to get.'

'*C'est la vie*,' Grace said, attempting to appear unconcerned.

Privately, she worried that Orly really had given up his pursuit of her. He had weighty matters on his mind: an ambassador to be eliminated, not to mention his own political aspirations. No doubt he was keenly anticipating being appointed president of France's first communist government. Why would his thoughts be dwelling on a mannequin?

Grace reminded herself that Ferdinand had said Orly would stop at nothing to get what he wanted. She tried to imagine the minister, distracted by his obsession with her, throwing down his fountain pen or kicking at a door in sheer frustration. She had to believe he still desired her.

Monday 4 July

'Giscard Orly is a power-hungry fantasist,' Nicole, the angular, middle-aged agent who'd been assigned to Grace, said coolly. Grace had just arrived at the anonymous townhouse tucked away in a quiet part of the Marais where her training had been taking place. Nicole added, 'Given his character traits, I predict he is already picturing you willing — no, begging — to be violated.'

Despite Nicole's even tone, Grace felt ill. All her confidence seemed to be draining away.

'It helps to disassociate yourself,' the agent advised. 'You are merely playing a part, like an actor in a play. But you must remember — it doesn't matter what Orly might say or do, your performance cannot take place any sooner than the eve of Bastille Day.'

'How can you be so sure this act of mine will take place at all?' Grace frowned. 'He's left me completely alone for nearly two weeks now.'

'Believe me, that won't last,' Nicole said. 'He'll have a plan. All you have to do is keep your nerve.'

Easier said than done, Grace thought as she left the townhouse. In fact, it had been exactly thirteen days since she'd heard from Orly. It was no use pretending she was some sort of femme fatale, she thought gloomily. Despite Nicole's prediction, she feared Orly's interest in her had been fleeting. At the same time, she couldn't help but be relieved that she'd gained a reprieve for another day.

Grace felt as if she was trapped on an endless emotional rollercoaster, and yet every morning she still had to turn up at the *maison*, ready for fittings, to show clothes and entrance clients. As she made her way home each night, she found herself trembling with the sheer strain of it all. Philippe was under pressure, too. He managed to see her several times a week, but it was difficult for either one of them to relax. They made love with a new, feverish intensity, as if every time they lay in each other's arms might be the last.

Wednesday 6 July

On the fifteenth day, a small package was delivered to the *maison*. Not daring to open it in the *cabine*, Grace hurriedly slipped it into her handbag. Only when she was safely in her room in the rue Dauphine did she discover what lay inside — a pair of diamond earrings from Van Cleef & Arpels.

She did not return the gift.

A mere twenty-four hours later, Grace received an intricate gold bracelet made by Boucheron. This, too, was retained. The *pièce de résistance* arrived on the following afternoon — one of Cartier's famous diamond-studded brooches in the shape of a panther with a large cabochon emerald clasped in its claws.

The next morning, she despatched a handwritten note to Orly. It said simply: *13 July, 9 pm, Maxim's. Mademoiselle D.*

Monday 11 July

Marguerite Carré stared at Grace, then at her little green book.

'Is it possible you have been eating more croissants than usual?' she said, wrinkling her brow,

Grace was puzzled.

'This toile is cut to your precise measurements,' Marguerite Carré said, 'yet it is not fitting as it should. Do you see, here at the waist it is pulling a little, and the line of the bust is not quite correct.'

'I'm afraid it must be our charming doorman who is to blame.' Grace grinned. 'Whenever we meet for coffee Ferdinand insists on tempting me with *viennoiseries*.'

'Well, you must learn to resist,' Madame Carré scolded. 'Imagine if you put on weight after the toile was approved — when the fabric was cut, it might not fit and the entire length would be ruined.'

'I'm sorry, madame, it won't happen again.'

Later that day, Grace fainted. Fortunately, she was in the *cabine* at the time, having just finished showing a selection of cocktail dresses to the vivacious divorcee Mrs Pamela Churchill. Grace had wriggled free from the final *modèle* and passed it to a dresser before collapsing onto a conveniently placed, frothy cloud of tulle petticoats.

When Grace opened her eyes, she saw she was lying on the sea-green chaise longue where the occasional exhausted mannequin would recline during stolen moments between parades. How she'd been moved there, she didn't know, but to her relief, save for Brigitte and Marie-Hélène, she was alone.

'Grace, oh, thank goodness. We were so concerned about you,' Brigitte said.

'I honestly don't know what came over me.' Grace sat up and attempted to smile. 'It must be because I was so light-headed. I haven't felt at all like eating lately, yet the odd thing is, Madame Carré says I've put on weight. Perhaps I should see a doctor?'

'Perhaps you should,' said Marie-Hélène. She glanced quickly over her shoulder before lowering her voice to a whisper. 'Is it possible you might be pregnant?'

Pregnant. The moment Marie-Hélène uttered the word, Grace knew it was true. In addition to her mysterious symptoms, she was about six weeks overdue, something she'd put down to the unremitting stress imposed by her nerve-wracking circumstances.

She had not given a moment's thought to the possibility she might be in an even more calamitous state, for although she'd taken no precautions during her two and a half years of married life, there'd been no sign of a baby. Stupidly, she had developed a false sense of security, and now she was paying the price. Ashen-faced, she looked at her friends with dismay.

'It's my fault!' Brigitte cried. 'I should never have introduced you to my cousin.'

Marie-Hélène adopted a more practical tone. 'I can see this is not welcome news, but you must not despair. There are ways of dealing with this kind of situation.'

'You mean … an abortion?' Grace had heard of such a thing, but the thought terrified her. She had visions of dirty back-alleys and unspeakable procedures.

'I do. You wouldn't be the first mannequin to find herself in this condition.'

Grace bit her lip. Her encounter with Giscard Orly was only two days away — she could not let anything stand in her way.

'Thank you both, I don't know where I'd be without you. Right now, though, I'm confused. I'll have to think about it.'

Marie-Hélène frowned. 'Don't take too long, will you?'

Although she understood her friend was trying to help, the idea of a termination filled Grace with horror. But what else could she do? She had to work, and the fitters were ruthless. The alarming notion occurred to her that perhaps Madame Carré already half suspected the truth.

Grace's head was swimming. As she closed her eyes she heard Brigitte say, 'Let's leave her now, she needs to rest. Anyway, we are wanted in the studio.'

Alone, Grace's anguish only increased. As her mind veered from one solution to another, a single fact became clear. Philippe Boyer was the love of her life. And now she had the power to become his wife.

Philippe was an honourable man. If she told him about her condition he would doubtless feel obliged to marry her. Yet Grace shrank from the idea. The last thing she wanted was for the man she adored to feel forced into marriage.

Suddenly, she sat bolt upright and groaned. How slow-witted she had been! The baby she was carrying could well be Jack's. And if that was the case, what possible solution could there be? No matter what befell her, she would not, could not, go back to him.

Grace hugged her knees to her chest. If only she hadn't foolishly agreed to Jack's request to come to her room. If only she'd refused his indecent proposal, been wiser, shrewder, stronger, *something*, she would never have found herself in this disastrous state.

Grace had believed she'd struck a simple bargain: one last sexual encounter in exchange for her liberty. Now, with a sense of rising panic, she realised how naive she had been — negotiating life's grey areas did not occur without penalties. Even if she wanted to, could she now say to Philippe with her hand on her heart that the baby was his? She could not. That was one lie she would never tell.

Grace heard a rustle of silk. 'My dear, I think you dropped off for a moment. Are you all right?'

She opened her eyes to see Madame Raymonde sitting next to her.

'Tutu told me you weren't well,' she explained.

'You're very kind. I'm so sorry to cause all this fuss.'

'Not at all.'

Grace thought quickly. She could not allow herself to dwell upon her plight. What she needed was time away from the *maison*. She was conscious that as each hour passed, her dangerous rendezvous with Giscard Orly drew ever closer. She had to gather her strength.

'It must be a virus,' she said weakly. 'I'm afraid I will need some time off. Perhaps just until after Bastille Day?'

Madame Raymonde studied Grace with her deceptively mild blue eyes.

'Take good care of yourself,' she replied.

CHAPTER THIRTY-FIVE

Tuesday 12 July

A rumbling mew emanated from the landing outside Grace's room. It could only be the little concierge's cat, which meant Madame Guérin herself must be close behind. Rising from her bed, Grace opened the door, watching as Tartuffe bounded in, leapt up and triumphantly settled himself on her armchair.

As she expected, a couple of minutes later the concierge appeared, puffing from the effort.

'*Excusez-moi, mademoiselle,*' she said between gasps. 'I know you are not well, but I have a note for you. The message was sent on here when it was discovered you were not at the *maison*. I thought it might be important.'

'Won't you sit down, madame?' Grace said. 'Perhaps you would like a tisane?'

'Thank you, no. My assistant and I must return to our work.' She scooped up the cat in her arms. 'Tartuffe, off we go. We will leave Mademoiselle Dubois in peace.'

Peace — if only such a thing were possible. To the contrary, she felt wretched. Although her spirits rose briefly when she saw that the note was from Philippe, its contents were far from welcome.

His father had come unexpectedly to Paris for a few days. Apparently he'd had a sudden yen to spend time in the company of his old Resistance brothers-in-arms and watch the Bastille Day parade. Philippe wrote:

> *I explained to Gaston that, regrettably, you and I had important commitments tomorrow as well as on 14 July, which means the only time we can see him is this evening. It would mean a great deal to me if you could join us. I know the timing is less than ideal, but hopefully it will provide some distraction.*

Grace frowned; the mere thought of going anywhere in her current condition was overwhelming. Yet how could she refuse? Philippe had been more understanding about her hidden marriage than she had any right to expect. He wasn't asking much of her.

In any case, how else was she going to spend the night? There was not a thing she could do about her pregnancy, at least not until after tomorrow's assignation. She would only lie in bed, stare at the ceiling and become increasingly agitated.

Philippe was right. If ever she needed a distraction, it was now. She might be feeling under the weather, but there was still enough time for her to have a short rest. Then she would bathe, put on a dress, meet Philippe and Gaston and drink a glass of champagne. Indeed, the more Grace contemplated the evening, the more she welcomed the respite she felt sure it would provide.

Grace took Philippe's hand as they walked towards the Boulevard Saint-Germain. 'You are unusually debonair tonight,' she remarked, looking him up and down.

She had never seen Philippe in a suit before, let alone one that was tailor-made and accompanied by a deep-blue and white striped silk tie by Charvet. She wondered how he had come by such expensive attire. Without his black leather jacket and motorcycle boots, Philippe seemed very polished, and, just possibly, even more attractive.

'I thought they might not let me through the door in my usual clothes.' Philippe grinned as he hailed a taxi. After opening the door for Grace he slid in beside her, then said to the driver, '*La Voiture Folle, s'il vous plaît.*'

'Paris's most exclusive nightclub, the one famous for its piano bar? That's unexpected.' Grace's forehead creased. 'I thought Gaston spent his time hidden away in the countryside. Are you quite sure he'll be comfortable in a place as smart as The Crazy Car?'

'You're right — you wouldn't usually catch Gaston somewhere like that. But apparently he and the owner go back a long way.'

A row of blazing lights ignited as Grace stepped out of the taxi. This was not unexpected; photographers were often stationed at the entrances of fashionable night-spots. In glamorous post-war Paris, there was an eager market for images of the stylish, well-connected men and women who were able to indulge once more in the city's many pleasures.

Knowing full well that Madame Raymonde was far more likely to lend a mannequin something pretty to wear if she thought a picture of her might appear in a smart publication, Grace offered up a dazzling smile.

Amid the blizzard of flashing bulbs, she realised Philippe had disappeared. She assumed he wouldn't want his communist comrades to see a picture of him entering La Voiture Folle — it was a very long way from the grubby alleys of Belleville.

Brushing past the huddle of photographers, Grace entered the club in her fitted, white faille dress, the angled panels of its skirt flying behind her. She found Philippe inside the door, waiting.

'I've just been thinking how fortunate it was that I didn't bring the motorbike. You would have had to ride side-saddle in that.' He inclined his head towards her.

'Do you think, just this once, you could put my poor little frock's unsuitability aside?' Grace demanded with mock irritation.

'What can I say? You are the most beautiful girl in Paris — whether you have clothes on or not,' Philippe murmured, kissing her lightly just below her ear, before adding, 'Mmm, how is it that you always smell so delicious?'

The two continued their flirtatious banter as they walked through La Voiture Folle's dark, velvet-lined vestibule. When they arrived at the entrance to the main room, a number of guests turned around to look at the glamorous couple. Grace caught the eye of Julia Child sitting with a man of modest stature she thought must be Paul, her diplomat husband; Lady Diana Cooper flashed her famous smile while her companion, one of the Mitford sisters, raised a champagne cocktail. Pablo Picasso simply saluted; he was sharing his table with his young mistress, Françoise Gilot.

'Darling,' Philippe said, 'you will have to ignore your admirers, especially Pablo. If I let you near him, he'll only go on again about wanting to paint your portrait — and, as you know, that undertaking inevitably leads to a scandalous outcome. It would be far safer all round if we found our table.'

Grace didn't move.

Someone had begun to play the piano. Blinded by the white glare of a spotlight, she found it impossible to see the stage. It didn't matter. Grace only needed to listen in order to know whose hands were touching the keys.

'Ah, that's Gaston!' Philippe exclaimed. 'Madame Marly has clearly had her way. She does love it when he plays Chopin. Of course, he is just as likely to launch into something by Dizzy Gillespie. Wait a minute — I'll go over and let him know we're here.'

Grace continued to stare. As her eyes adjusted, she was able to discern the outline of the large, thick-set man seated at the piano, a hat pushed to the back of his head. His distinctive appearance only confirmed what she already knew. It was Reuben.

Grace felt faint. Her chest was tight; she could barely breathe. Nothing made sense.

How could Gaston and Reuben be one and the same? Unless, unless ... she made a rapid calculation. Reuben could well have fathered a child while he'd been in France during the last year of the Great War. Philippe had just turned thirty — the dates aligned.

But why did he call Reuben by the name of Gaston? A piece of the puzzle was missing.

If it were true, though, if Gaston was Philippe's father, then — no, she couldn't bear it. What she and Philippe had done together was not just an act of adultery, it was a perversion. Worse, she could well be carrying the blighted fruit of their union.

Choking, Grace whirled around. She rushed through the shadowy vestibule towards the door. Suddenly, an exotic-looking woman appeared. 'My dear, I am Madame Marly, the proprietor of La Voiture Folle. Can I be of assistance?'

There was a fox fur hanging around the woman's neck. The animal's tail was clenched in its jaws, held there by two rows of sharp, pointed teeth. Grace had seen that same fur somewhere before. Now, like the fox, she too was caught in an impossible snare.

The door opened. New arrivals descended from a limousine. The photographers' flashes exploded; a brilliant, staccato light flooded in.

'Please tell Monsieur Boyer that Mademoiselle Dubois is not well,' Grace cried, her heart pounding.

Then she ran out of the club, turned away from the cameras and fled.

CHAPTER THIRTY-SIX

Wednesday 13 July

'I am perplexed,' Ferdinand confessed. 'It seems so unlike her.'

In the absence of his usual early morning companion, the doorman was sharing a coffee at Café Bertrand with Madame de Turckheim.

'Mademoiselle Dubois is a charming, vivacious beauty,' he said. 'It is only natural she would attract many admirers. But I know for a fact that she declined the attention of the Baron de Gide. She even insisted I return his ruby and diamond necklace.'

'Did she, indeed?' Tutu said. 'That takes a strong will.'

'I agree. Of late, she has been seeing a young man — some sort of journalist, I believe. He might not be wealthy or terribly well connected, but he is handsome and she certainly appeared to be in love with him.'

'Ah, yes, we have all seen that distracted look in her eyes,' Tutu agreed.

'Well then, I am sure you will be interested to hear that Minister Giscard Orly, having first besieged Grace with flowers, has now sent her several pieces of expensive jewellery — I recognised the makers' packaging immediately.'

'Which she has also returned?'

'*Au contraire*! I asked her if she wished me to do so, but she declined. I must confess to being rather shocked. It is completely out of character. Now she seems to have fallen ill and, I can assure you, that one is never ill; yet this is the third day she's been absent.' Ferdinand shook his head. 'Something is not right, Tutu. I have heard things, disturbing things about Orly and his inclinations.'

'Ferdinand, you appear quite concerned.'

'You are correct. I cannot explain why, but I am very much afraid that our little Australian is about to find herself in a dangerous situation.'

Grace waited for nightfall with the keenest anticipation and a crystal-clear mind. It was as if the devastating events of the past three days had never happened. She did not dwell on the future of her pregnancy, the identity of the child's father or the nature of the relationship between Philippe and Reuben — she could not. Instead, she concentrated only on what needed to be accomplished.

Nicole had spent hours with Grace, reviewing every detail of the operation. She had coached her not only on administering the drug and the mechanics of the safe, but on exactly what she should say and do at every step along the way. Yet Grace knew far more would be required of her than this training could ever provide. Everything she had ever learnt in her twenty-six years would count. Success would not depend on her physical beauty; not really. It would be a test of her wits and her will.

All the same, Grace was aware that her appearance was vital. She had a picture in her mind of the impression she wanted to create — that of a woman who, although sophisticated, was undeniably, irresistibly seductive.

When the clock at last displayed the appropriate hour, she began dressing in a methodical fashion. She clipped on a strapless black brassiere, slipped into a pair of matching silk briefs and then laced up her *guêpière*, the narrow corset all the mannequins wore to cinch in their waists. Next, Grace eased fine nylon stockings over each leg until they sat smoothly against her thighs. Having fastened the stockings to her suspenders, she removed a full-skirted, black lace cocktail dress from its hanger. As she stepped into the dress she bent forward so the scalloped edges of its low-cut bodice hugged the swell of her pillowy breasts. Her shoes were black suede with a pointed toe and a high, fine heel. 'Follow me home shoes', the girls in the workroom called them.

Grace had already perfected her make-up, which included a Helena Rubinstein lipstick in a shade of red that might have seemed outré if applied by a less expert hand. Now she attended to her coiffure, arranging her dark curls on top of her head in such a way that the removal of a single jewelled pin would be all that was required for them to come loose and tumble down. Finally, Grace added the Van Cleef & Arpels diamond earrings, placed the Boucheron bracelet on her wrist and pinned the spectacular Cartier panther brooch at the precise point where the top of her dress met her revealing décolletage.

Despite the hazardous nature of the evening that lay ahead, Grace felt only a sense of professional detachment as she stood in front of her long mirror and studied the result of her careful preparations. She scrutinised herself from the front, and then, turning to peer into a small mirror she held in her hand, from the back.

The finishing touch was a very liberal spray of perfume behind her ears, between her breasts, in the crook of her arms and on the nape of her neck. She had not selected the demure Miss Dior, but Elsa Schiaparelli's signature perfume, Shocking. It would suit the occasion, she thought.

After picking up her satin evening bag she walked briskly towards the door. Then she hesitated. She went back to the mirror and looked at herself once more.

'*Bonne chance*,' she said to her reflection.

In Maxim's gilded Art Nouveau dining room, an empty bottle of Pol Roger stood on Orly's table beside a barely touched dish of quail and Iranian caviar. He leant forward, his eyes roaming from Grace's full crimson lips to the line of her throat and then the curve of her breasts. 'I confess, I am a man of some experience,' he said silkily. 'Yet I have never met a woman like you before.'

'But, surely, each woman is unique.'

'Not really. When Shakespeare referred to Cleopatra's "infinite variety", I think he had someone very much like you in mind.'

'Is that so?'

'It is, and I shall tell you why. First, I admit, I can't stop looking at you.'

'Thank you, Giscard — I had detected your interest,' Grace teased.

'You are an immensely desirable woman. I might have seen you just twice before, but on each occasion your appeal has only increased. Tonight, wearing jewels befitting your beauty, you are even more alluring.'

He's reminding me that he has met my price, she thought.

'Second, although it is clear you do not shy away from attention, there is an air of mystery about you. I feel I have spent all evening talking, while you have said barely a word about yourself.' He regarded her with a speculative expression in his ebony eyes.

'Never mind, there is a perfect way for me to get to know you much better,' he said. 'We will have cognac in my townhouse.' It was not a question but a statement of intent.

Good, his defences will be down if he believes he has the whip hand, Grace reflected.

'There is nothing I would like more than to share an intimate after-dinner drink with you.' She gave Orly an enticing smile. 'But, I regret,' she said as her smile faded, 'that your townhouse, magnificent as it may be, is of no interest to me.'

'Let me assure you, I can arrange a private suite at the Crillon or, if you prefer, the George V Hotel, at a moment's notice,' Orly said quickly.

'I do not wish to go somewhere you have been with other women.'

'Where, then?'

Grace lowered her voice. 'I propose we go to your office.'

'What, you mean at the ministry?' Orly raised an eyebrow.

'Exactly. I'll be frank. There are many men who would like to spend time with me — rich, handsome men with great charm. They don't interest me. Now I will tell you why you do.'

Orly preened. 'Go ahead.'

'Giscard, it goes without saying that you are also handsome, rich and charming. But you have something extra. It is the aura of power. Partly it is your position, although I feel it is something more, something innate. Yes, you are a minister now, but I predict that one day you may well become the President of France. I find myself immensely attracted to that power.' Grace flicked her tongue over her lips. 'I felt it as soon as we met.'

Before Orly was able to respond, Maxim's head waiter appeared at his side.

'I trust everything has been to your satisfaction, Minister,' he said, bowing slightly. 'Perhaps you and mademoiselle would enjoy a brandy after your coffee? We have some very fine vintages.'

'Not tonight, Georges. Just the bill, please,' he said briskly as he waved the man away.

'Now, where were we? I believe you were saying you wished to come to my office,' Orly prompted.

Grace whispered, 'I want to give myself to you in the place where you exercise power, so that each time you enter the room, take a telephone call or receive a colleague, you will be stirred by the memory of what I have begged you to do.'

Not a bad start, not bad at all, Grace decided. Seated next to Orly on the back seat of his chauffeur-driven limousine, she was contemplating her satisfactory progress when Orly began to stroke the inside of her thigh. Although warned that this was to be expected, she still had to fight the urge to scream and squirm away. It was as if she were a child once more, the same child whose skin had crawled when she'd felt the smooth body of a snake slide against her. The difference was, she thought grimly, there was no one to save her now.

After the uniformed driver manoeuvred the limousine through the ministry's towering black and gold gates, he pulled up on the far side of a cobblestoned courtyard. The chauffeur, his expression impassive, opened the door for Orly and then Grace. After the minister helped her out, the chauffeur resumed his place behind the steering wheel and drove away.

Orly unlocked the front door of the grand eighteenth-century *hôtel particulier* with a large brass key, before escorting Grace into a lofty hall, empty save for the solemn portraits of former government ministers. Taking her arm, he led her down an echoing corridor until he reached a set of doors. Orly opened them with a second, slightly smaller brass key, then stood aside.

'After you, mademoiselle,' he said.

Grace found herself in a vast, high-ceilinged room decorated in the imperial style favoured — no matter the political persuasion of the government — for France's most prestigious public buildings. There were heavy red velvet curtains trimmed with gold fringes hanging in front of floor-to-ceiling windows; a wide blue and maroon patterned Aubusson rug on the parquetry floor; and an abundance of gold and white panelling.

Grace was relieved to see that the minister's desk, chairs, coffee table and drinks cabinet, which stood on one side of a black and gold Coromandel screen, were all exactly where the diagram Nicole had supplied indicated they would be. Most important of all, a misty landscape by Corot was hanging on the back wall.

'You spoke of the place where I exercise power. Is this what you had in mind?' Orly asked with an expansive gesture.

'It's perfect,' Grace replied. 'All I require is for you to sit down, Giscard, behind your desk, if you please. I would like to fetch our drinks.'

'Shouldn't I be attending to that?' Orly said, frowning.

'Oh, do allow me,' she pouted coquettishly, 'I want to give you a little surprise.'

Grace glided behind the Coromandel screen. What she was about to do had not formed part of Nicole's briefing, yet she had the strongest feeling that her success — and her safety — would depend upon captivating Orly in the most persuasive way possible. Taking a deep breath, she quickly removed her lace dress and drew the tiny vial from its hiding place inside her corset. After emptying the contents into a glass, Grace placed the vial in her bag, poured two drinks, and then stepped away from the screen.

Wearing only her stiletto shoes, her stockings and provocative black lingerie, and carrying a brandy balloon in each hand, Grace posed much as she would when entering the salon at the beginning of a show. *Let him see what he thinks he's bought*, she thought.

'Mademoiselle Dubois, you continue to both arouse and astonish me,' Orly said with approval.

Grace felt the intensity of his gaze as, with a tantalising undulation of her hips, she crossed the room. Handing him one of the brandy balloons, she said, 'To a memorable evening.'

'Indeed.' Orly drained his glass.

With that, his charm slipped away, much as a snake might shed its skin. His expression became cold; his manner acquired a brutal edge. This change in demeanour would have been of no consequence, if only Orly had been displaying the effects of the drug she'd put in his drink. Grace felt her first sting of fear.

'It is time, Mademoiselle Dubois,' Orly said impatiently. 'We will begin.'

'As you wish, minister.' She was determined to hide her mounting anxiety.

'Sit on my desk, facing me,' he commanded.

Grace did so, arranging her legs in a way that indicated just how wanton she was prepared to be. No matter what happened, she reminded herself, she had to maintain her nerve and continue to play the role of a practised courtesan.

'Let your hair down.'

Grace removed the jewelled pin and shook her dark curls free.

Orly kept his glittering, cobra eyes fixed on her. 'Now take that off,' he said, pointing to her brassiere.

Grace slowly unfastened the scrap of black silk and let it fall.

CHAPTER THIRTY-SEVEN

Giscard Orly sat slumped in his over-large Napoleonic chair. His eyes were shut, his head with its swept-back, brilliantined black hair hung limply to one side and a small trail of drool spilled from the corner of his lower lip. Grace bent over the slumbering man. She would have to search him.

Stealthily, she inserted one hand into Orly's right trouser pocket. Then, to her horror, she heard a faint scraping sound. It was a key turning in a lock.

'Security!' a harsh voice announced.

Grace had just enough time to adopt an orgasmic expression and, despite her revulsion, to press Orly's face against her bare breasts. Beams of light bounced off the gold and white panelled walls. A moment later, a uniformed guard appeared, wielding a torch. In the flickering half-light his features were grotesque; he might have been one of Notre-Dame's gargoyles.

Despite her hammering heart, Grace forced herself to continue her masquerade. As a consequence, it was not a shocked and embarrassed Grace Woods but Mademoiselle Dubois, near-naked courtesan, who produced an impudent wink.

Thank God, she thought, the minister's penchant for nubile young women was widely known.

'*Excusez-moi*,' the guard muttered with a barely suppressed smirk. He hurriedly retraced his steps and left, closing the door behind him.

Grace released Orly, whose head flopped back against the chair. She remained where she was, though, listening intently until she heard the footsteps fade away. Only when she was certain of the silence did she return to her search. She gingerly felt around the pocket. It was empty. Willing herself to remain calm, she turned her attention to another pocket.

As Grace felt the folded piece of paper, she knew this time fortune had smiled. Grasping it between her thumb and forefinger, she cautiously eased it out. Orly coughed and she jumped, almost dropping the paper. Again she waited, tense and motionless. When his even, sonorous breathing resumed, Grace triumphantly held the piece of paper up to the light.

The code was — no! She couldn't believe it. The only thing written down was her own name and the telephone number of Maxim's. Her elation faded as quickly as it had arrived. She had no choice but to keep searching.

Her frustration mounted as, methodically, she continued to explore Orly's coat. She located his wallet, a small silver pen, a tortoiseshell comb, an initialled handkerchief and a slim leather diary. There was nothing else. Then her hand closed over a piece of card tucked behind a loose corner of lining. Grace drew it out slowly. Here, at last, was the safe's combination.

As Philippe had promised, having memorised the diagrams and practised with an identical safe, she could perform her next task in the dark — which was just as well, as, save for the illumination provided by a single desk lamp, the room was dim. She couldn't turn on any more lights for fear of waking Orly. Instead, she reached up and cautiously removed the Corot landscape. There, flush against the wall, was the safe.

Grace tucked her loose hair out of the way, behind her ears. *Focus*, she told herself. She tried to steady her breathing, to keep her hand perfectly still. All the same, her fingers quivered as she spun the black dial once to the left, stopping at the number four. Two rotations to the right and then a stop at seven came next, followed by a final three spins to the left, until the dial rested on a nine. She heard a gratifying click. The door swung open.

'Dammit,' she whispered under her breath as one of her diamond earrings fell to the floor. After a quick look at Orly, she swiftly picked up the sparkling clip and reattached it. There was no time to lose. She had to examine the safe.

Inside were several leather boxes, two passports, various documents and a thick pile of cash. But there was just one unsealed envelope. A glance at the single sheet of paper it contained was enough to confirm that here were the assassin's instructions, written in the minister's own hand.

She turned towards the Coromandel screen and slipped the envelope into her handbag. Only then did it occur to Grace that she was still wearing nothing but her briefs, corset and stockings. Her brassiere was resting where it had dropped on the ministerial desk. Grace snatched it up and put it on, rapidly followed by her dress.

Then, with her heart racing, she returned to the safe, quietly closed the door, spun the dial and rehung the Corot. Finally, she inserted the card bearing the safe's combination back into its hiding place behind the loose lining in Orly's jacket.

Grace gave a sigh of relief. Hopefully, it would not be until many hours later that the traitorous minister would wake up from his drug-induced sleep, confident that the

Soviets' plan was secure. He'd feel confused and unwell, but would simply assume he had overindulged. Just in case he became concerned by gaps in his memory, she scribbled a hasty note and left it on his desk: *Giscard, what a man you are! The evening was unforgettable. Mademoiselle D.*

Warily, she poked her head out into the corridor. All was still and quiet. With her shoes in one hand and her handbag in the other, she walked noiselessly towards the front door. She had nearly reached the entrance hall with its dour ministerial portraits when she stopped. She'd seen a flash of light.

It must be that vile security man doing another circuit of the floor. Grace looked around. There was nowhere to run, nowhere to seek shelter. Then she saw a door — painted the same colour as the wall. Hoping desperately that it would not lead towards danger, she hurriedly stepped inside.

Grace shut the door behind her. She was in darkness. Suddenly, there was a crash as something hit her leg. Groping about in the dark, she realised she had collided with a tin bucket. She ran her hand up one wall and then another as she searched for a light switch, finding a row of small levers. Praying the one she selected was not a master switch that would suddenly illuminate the entire building — and bring the guard straight to her hiding place — she pressed down the first of the line. The single bulb above flickered weakly into life. Listening intently, she waited for the sound of running feet. She heard nothing.

Grace was standing in what appeared to be a large cleaners' closet. Overalls hung from hooks along one side; a mop and broom were propped in the corner; the shelf opposite contained various soaps, brushes and cloths.

Grace turned off the light. Then, very slowly, she opened the cupboard door by the smallest of margins.

'It's two o'clock,' she heard the security guard say. 'So you're on until ten.'

Then another man. 'How about you?'

'I'm on a double shift,' the guard grumbled. 'Still, the money's good. The boss is in a bit of a panic over Bastille Day. Wants one of us at the front door from now on. We can take it in turns till the cleaners get here at nine. No one else is expected. The minister is in, by the way, but I wouldn't go disturbing Romeo if you know what's good for you.' The man sniggered. 'He's fully occupied.'

Grace heard the screech of a chair being pulled over to the front door. Peeping out, she could see that the same security guard who had burst into Orly's office had settled himself by the entrance with several newspapers and a thermos flask.

She was trapped. Grace shut the door and sank to the floor. *I should have known it wouldn't be as easy as it seemed*, she berated herself. *How on earth could I have thought that managing to pass myself off as a fashion mannequin was going to equip me to steal enemy secrets?*

She hugged her knees to her chest while she considered her options. If she left her cramped sanctuary and tried to find an alternative way out of the building, she risked running into the second man. But she couldn't leave by the front door without passing the security guard stationed there.

Grace's mind raced. She considered, and rejected, half a dozen increasingly desperate, far-fetched plans. Then she went through them again. There was one idea that had a slim possibility of success. All she had to do was to assume yet another persona.

Grace removed her dress. It was for the second time that night, she thought wryly — at least being a mannequin had prepared her for slipping in and out of her clothes at a moment's notice. She turned on the light again and pulled on a pair of the overalls, followed by the smallest plastic shoe covers she could find among the row on the floor.

Grace put the official French credential into the overalls' only pocket. She squashed her jewellery, shoes, dress and handbag into the metal bucket, then rubbed off as much make-up from her face as she could with one of the cleaning cloths. She placed another, larger cloth over her hair and tied it under her chin. It wasn't exactly an Hermès headscarf, but at least it suited her purpose. Finally, she turned off the light. There was nothing else to do — except wait.

CHAPTER THIRTY-EIGHT

Thursday 14 July

It felt as if she had been in the cupboard all night, yet when she checked the time on her wristwatch, it was still only half-past three in the morning. Four came and went, then five. Grace tried to ignore the occasional noise she heard outside. If only she could remain undiscovered, perhaps she could still save the American ambassador's life. She was terribly tired, couldn't remember ever feeling so weary. No matter how hard she willed herself to stay awake, her eyelids kept fluttering shut.

Grace blinked. *I'll just have one more look*, she thought, dragging open her eyes. She started in horror. It was nearly nine o'clock. Springing to her feet, her heart beating rapidly, she opened the door by a couple of centimetres, and listened.

Nothing. Now she craved noise, action, people. She needed bustle and she needed workers to arrive. Then, at five past nine, she heard the chair by the entrance screech as it was dragged back to its proper place. This was followed by the sound of the front door being unlocked and pushed open. At last, there was a laugh, an exchange of greetings — *'Joyeux quatorze juillet*' and '*Bonne fête nationale*' — then the clatter of several pairs of feet walking down the hall.

Grace slipped out of the closet, carrying the bucket and a mop, her collar turned up, head down, the cloth scarf pulled forward.

'You're keen,' a woman with a guttural accent said.

'Got in early,' Grace muttered. 'They've asked me to mop the footpath outside, it being the national holiday. All right for some,' she added gruffly.

Still hanging her head and with a forbidding scowl on her face, she passed unhindered by the lecherous security guard and shuffled through the door.

She was very nearly free. But would she be too late? Pushing the mop in front of her, Grace walked as fast as she could without arousing suspicion. It was midsummer and the day was already hot. She felt the sun on her neck, a trickle of perspiration run down her back.

At the corner, Grace peered around furtively. Nobody paid her any attention. She was used to being gazed at, admired, even ogled — now she was grateful that thanks to her disguise, she was close to invisible. After one last look, she swiftly escaped down the side street. She was out of sight at last, and there, chained to a railing, was Philippe's motorcycle.

Fumbling inside the bucket, she located her handbag and grabbed the keys. Yet, when she tried to unlock the bike, her hands wouldn't stop shaking. Grace forced herself to concentrate. She thought about the men and women who had fought with Philippe in the Resistance. They had faced perilous situations over and over again. She had just this one task to complete.

Grace undid the lock. She flipped open one of the bike's panniers and threw in the contents of the bucket before hoisting herself onto the powerful machine. She revved the engine, pulled away from the kerb. As she roared down the street, she felt her nerves subside. Her sole remaining fear was that she would not reach David Bruce in time.

Grace accelerated hard as she drove into avenue d'Iéna, then came to an abrupt stop in front of the ambassador's grand residence. She hurled herself off the bike, pushed it against a wall and ran to the front door, where a massively built US marine blocked her way.

'I have to see Ambassador Bruce.'

'Sorry, ma'am, no one gets in without the proper authority.'

'Don't worry, I have it right here.' She plunged her hand inside her overalls' single side pocket only to find it empty. She groaned. The rush of wind during her reckless motorcycle ride must have blown the desperately needed credential away. 'I'm sorry, it's gone,' she said. 'But you must understand. I have a top-secret, urgent message for the ambassador. It's a matter of life and death!'

The marine began to laugh. 'Pardon me, ma'am, but from the look of you I'd say you're most likely in charge of a broom, not top-secret material. I guess this must be a fourteenth of July joke, sort of like our April Fools' Day.'

He was still chuckling as the front door swung open. When two officials wearing pinstripe suits strolled out, Grace saw her chance. She sprinted inside, with the now furious guard in close pursuit.

'Stop! Stop!' he called, hurling himself in her direction. Grace was no match for the enormous man. He clamped one hand on her arm and blew a whistle with the other.

While Grace struggled to free herself, she saw several hard-faced men wearing dark suits rapidly approaching. Boiling with frustration, she could see no hope of escape when, from the corner of her eye, she caught a glimpse of a tall elegant woman with hooded eyes.

'Mrs Bruce!' she cried.

For a moment, the woman paused, before an escort began hurrying her towards the front door.

'These agents are going to question you,' the marine growled at Grace.

'No bloody way!' she exploded.

Mirage-like, Mrs Bruce's face appeared before her eyes. 'Please, gentlemen, you can release this woman. I know her,' she said, turning towards Grace. 'Miss Dubois, I didn't recognise you at first in that … what is it, fancy dress? But when I heard you call out — well, I couldn't mistake the accent. What on earth is going on?'

Grace quickly explained the problem.

'My God!' Mrs Bruce's eyes filled with horror. 'David has already left.'

'He's gone?'

'Why yes, some time ago. He should be with the French President on the podium at the Place de la Concorde by now. In fact, the parade will reach them in less than twenty minutes. I was planning to join David later, when the aerobatic display began.'

'Look, I have a motorbike outside,' Grace said. 'I'd better leave straight away.'

Mrs Bruce shook her head. 'You don't have a hope of making it through. There's security everywhere and they'll never let you past the barricades. If only we could make contact!'

'What's the problem?'

'The entire phone exchange has gone down. Since the war, it's been held together by Scotch tape and blind faith. Hell, why did it have to happen today of all days?'

'Sounds more like sabotage to me,' Grace said with alarm, acutely aware that as every minute passed, the threat to the ambassador's life grew closer. 'There must be something I can do!'

'I have a diplomatic pass with photo ID that will at least get me through any checkpoints,' said Mrs Bruce. 'But with the traffic the way it is, if we go in an embassy car, it will take far too long.'

'Looks like the bike is the best bet, after all,' Grace said.

Mrs Bruce nodded. 'As long as I come with you.'

CHAPTER THIRTY-NINE

Grace regarded the ambassadress with a dubious expression. She was patriotically attired in the colours of France — which also happened to be those of the United States — in a blue Dior dress with a wide white collar and double cuffs. On her head was a pert blue pillbox hat trimmed with long scarlet ribbons.

'Don't worry about the outfit,' Mrs Bruce said. 'I know how to handle myself on a motorbike.'

Grace grinned. 'In that case, let's go!'

Like a film running at double speed, everything that happened next seemed to acquire a faster pace. Grace bolted out of the residence and flung herself on the motorcycle. After a quick word with her protesting security detail, Mrs Bruce followed close behind. The two women sped out of avenue d'Iéna; Grace gripped the handlebars as Mrs Bruce clutched Grace, her hat's scarlet ribbons streaming behind her.

Pont de l'Alma, Pont des Invalides ... one ornate bridge after another flew by. As Grace raced down avenue de New York, the sparkling river, the poplar trees and the urns filled with bright summer flowers became one indistinguishable blaze.

Thanks to Mrs Bruce's official pass, the pair were waved through each new section of road — Cours Albert 1er, then Cours de la Reine. But as they passed the steel and glass domes of the elaborate Grand Palais, Grace felt a tap on her shoulder.

'Only twelve minutes left!' Mrs Bruce yelled.

They were approaching another road block. There was no time to stop. Ignoring the gesticulating officials, Grace swerved to the right. The bike began to lose traction: if she didn't act quickly, they were sure to crash. She leant over to one side and Mrs Bruce did the same. Instead of slowing down, Grace opened the throttle and accelerated hard. There was the smell of rubber burning. The two women braced themselves. They felt the bike shudder, heard its tyres scream. Then, a split-second later, it was upright and they were speeding forward again, albeit chased by a car filled with several angry policemen.

'Are you okay, Mrs Bruce?' Grace yelled over her shoulder.

'Yes, but I think under the circumstances you should call me Evangeline.'

'Where'd you learn about bikes?'

'London, in the war. I was with the OSS.'

'What?' Grace shouted.

'It's got a new name — CIA.'

As they skidded to a stop beside l'Orangerie, Evangeline leapt off and grasped Grace's hand. 'It's over to you now,' she said. 'I'll explain everything to those *gendarmes*.'

Grace marvelled at her aplomb.

'I'm going to stand with David,' she added, quickly righting her hat. 'He won't change his plans, but at least I'll be by his side should the worst happen.'

'It won't — not if I can help it!' Grace cried. She'd caught sight of Philippe and was already sprinting towards him. 'Quick!' she called out. 'The assassin is on top of the Jeu de Paume.'

'What? How?'

'See the scaffolding? It was put there this morning. Four men were detailed to carry out the construction. Only three came back down. The fourth is our man. When the band starts playing the French national anthem, he will shoot the ambassador.'

'Right. I'm going up.'

'Not without me you're not.'

'Stay on the ground. It's far too dangerous!' Philippe hooked his foot into the first metal bar and began pulling himself up.

Grace had no intention of leaving Philippe to face the killer alone.

By the time she reached the second storey, Grace was wet with perspiration. She chanced a look down. It was a mistake. Her legs gave way and she was suspended in midair, hanging on to the scaffolding by her slippery, sweat-soaked hands alone. With the plastic over-shoes still on her feet, it was impossible to regain a foothold.

Time stopped. The noise from the square below disappeared. *I am alone and with child*, Grace thought. It would be so easy to let go.

Then she felt her right foot hit a crossbar, gain traction. Her left foot was next. Swallowing back the bile in her mouth, Grace hauled herself up the remaining few metres and staggered onto the Jeu de Paume's roof.

She almost fell over a huge, bald man lying collapsed on his side. Blood trickled from one nostril and there were angry marks around his neck. Philippe stood over him, breathing hard, a garrotte dangling from one hand.

'Thank God,' Grace said. 'You're safe, and so is Ambassador Bruce.'

There was a sound, the scrape of a boot against metal. Grace spun around. Another man, his faced masked by a black balaclava, leapt onto the roof. He shoved her out of the way before picking up the first man's rifle and launching himself at Philippe.

Grace was stunned. There'd been nothing in the instructions about a second assassin. Worst of all, now he was armed. The only reason he hadn't used the rifle on Philippe straightaway, she thought feverishly, must be because the parade hadn't reached the square yet. He needed the sound of drums and trumpets to muffle the gunfire.

She watched in shock as both men traded brutal blows. Every muscle in her body was rigid. She couldn't move, couldn't scream. It was as if she were inhabiting the worst kind of dream. Philippe tore an arm free and swung at the man; the rifle gleamed in the sunlight as it spiralled out of his hand. Grace heard it fall with a clatter, but the killer didn't stop. He knocked Philippe to the ground. His hands went around Philippe's throat. He was choking him to death.

A surge of adrenaline snapped Grace into action. She leapt for the gun, grabbing it just as the Republican Guard rode into the Place de la Concorde. In the distance, there was a blur of black and gold uniforms, of red plumes flying from gleaming centurions' helmets. A military band struck up 'La Marseillaise'; the rousing anthem boomed from a score of loudspeakers.

Grace saw not a man, but a deadly snake poised to strike. She pressed the trigger.

Racing over to the fallen would-be assassin, Grace tore the balaclava from his head.

'You!' she screamed.

A pair of glittering black orbs half opened. 'Next time you try to outwit a man like me, make sure you don't leave a stray diamond behind.'

Of course. A stone must have come loose when her earring was dislodged. Orly would have seen it, sparkling beacon-like on the floor right in front of the safe, and become suspicious.

'You're a dead woman,' he hissed, as his eyes shut.

Grace felt a familiar touch on her cheek. 'Darling,' Philippe said tensely, 'thank God you're all right.'

She was numb, couldn't look away from the dark stain spreading across Orly's chest.

'Listen carefully,' Philippe was saying, slowly and clearly, though she could barely take his words in. 'Your job is done. Right now, we have to get down as fast as we can.' He scanned the rooftop with his one good eye — the other was swollen almost shut. 'It's not safe here. There could be other gunmen nearby. You go first, I'll follow.'

Once they reached the ground, Philippe held a trembling Grace tightly in his arms. 'It's over, all over, my darling,' he murmured. 'You have been exceptional. And, by the way, thank you.' He gave her the special smile she adored. 'It is not every day that a beautiful, clever woman — let alone a Paris model — saves one's life.'

A group of *gendarmes* ran towards them. Grace watched as Philippe shouted a few words and pointed at the Jeu de Paume's roof. Then he turned back to her.

'Philippe, I'm sorry about the other night —' Grace began.

'What, with Gaston? It's me who should be apologising. You must have been terrified, thinking about what you would have to do the next day. My God, I can't believe what I put you through.' He looked into her eyes. 'Let me take off that awful headscarf so I can kiss you.'

Despite all she'd been through, the feeling of his mouth on hers made Grace flicker with desire. Grace realised then with a dreadful certainty that, although their love was forbidden, she would never be free of her yearning for him. Despite the action she knew she must take, his would always be the only caress that she craved.

Philippe broke away. There were at least a dozen dark-suited men approaching. 'CIA,' he said. 'I must speak to these agents urgently and you have to go somewhere safe.' He grasped her by the arm. 'Do not under any circumstances return to the rue Dauphine or, for that matter, go near any of the Saint-Germain cafés. You heard what Orly said. Already his men must be out on the streets hunting for you.'

He nodded in the direction of a couple of policemen. 'I'll arrange for one of those officers to take you to Brigitte's place on the Île Saint-Louis. Stay there for the rest of the day. Later on, he can bring you to the bistro we went to in Belleville. Remember the one?'

Grace nodded.

'No one will think to look for you there. Meet me at five o'clock. I should have something worked out by then.'

There was no chance to say more. Ambassador Bruce was coming towards them.

He shook Philippe by the hand. 'Thank you, young man. That was a mighty courageous thing you and this young lady did,' he said. 'And I hear Mrs Bruce had some involvement? Well, you have probably realised by now that my wife is a law unto herself.' The ambassador's light-hearted remark could not mask the worry etched on his patrician face.

'I'm returning to the embassy immediately,' he said. 'A full security alert has been issued, and now that communications have been at least partially restored, we're putting together a team to deal with the situation. Captain Boyer, I'm afraid that means you will have to say goodbye to your friend. You're needed for an urgent debriefing.'

'Yes, sir.' Philippe turned back to Grace. 'It seems I have to leave you,' he said. Then he whispered, *'Je t'aime,'* before adding, *'à tout à l'heure.'*

'Until later,' Grace said, echoing his words. With tears streaming from her eyes, she watched him walk away.

CHAPTER FORTY

The fatigue enveloping Grace was so profound that merely lifting one leaden foot after another required the greatest determination.

'Oh, no!' Brigitte cried when she answered the faint knock on her door and saw Grace, pale-faced and swaying. 'Come, lean on me. Marie-Hélène is here too; we will both take care of you.'

Kicking off her plastic shoe covers, Grace limped across the room and collapsed onto a sofa.

'Thank you. I … I'm exhuausted,' she murmured.

'My dear, whatever have you been up to? And where did those bizarre clothes came from?' Marie-Hélène wrinkled her *retroussé* nose as she eyed Grace's overalls. 'Never mind. When you're feeling better, I'm sure Brigitte will lend you something to put on.'

'Why, of course, and in the meantime I will bring you tea,' Brigitte said. 'I know that is what the English drink at times like this, so I imagine it is the same for Australians. I hope you like Darjeeling.' She busied herself in the kitchen, then reappeared carrying a tray bearing a worn silver teapot, three pretty cups and a plate of golden madeleines.

'I just received a garbled message from Philippe.' Brigitte

frowned as she set the tray down. 'I gather there's been some kind of political incident and — oh, Grace, he said your life was in danger! He didn't mention your condition, so I assume you haven't told him. Otherwise, I'm sure he would never have involved you in this dreadful business.'

Marie-Hélène tapped one high-heeled shoe on the parquetry floor. 'Before we get onto whatever has been going on, I'd like to know precisely why you haven't informed Philippe that you are pregnant with his child.'

Grace blinked away the tears gathering in the corners of her eyes. Now that her part in the perilous events of the past twenty-four hours was over, every anguished thought she had previously suppressed threatened to engulf her. Yet somehow she would have to remain strong.

'Because the baby might not be his,' she said.

Seeing Brigitte's and Marie-Hélène's shocked expressions, Grace realised she could no longer avoid divulging at least one of her secrets — her loyal friends were due some sort of explanation. Summoning what little energy she had, she began slowly, determined not to become emotional as she revealed that a large part of the reason she had travelled to Paris was to escape her marriage.

Ignoring both Marie-Hélène's raised eyebrows and Brigitte's rapid intake of breath, she went on to relate the torrid events that had taken place on the night of Jack's visit.

'And then he ... he called me a trollop and stormed out,' she said, unable to prevent a quaver from entering her voice.

'The man must be a monster!' Brigitte cried.

'I don't know.' Grace steadied herself. 'It's true, there wasn't much of a choice, but all the same, I did agree. And it was hardly the first time we'd had sex when I didn't want to — I always thought it was what wives were expected to do.'

She picked up her teacup. 'Foolishly, I believed that making love one last time would solve a big problem. Now I can see that all I did was make everything a hundred times worse.'

'*Oh là là!*' Marie-Hélène said. 'I had a feeling you had left somebody behind, but I must admit I wasn't expecting this. Never did I imagine, when I first set eyes on our new Australian model with her black curls and lovely face, that her life would turn out to be so, shall I say, complex.'

Grace silently reflected that her friends had no idea just how complicated her life really was. And that was the way it must stay. She felt dismayed as she imagined their horrified reaction should she ever reveal that, to her shame, Philippe had turned out to be her own brother.

'Darling, you have to be sensible about this,' Marie-Hélène insisted. 'Simply tell Philippe you are having his baby. This is not the time to worry about a single episode of love-making or whatever it was. I advise you to forget it ever happened.'

'Even if I could,' Grace said, 'it would make no difference.'

Gripping her cup, she tried to steel herself. Grace was aware that the words she would say next were necessary, even though they were certain to destroy any chance of a future life with the man she loved so passionately.

'Philippe is an attractive man,' she remarked, striving to appear blasé. 'I suppose that's the reason I allowed myself to become swept away. But after what he's put me through during the past few days, I have decided he comes with far too many risks attached.

'What *has* Philippe mixed you up in?' Brigitte asked. 'All I know is it sounded serious.'

'That's an understatement. I'm not sure if you're aware of what his job really is, but let's just say he involved me in a terrifying life and death situation.'

'I can't believe it!' Marie-Hélène exclaimed.

'There's more. As a result, Minister Giscard Orly — a man who's turned out to be as savage as he is corrupt — ordered a gang of murderous thugs to scour Paris for me. So, yes, my life is in danger — and all because of Philippe.'

Grace forced down a mouthful of tea. 'As a matter of fact,' she said, 'I would appreciate it if you would inform Philippe Boyer that I never want to see him again. And, for that matter, I don't wish to hear a word about him — ever.'

There. She'd made herself plain. Now there was no hope.

For a few minutes, nobody spoke. The apartment sat high above the Quai d'Anjou, a narrow, cobblestoned street situated so close to the Seine that the three friends could hear the sound the water made as it slapped against the prows of the passing *bateaux mouches*.

Brigitte broke the silence. 'There is only one thing for it. You must leave Paris,' she said.

'I know you mean well,' Grace replied dejectedly, 'but that's easier said than done. Where would I go? How would I live?'

'It may not be as difficult as you think. My late father can help you.'

'That makes no sense.' Grace propped herself up on a faded pink cushion.

'I seem to recall you once saying that we all have our secrets.' Brigitte took a breath. 'Well, here is mine. My papa was the Count d'Andoise.'

Marie-Hélène whistled.

Grace looked blankly at her friend.

'Tomorrow you must go to Charincourt; it was his château. You will be safe there. Orly's men will never find you.'

Fear clutched at Grace's throat. She hoped Brigitte was right.

'It's near an abbey and I know the abbess well.' Brigitte paused. 'How would you feel,' she said gently, 'if after the baby is born, she were to find a family who would take in the child?'

Marie-Hélène did not wait for Grace to respond. 'If you won't terminate your pregnancy or tell Philippe he is the father, well then, that is exactly what you must do,' she said. 'Brigitte has come up with the perfect solution for each of your problems. And I will deal with Madame Raymonde. I'll say there has been a crisis in Australia, that your mother has fallen ill and you must depart immediately. Don't worry, I will tell your nice little concierge the same thing. Later, you can write to Madame Raymonde and let her know the crisis has passed. As she is well aware that the clients positively fight among themselves to purchase whatever they see on your elegant back, an invitation to return to the *maison* is certain to follow.'

With a blithe expression, Marie-Hélène added, 'In less than a year, all will be just as it was. This political situation will be sorted out, you will have recovered your usual *joie de vivre* and nobody will suspect a thing.'

Grace's shoulders drooped. Alfred was dead. Philippe was lost to her forever; so, it seemed, were Reuben and Olive, and soon her poor tainted child would be as well. Despite Marie-Hélène's optimistic prediction, she doubted she would ever be happy again.

The three young women were finishing a simple supper of *oeuf mayonnaise* when Marie-Hélène announced she was departing for Grace's attic.

'Don't be concerned, it won't take more than five minutes to collect everything that's needed,' she assured her apprehensive companions. 'And anyway,' she tossed her luxuriant titian hair, 'nobody is looking for a redhead — at least, no one from Orly's gang.'

With that she picked up her Louis Vuitton handbag and whirled out of the door.

Grace turned to Brigitte. 'You've both been so kind. Is there anything I can do for you?'

'Just come back from Charincourt cheerful and well, with all your troubles behind you.'

'But surely there must be something else?'

'You could always help me clean up.'

Grace was drying a dish when she noticed it bore the faint imprint of an elaborate family crest. 'Now I understand why you were so reticent about your father's identity,' she said. 'It's because you didn't want to, well, at home we'd say "show off".'

To Grace's surprise, Brigitte's refined face was contorted by a sudden scowl. She spun around, her hands still soapy and wet.

'It's not modesty that prevents me from claiming his name,' she declared. 'It's shame! My father was one of France's most notorious Nazi collaborators.'

'Brigitte, I'm sorry. I had no idea.'

'Well, unfortunately for me, his reputation in this country is all too well known.' She reached for a cloth and began to dry her hands. 'The racial prejudice of the noble line of Andoise males is a long and horrible family tradition. I'm sorry, I promise that after tonight I'll never mention Philippe again, but right now it's the only way I can explain. Remember I told you that he and I were related?'

'Vaguely.' Grace felt her pulse quicken.

'Philippe's grandfather, Emmanuel, was my grandfather's younger brother. When Emmanuel married a woman of the Jewish faith, Grandpapa accused him of defiling the precious Andoise blood line. He refused to allow him or any of his descendants to come near the château again. That is why I didn't see Philippe, and I still know almost nothing about his parents. I heard that his mother was killed during the war, but that's about all.'

Brigitte walked out of the kitchen. 'Let's sit down. There is something else I'd like to share with you.'

With her muscles aching, Grace sank gratefully onto the soft, cotton-covered sofa. 'Tell me about it,' she said.

As Brigitte spoke she twisted a strand of fair hair in her long fingers. 'My own mother died in a hunting accident when I was very young,' she began. 'Even after that, Papa made it quite clear that I wasn't worth bothering about. You see, he always felt I should have been a boy, someone to inherit his title. As you can imagine, I never felt close to him, and anyway, I hated his ideas. As soon as I could, I left Charincourt and went to live in Paris. Grandpapa was already dead; I swore I would never set foot in the château until my father was in his grave too.'

'What happened to him?'

'He was executed by some local people just as the war ended. It was brutal, rough justice, but the truth is, I found it impossible to grieve for him.'

'You poor darling, what a lot you have been through.' Grace struggled to reconcile the traumatic events her friend spoke of with the serene image the ethereal blonde maintained; Brigitte was usually so unruffled, so self-contained.

'It could have been worse,' Brigitte said. 'Do you remember what I told you about the head-shaving? A few days after I returned to the château, a group of angry local citizens arrived. They wanted to inflict the same punishment on me.'

'No! Why?' That Brigitte might have been subjected to the same retribution she'd described while they drank chablis in the rue du Faubourg Saint-Honoré had never crossed Grace's mind. Recoiling, she pictured Brigitte in the hands of a crazed mob, their faces distorted by hatred, as a razor was produced and her lovely hair was brutally shaved off.

'It was a strange, fearful time — there was a sort of madness in the air. I heard later that some of the villagers who denounced me the loudest were themselves guilty of helping the Germans — I suppose they were keen to cover up their complicity. But then, I hadn't been around for years; perhaps everyone simply assumed that, just like my father, I too was a collaborator. Because of his Resistance sources, Philippe knew it wasn't true. When he heard about what had happened to Papa, he grew concerned about the cousin he had never seen. Thank God, he turned up at Charincourt just in time.' Brigitte shuddered. 'Furious people were holding me down. They had already begun to tear at my clothes — I was terrified. Philippe confronted them, demanding they see reason. I will never forget what he said: "Why should the sins of the father be visited on the head of his innocent child?"'

Brigitte's words resounded in Grace's mind. She knew how it felt to be an innocent child, to be trapped in a world of deceit not of her making. But by giving up her baby, wouldn't she be committing the same crime?

For her friend's sake, she tried to smile. 'Thank you. I'm very grateful for your offer to stay at the château, and yes, you're right about the outcome of this pregnancy. I will take your advice.'

Grace felt as if she had no more ability to change the course of her life than a leaf being carried along by the swirling current outside.

Philippe rode his motorcycle slowly down Belleville's grimy streets. The usual rotting garbage lay in the gutters where it was fought over by starving cats. But where were the inhabitants? As a rule, the French made the most of their national holiday, yet the quarter was unnaturally quiet. Perhaps the residents of this decaying corner of Paris felt they had little to celebrate.

Pulling up at the kerb, he chained his bike to a lamppost, crossed the cobblestoned lane and walked into the café.

'An Armagnac,' Philippe said to the barman. 'Better leave the bottle on the table.' He noticed they were the only people in the room. 'Where is everyone?' he asked, but received only a shrug in return.

Philippe couldn't say why exactly, but something in the atmosphere caused a spike of alarm in his belly. Telling himself it was a reaction to the events of the day — he often felt a charged hyper-vigilance after a dangerous mission — he sat down and dealt with his anxiety in the best way he knew, by downing a glass of the fiery brandy.

Still, he couldn't relax. He glanced at his watch. It was well past five o'clock, yet Grace hadn't appeared. His eye was throbbing; he decided another glass of Armagnac might help. He did his best to peer through the window. Where was she? What could have caused the delay?

He tapped his fingers on the table as a variety of dire scenarios played out in his mind. Grace had been waylaid. Kidnapped. Assaulted, attacked or worse. No. He forced himself to dismiss his fears. Other than the policeman he'd assigned to her, there wasn't a soul who knew where she'd been staying today, or that she was coming here to Belleville.

What, then? As he filled his glass once more Philippe was struck by a sickening thought. Maybe nothing untoward had occurred. She had simply come to the decision that she didn't want to see him again. Groaning, Philippe put his head in his hands. After what he'd put her through, she was probably arranging a passage back to Australia. Perhaps she had even decided to return to her husband.

He wouldn't blame her. Grace had prevented the deaths of Ambassador Bruce, himself, and who knew how many others. Yet, at the same time, she may well have killed a man. It didn't matter how treacherous Orly had been, this was likely to create unimaginable trauma. And that is what he, Philippe Boyer, had done to her.

Grace wasn't a professional agent, let alone a trained soldier or a resistance fighter; she'd never known war. It was only natural she'd want to escape the horror of it all, to return to the safety of life with her husband in her own sprawling country on the other side of the globe.

What folly, he thought bitterly. *In my arrogance, I was bent on a mission to save the world, but who could tell what lay ahead?* There were no guarantees. The one certainty seemed to be that he had driven away the woman of his dreams, the only woman he would ever love.

Over an hour had passed. Philippe paid his bill, then rose unsteadily to his feet. He had to face facts; Grace wasn't coming. Either something grievous had happened to her, or she'd made up her mind to leave him. Either way, the situation was urgent. He had to find her.

With his heart pounding and his eye on fire, Philippe charged out of the café. He tried to avoid the rank pools of stagnant water on the ground, to ignore the sulphurous smell.

He had just reached his bike when the shot rang out. As he staggered, then fell, only the savage alley cats heard him cry, 'Grace!'

BOOK THREE

La Femme

The Woman

CHAPTER FORTY-ONE

Loire Valley, 15 July 1949

Grace stared out the window of the rocking carriage. As the train gathered speed, billowing white clouds flew past, then vanished. She was fleeing Paris.

Sitting huddled in a corner, Grace bitterly recalled the boundless optimism, the sheer self-belief she'd had when she'd arrived in the City of Light. She had thought she could conquer a new world, be reunited with a loving father, that a golden future lay stretched out before her. Since those innocent days, her hopes had proven to be as insubstantial as the clouds outside. One by one, each precious dream had been torn away. Worst of all, she'd fallen in love with an extraordinary man and now she couldn't even allow herself to see him. Philippe probably hated her, anyway, for the way she'd left him so brutally. At the very least, he would despise her for lacking the courage to face him and explain her decision.

Grace told herself she'd been nothing but a naive fool: a girl from the bush, out of her depth, beset with delusions. How the hell had she imagined she could escape her past, let alone her own limitations?

That she was now rattling through the lush countryside in the very same region where the Tatin sisters had prevailed over what they had thought an irreversible disaster, was a cruel irony. So much for Mademoiselle Elise's inspirational stories. For, hard as she tried, Grace could not see how she could produce something splendid from her ruin. It would take more than ingenuity, or determination, or even luck. It would require a miracle.

From a distance, Charincourt appeared to Grace like a shimmering castle that belonged, not in this troubled world, but in the pages of a fairy tale. With its clusters of turrets, slender towers and silvery spires, it might have been the setting for an improbable fable.

Yet as the fanciful citadel grew nearer, Grace's eyes widened with alarm. Its creamy limestone walls were infested with knotted spools of ivy, elaborate chimneypieces were shattered, windows smashed, and several of the statues of *chevaliers* that had previously stood guard atop the parapet now rested like fallen warriors on the unkempt ground. It was as if a malevolent spirit had laid waste to all that had once been noble and grand.

Hunched on the seat of the old-fashioned pony trap she'd travelled in from the nearby town of Orléans, Grace tried not to show her dismay. However, by the time Claude Devreaux, the aged driver, brought the trap to a halt in front of the derelict structure, her eyes brimmed with tears.

'I know what you're thinking,' Claude said in a kindly tone as he put down the reins. 'The old place is a sorry sight.'

Grace remained seated. She was in no hurry to enter the deserted château where, at least until her baby was born, she was sentenced to live a desolate life.

Claude climbed down from the trap, slowly straightened up, then held out a gnarled brown hand to steady Grace as she stepped onto the ground.

'Charincourt was at its best when Mademoiselle Brigitte's mother was still alive. In those days, there wasn't so much as a stray leaf on the driveway,' Claude said wistfully. 'And you should have seen her rose garden. Those overgrown bushes at the front are all that's left.'

'Where do you and Madame Devreaux live?' Grace asked hopefully.

'In the gatehouse. Perhaps you noticed the cottage when we passed through the big stone posts covered with moss?' Claude inclined his grey head in the direction of Charincourt. 'Never mind,' he said. 'You'll be all right. Marie and I have sorted out what used to be the housekeeper's rooms. They're around the back. Come on, I'll show them to you.'

Grace reluctantly followed Claude as he hobbled along a pathway that led to the rear of the château. Just as he'd said, there was a sizeable, largely wild vegetable garden, although it did appear that one corner had benefited from the elderly caretaker's attention. Grace smelt the aroma of freshly turned earth as she walked beside rows of thriving tomato vines, beans and courgettes. There was even a flourishing strawberry patch.

'Here we are,' Claude said, letting Grace into a cool, stone-paved hallway. 'Just go through that door on the left.'

Grace did as he said, then came to a sudden halt. 'This is not what I expected!'

The housekeeper's quarters consisted of a bright, cheerful sitting room — Grace noticed someone had placed a blue jug filled with vivid red poppies on a table under its bay window — and an adjoining bedroom of about the same size. Further exploration revealed there was a lavatory down the hall and, in the next room, a huge ceramic bath with gleaming taps. On the other side of the corridor was a butler's pantry with a larder, sink, a small stove and shelves for a few plates and glasses. A closed door was at the end of the hallway.

'It's all clean and fresh,' Claude said. 'Marie's washed everything; she's only just rehung those red and white checked curtains. We've left bread and milk in the pantry, and there's a bit of cheese and some newly laid eggs as well. Now, what else? Oh, yes, you can help yourself to anything growing in the garden. I can recommend the tomatoes — this year's crop is the best I've had. And there are some fine peaches and cherries still on the trees.'

For the first time in days, Grace felt her spirits rise. Touched by the old man's thoughtfulness, she said, 'Thank you, you've been very kind. Would you like to rest for a minute?'

Claude nodded. 'I don't mind admitting, lately I do find myself getting tired.'

After settling himself in one of a pair of generous blue armchairs, he confided, 'The housekeeper left only a year ago — she was the last person to actually live in Charincourt. All Marie and I had to do was give her rooms a good airing and a going over with the mop and duster. As for the rest of the place, well, as you've seen from the outside, it's in quite a state.'

'Why *is* that? What on earth happened?'

Claude scratched his head. 'It's hard to believe, I know, but the count thought Adolf Hitler was a kind of messiah. When the war ended, some of the local people took their revenge on him. Then they set about wrecking Charincourt.'

'What a dreadful time that must have been. All the same,' Grace said, 'I'm looking forward to exploring the rest of the château.'

'Oh, you mustn't do that,' Claude warned. 'There's broken bits of furniture and what have you everywhere, and the structure is far from sound. That's why, other than these few rooms, it's all locked up — I wouldn't like to see anyone have an accident.'

'Who owns Charincourt now? Brigitte said she wasn't sure.'

'The family's lawyers up in Paris pay me my wages, but the inheritance itself seems to have become a bit of a mystery.' Claude hauled himself to his feet. 'I'd best stop running on and let you settle in.'

The little bay mare tossed her head and whinnied when she saw Claude approaching. He withdrew a withered apple from his pocket, saying, 'If you give this to Jezebel, you'll make a friend for life.'

While Grace fed the pony, Claude added, 'Now, before I forget, I left the keys on the table by the window and' — with an effort, he swung Grace's suitcase down — 'you'll be wanting this. Can I carry it in for you?'

'Thanks, but I'm sure I can manage.'

'Well then, Marie and I are not far away. If you need anything, just knock on our door. Tomorrow you can explore the village; it's called Sainte Jeanne, after the abbey.'

'Brigitte mentioned the abbey to me.'

Claude nodded. 'She made a point of saying that I was to introduce you to Mother Francis Xavier as soon as possible.'

He hoisted himself into the trap, took the reins in his weathered hands and set off down the driveway.

CHAPTER FORTY-TWO

Sainte Jeanne, 16 July 1949

'That is a very sad, tragic story,' the abbess remarked, coolly observing the nervous young woman who sat opposite.

Grace said nothing, merely continued to twist the newly acquired silver ring that encircled the third finger of her left hand.

'But it *is* a story, isn't it?'

Grace shifted uncomfortably in her straight-backed chair.

'During the past decade I have seen many women with the same expression you have on your face,' the abbess said in a gentler tone. 'But let me assure you, within these walls, there is no place for shame. The world has known too much suffering, and far too many members of our sex have endured desperate circumstances not of their making. In any case, it is not for those on this earth to pass judgement. The sisters and I leave that to God.'

The abbess's study was austere. Painted white, it had a dark timber floor and a row of narrow windows that allowed in only slivers of light. On the wall opposite was a wooden crucifix; below that, a striking painting of the abbey's patron saint, Joan of Arc, resplendent in a suit of armour.

Grace studied Mother Francis Xavier's face. Framed by a stiff white wimple, it had an oriental cast. The colour of her complexion was reminiscent of old ivory; she had prominent cheekbones and almost lidless, elongated black eyes.

'Madame Dubois,' the abbess said steadily, 'you have told me you are to have a child in February. You have also said your husband died just a month ago while defusing a bomb. Only one of those statements is true, isn't it?'

Grace's cheeks coloured.

'Perhaps you should start at the beginning,' she said. 'Let us walk together, and you can tell me the real reason you have come to the Abbaye de Sainte Jeanne.'

The two women, one robed in a dove-grey habit, the other wearing a pale blue summer dress, strolled side by side beneath the abbey's stone cloisters. A light rain had begun to fall, filling the courtyard with a fine grey mist.

Grace wondered anxiously how the abbess, a woman who'd spent her life sequestered in holy orders, could possibly react with anything other than horror to what she was about to reveal.

She took a deep breath. 'I may have killed a man,' she said.

Grace could detect neither the shock nor condemnation she had expected. Mother Francis Xavier simply questioned Grace closely about the events that had led to such a violent act, then nodded her head.

'The taking of a life is indeed a serious matter,' she said solemnly, 'although it would seem you had no choice. Remember that five centuries ago, not far from here, the holy Maid of Orléans herself acted similarly when she fought to save France. In recent years many other French women have, by necessity, done the same. I trust this abbey, and the village of Sainte Jeanne, will provide you with sanctuary.'

Grace was flooded with relief. Here, at last, was a person to whom she could unburden herself.

As if she had been able to read Grace's mind, the abbess added, 'Now, tell me about the child you are carrying.'

'You were right,' Grace said, straining to speak above the sound of the downpour. 'The name Madame Dubois, the French husband, the ring — it's all a masquerade. I did marry, in Australia, but now my husband and I are to divorce. Only, he forced me into a single, awful encounter when he came to Paris a couple of months ago. Now I honestly don't know if my child is a product of that wretched experience, or the result of a serious affair with a man I love very much.'

It was raining harder now; sheets of water beat against the convent's medieval walls.

The abbess gave Grace a penetrating look. 'Have you spoken about this to either of the men concerned?'

'No, and I don't intend to — ever.'

'But the man with whom you have had a loving relationship — isn't there a chance he might want to take on the child?'

Grace's mouth became dry. She felt a wave of nausea and swallowed hard. Nothing she had disclosed up to now compared to the sin she was about to reveal. Yet she knew she must continue, that only by confessing would she have any chance of respite from her current torment.

'It is impossible. When we began seeing each other, I had no idea. But recently, something happened that has led me to believe …'

'Yes?' the abbess inquired gently. 'What is it that you believe?'

For the first time, Grace forced herself to share the grave suspicion that haunted her. 'That my lover and I have the same father.'

Grace omitted to say that she still longed for Philippe's presence, that no matter what she now knew, if he came to her, she would sin again.

Mother Francis Xavier's calm gaze didn't alter. Placing her hand on Grace's arm, she said, 'Come, let us retire to the chapel.'

The pair sat in silence on a long wooden pew in front of a simple altar draped with a white linen cloth. Four slender candlesticks and a silver cross were its only ornaments. The rain had stopped abruptly; weak sunshine filtered through the chapel's stained-glass windows, tinting the paved floor with squares of amber, ruby and emerald.

'You carry a very heavy burden,' the abbess said at last. 'I see how much you suffer. In my experience, prayer never fails to provide succour, even when one is enduring the state of extreme distress in which you now find yourself. No matter what the nature of the transgression, even if it be grave indeed, you will always be welcome in this holy place. Yet despite what you may think' — she searched Grace's face with her black eyes — 'I am not so unworldly that I believe prayer alone will resolve your current dilemma. A way forward is needed.'

Falteringly, Grace explained Brigitte's proposal. 'Would you help me?' she asked.

Mother Francis Xavier said nothing. Instead, her hands moved towards her rosary as she knelt before the cross.

Grace waited, struggling to keep her unruly emotions in check. The plan was the only sensible, realistic course, she told herself — it would solve so many problems. And yet something hot and fierce within her heart rebelled. To abandon a child — she knew from her own painful experience just how anguished that child might be one day.

At last, the abbess regained her seat. 'I agree,' she said. 'I will seek out a family who will take the baby. That is the path you must follow.'

Overcome by sadness and regret, Grace bowed her head.

'My dear, it is clear to me this decision has caused you great unhappiness,' the abbess said. 'But, save for divine intervention, I see no alternative.'

CHAPTER FORTY-THREE

August 1949

The landscape was nothing like the one that she knew. Gone were the familiar dusty plains and muted green bush, the golden wattle and scarlet bottlebrush of her homeland. Absent too were the grey wallabies and red kangaroos, the ears of their young and perhaps a soft paw or a nose visible above their mothers' furred pouches. Like the raucous, sulphur-crested cockatoos gliding on air currents, their chalky feathers spread wide, or the kookaburras, eyes masked like bandits, ceasing their laughter in order to seize an unwary reptile, these sights and sounds existed only in Grace's memory.

Now, as one balmy summer day in Sainte Jeanne faded into another, she came to know a very different environment. During long walks Grace picked wild blackberries, savouring the tiny fruits that stained her lips and her fingers with their purple juice; often she'd gather armfuls of poppies, bright blue salvia, yellow foxgloves and star-like daisies. Soon, the vibrant flowers spilled from vases and jars on every spare surface of her two sunny rooms.

To her delight, Grace saw squirrels scamper up oak trees and descend hugging acorns, long-legged plovers strut through the grass, and wood pigeons take sudden flight, their dusky pink breasts catching the light. Sometimes, in the forest, deer veered so close she might have extended her hand and stroked their smooth hides. Instead, Grace sensed the air shift as they cantered by.

She soon discovered that in this northern realm, twilight lasted significantly longer than in the great southern land of her birth. She grew to treasure the softly lit hours, frequently spent in the company of Claude and Marie. Beneath the spreading branches of the old lime tree that stood behind the gatehouse, time would slip by as the three of them, talking and laughing, played draughts or dominoes.

Sometimes Monsieur Huppert, Sainte Jeanne's sole schoolmaster and part-time mayor, would find himself in the mood for chess, although as the man was not to be rushed when pondering either his opening gambits or subsequent strategies, the *denouement* would, as a rule, require a long wait.

During these companionable evenings, pyramids of local cheese and wood-fired bread, peaches and pears and slices of Anjou plum pie were eagerly consumed, washed down with sparkling spring water for Grace and, for the others, chilled carafes of Sancerre's justly famous white wine.

She had been briefly alarmed when, on one rare overcast day, she'd caught sight of two suspicious-looking men in dark suits prowling around the château's grounds. Her heart had thumped wildly as she took to her heels, attempting to dodge between trees and stay in the shadows as she ran for her life to the safety of Claude's cottage. But when she'd arrived, distraught and out of breath, he'd explained that the men were merely notaries who had been sent by the law firm that represented the late count's interests.

'Don't worry — they're not after you,' Claude had said reassuringly. 'Remember I mentioned that the estate had never been settled? There are legal matters that need sorting out and they can't locate Brigitte's cousin Philippe. It seems they've sent off letters to various places, but there's been no response.

'Apparently, they heard a rumour about someone living in the château. I told them Captain Boyer wasn't here, but they insisted on seeing for themselves,' he'd complained.

If only Philippe *were* here, Grace had thought. The one piece of good news was, at least for now, she had nothing to fear from Orly or his men. As to what her future might hold, lulled by the comfort derived from simple pleasures, surrounded by friendship and bucolic tranquillity, it was easy for Grace to imagine that time itself had been suspended.

September

She pulled back her hair, now grown long and unruly, pushed a wide-brimmed straw hat onto her head and tied its red ribbons under her chin. Humming happily, Grace set off as she did every morning to work beside Claude in the now much-expanded vegetable garden. As she applied herself to weeding and watering and the removal of yellow caterpillars, Grace realised how nurtured she'd been by her life on the land in Australia. With the sun warming her back and the feel of damp soil on her fingers, it was good to recapture the sense of wellbeing that tending the earth had brought her.

'*Vraiment*, I think you have *la main verte*,' Claude declared. He was peering inside a basket brimming with the runner beans she'd just finished picking.

'A green hand? That's so funny! In English we say a green thumb.'

'Ah, the English — they have no generosity of feeling. Why stop at the thumb?' Claude grumbled. 'You are a much better gardener than that!'

'Well, if that's the case, I think I'll tackle those roses at the front of the château,' Grace said. 'I helped my mother with her rose garden often enough. Let's see what I can achieve at Charincourt.'

'Do you write to your mother?' Claude asked, tilting his head.

'We've had a falling out.'

The old man regarded Grace with his rheumy eyes. 'Even so, send her a letter. You only have one mother, you know.'

A letter. At first she'd been too angry. Then she'd decided she would respond if Olive made contact, but no word from her had ever arrived. And now — how could she write to her mother, with all that had happened? What would she say? She'd be too ashamed. Better to wait; she did so much waiting these days.

As summer cooled and became autumn, her body swelled. Grace saw the trees turning scarlet and tangerine, watched as the papery beech leaves were whirled by the wind into golden drifts. At night, alone in her silent room, without so much as a rustle of grass or the coo of a wood pigeon to distract her, she'd marvel at the sensation of butterfly wings fluttering deep inside her.

Those were the moments when she missed Philippe most.

Soon it was too cold to spend evenings outside. Instead, Grace sat by her pine-scented fire after a day spent helping Marie make jam and bottle late-season apricots and peaches. It was the good-natured Marie, with her silvery hair wound on top of her head and her cheeks flushed pink by the heat of the oven, who taught Grace to cook local specialities such as delicious pork rillettes, fragrant coq-au-vin and a few favourite recipes from her native Normandy.

'Delicious! I couldn't do better myself.' Marie's highest accolade was proclaimed on a cool November day she'd deemed ideal for Grace to perfect the golden shortbread known throughout France as *sablé*.

On an impulse, Grace decided to present Mother Francis Xavier with the biscuits; she had the feeling the abbess rarely permitted herself a treat.

'The ones on the left are flavoured with lemon, in the middle they're almond, and those others I made with orange zest.' Grace smiled.

The abbess placed a single lemon biscuit beside her glass of mint tea. 'You continue to be well?' she asked.

'Very well,' Grace replied.

'You have been happy enough here, I think, safely tucked away in the château. But your stay in Charincourt will soon come to an end,' the older woman reminded her. 'After the birth of the infant, you must return to the world. You should know that I have made contact with a suitable family. They have two children of their own but are very happy to take in another.'

Her words shook Grace out of her complacency. It was true, she had been wandering about as if her dreamy life in the glorious countryside would go on and on. It would have been perfect, if only she could stop hoping that one day

Philippe would stride into the château, clasp her in his arms and declare that neither the law of God nor man could stop them from being together.

She had no wish to contemplate the birth of her baby — the time to do so would arrive quickly enough. Determined to change the subject, she cast her eyes about the room until they came to rest on the picture of Joan of Arc.

'I see you are looking at our patron saint,' the abbess said. 'The painting is a good enough copy, but it doesn't compare with the original.'

'What do you mean by that?' Grace asked, intrigued.

'Many years ago the abbey was blessed with the gift of a masterpiece by the great seventeenth-century Dutch artist Rembrandt van Rijn,' Mother Francis Xavier said. 'But as you might know, during the war the Nazis looted every treasure they could find.'

'You're saying they stole the abbey's Rembrandt? I heard a little about their enthusiasm for art — other people's, that is — when I visited the Jeu de Paume. Is that where the painting was taken?'

'I don't think so. There was a rumour that it was sent to a warehouse in Paris, apparently intended for the Führer's personal collection, but' — the abbess shrugged — 'nobody really knows what became of it. The image you see on our wall is but a reminder of what we have lost.'

'The original must be worth a great deal,' Grace said.

The abbess regarded Grace with her lidless eyes. 'Sainte Jeanne is priceless,' she replied.

CHAPTER FORTY-FOUR

November 1949

Grace lowered herself onto a rusty wrought-iron bench that sat in the thriving rose garden she'd worked so hard to bring back to life. She was proud of her efforts, but what would happen to it when she left? Would this scented haven revert to the tangled thicket of thorns she'd found on her arrival?

What a ridiculous question! She shook her head. *Why on earth am I preoccupied with roses when I should be worrying about myself?*

Grace jumped to her feet. Brandishing her scissors, she began snipping the stems of the full-blown red blooms, before tossing them into a wicker basket. Perhaps Marie-Hélène's optimism had been misplaced — Madame Raymonde might not take her back. Then what would she do?

Grace paused as, one by one, she imagined the faces of her friends from the House of Dior: Madame Carré and Tutu; Victoire, Corinne and the other mannequins. It seemed so long since she'd seen any of them.

Then a calamitous thought struck. *Le patron* might already have his eye on a new *jeune fille*. He could be in his studio right now, discussing this beauty's merits with Madame

Raymonde. If a permanent appointment was made, there'd be no chance for her to return.

Ferdinand would know, she thought. Oh, if only she were still his confidante!

It was all too depressing. Grace returned to the wrought-iron bench and sat, balancing the basket on her knee. Although Brigitte and Marie-Hélène had visited, even they had seemed unusually subdued. Afterwards, she'd felt more dispirited than ever.

Brigitte's attempt to talk about Philippe hadn't helped. 'Please don't,' Grace had warned. 'Remember what I said in Paris, about the way he placed me in such danger? That was unforgivable. In fact, as far as I know, my life is still at risk.'

'All the same, there is something I need to tell you —'

'Honestly,' Grace replied, 'I don't want to hear his name, let alone learn what he's been up to. What with this pregnancy I'm … well, I'm already overwhelmed.' She knew if she listened to another word about Philippe she would be likely to dissolve into tears, abandon all restraint and beg to see him.

'But it's very important,' her friend insisted.

Grace felt stricken. Why was Brigitte, of all people, pressing her at a time like this? 'I'm sorry,' she said. 'I couldn't bear it.'

And there the subject had been left. Grace didn't reveal that, try as she might, she could not extinguish her desperate longing. Nor did she confess that, each morning, she caught herself hoping this would be the day when Philippe would come to her.

Yes, he'd been told that Grace never wanted to see him again. But she knew Philippe too well, his fierce determination. If he had a genuine desire to find her, nothing Brigitte or anyone else said would stop him. His continuing absence surely proved, in the bluntest way possible, that despite his former declarations of love, in reality she meant little to him. People spoke all the time about having a broken heart, but she had never reckoned on the all-consuming physicality of the pain. It was an ache that never ended.

The noise made by the clattering trap as it trundled down the driveway disturbed Grace's melancholy reflections. She looked up, amazed to see who it was in the smart grey suit and hat sitting next to Claude. Her basket of roses went flying as she ran forward to greet the unexpected visitor.

'Ferdinand!' she cried.

'The very same,' he replied, stepping down from the trap before embracing her warmly.

'I was only just thinking about you and now here you are — I seem to have conjured you up!' Grace said.

'Apparently so. As it happens,' Ferdinand added while fastidiously brushing dust from his trousers, 'I felt an irresistible urge to once more share coffee and conversation with my favourite *petite Australienne*. Of course, I'm not used to having to travel quite this far in order to do so.'

He stood back, nodding his head in approval. 'You look wonderful, my dear, in your sunhat with the ribbons and your pink shift. And I see,' he said drily as he gestured towards the towering château, 'you have found a nice little place to hide yourself away.'

'But what are you doing here?' Grace asked.

'First, I will help you collect all those pretty roses I have just observed sailing through the air. After that, I would like to sit somewhere comfortable with a pleasant drink in my hand and then — why, then I will tell you everything.'

Grace turned around, her hands on her hips and a smile on her lips. 'Right. The flowers are in water, you're sitting down and I've poured you a glass of wine — although there's coffee, too, if you'd like it. Now, you must reveal all!'

Ferdinand raised his eyebrows. 'What can I say? Other than that last week, the Duchess of Windsor left the atelier in a huff.'

'But surely there was something Madame Beguin or Madame Luling could do?'

'Apparently not. She wouldn't be stopped. And she's not the only one of the clients who's unhappy,' Ferdinand continued. 'So far, I believe there have been complaints from' — he ticked the names off on his fingers — 'the Countess de Ribes, Rita Hayworth and even the delightful Mrs Churchill.'

Grace was shocked. 'But whatever has happened? What do they say?'

Ferdinand gave a theatrical sigh. 'Well, that's just it: always the same thing. They ask, "Where is that beautiful model with the lovely dark hair and emerald eyes?" It seems our fine ladies cannot imagine themselves in a gown or a dress, or even a suit unless this particular mannequin inhabits the garments first. They claim only she gives them animation, brings them to life, if you will. There is nothing else for it. As soon as you can' — he glanced at Grace's belly before looking tactfully away — 'you must return in order to rescue the House of Christian Dior!'

Grace burst out laughing. 'Really, Ferdinand, you are impossible. What you have just said cannot be true.'

'On the contrary,' Ferdinand protested with a flamboyant flutter of his hand. 'I might have exaggerated just a little, but let me assure you, the atelier is not at all the same without you.'

'Believe me, I'd give anything to go back to the *maison* when my life settles down.' Grace sighed. 'But how did you know I was here at Charincourt?'

'Your friend Ferdinand knows more than you think,' he said with an inscrutable expression.

'So I don't have to explain anything to you?'

'Not if you don't want to. Perhaps you would prefer me to pass on the latest gossip from Paris?'

'Yes, please.'

There followed a pleasant hour during which Ferdinand told of the Parisians' view of Philip of Greece — 'handsome as a God is the collective opinion' — who was about to be joined in Malta by Britain's Princess Elizabeth, before traversing the state of Picasso's liaison with Françoise Gilot — 'nobody knows how she puts up with his dalliances'.

Next, Ferdinand expounded on the continuing social triumphs of Evangeline Bruce. 'She's reputed to host her soirées at the American Embassy with just as much charm as she rejects would-be lovers,' he said, before concluding with a description of the notorious affair between Pamela Churchill and the handsome young Fiat automobile heir, Gianni Agnelli. 'I know for a fact he takes care of all madame's accounts, including those very substantial bills from our very own *maison*,' he confided with an arch expression.

Ferdinand's droll remarks provided just the diversion Grace needed. For a short time, at least, she forgot her troubles, but when it came time to say goodbye, she frowned anxiously.

'Do you really think the *maison* will give me back my job?' she asked.

'They would be foolish not to,' Ferdinand said brightly as he climbed into Claude's waiting trap.

Grace was grateful for his reassurance. However, as she watched his elegant form disappear into the distance, she realised that her loyal friend, who knew all there was to know about life in the Dior atelier, had avoided giving her an answer.

CHAPTER FORTY-FIVE

December 1949

While new life grew within Grace, each day stronger and more vigorous, the surrounding landscape became increasingly barren. With the exception of the conifers' defiant needles, the trees were stripped bare, their exposed limbs clawing at the pale sky in a menacing fashion.

By Christmas Eve the weather had turned very cold. Grace usually loved this time of the year, yet now she struggled to join in the merriment. Although she tried to smile during the aromatic dinner of roast goose and chestnuts she shared with Claude and Marie, it was not without effort. Afterwards, during midnight mass in Sainte Jeanne's freezing chapel, she found it impossible either to keep her mind on the service or to stop shivering.

The nuns' songs of praise for the Christ child receded as Grace thought longingly of Christmases spent at home during days of scorching heat. She missed the bunches of flowering red gum on the gaily decorated table, the ridiculously hot, heavy meal that always finished with a chilled, passionfruit-topped pavlova, the blessedly cool swim in the dam that would follow a doze on the veranda. She missed Alfred. And she missed her mother.

February 1950

Snow began falling.

'What a glorious sight!' Grace called out to Claude. As she gazed at the sparkling landscape, the low mood that had clung to her during the past weeks drifted away.

Claude paused as he unloaded a bundle of firewood from the back of the trap. 'That snow is too heavy for my liking.' He frowned. 'If it keeps coming down like this the roads will be closed. I've cleared the path for you,' he added, 'though I doubt it will stay like that for long.' The pony snorted, creating a plume of steam. 'If you ask me, it's a good day to keep inside — even Jezebel agrees.'

Bundled up in a heavy brown woollen overcoat she'd discovered at the bottom of the former housekeeper's wardrobe, Grace waited until the trap had rattled away before she began walking around to the front of the château. Regardless of Claude's advice, she wanted to see how Charincourt looked in the snow.

After plodding for only a few metres, she felt one of her boots begin to slide on an unexpected stretch of ice. She cried out and had a vision of herself flying through the air but, by planting the other boot firmly down on a patch of more stable ground, she managed at the last minute to right herself.

I should probably be more careful, Grace thought, but she couldn't help smiling. Something about this new white world made her excited rather than fearful.

'What a sight,' she murmured as she reached the driveway.

With a thick layer of glistening snow on the roof, the parapet, the deep reveals of the windows and the great front door's threshold, with its turrets and silver spires shimmering in the winter sunshine, Charincourt was no longer a ruin but an enchanted castle of light.

After a week, Grace changed her mind.

'This is unbearable!' she declared, pacing restlessly up and down the paved floor. For several days now, fresh snowfalls had made it impossible for her to leave her two lonely rooms.

She tapped her fingers impatiently against the bay window. The frost prevented her from even glimpsing the outside world; the icy glass had become a mirror. *I'm trapped*, she thought. *Rapunzel was better off than I am.*

What could she *do*? She couldn't settle down to answering Charlotte's latest letter, nor to drawing or reading in front of the fire. The thought of cooking was unappealing. Grace sank into one of the armchairs and rested her head in her hands.

Enforced confinement had given her a great deal of time to think. Without either company or distraction, she could not avoid returning to the painful conclusion she had reached. She'd acted in a manner as impulsive as it was foolish, not just once, but over and over again.

Why hadn't she given Olive a chance to explain her past? Instead, she'd been hot-tempered and quick to judge. Then, when she'd seen Reuben at La Voiture Folle, the shock had been so great she had fled from the club. What was even worse, afterwards she'd lacked the courage to question Philippe about his father. If only she had, she might have uncovered the vital missing piece of the puzzle that had caused her so much grief. She loved Philippe more than ever. Yet now, because of her actions, the riddle of how her life and his intersected would never be solved.

Grace groaned. *Each time I had the chance to learn the secrets of my past, I ran away. I squandered every opportunity to discover what really happened.*

She'd made assumptions, guessed at the truth — but what if she'd been wrong? Now it was too late to do a thing about any of it; she had no choice but to live with the grim consequences of the rash decisions she had made.

Grace left her armchair and walked back to the window, but still she could see nothing other than her own reflection. She turned sideways, tracing the outline of her great swollen belly with one hand. Suddenly, she felt tears prick her eyes. She had tried not to become attached to the babe, told herself that to develop affection would only make their inevitable parting more painful.

She had not been successful. Nor could she quell her fears. As birth became imminent, her anguish increased. Would the child bear the mark of her parents' sin? Lately, Grace's nights had been plagued by terrible dreams. Her baby born dead. Or alive, but of monstrous appearance. Now, with nothing to do but wait, she thought only of what would become of the mite.

In an effort to rid herself of these desperate thoughts, Grace gazed around the room — there had to be something that would provide diversion. Her eyes came to rest on the shiny circle of keys Claude had given to her when she'd first arrived at Charincourt. She picked up the brass ring, then examined each key in turn. There was one she had never used. Small and silver, it gleamed invitingly. Her mind turned to the door at the end of the stone-paved hall. Perhaps that was what it was for?

Claude had warned her not to go off exploring. Grace put the keys back where she'd found them.

Although … surely a peek inside wouldn't hurt? *I'll just see if it fits in the lock*, she decided.

The sliver of metal turned smoothly, yet the door itself remained stubbornly shut. Having rattled the handle to no avail, Grace pushed against the door with her shoulder. It sprang open so abruptly she would have fallen to the ground if she hadn't grasped the corner of a handsome brass-inlaid cabinet.

She gasped. The room was enormous, with high moulded ceilings, the delicately carved wood panelling known as *boiserie* on the walls and fine parquetry on the floor. Yet so much else had been ruined. The glass in one of the huge mirrors was shattered, some of the beautiful antique furniture was damaged and almost all the gold brocade seat covers were badly torn. Several windows had been broken, letting in a draft so icy that each time she exhaled the air turned white and vaporous. Still, a fine tapestry depicting nymphs and a shepherd, as well as a set of portraits and several landscapes, seemed largely undamaged, if only it were possible to see them properly beneath their shroud of cobwebs.

Grace sneezed — dust lay everywhere. It clung to the folds of the pale green taffeta curtains that rustled gently in the chill breeze, hung in strands from the crystal chandeliers that dangled tipsily above her, and coated the limestone mantelpieces.

As she wandered across the deserted room, picking her way through the debris, Grace tried to imagine what it would look like if she could wave a magic wand. With the furniture mended, the shattered glass replaced and everything given a thorough spring cleaning, it would be magnificent. All that was required was the means, the will — and love. *Love transforms everything*, she thought forlornly.

One by one, she pulled out the drawers of a handsome marquetry chest, although all she discovered was a pile of mildewed linen and some cracked gold-edged porcelain. She was examining a plate when, from across the room, she heard a muffled sound. It seemed to be coming from a large, rickety armoire of surprisingly poor quality.

Her curiosity piqued, Grace drew closer. There was a gap where the armoire's two ill-fitting doors should have met — just a single rusted lock held them in place. Grace was attempting to prise the doors apart when, suddenly, the lock broke and they sprang open. She peered into the dark interior, then jerked back with a scream. A pair of monstrous, ruby-eyed rats, which had been gnawing on piles of old newspapers, were glaring at her. Horrified, Grace backed away.

She then found that she'd stumbled into a soaring entrance that boasted a grand marble staircase with a black wrought-iron balustrade and, high above it, a painted ceiling depicting a heavenly scene. Though sorely tempted to explore the upper floors — for dear Claude had clearly overestimated the château's danger — Grace walked only to the landing at the top and no further. Congratulating herself on her willpower, she turned around. *I'll go back to my room and do something useful*, she vowed, recalling her unwritten letter.

As she descended the sweeping staircase her mind wandered back to the dazzling entrance she and Philippe had made at Count de Beaumont's glamorous ball, the way his guests had applauded as the two of them entered the salon in their dramatic costumes. She could almost hear the orchestra's romantic music wafting towards her, feel Philippe's intense presence by her side. How carefree, how blissfully happy she had been. Now it seemed more like a dream.

With her thoughts on that thrilling night, Grace trod heavily upon the next step. She cried out as a sharp piece of marble sheared away. Grace lost her footing. She flung her arms out wide, scrabbling frantically for the wrought-iron balustrade, only for the tips of her fingers to glide past its smooth rail. She felt herself falling, plunging through space.

CHAPTER FORTY-SIX

It was so very pleasant to be lying on the big rock next to the creek and the gum trees. Just for a moment she'd felt alone — even a little frightened. But now that her father was near, Grace knew she would be all right.

At first she'd been sure she had imagined his voice. Sometimes, when a southerly blew through the silver-grey leaves of the eucalypts, they made a fluttering, ghostly sound. She wondered if the murmur she heard was really this unearthly noise, carried to her ears by a willy-willy's gusty spin.

Grace felt a chill spiral of air pass over her face. *Open your eyes*, her father's voice seemed to whisper. *It's not your time yet.*

Her eyelids quivered. She looked about. The creek, the rock and the trees had disappeared. Instead, Grace saw cherubs frolicking on fleecy clouds hovering overhead. Where *was* she?

With a jolt, it came to her. She'd fallen from the stairs onto the château's parquetry floor. Rubbing a tender lump on the side of her skull, she attempted to stand. Then she felt a wave of pain.

'Damn!' Grace exclaimed, kneading the base of her spine. She must have injured her back as well as her head when she fell. But what if she'd hurt her baby too? She needed help urgently, yet not a soul knew of her predicament and she'd freeze — or worse — if she couldn't reach her room. Cautiously, she crept on her hands and knees over to the balustrade and hauled herself to her feet.

'Thank God,' she muttered. Now, if she could just take the first step ...

It wasn't possible. The jabbing back spasm had returned, much stronger this time, as if a blade was twisting deep inside. That was when she knew she'd been mistaken. The excruciating pains were not the result of her fall. She was in labour.

Grace clenched her jaw. She would not panic. *If I have to give birth to this child alone, and in the condition I'm in, then I damn well will*, she told herself.

Half staggering, half crawling, she slowly made her way out of the hall, back across the cavernous reception room and through the door that led to the paved corridor. Finally, she reached her bedroom, exhausted and in pain, yet with an unexpected sense of profound exhilaration.

Grace had been in labour for hours when she saw a blurred face at the window. She felt weak and feverish, had endured her agony for so long she couldn't tell whether she was hallucinating. One minute it was there, the next it was gone. Grace screamed with terror. The face belonged to a man sent by Orly to kill her. They had found her at last, just when she was utterly defenceless.

No. Grace was overwhelmed by joy and relief. Finally, when she needed him most, Philippe had come.

Again, she was wrong. It was Claude who stomped into the sitting room, a sprinkling of snow lying white on his shoulders.

'When you didn't answer my knock I used my spare key. I hope that was all —' Claude broke off, as he stared through the open door of the bedroom at Grace, white-faced and writhing. 'Do not worry!' he shouted. 'My wife will attend you.'

Marie arrived just in time. Not more than fifteen minutes after she entered the room, Grace gave birth to a tiny daughter.

'What will you call her?' Marie asked as Grace cradled her child.

'Serena,' Grace murmured. 'I pray that her life will be blessed with more serenity than mine.'

The abbess was among Grace's first visitors.

'I am glad your child has been safely delivered,' she said evenly, 'especially after your lucky escape. It is fortunate that you are so tenacious.'

Grace looked away, towards the bleached world outside. She dreaded hearing what Mother Francis Xavier would say next.

'But you do understand,' the abbess continued, her face an ivory oval against the white of her wimple, 'that the arrangements we discussed are in place.'

Grace didn't answer.

'Remember when we first spoke about relinquishing the baby, in the chapel on that grey rainy day? At the time, it occurred to me that once you held your child in your arms, your decision would require great courage,' she said gently. 'Now, for Serena's sake, are you still prepared to make that sacrifice?'

She laid her hand on Grace's. 'I wish circumstances were different, but there is also a family to consider and they are waiting to welcome a new baby into their home. It isn't fair to you, to Serena or to them to draw this process out — it can only cause pain for everyone.'

'How long do I have?' Grace whispered, her cheeks wet with desolate tears.

'One week,' the abbess said.

The plan had sounded so prudent, so rational, so *acceptable* when Brigitte had first suggested her baby be adopted. But with Serena in her arms, gazing up at her from beneath her faintly etched brows and pursing her tiny pink mouth, Grace knew she could not let her go. She loved the child, in her breath and her blood and her bones.

Yet it was impossible to stay in the château forever, and Alfred's small legacy had all but run out. Alone and penniless, how could she care for Serena, let alone protect her from the shame of having an unknown father who might be her own mother's brother?

Then it hit her; the realisation that there was, in fact, a way to keep her baby. When she'd discovered she was pregnant she had sworn that, no matter what, she wouldn't go back to her husband. But that was before she'd given birth to this wondrous tiny being. Despite everything that had happened between them, if she told Jack that Serena was his, the result of their final tryst, he would take her back, she was certain of it. But could she bear to return to Merindah and to a relationship that had been irredeemably poisoned? Her throat constricted as she considered the prospect of being bound forever to a man who had chosen to exercise his power over her in the most unspeakable way. Grace let out a strangled moan. In her desperation, she'd actually been contemplating trapping Serena in exactly the same deceitful situation as the one in which Olive had placed her. She would be allowing her child to think one man was her father, when all the time it was very likely someone else. *At least,* Grace thought bitterly, *Olive knew the identity of my true father. I don't even have that certainty.*

As she suckled Serena, Grace felt fresh tears spill onto her cheeks. The abbess had been right. There was only one alternative.

Grace didn't want to open her eyes. If she did, she would be forced to acknowledge that the day — this awful day — had begun.

As if sensing an impending catastrophe, Serena emitted a piteous wail. Grace rose from her bed. She picked up her baby then lifted the lid of the little music box, that long-ago present from Reuben. Grace hoped that the last time her daughter gazed up at her she would not see a face marked by misery. Yet, try as she might, as the ballerina twirled in endless circles and the tinkling tune played on and on, she could not stop her tears from falling.

She changed Serena and dressed her, then held her close. The past week's rising temperature meant a thaw had set in; melting snow dripped past the window in silvery streams.

'Look outside, can you see?' Grace said to her child. 'Soon it will be spring.'

She told Serena she would love her forever, kissed her tender neck and her cheeks, soft as petals, but knew she couldn't put the moment off any longer.

Grace wrapped her daughter in the rose-pink shawl she had found in the mysterious polished box. Then, with the babe in her arms and the heaviest of hearts, she trudged grimly through the mud and the slush to the Abbaye de Sainte Jeanne.

CHAPTER FORTY-SEVEN

Grace stumbled, then stumbled again. She was so blinded by tears she could barely manage the short walk back to Charincourt. When she reached the château, she wiped her eyes and looked up blearily at the place where she had sought shelter. Without the camouflage of snow, the château had resumed its desolate appearance. The great decaying structure, dank and broken, emanated malevolence.

Grace fled back to the safety of her solitary rooms. With shaking hands she unlocked the door, blundered inside and threw herself, sobbing, onto the bed. When at last there were no tears left to shed, she lay where she was, unmoving. How could she ever come to terms with what she'd done? Her body ached for the child who had so recently been a part of her. She hadn't been prepared for this terrible raw pain. It was as if something essential — a hand, an arm — had been brutally torn away.

Time passed. It might have been minutes or hours, Grace didn't know. During the past week, each day had been marked by Serena's cycles: when she slept, when she suckled, when she was bathed. Only a week! She would never again smell her sweet scent, feel her tiny fingers curl around her own, stroke her downy head. What she wouldn't give for another day, an hour, a few precious minutes with her beloved child.

The room was too quiet. She'd grown used to Serena's cries, her whimpers and gentle coos. Now there was nothing, only silence. The void was unbearable.

Still, she lay there. The fire was unlit but she barely noticed the cold. Grace wanted only to remember, tried to recall every moment she'd spent with her daughter during the past seven days. Yet already she felt the memories begin to disappear; they were no more tangible than melting snow.

Grace glimpsed a shadow passing the window, then heard a knock at the door. It would be dear Claude again. She did not wish to see a living soul; she only wanted to be left alone with her grief. All the same, it was kind of the elderly caretaker to come and see how she was faring. She forced herself to rise from her bed.

'Bonjour, Claude,' she said dejectedly as she opened the door.

'Bonjour, Grace.'

She gasped, then staggered back into the sitting room before collapsing into one of the armchairs. This phantom was surely another cruel hallucination.

'Philippe,' she managed to whisper. 'Is it really you, or have I lost my mind?'

He was as handsome as ever, his eyes still a vibrant blue, his dark hair brushing his collar. Yet he had two faint lines on either side of his mouth that Grace had never seen before.

'It's me, all right,' he said with an expression of concern. 'I'm so sorry, I know this must be a shock, but I can't tell you how wonderful it is to finally see you.' He looked at her lovingly. 'I came as soon as I could.'

'What are you talking about?' Grace said, faint and confused. 'I've been here in the château for months.' Although she longed for him to hold her in his arms, when he moved towards her she forced herself to look at him coldly.

'You have every right to be angry with me,' Philippe said, obviously dismayed. 'But I can see you're not well, and it's freezing in here. Let me light the fire, or at least bring you something to drink that will warm you up a little.'

'Don't bother,' she replied curtly. 'Just tell me what has brought you to Charincourt.' Philippe's presence was almost more than she could bear, yet her dearest wish was that he would never leave her.

He sat down in the armchair opposite Grace. 'First, I need to tell you what happened on the night of Bastille Day,' he began, 'when the communists discovered I had betrayed them.'

'How did they find out? I thought your cover was completely secure.' Grace drew her brows together.

'Remember when we went to La Voiture Folle and there were all those photographers outside? I was convinced I'd eluded them, but apparently I was wrong.'

Grace's heart skipped a beat. She would never forget the moment she discovered that Reuben and Gaston were one and the same.

'As soon as Orly realised his safe had been opened, he instructed his men to eliminate you. They were provided with a photo from a newspaper gossip column. Unfortunately, when the thugs spotted me in the same picture, they realised I was leading a double life, that we were accomplices.'

'So they began to look for you too.' Grace said.

'Yes. When you didn't turn up in Belleville, I was terrified something awful had happened to you. I was about to jump onto my bike and start searching, but' — his voice faltered — 'that's when they made their move. I was shot.'

'I had no idea!' Grace felt ill. This was the reason why he'd never come to her, and it had been all her fault.

'Grace, you're shivering,' Philippe said, looking worried. 'Do you have any brandy?'

Unable to speak, she pointed to the pantry.

A few minutes later he returned with two glasses. 'Drink this,' he said, 'while I light the fire.'

He handed Grace a glass, then struck a match to some kindling. As the wood began to crackle and flare, she swallowed a mouthful of the burning liquor. 'This attack on you. How bad was it?' she asked anxiously.

'Bad enough. Fortunately, an ambulance arrived quickly — apparently the barman called it — and took me to Emergency. By the time I'd been operated on, word had reached my superiors about what had happened. I was transferred to a secure military hospital where I drifted in and out of consciousness for ages. Ironically, the former Minister of the Interior was one floor below me.'

'Giscard Orly is alive?' Grace grasped her glass so fiercely her knuckles turned white.

'He is. But you have nothing to fear. Together with every one of his foul accomplices, our murderous ex-minister now resides in France's most unpleasant, high-security jail.' Philippe gave a contemptuous laugh. 'I don't think a man like Orly will adjust very well to the rigours of prison life, do you? On the other hand, he will have a very long time to get used to it. Imagine — no women, no fine wine and no gourmet cuisine, just a regime that would challenge a Spartan.'

'That's good to hear.' Grace drank some more brandy. 'Not long ago, I thought his men had found me; I was terrified. Orly is the first truly evil person I think I've ever come across. All the same, I'm relieved I didn't take a life.'

No, she thought, staring miserably into her glass. *I have created a life instead. And what a world of woe I have unleashed by doing so.*

Philippe frowned. 'Something has happened to you since you came to Charincourt, hasn't it?'

She nodded.

'Well, perhaps this should wait until you feel stronger …'

'Philippe, for God's sake, tell me what you're doing here,' Grace pleaded.

'All right. When Brigitte revealed you had no feelings for me, that you didn't ever want to see me again, I felt as if my world had come to an end. But I wasn't surprised.' He groaned. 'I was sure that after everything I had put you through, you must have loathed me — and how could I blame you? I reached the conclusion that you had returned to the safety of your home, and quite likely to the warm embrace of your husband. I convinced myself it would be pointless to look for you.'

Philippe stood abruptly and walked over to the bay window. Turning towards Grace, he said, 'Remember, I was in hospital, ill and confused. Brigitte was the only person in Paris permitted to see me — she was recorded on my service file as next of kin.'

Grace was mortified. Brigitte had begged her to listen to something very important she had to say concerning Philippe, but Grace had rejected her every attempt to do so.

'I asked my cousin if she believed you might ever want to see me again. Brigitte said there was no hope. I tried to forget you, tried to stop loving you — it was impossible.'

The fact that Philippe still cared for her made everything worse; Grace felt as if a shard of glass had pierced her heart.

'Then, one day, Brigitte brought Jacqueline Bouvier with her. She was only allowed to see me because the US Embassy interceded. Things started to change after that.'

'I'm sorry,' Grace said. 'My head is swimming. You're saying that *Jackie* had something to do with you turning up here?'

'She wanted to share a remark her Australian friend had made. I said I didn't wish to hear a word about you — it would hurt too much. But Jackie insisted.' Philippe smiled ruefully. 'Apparently, you told her that if one never took a risk, one would be unlikely to make a mistake; as a result, one's life would be small and very safe. She asked me if this was what I wanted.'

He sat down again and drained his brandy. 'Seeing as I didn't think my life had been small, and it certainly hadn't been safe, I put what she'd said down to the boundless naivety of a rich American girl. Jackie clearly didn't have a clue what I'd been through.' Philippe looked forlornly at Grace. 'It was only some time afterwards that I realised I *was* doing everything in my power to stay safe.'

'I'm so sorry I hurt you,' Grace said in a low voice.

'You were the first person outside my secret world with whom I dropped my guard,' he explained. 'But I am ashamed to say, when you ran from me, when Brigitte delivered your message, I attempted to shut off my feelings behind a set of iron doors.' He ran his fingers through his hair. 'I was a fool.'

'So you decided to find me. I can't believe Brigitte would have revealed where I was.'

'You're right — she refused. But it wasn't hard to work out that if there was a chance you had not returned to Australia, it was likely she had hidden you safely away in Charincourt.'

Philippe paused. 'Believe me, I would risk anything, do anything, to have our life back, exactly as it was before I involved you in that political madness.'

Despairing, Grace clasped her hands together. Her love for Philippe had never diminished; if only it was possible to obliterate the past, if only their story could be rewritten.

'As soon as I was more or less recovered, well, as you can see — here I am, pleading with you to return to me. Only, I must tell you, I am not alone.'

Philippe stepped into the hall. Grace heard a few muffled words being exchanged before, wearing an enormous greatcoat and carrying a battered felt hat in his hands, Reuben Wood strode into the room.

Grace jumped up, her heart beating wildly. 'What are you doing here?'

'I've come to set you straight, Princess,' he said. 'It's something I should have done a long time ago.'

'And that makes it okay for you to turn up, out of the blue?' Grace demanded. She was shaking with anger.

'I'm sorry — '

'*Sorry*? Having stayed away from me all these years, you come waltzing in as if nothing had changed, and on a day that — thanks to you — happens to be the worst of my life. I can't believe you have the hide to show your face.'

'My God, you poor girl. It's all my fault,' Reuben cried. 'You've been living in — you know at fun fairs, where they have a Hall of Mirrors? Everything is distorted, all the bits are in the wrong order. Trust me, nothing is the way you think it is, nothing.'

Grace's rage was replaced by a wave of fatigue. 'I have no idea what you're talking about,' she said, sinking back into her armchair.

Reuben pulled up a seat. 'Identity,' he said, leaning forward. 'Yours, mine, and that of just about everyone who has ever loved you. I'm talking about who we really are.'

Grace couldn't help it. Shocked, overwhelmed and exhausted, she began to cry.

'The only thing I'm certain of is that you are my real father,' she sobbed. 'Olive confessed before I went to Paris. But because you walked away, because of your silence, the most terrible thing has happened. Didn't it ever occur to you that I deserved to know the truth?'

Reuben rubbed his chin. After a moment, he began to speak. 'Every single time I looked at you I wanted to tell you who I was, what you meant to me. Only I couldn't.'

Philippe coughed. 'This is between the two of you. I'm walking over to the village for a coffee but, please, come and fetch me when you're finished.'

Reuben nodded.

'Well?' Arms crossed, Grace looked at her father.

'I'm not asking you to forgive me; I know it's too late for that,' he said. 'But perhaps if I tell you what happened, you might begin to understand how it all went wrong.'

CHAPTER FORTY-EIGHT

Sydney, March 1922

Reuben Wood scuffed the turf beneath his feet as he inhaled the familiar smell of Smith's saleyards, a distinctive combination of horse sweat, manure, waxed leather and fresh hay. At just twenty-four, he was large and well built, with a shock of black hair and brawny hands.

He ambled a little closer to a lively grey colt he'd seen.

'You won't find a finer prospect,' Smith said, running his fingers over the animal's glossy hide.

'Is that a fact,' Reuben responded coolly, pushing his hat to the back of his head.

His friend Alfred Woods was looking for a swift horse of just this colt's type, but Reuben wasn't about to reveal any interest to the vendor. That wasn't how a good deal was done.

Reuben was determined to do his best by Alfred. At first, they'd had a strictly professional association. But, over time, it had become much more than that. Despite Alfred's wealth and education — Reuben had left school at fourteen himself, and never seemed to have much cash — the two men soon discovered they shared a similar outlook on life.

It wasn't only horses they had in common. Each was as much taken with music as the other, especially the classics, and they both agreed there were few poems that captured the great Australian bush better than those penned by Henry Lawson and Banjo Paterson. They also shared a philosophical turn of mind, and were wont to converse well into the night about such matters as the morality of war, and how far a man might go to do what he knew was right.

Reuben looked up, surprised to hear his wife's voice. 'Rae, what on earth are you doing here?' he said.

The pretty young woman ran over to him, kicking up puffs of dust with her feet as she crossed the yard.

'You'll never guess!' she announced, tossing her curls.

'Well, it must be something special, considering I'm busy talking to Mr Smith about this colt of his.' He turned towards the vendor, slightly embarrassed. 'My apologies, I'll just be five minutes. It seems Mrs Wood's got a bee in her bonnet.'

Reuben took Rae to one side. 'What's going on?'

'I'm sorry to break in like this, but I was so excited I just couldn't wait. It's definite. Oh, darling, we're going to have a child.'

Although the bar at the Hotel Australia was crowded, it wasn't difficult for Reuben to pick out Alfred. The man's elegant bearing, his perfectly tailored pin-striped suit and finely wrought features set him apart, even from the well-heeled clientele of this exclusive watering hole.

Reuben elbowed his way towards his mate with a broad smile on his face.

'Hello, my boy, you look as pleased as Punch,' Alfred greeted him. 'You must have bought that colt for a damned good price to be as cheerful as this.'

Reuben took off his shabby hat. 'I reckon I did. But I've even better news than that.'

'Do you now? Happens I've a bit of news myself. What's going on in your neck of the woods?'

'A baby, that's what!' Reuben announced, beaming. 'Rae's due to give birth in early September.'

To Reuben's surprise, Alfred emitted a hearty laugh.

'What's so funny?'

'It looks like our names are not the only way in which we are alike. Olive's pregnant too and —'

'Don't tell me she's due at the same time.'

'You're right! Well, well, this is a fine coincidence.' Alfred clapped his strapping friend on the back. 'Good God, man, if anything calls for a drink, it's this.' Alfred signalled to the barman. 'I'd like two of the best whiskies you have — let's make it doubles.'

'Happy days,' said Reuben when the tumblers of amber spirits appeared.

'I'll drink to that.' With a smile, Alfred touched his glass to Reuben's.

Charincourt, February 1950

As Reuben spoke, the web of lines on his face appeared to deepen. Grace could see how much he'd aged during the past decade.

'Alfred rang me at home in Surry Hills from the women's hospital in Paddington to tell me Olive was in labour. He was thrilled, declared he'd already bought the finest Cuban cigars, ready for us to smoke when the baby arrived. I was pretty excited myself, knowing Rae's time couldn't be far away.'

'I've never heard anything about this before,' Grace said.

'Anyway,' Reuben continued, 'we waited and waited to hear back until eventually, Rae said she couldn't stand it. So I decided we should take a little walk. Mind you, she couldn't go far. 'We went up to the corner shop and bought a copy of *The Sun* newspaper — it's funny, I still remember what was on the front page. It was something about Lloyd George, the British Prime Minister, laying down the law about the Turks and the Greeks all over again. As soon as I opened the door of our cottage I could hear the phone ringing. I sprinted over, but I was too late. Then I recall saying something like, "Not to worry. If that was Alfred, he'll be bursting to tell us the good news. I bet he rings again in a minute."'

Grace stared at Reuben. 'What are you saying? That you calmly sat by, with your pregnant wife at your side, while you waited for news from another man who was just a few miles away about the birth of a child he thought was his — but that you knew was your own? That's one of the most cold-blooded, duplicitous acts I could ever imagine! And to think I was that child.'

'No, Grace.' Reuben's mouth set in a firm line. 'You were not.'

'What on earth are you talking about?'

'Olive delivered her child, but the cord was wrapped tight around its neck,' Reuben said. 'The baby never drew breath.'

CHAPTER FORTY-NINE

Sydney, 31 August 1922

Reuben tried to comfort Rae, to assure her that just because a terrible tragedy had struck poor Alfred and Olive, it didn't mean their baby would suffer the same fate.

'There, there, darling,' he murmured as he lay in bed with her that night, smoothing her curls back from her damp forehead. 'Get some rest. You'll be glad of it once our child is born.'

'I don't know how I'll sleep after hearing something like that,' she said. 'Poor Olive, and Alfred too — it's heartbreaking news.'

Exhausted by worry, she swiftly slipped into a deep slumber. Reuben also slept, until Rae woke him just before midnight. The sheets were wet.

'Dearest,' she said, 'it's time.'

'Time?' Reuben was still half asleep.

'The baby's coming.'

He scrambled out of bed. 'Cripes! Where's your bag?'

Rae pointed to a small leather case sitting in the corner of the room.

'Righto, I'll just get dressed.' Reuben pulled on his clothes while Rae changed into a fresh nightdress, slippers and a dressing gown.

'Here we go,' he said, picking up his wife's bag in one big hand and putting the other around her delicate shoulders. 'Easy does it, darling.'

'I wasn't expecting it to be like this,' she said, grimacing. 'The pains have come on so quickly.'

'Ah, that's because our baby's keen to meet us,' Reuben said with a comforting smile. 'And, just think, it will be on the first day of spring.'

Charincourt, February 1950

Grace watched Reuben closely. Despite the ache in her own heart, she couldn't help feeling for the enormous man who was in such obvious distress. He'd tried to restart his story twice, but had been so overcome by emotion that he'd not been able to continue.

Reuben had the look of a man who was struggling in a perilous sea. 'Princess,' he said, breathing heavily, 'even though this all happened so long ago, it's damned hard to talk about.'

Grace neither encouraged nor discouraged him. She didn't know what to think.

'Rae's labour wasn't long, not like poor Olive's. I'd gone back home, thought playing the piano for a bit would distract me. Sure, I'd told Rae not to be concerned, but the fact is, I was in a hell of a state. All I could think of was, what if something happens to our baby?'

'And was the child all right?'

'I'm not ashamed to say I broke down and cried like a baby myself when I saw the wee thing, I was that relieved,' said Reuben. 'Such a bonny babe, with pink cheeks and whisps of soft dark hair. A beauty, even then. Princess, that baby …' He touched Grace's hand. 'It was you.'

Once more, like an upended jigsaw, Grace felt the pieces of her life fly into wild disarray. 'You mean,' she said slowly, 'all the time I thought that Olive was my mother, it was really Rae?'

'If by mother you mean the woman who gave birth to you — yes,' Reuben said.

'I can't follow any of this,' Grace wailed. 'Are you saying Rae abandoned me?'

Reuben shook his head. 'She would never have done that, not willingly. I knew something was very wrong as soon as I walked into her room. Rae was so pale … The midwife called for the doctor, but even when he arrived, there was nothing that could be done. You see, they couldn't stop the bleeding.'

Reuben continued, his voice trembling. 'At the end, poor Rae was very weak. Her breath was so shallow she could hardly say a word. She motioned for me to come close. I stroked her hair as she whispered, "Do what is best for our precious child." Then your mother died.'

Reuben covered his face with his hands, his shoulders shaking. After several minutes, he mopped his eyes with a handkerchief and said huskily, 'You need to hear the rest. I decided to call you Grace. That was your mother's real name. When she was a little girl she called herself "Rae" — I guess it was easier — and soon everyone else did the same. She was the love of my life, the dearest thing, and still only twenty-two on the day she left me. I was broken-hearted, but at least I had you, my little Grace.'

'Then why not keep me with you?' Grace burst out, although even as she uttered the words she knew condemnation was unwarranted. Her own bitter experience had taught her that sometimes the fates conspired to tear apart parent and child.

'I took you with me from the hospital, only I couldn't face going home again. Everywhere I looked, I knew I'd see reminders of your mother: her apron hanging on the hook next to the stove, her empty shopping basket on the kitchen table. I would've waited to hear her lovely voice singing away over the ironing, her footsteps pattering down the hall. So I checked into a small boarding house, just near Central Station. I don't know what I was thinking, but I soon found out I had no idea how to take care of a baby. There wasn't a crib so I put you in a drawer that I lined with a clean horse blanket. I had a go at feeding you with a little milk and boiled water; I even tried a bit of juice from some meat with an eye dropper, but you, poor wee thing, screamed and screamed. The people in the next room complained. The landlord said we had to leave. You were weak and growing weaker. I was at my wits' end and half mad with grief. But I knew I had to do something quickly or my darling baby girl would die too.

'Then it came to me. There was one person who, despite everything, might be able to help. I wrapped you up in a pink shawl — it was Rae's favourite — and took you to the Hotel Australia.'

CHAPTER FIFTY

Sydney, 2 September 1922

Reuben Wood strode across the shining granite foyer, acutely aware of the disapproving eyes of guests and staff alike. It was only too apparent that the sight of a big, rough-hewn man cradling an inconsolable baby in his arms appalled them.

Mortified, Reuben wondered why he had ever thought it a good idea to bring his baby to this place. And he felt as if each person that he passed — the woman in a green dress and hat who abruptly ceased her conversation with a friend, the frowning concierge, the bellboy with his brass-buttoned livery and embarrassed stare — wondered too. Wishing only for invisibility, he chose not to take the hotel's great central staircase. Instead, he hurried over to the bank of elevators more discreetly located at the rear of the foyer.

Once there, however, Reuben hesitated. He watched, mesmerised, as the translucent skin on the crown of his baby's head quivered with each fluttering beat of her pulse. Perhaps there was still time. Then the sharp clang of the lift doors brought a return to harsh reality. There was no other way.

'My God, who could have imagined such tragedies would befall the two of us?' Alfred groaned with despair as he stood with Reuben at his wife's bedside.

Olive lay still in the darkened room. Her eyes were open, yet it appeared she saw nothing, not the heavy swagged curtains, not the velvet-covered chairs or the tasteful watercolours on the wall — not even her own husband.

'After the baby died, Olive refused point blank to stay in the hospital, but it's been two days now and just look at her,' he said, distraught. 'The doctors say it's the shock, but they don't seem to have any idea what to do about it. She doesn't eat, doesn't sleep. I'm terrified that I'll lose her too.' Alfred rubbed his temples. 'I don't know, perhaps your idea might work. Maybe if she sees little Grace, it will bring her back to us.'

Reuben's baby daughter lay limp in his muscled arms. He bent down and placed her carefully on the quilt next to Olive, then waited. The woman's eyes remained vacant. It was as if Grace didn't exist.

'I'm sorry,' Reuben said. 'I suppose it was worth a try, but Olive seems to be in another world. I'd better take my little one and leave. Somehow, I have to find a way to stop Gracie following her mother to the grave — though Christ only knows how I'll do it.'

As an ashen-faced Reuben picked her up, the baby whimpered.

Very slowly, as if emerging from a trance, Olive turned towards the faint cry. She reached out her arms and took Grace from Reuben. Then, ever so gently, she held the starving baby to her breast and smiled.

It was obvious to Reuben how best to save Grace — and Olive. Yet once more he wavered.

How could I give up my child? Foolish man, he thought. *The question should be, how could you not?* At least this way, he would know she was being cared for by two fine people.

Grace lay peacefully in Olive's arms, her tiny face content. 'Please, Reuben. Leave her with me, I implore you,' she said. 'At least while she's so young. I promise I will treat Grace as my own, devote myself to her. Then, perhaps one day ... well, you might be able to look after her yourself.'

Shocked and grief-stricken, aching for his wife, Reuben tried desperately to reconcile himself to the action he knew he must take.

Finally, he nodded. 'Only, promise me something,' he said. 'Yes?'

'When Grace is old enough, let her return to me. Let me tell her the truth.'

Charincourt, February 1950

'I gave Alfred and Olive the form for your birth certificate. I'd already written your name in, but nothing else. Then I left.'

Grace tried to picture the scene in that hotel room: the traumatised woman; the ailing baby; two men making a decision that would affect the course of each of their lives forever.

'I can understand why you handed me over to Olive, I really can. I think it was a brave, selfless thing to do,' she said. 'But why did you never disclose your true identity? It meant I grew up without knowing who I really was. Did you decide you didn't want to be a father to me after all?' Grace's voice dropped to a whisper. 'Rae only died because of my birth.'

Reuben pushed his hair back from his forehead. It was still thick, although now streaked with grey. 'I didn't blame you, not for a minute. All I wanted was to fulfil Rae's last request: to do what was best for our precious child.

'But I never stopped wishing you could be with me. Once, when you were all staying in Sydney, I even confronted Olive at the hotel.'

'I remember that day.'

'You do? How's that?'

'I overheard you arguing. But I was still a child — I didn't know what it meant.'

Reuben sighed. 'I pleaded with her to give you up, but she wouldn't hear of it. She said I should remember our agreement. You were a twelve-year-old girl — how could a rough type like me take care of you properly? How would I be able to give you the sort of care that only a woman could? I knew she was right. Then, each time I saw you, well, you were blooming. Olive and Alfred loved you dearly and had the means to provide you with every advantage in life. Compared to them, what could I give you? Very little.'

He swallowed. 'I saw you whenever I was able to, but Olive insisted I wasn't to visit Brookfield. She was good about writing me letters, though, letting me know about your progress. I was always so proud of my beautiful daughter, my only child. In the end, I got to thinking, what would she want with a poor specimen like me? It didn't stop me from loving you, Princess. You're an honour to your dear mother's memory.'

Two sets of parents, both friends, both with the same name — save for a single letter. One baby dies at birth, one mother perishes while giving birth. The motherless babe is given to the childless woman. An unknown hand adds an 's' to the child's name and she is born anew, with another mother, another father and a different life.

It was impossible. This was surely a myth, a fable, a fairy tale. Yet, in her heart, Grace knew that every word Reuben had spoken was true.

'My poor mother, to die in such a way.' She shuddered. 'And Olive, who only ever cared for me with love — oh, the things I accused her of!'

Grace gripped the arms of her chair. She could not succumb to her anguish — not now. Nothing could be done to alter the past, but it was just possible that she had a chance to change the future.

'Reuben.' Her voice had a new urgency. 'I have to ask you something of the utmost importance. You just said I was your only child. That doesn't make sense. Philippe told me you were his father.'

'But not his real father.'

'What? What do you mean?' She tried to resist the feeling of hope coursing through her, barely breathed as she waited for the answer.

'Exactly what I said. I'm not his real father. It's a long story, goes right back to the beginning of this last war —'

'I'm sorry, Siddy,' Grace said, jumping up. 'I have to leave right away.'

She grabbed a coat from a hook on the wall and ran to the door. 'Fetch Philippe,' she called over her shoulder. 'I'll explain when I get back.'

'Princess, wait. What's going on?'

'I've made a terrible mistake!'

CHAPTER FIFTY-ONE

Grace flew down the driveway and across the meadow to the Abbaye de Sainte Jeanne. Frantically ringing the bell, she shouted, 'Let me in, please, let me in!'

One of the novices opened the door with a bewildered expression. 'Whatever has happened?' she asked.

Grace burst into the courtyard. 'Please, I implore you. I must see the abbess.'

The novice looked uncertain. 'I don't know —'

'Don't worry, there she is!' Beneath the cloisters, Mother Francis Xavier was shepherding a group of little girls in the direction of the chapel.

'Mother, oh Mother!' Grace sprinted towards her.

The abbess turned around. 'You had best come with me and explain the reason for this disturbance.' Waving to the novice, she said, 'Josephine, could you take charge here? These young ladies are preparing for their first communion.'

Grace spoke in a rush. 'Thank you so much. I'm terribly sorry to cause such a scene, but I need to talk to you urgently. It's about Serena — everything has changed.'

The abbess sat behind her oak desk, looking searchingly at Grace. 'So, after all these years, at last you know who your real parents are. I am sure that is a very great shock. It will take time to adjust. And you tell me that Reuben is not Philippe's father, although as yet you have not received an explanation as to why this is the case.'

Grace heard the click of Mother Xavier's rosary.

'You must leave Serena in our care until the truth is established.'

'But —'

The abbess let her rosary slide through her fingers. 'My dear, I can imagine how painful this is for you, but as you know, my greatest concern is Serena's welfare. I am also mindful that there are two kind-hearted souls who will arrive at the abbey today at five o'clock and be expecting to leave with their new baby daughter.' She clasped her hands together. 'If you are unable to persuade me that Serena is not the product of an incestuous union before that time, then I am deeply sorry, but for the good of all parties, the adoption must proceed.'

Panting and out of breath, Grace found Reuben and Philippe waiting by her door when she returned to the château.

'Good, you're both here,' Grace said, hurrying them inside.

Minutes later, she set down steaming mugs of hot chocolate on her round table. As the three of them took their places, Reuben remarked, 'They're warm-hearted people, the Devreauxs. It was kind of them to put us up for the night.'

'Siddy,' Grace said, leaning forward. 'I'm afraid there's no time to chat. I have to know why you call yourself Gaston, and what exactly your connection to Philippe is.'

Reuben picked up his mug. 'Like I said, it all started at the beginning of the war, during the Germans' advance across the

Ardennes. Our battalion was completely overrun by Panzer tanks. I ran through a forest until I'd almost reached open ground. That was when I found an identity card. It was lying on a bed of fallen leaves as if it had been left there for me.'

Grace began tapping her foot.

'I snatched up the card,' Reuben continued, 'raced like a hare until I found cover, then took a chance on approaching one of the villagers. Luckily for me, he turned out to be a Good Samaritan. He said the card's owner had been shot by the Gestapo. He gave me some old clothes and promised to burn my uniform.'

Reuben drained his hot chocolate. 'I took a closer look at the picture on the card and realised the bloke was around my age and, fortunately for me, he had a mop of black hair. It didn't take me more than a minute to decide my best chance of survival would be to pass myself off as him — Gaston Villeneuve. I smeared his picture with dirt so the features were blurred. I stole his identity.'

'But I don't understand,' Grace broke in. 'What has this got to do with Philippe?'

'Sorry, Princess,' Reuben said. 'I'm getting to that.'

Grace's foot was tapping again; she felt as if the walls of the sitting room were closing in. 'Okay,' she said, rising to her feet. 'But I'm going crazy in here. Let's walk as you talk and please, Siddy — hurry!'

'Have you been to Burgundy?' Reuben asked.

Frowning, Grace shook her head.

They were walking side by side through a grove of birch trees, with Philippe — he'd yet to say anything more than a greeting — following close behind. It was so quiet she could hear the sound of her pulse, thudding in her ears like a drum.

'I was travelling through the region, heading south,' Reuben said. 'When I came across a deserted farmhouse — or at least, I thought it was. There was a half-starved woman inside.'

Behind her, Grace heard a sharp intake of breath.

'Annette was her name,' he continued. 'After I'd convinced her I could be trusted, she told me she and her son had worked for the Resistance in Paris. One day, she'd walked into a trap. Annette ran for her life and, well, with the help of the Resistance along the way, that farmhouse was where she ended up. I'd seen your mother die; here was my chance to save a life. Annette's husband had been shot early on. With a Jewish mother, he didn't stand a chance. Seeing as Annette was so well known to the Nazis, I thought that if I married her, and gave her my name, she'd be safe.'

Reuben paused. 'Names — I never thought about it once, but they can change a lot, can't they?'

'So it seems,' Grace said tensely. 'Please go on.'

'Only a week after our wedding, Annette contracted a fever. There was no medicine, and with her so weak from all she'd been through, she couldn't fight it. I had to stand by and watch another woman pass away,' Reuben said, grim-faced. 'And just like Rae, before Annette died she asked me to do my best for her child. She gave me a secret address and begged me to find her son. "Care for him," she said, "as you cared for me."'

Grace stopped walking abruptly. 'The son, it — '

'Yes, it was me,' Philippe said. He lengthened his stride to draw level with her. 'Gaston — I mean Reuben — became a member of the Resistance, and saved my life more than once. He may be my stepfather, but he is as dear to me as my own *papa*.'

'But I thought that night, in La Voiture Folle, when I saw the man you called your father, I thought we must be brother and sister,' Grace said in a rush.

'God above, it's little wonder you didn't want to see me again.'

Grace felt overcome with relief but at the same time, yet again, furious with herself. If she hadn't been so quick to jump to conclusions, everything might have been different. Perhaps it still could be. They could pick up where they left off, maybe even marry. For a brief moment her spirits skyrocketed before she reminded herself that Philippe still knew nothing about Serena. And time was running out.

He went to put his arm around her, but she shrank away. 'What is it?' he protested.

Reuben looked from one to the other. 'Seems to me you both have a few things to sort out,' he said. 'I'll see if Claude and Marie are about.'

Without waiting for a response, he set off through the trees.

'Philippe,' Grace said, unsteadily, 'It's all been such a shock — I'm not sure I can stand.'

He pointed to a fallen log. 'Let's sit on that.'

Once more he attempted to put his arm around her but again she drew back.

'Of course you're shocked,' he began, 'and I can see why you're angry with me. You think I deliberately led you astray. But Gaston wouldn't speak about his former life. It would have been all too easy to make a passing reference, to slip up and give himself away.'

There was a weary sadness in his voice that made Grace yearn to comfort him, to say whatever was needed to make his pain go away. 'It was only after I left the hospital that

I broke down and confessed to Gaston that I was in love with a glorious green-eyed woman called Grace. When I told him she'd grown up on a huge sheep and wheat farm in Australia, he realised immediately who that woman must — could only — be. Then, for the first time, he revealed his true identity. You have to believe me, when I told you last year that I couldn't find Reuben Wood, I never knowingly deceived you.'

'And I have no intention of deceiving you now,' Grace said.

'What does that mean?'

Secrets and lies; subterfuge and masquerades; on and on for year upon year. They had caused so much grief. No matter the cost, now was the time to tell Philippe the whole truth.

'I have had a child.'

'A child? You mean — I am a father?' His jaw dropped. 'My God, I … I had no idea.' He turned towards Grace. 'Darling, now I understand. You've been worried about how I'd feel — but I couldn't have better news! Tell me, is it a boy or a girl?'

'A girl. Her name's Serena.'

'A baby girl — it's hard to take in,' he said breathlessly.

Philippe punched the air and gave an excited whoop. His euphoria only made Grace feel more wretched.

'I can't believe you did it all alone, darling, with such a terrible thing on your mind. You are even braver than I already thought.' Then he paused, his forehead creasing. 'But I don't understand.' He looked at her intently. 'Where is our baby?'

She dropped her gaze.

'Grace?'

Still she was silent.

'Look, I know you've been through a lot,' he said, 'more than I could ever imagine. But can't you see? This is the perfect time to start again, to put all our problems behind us. They're over.'

'They're not.'

'What are you talking about?'

Grace took a deep breath. 'I don't know if you are Serena's father — or if it's Jack.'

CHAPTER FIFTY-TWO

Philippe gripped her arm. 'I've been trying to work out why each time I try to touch you, you flinch. You can't even look at me, can you?' His eyes blazed. 'And no wonder. What the hell have you been up to?'

His anger was like a blow, a punch to the head that left Grace reeling. She had to force herself to speak. 'You remember that night when you arrived and saw Jack?'

'Yes.' Philippe folded his arms.

'Well, earlier, Jack said he would only sign the divorce papers if I had sex with him. Even though the mere thought made me sick to my stomach, I had no other option, so … I agreed.'

Philippe's face darkened.

'No matter what you imagine, I just wanted Jack to disappear from my life.'

Philippe's silence confirmed Grace's worst fears.

'Don't worry. I've made up my mind,' she said.

'About —'

'About my daughter, Serena.'

'What are you saying?'

'I thought I had no choice but to give her up for adoption. Now I wouldn't dream of it. But just in case you have the wrong idea, I don't want anything from you. Somehow, I'll find a way to take care of her myself.'

Grace glanced at her wristwatch, then sprang to her feet. 'I have to leave now. Please don't follow me.'

She hesitated for only a moment. 'For what it's worth,' she said, unable to stop her voice breaking. 'I love you. You're the only man I have ever loved.' She turned on her heel and began to run.

'Wait, Grace, hear me out,' Philippe yelled as he came after her. Catching her by the shoulders, he spun her around. 'You're such an impetuous woman! I don't care who Serena's father is. If you will marry me, she will be our child and that is all that matters.'

'*Marry* you?'

'If you are free to do so, yes.'

'But I saw the look on your face. You were appalled, furious.'

'That was before I knew about the loathsome position you were put in.'

'I don't want you to marry me out of pity!' Grace cried.

'That's not the case at all!'

They glared at each other.

Grace looked away.

Philippe groaned. 'I've gone about this in completely the wrong way. What I should have begun with, back in the château, is very simple. I love you too. In fact, I adore you, body and soul.' His voice steadied. 'And before you say anything, I want to marry you for an entirely selfish reason. It is because you are simply the strongest, most courageous, most surprising and enchanting person I have ever met, and if you don't marry me, then my life won't be worth living.'

'Well, in that case …' She looked into his remarkable eyes. 'Yes.'

'Yes? You mean that you will?' Philippe grinned. 'Just as I said, impetuous, through and through. And thank God for that.' He pulled Grace towards him, murmuring, 'Darling, you cannot imagine how I have longed for this moment —'

'Philippe, so have I, but there's no time!' she cried, struggling free. 'If we are not at the Abbaye de Sainte Jeanne within the next twenty minutes, I will never see Serena again.'

Once more Grace found herself in Mother Francis Xavier's shadowy study, with the crucifix on the wall and the picture of the Holy Maid gazing down.

'You have both been through much,' the abbess said, looking from Grace to Philippe. 'Some of life's greatest challenges, its most terrible tragedies, have enveloped you. Yet somehow, you have survived and, though cruel circumstances have driven you apart, you have found your way back to each other again. One might say,' she glanced at the painting, 'that it is a miracle. Of course,' she allowed herself a fleeting smile, 'such things have been known to happen in this part of the world from time to time.'

'Does this mean you accept our explanation, that we may take Serena away with us?' Grace asked, yearning to hold her child.

'It does. In fact, I believe I can see Josephine at the door with her now.'

Grace gently took her baby, still swaddled in the pink shawl, from the earnest novice.

Philippe's face lit up. 'Hello, my little angel,' he said softly. 'It's me, your papa.'

Grace felt him place a protective arm around her shoulders, watched as he kissed the top of Serena's downy head. They were three now; a family.

'My children, go with God's blessing,' Mother Francis Xavier said.

There was much excitement when Grace and Philippe announced their good news at the gatehouse.

'A wedding?' Claude exclaimed, grasping Marie and attempting an arthritic jig around the room. 'But how has this all come about?'

'The story is terribly long and complicated.' Grace smiled. 'Let's leave it for another time.'

'In any case, there's more to celebrate,' Reuben declared, looking happier than Grace thought she had ever seen him. 'Don't any of you realise — I'm a grandfather!'

'Well, we must do something to mark the occasion,' an out-of-breath Marie said. She bustled away, returning with a bottle of wine from Sancerre and a chocolate gateau she had fortuitously baked only that afternoon.

By the time toasts had been made and a date for the nuptials discussed, night was drawing in.

'You're tired,' Marie said to Grace. 'I can see shadows under those lovely eyes of yours, and I'm sure you want to take your little one home.'

Grace yawned. 'You're right, it's been a very long day. But first I'd like to clear these things away,' she said, casting a meaningful look in Reuben's direction.

'I'll help,' he replied, following Grace into the kitchen.

'I suppose you're wondering why I didn't come back to Australia, or at least let you know I was alive,' Reuben said, his frame dwarfing the doorway.

Grace nodded. 'It's the only thing left I don't understand.'

'All I can say is that, technically, I was a deserter. I was afraid that if I came home, at best it would be in disgrace, at worst I would be thrown into jail. I was ashamed.'

'But you never tried to make contact,' Grace said sadly. 'What happened, Reuben? All I had was the box Olive finally gave me with the letter from Lieutenant Carruthers, the shawl and the photograph. The woman in the picture — it was my mother, wasn't it?' Thinking of the poor sweet creature who had brought her into the world, Grace felt overcome by grief.

'Yes, that was Rae. It's harder to explain the rest of it. By the end of the war, I'd decided you were well rid of me. What would you want with a criminal? Now I can see I should have taken whatever was coming.' Reuben sat down heavily on a wooden stool, his oversized head slumping forward. 'Princess, I made a terrible mistake.'

'Oh Siddy, you're not the only one to have made a mistake — I've made more than my share,' Grace said, kneeling beside him. She took his large hand in her own. 'This morning you said you knew I couldn't forgive you, but you hoped I would understand. There is nothing to forgive. There never was.'

After Reuben and Grace returned from the kitchen the five of them wished each other a fond good night at the door, hugged and exchanged kisses.

Claude took Grace aside. 'Now is the time,' he said.

'The time for what?'

'To write to your mother. Tell her what's happened.'

CHAPTER FIFTY-THREE

In the morning, Grace tenderly kissed Philippe and Serena before sending them off to meet Reuben at the caretaker's cottage. So much had changed so quickly that she needed solitude in order to gather her scattered thoughts.

Just twenty-four hours earlier, she had believed her life was destined to be as empty as it was desolate. Yet, astonishingly, in the space of one extraordinary day, her treasured daughter, the man she adored and her dear missing father had been returned to her. Now there was just one much-loved individual from whom she was estranged: Olive, the woman who had surmounted her own searing tragedy and, in so doing, become Grace's doting mother.

Taking a seat by the bay window, Grace looked happily at the brilliant yellow daffodils that stood in the blue jug on the table. There was something life-affirming about them, like a handful of golden wheat or a stray patch of the sunlight that dappled Brookfield's creek. Buoyed by these childhood images, she reached for a pen and a piece of notepaper.

Grace expressed her sorrow and regret over what had passed between her and Olive. She provided a brief account of the dramatic events that had transpired since she had arrived in France, revealed she was to marry, and that she had recently given birth. Finally, she wrote:

The fact that you kept the circumstances of my own birth a secret no longer matters — I am sure you had your reasons. What is important now is that you, my dearest mother, know that I feel truly blessed to have received your and Alfred's devoted care all my life.

With fondest love,

Your daughter Grace

PS I have missed hearing from you so much. Please do write, care of Monsieur Claude Devreaux, Charincourt Cottage, Sainte Jeanne, France.

After a month, Grace became anxious. She reminded herself that, even by airmail, it would take more than two weeks for her letter to reach Olive at remote Brookfield station, and at least that amount of time again for a reply to arrive in Sainte Jeanne.

Philippe had already returned to Paris. 'Sadly, I must go back to work, which means I can only stay at Charincourt with you and Serena on Saturdays and Sundays', he'd explained as he held Grace in his arms on the first night in the château. 'As I'm living in one rented room, I have to find somewhere for us to live — that's not so easy these days.'

She'd felt tiny ripples of pleasure as he kissed her neck and her cheeks and her lips. Then he'd added, 'Although one thing is certain, my darling — wherever we end up, I can promise you this time it will not be on the sixth floor.'

Grace was eating a lonely breakfast of crusty bread and hot chocolate when she saw Marie hurry past. 'Good morning, would you like to join me?' she said, opening the door.

'Sorry, I'm in a bit of a rush,' Marie responded. 'It is market day and that special goat's cheese Claude likes always sells out quickly. I really only stopped by to give you this.'

She presented Grace with an envelope. 'Enjoy your day!' Marie called as she hastened away.

Grace thought her heart would burst. At last, here it was: the longed-for letter from her mother. Yet, disappointingly, she saw that the writing on the envelope was not Olive's neat script, but Charlotte's looping hand. She opened it quickly and began to read.

Dear Gracie,

What I have to say will probably shock you, so prepare yourself. Yesterday, I married Jack Osbourne.

There, I knew it would be a surprise! Jack and I have spent a great deal of time together during the past few months, and the friendship we have always shared has deepened. Jack is the kind of man who needs a wife, and now that your marriage has been officially dissolved, we couldn't see the point of waiting.

I know Jack isn't head over heels in love with me — not the way he was with you, anyway — and he's not always the easiest man but, believe it or not, together we make a pretty good team. We like the same way of life and I think we will make a go of it out here at Merindah.

My darling friend, I know this is an unexpected, rather odd situation, but my dearest wish is that my marriage to Jack will not come between you and me.

With much love,

Lottie

The flimsy, pale blue sheet of paper slipped out of her grasp as she stared straight ahead in amazement. Grace shook herself, snatched the letter from the floor and read it again, this time reflecting upon every word.

Jack and Charlotte. Grace had never imagined them together. Yet the more she thought about it, the more obvious the match seemed. As long as Jack kept his drinking under control, she could see they could make each other happy. She hoped with all her heart that, for Lottie's sake, the marriage would be a success.

Grace had swallowed the last of her chocolate-soaked bread when a sudden thought struck her. She'd felt far too humiliated to write to Charlotte and confess that sex had been the price of divorce Jack had demanded from her on the night he came to Paris. 'Thank God for that,' she murmured as she sat staring at the daffodils in the silent room.

The next morning Marie appeared at the door once more. 'I have some time today — we could have that coffee now,' she said, smiling. 'Oh, and I have another letter for you.'

'Would you mind terribly if we postponed?' Grace said, trying to contain her excitement after at last spotting her mother's handwriting on the envelope. 'I've been waiting for this moment for an awfully long time.'

Grace sat curled up in an armchair reading Olive's loving response. She experienced a wave of joy and relief. Now that she, too, was a mother, and having come so close to losing her own baby, she realised the suffering Olive had endured. She could also imagine the pain she had inflicted upon the woman who had looked after her so selflessly. Olive's forgiveness made Grace's heart soar, yet the letter's postscript perplexed her: *I do not understand why you never received my letters,* she wrote. *I posted them all to Paris, care of Christian Dior.*

Here was yet one more puzzling question, although, this time, Grace was certain she knew just the man to provide the answer.

'*Mon dieu*,' Ferdinand said, clapping his head with his hand.

Having first treated herself to an expert manicure and a chic new hat adorned with an oversized black velvet bow, the first place Grace went when she arrived back in Paris was to the atelier to introduce Serena to her friends.

She'd waited until each of Dior's glamorous mannequins, the various mesdames and a long line of other staff members had filed through the *cabine*, clucking and cooing, before asking Ferdinand if he knew anything about some unclaimed correspondence.

'As a matter of fact, I do. I had no idea what to do with all these letters addressed to a Mrs J. Osbourne that arrived every month with the regularity of a Swiss watch.'

'So, what happened?'

'I kept them.' Ferdinand shrugged. 'I decided there must be some connection to the *maison* and that one day, whatever it was would eventually become clear.'

He immediately disappeared, returning a few moments later bearing a bundle of pale grey envelopes tied with satin ribbon. '*Voilà*,' he said with a flourish.

'I'm sorry, darling Ferdinand,' Grace said, 'I don't want to appear rude, but would you mind awfully if I took a peek right away?'

'Be my guest,' he said as he proceeded to tickle a delighted Serena under her dimpled chin.

Grace undid the ribbon, seized the envelope with the earliest date stamp and swiftly tore it open. Tucked behind the letter was a photograph of her mother, taken at a long-ago ball. Although the first page of the letter gave a similar account of events to the one she had already received from Siddy, the second contained an unexpected, poignant revelation.

> *You might think it strange, but from the moment I held you in my arms I was convinced you were a gift from a munificent God, that your presence in my life was a matter of fate. It was with this belief in mind that one night, when you were still just a couple of weeks old, I stole into Alfred's study. I removed your birth certificate from the desk drawer, took up a fountain pen and altered your last name.*
>
> *I told myself that, thanks to Providence, a terrible wrong had been righted, whereas all I had done was make a single small mark on a sheet of paper. After that, it seemed only natural to print Alfred and Olive Woods in the spaces headed Father and Mother. At the time, it felt as if it had been preordained.*

Slowly and carefully, Grace folded the letter. When it came to her own identity — if not her child's — no more mysteries remained.

CHAPTER FIFTY-FOUR

July 1950

Grace flinched. Once more, she stood in the atelier's studio, the recipient of a stabbing pin.

This time, however, the tense discussion taking place between *le patron* and Madame Carré did not concern a sumptuous design for an English princess, a Hollywood film star or even the wife of a South American dictator, but focused solely upon the merits of her own wedding dress. After one final adjustment, Monsieur Dior announced that the gown met with his approval.

Grace thanked him profusely. 'I couldn't be happier, monsieur. The dress is perfect.'

Le patron bowed his head to one side. 'It has been an honour, Mademoiselle Dubois.'

Grace watched on as four white-gloved apprentices carefully lined each of the billowing folds of her dress with clouds of pale grey tissue, before placing the entire confection into an enormous cardboard box with all the respect rightly accorded a masterpiece. Finally, the carton was tied with spools of trailing satin ribbon that had been stamped, over and over, with the most revered name in the world of fashion.

'It's hard to believe,' Grace said to Ferdinand as the great white carton was borne through the atelier, 'that only a year ago I ran away from Paris. I thought I'd never be happy again. And now, it's as if I am living in a fantasy. Everything — well, almost everything — is exactly as I'd most want it to be.'

Just before they reached the door, Ferdinand snapped his fingers at the apprentices. 'I'll look after that,' he said, taking the box from them. 'Haven't you forgotten something?'

The boys scurried away, returning a moment later carrying teetering piles of beautifully wrapped gifts in a variety of shapes and sizes.

Grace raised her eyebrows. 'What's this? Who are they from?'

'I believe some were sent by clients; others were delivered to Dior by your friends and admirers,' Ferdinand replied.

'I'm very touched,' Grace said. 'It is so kind, and completely unexpected. For one thing, how did all these people find out about tomorrow's wedding?'

'Secrets travel fast in Paris.' He laughed. 'Actually, that is not an original *bon mot*. I was quoting Napoleon Bonaparte.'

Their arrival in the avenue Montaigne coincided with the appearance of two chauffeur-driven black Cadillacs, provided courtesy of the American Embassy. At a signal from the doorman, the gifts, followed by the wedding dress, were loaded into the first gleaming car.

'By the way,' Ferdinand said to Grace as he helped her into the second limousine. 'Did you know that Napoleon had a plan to conquer Australia?'

Grace smiled at him through the open window. 'I can't say I did.'

'It is curious,' he said wistfully, 'that such a lovely young Australian came to France and captured our hearts instead.'

The caravan of vehicles and horse-drawn carts made its way down country lanes bordered by orchards and meadows. Some transported chairs, tables and market umbrellas; others brought cutlery and tablecloths; still more hauled wine, boxes of glasses and wooden boards for a dance floor; one delivered a magnificent grand piano. Finally, a large truck drew up at Charincourt laden with cut flowers, crates of fruit and vegetables, seafood and meat, loaves of bread and wheels of cheese.

'You know, darling,' Olive said to Grace as they watched the arrival of this cavalcade. 'I have a confession to make.'

'Really?'

'When Marjorie and I left Australia, I was brimming with confidence. I couldn't imagine anything I'd rather do than oversee arrangements for my daughter's wedding.'

'But that's exactly what I would have expected,' Grace said with affection.

'Yes, only I have to admit, by the time we caught the train from Paris — what with the language issues and not knowing precisely how the French go about their wedding celebrations — I felt quite overwhelmed.'

'That doesn't sound like you, Mum.'

'Oh, I'm back to my usual self. As soon as I met that capable Marie Devreaux, I knew everything would be as right as rain.' Olive turned her head. 'As a matter of fact, here comes Marie now, with Marjorie.' She gave Grace a quick kiss on the cheek. 'Excuse me, darling. I'd better see what's going on.'

Rather like two generals and a loyal lieutenant, the trio surveyed their field of battle.

'Not there!' Olive called out as a man began knocking in tent posts.

'*Ici, ici!*' Marie shouted, waving at a woman who was struggling beneath the weight of myriad peonies.

'Goodness!' Marjorie exclaimed, as one of the truck drivers presented her with both an impertinent wink and a box of fresh snails.

Smiling to herself, Grace left the three comrades-in-arms to direct operations and made her way inside the château. Soon it would be time for her to apply make-up, do her hair and, of course, don the glorious Dior dress. As she walked into the sitting room, she cast a glance of approval at the bridal bouquet of wild grasses, white lilies and pale yellow roses that stood waiting in a vase on the table. Propped up against it was the photograph of herself Olive had sent.

Grace looked lovingly at the picture. *Dear Mum*, she reflected. *Where would I be without you?*

A group of violinists in tailcoats who had been playing a spirited air put their instruments down. Guests stopped chattering. Even Jezebel, tethered to a nearby tree by a garland of yellow and white flowers, ceased whinnying.

For a moment, the only sound that could be heard was the faint swish of leaves. Then the nuns from the Abbaye de Sainte Jeanne raised their voices in song.

Led by Brigitte and Marie-Hélène, the House of Dior's mannequins began to float slowly across Charincourt's lawn. They could not borrow couture gowns for the occasion — naturally, these precious dresses had to remain safely in Paris. Instead, as a result of an inspired suggestion from Madame Carré, each beauty was attired in an enchanting, floor-length creamy toile.

The models took their places on either side of a scalloped white awning. In its shade, Mayor Huppert stood waiting stiffly, wearing an ancient top hat and a scarlet sash. Mother Francis Xavier, in her dove-grey robes, was to his right, her face reflecting its usual serenity.

Philippe stood before the abbess. His charcoal-grey suit was perfectly cut, his silk Charvet tie displayed suitable restraint and, if he wore his dark hair perhaps a shade too long, the mannequins were united in silent agreement — he was unquestionably handsome. For his part, Philippe barely noticed the bridesmaids or the guests. Only one person captured his attention.

'Grace,' he murmured. 'Oh, Grace.'

It is said that every bride looks radiant. All agreed, however, that today the bride was bewitching. The guests gasped as Grace, on the arm of a beaming Reuben, wafted towards them. Her exquisite full-length, white satin gown had a tightly fitted bodice, an off-the-shoulder neckline trimmed with pearls and a gently belled skirt finished with a train. With her black curls drawn back in a loose chignon and a long chiffon veil drifting behind her; with her emerald eyes shining and her full mouth curved into an enchanting smile, there was something other-worldly about her.

'You look divine,' Marie-Hélène whispered as she passed. 'That poor man — he will fall in love with you all over again.'

Grace handed her bouquet to Brigitte, then took her place by Philippe's side.

The nuns' voices were stilled. Monsieur Huppert stepped forward. Suddenly, the quiet solemnity was pierced by a high-pitched squeal. All eyes turned to Serena who, held by her flush-faced grandmother, bestowed a toothless grin upon the crowd and waved her little hands excitedly.

The tension was broken. There was laughter and smiles; even the mayor visibly relaxed. He proceeded to conduct the official French ceremony with unexpected élan before Mother Francis Xavier recited a prayer.

Despite her apparent composure, Grace was dazed, even numb; the day seemed unreal. When she heard Mayor Huppert announce, 'You may now kiss the bride,' it sounded to her as if his words came from somewhere far away.

Only when she felt Philippe's lips on her own did her senses come alive. As she was engulfed by a wave of pleasure, it occurred to her this must be what it felt like when a spell had been broken.

Rendered golden by the mellow summer light, Charincourt's glowing walls provided a striking backdrop to the vibrant throng of people mingling on the adjoining lawn.

'That's unexpected,' Philippe said to Grace as they stood hand in hand in the midst of the crowd. 'As you know, it is rare for the French to seek out the company of those outside their own social strata, yet our wedding guests, who — let's agree — are nothing if not diverse, seem to be positively embracing one another.'

'Perhaps,' Grace remarked with a mischievous grin, 'it has something to do with the fact that the bride is Australian.'

The two looked on with contentment as writers and artists talked animatedly with farmers and shopkeepers; Reuben's friends from Burgundy exchanged views with members of the Paris *bon ton*; Resistance comrades worked their charm on the mannequins; and Philippe's counter-espionage colleagues discovered a new world, thanks to Tutu and Mesdames Raymonde, Carré, Luling and Beguin.

Grace had known not to expect Jacqueline Bouvier, although the Countess de Renty had passed on her present: an engraved silver cocktail shaker she'd sent from Tiffany's.

'Poor Jacqueline,' the countess said. 'She so wanted to be with you but her mother insisted she'd had quite enough of the high life in Paris and refused to allow her to leave.'

Baron Édouard de Gide was also unable to attend. He had explained that, regrettably, his presence in Mexico at a performance of *Aïda* starring that exciting young Greek singer Maria Callas was the reason. Nonetheless, as Ferdinand had pointed out, 'Considering the baron's broken heart, despatching six cases of Cristal shows admirable panache.'

In deference to the summer day, Madame Marly was without her ubiquitous fox, although she made up for it by donning a striking lilac-feathered hat. 'I remember when I first saw you, Grace,' she reminisced, 'in the Hotel Australia when you were just a little girl. I have always been so fond of Reuben; what a feeling for Chopin he has!'

Earlier, Grace had seen Evangeline Bruce and Julia Child arrive in the official US Embassy car, the Stars and Stripes flying gaily from its bonnet. During the previous week, an attaché had hand-delivered a personal message from the ambassador himself, expressing his thanks on behalf of an indebted US Government for the heroic actions taken by Captain Philippe Boyer and Mademoiselle Grace Dubois. The letter mentioned forthcoming medals.

The man had also brought a cut-crystal Baccarat punch bowl, a gift from the grateful ambassador and his wife. Now it contained a modified version of Olive's famous concoction.

'Marie and I decided that peaches and brandy were the perfect substitutes for pineapple and rum,' Olive informed her daughter.

'If it's anything like the original,' Grace said, 'our guests will be dancing on the tables.'

She smiled as she watched the two happy warriors gaze with satisfaction at the long trestle tables displaying the wedding banquet they had masterminded. Guests helped themselves to glistening oysters and poached salmon, roast goose and turkey, dishes of waxy potatoes, green beans and asparagus, and a fine selection of local cheeses.

'You've outdone yourself, Mum,' Grace observed, 'but it's high time you relaxed for a bit and met some of the guests.' Spying Julia Child on her way to the buffet, she seized the opportunity to introduce her mother, then added, 'Mrs Child is learning to master French cuisine.'

'Well then, you're just the person I need,' Olive said. 'Those snails — what do you find is the best way to tackle them?'

'I'm yet to get the hang of it myself,' Mrs Child hooted. 'An *escargot* shot off my plate only the other night when I was dining at the Élysée Palace. My husband was convinced I'd caused a diplomatic incident!'

In the late afternoon a counter was laid out with bowls of raspberries and a large ice bucket filled with whipped cream. Yet before there was time for anyone to touch so much as a berry, Mayor Huppert clapped his hands. At that, three women appeared.

'Mademoiselle Elise!' Grace had been thrilled when she'd learnt her former governess intended making the trip from her home in the Alps where she now ran a select finishing school. Elise smiled as she carried a particularly large and fragrant *tarte tatin* to the table.

Behind her, Grace saw *le patron*'s personal chef, renowned as much for the distinction of being the only cook in Paris dressed by Christian Dior as she was for her outstanding cuisine. Madame Denise held a great platter on which a towering croquembouche shimmered. This pyramid of profiteroles, filled with *crème pâtissière* and drizzled with toffee, prompted Ferdinand to remark, '*Regarde, la pièce de résistance.*'

Only a moment later, however, he appeared to have changed his mind. '*Oh là là là là! C'est magnifique!*' he cried when, held aloft on a silver tray by the bride's triumphant mother, a markedly different creation materialised.

It occurred to Grace that few of her guests would have ever before encountered a traditional, three-tiered wedding cake of the type that Olive had perfected. Covered in gleaming white royal icing, embellished with rosebuds and topped with a miniature bride and groom, its appearance led Ferdinand to declare that this tour de force was the banquet's indisputable highlight.

The feast had been consumed, toasts exchanged and speeches made when Mayor Huppert proclaimed, '*Mesdames et messieurs*, friends one and all, it is my honour to announce the bridal waltz.'

Madame Marly signalled to the violinists. Reuben struck a resonant chord on the grand piano. But the bride and groom had danced no more than a few steps when a large automobile swept into the driveway.

Philippe frowned. Grace was confused. Everyone turned and stared.

A pair of men in black suits carrying briefcases emerged from the limousine. After making their way across the dance floor, they came to a halt in front of the groom.

'Captain Boyer?' the taller and thinner man inquired.

'Yes. Who the devil are you?'

'We are notaries and act with the authorisation of the government of France. I am Monsieur Caron and this is my colleague, Monsieur Bardot. There are important matters to discuss.'

'I remember those two,' Grace said to Philippe. 'They came to the château once before, looking for you.'

'That is quite correct, Madame,' said Caron. 'We have been trying to locate the captain for some time. Recently, it came to our attention that a wedding was to take place at Charincourt.'

Ferdinand was right, Grace thought. *There really are no secrets in Paris.*

'Accordingly,' the man continued, 'we surmised that if this were the case, we might well discover you here.' He gave a self-satisfied nod.

Philippe began to laugh. '*Mon ami*, I'm afraid whatever you want to talk about will have to wait. As you can see, I am tied up at the moment.'

Caron rummaged in his briefcase. 'All the same, I think you will want to hear what we have to say.'

Philippe exchanged a bewildered glance with Grace. 'Out with it then.'

'Captain Boyer, I suggest we retire somewhere a little more private.'

'Monsieur Caron, you don't seem to realise you and your colleague are interrupting my wedding celebrations. What *I* suggest is that you state your business as quickly as possible.'

'As you wish,' Caron said peevishly. 'The matter concerns the will of the late Count d'Andoise. It was lost, you see, and had been for years, but when a rather fine Boule desk recently went up for auction, the document was discovered in the top right-hand drawer.'

'I recall that desk,' Brigitte said, having come to see what the disturbance was about. 'It used to sit in Papa's library.'

'But how does this concern me?' asked Philippe.

Monsieur Bardot spoke for the first time. 'It concerns both you and your cousin. It seems the late count named his daughter' — the man nodded in Brigitte's direction — 'and yourself as his sole heirs.'

Passing papers to Philippe, Caron announced, 'The late count's assets, including Château Charincourt, all the objects within it and the attached land now belong to you and your cousin equally.'

'*What?*'

'In addition,' the notary continued, 'as his closest male relative you will inherit his title. Accordingly, despite the fact France is, of course, a republic, you and Madame Boyer may, if you wish, be known as the Count and Countess d'Andoise.'

'I can just imagine how that will go down around Parkes.' Grace giggled.

'Be that as it may, madame,' Caron said primly, 'there is one other matter we are obliged to bring to the attention of Captain Boyer and his cousin. Something of an irregular codicil has been attached to the will.' He retrieved the appropriate document from Bardot. 'It states that an item of great interest to a certain party lies hidden within Charincourt in a locked piece of furniture notable solely for its complete lack of distinction. A key has been provided, together with another for the château's front door. I can tell you nothing more.'

Amid the general intake of breath, exclamations and shaking of heads, Grace clutched Philippe's arm. 'I have an idea,' she said.

Throwing her satin train over one arm, Grace hitched up her dress and took off for the château, her veil billowing behind. Philippe, muttering about his adorable new wife's impulsive nature, ran after her. Brigitte was next, then

Marie-Helene, followed by a parade of mannequins, nuns in flapping habits, farmers with flying jackets and a posse of wildly excited Parisians. Grace opened Charincourt's great front door and rushed towards the grand reception room. A moment later she was joined by Philippe and then everyone else who had followed him.

'Stand back!' she cried.

Grace went straight to the rickety armoire, noting as she did so that the lock she'd broken previously was still lying where it had fallen. Cautiously, she opened the two doors, then discovered to her relief that the former hideous inhabitants were not in evidence — presumably the rats had heard the commotion outside and scuttled away. Only the piles of gnawed newspapers remained.

'I think whatever we're looking for could be buried somewhere under all that,' she said to Philippe.

'Let me help.' He began hurling armfuls of paper onto the dusty parquetry. But to Grace's dismay, once the armoire had been emptied, there was nothing to be seen.

While their guests exchanged bemused glances, she murmured to him, 'I have a horrible feeling I've just confirmed everything our French friends no doubt already think about the untamed nature of Australians. It looks like I've led everyone on a wild goose chase.'

'I'm not so sure,' Philippe said. 'Sometimes these old armoires have secret compartments; during the war we occasionally used them to conceal messages — even guns. See if any of the panels feel different, whether they have any give.'

Concentrating hard, Grace ran her fingers around the interior. Finally, after several uncomfortably long minutes, she thought she detected a slight movement in the top left-hand corner. On an impulse, she pressed down firmly with one hand, then stared with delight as she saw a section of the rear panel slide smoothly away. There, on what had been a hidden shelf, lay an elongated parcel.

Everyone crowded closer. Grace and Philippe heaved the mysterious package onto the floor, knelt down and began undoing its oilskin cover. Next, amid a growing buzz of excitement, Grace removed a cylinder of cardboard, followed by a thin layer of soft chamois leather. All that remained was a roll of canvas.

She took hold of the exposed corners; Philippe grasped the two he found coiled inside. Then the pair stood up and, facing one another, each took a couple of steps back so that the roll unfurled.

'Blessed Mother of God.' Mother Francis Xavier made the sign of the cross.

The abbess had only just arrived, arm in arm with Madame Guérin. Now, she stared in shock and disbelief.

'It's the Rembrandt,' she said. 'Our own Sainte Jeanne.'

Having complained of feeling temporarily faint, Mother Francis Xavier accepted a glass of the baron's excellent champagne. 'My dear Grace,' she observed as shadows crept across the lawn, 'the nature of the mind, or should I say, soul of a human being, rarely surprises me.'

The abbess took a cautious sip of her drink. 'Yet,' she continued, 'the note enclosed with the painting made it clear that the count was solely responsible for its removal. Not only that, he acknowledged it was owned by the abbey and that he had personally hidden it from the Nazis for safekeeping.'

Slowly she shook her head. 'May God have mercy on my soul,' she said in a tone of regret. 'I did not believe the Count d'Andoise was capable of such goodness.'

'Well, I'm just pleased for Brigitte,' said Grace. 'At least now she knows her father performed one noble act. And, of course, I'm thrilled that Rembrandt's Sainte Jeanne has been returned to its proper home.'

'The sisters are saying it's one of God's miracles,' the abbess observed.

'And what do you think?'

'That He continues to move in mysterious ways.'

Grace was considering this enigmatic response when she felt a hand on her shoulder.

'Would you mind, Mother Francis Xavier, if I stole my bride away?' Philippe asked.

As he led her towards the dance floor, Grace reflected, 'This inheritance — there's so much to think about.'

'True, although I have something a little more immediate on my mind.' Philippe gazed into Grace's eyes. 'All day, the only thing I have wanted to do is to take my desirable wife in my arms. Remember our first waltz, at the Count de Beaumont's? That was interrupted by our little charade and now we have been disturbed yet again. Do you think there is any chance we will be left alone this time?'

'I believe we will,' Grace murmured as Philippe, holding her close, began to sweep her around the floor. 'This time, the stars are aligned.'

CHAPTER FIFTY-FIVE

Paris, February 1951

The salon was crammed with women wearing couture suits and witty hats together with expressions of rapturous approval. As Grace paused, her face luminous beneath a glittering chandelier, she basked in the applause.

This was the moment that meant the most to all Dior's mannequins. For only after the completion of the new collection's first show were they able to ascertain whether they had done justice to *le patron*'s vision.

Wearing a dramatic black velvet sheath with faux-diamond earrings, Grace executed an effortless turn, before gliding back to the *cabine* with the other models.

'Won't you miss all this, darling?' Marie-Hélène said as she slipped out of a red lace cocktail frock. 'You were so thrilled when Madame Raymonde asked you to return.'

'That's true.' Grace handed her own ensemble to a waiting dresser. 'It's just that so much has changed.'

'*Mais oui!* If I had a husband as unusually attractive as yours and an adorable baby, even I might consider leaving.'

'And now there's Charincourt to restore,' added Brigitte. She smoothed cold cream on her face and began removing her make-up. 'You know I couldn't do it without you.'

Grace smiled. 'The fact is, girls, I don't think I'm going to have much choice.'

'But surely Philippe won't prevent you from working.' Marie-Hélène picked up a brush. 'I know men, and he's just not that type.'

'Oh, it's not Philippe I'm worried about. It's Madame Carré. She's a demon for measuring one's waistline.'

Two weeks later, having been toasted with champagne by the mannequins in the *cabine* under the supervision of Tutu and a doleful Ferdinand, Grace left the *maison*. She walked out of the famous front door dressed in the atelier's parting gift, an immensely flattering forest-green coat with a mink collar and cuffs.

As Grace felt the late winter sunshine warm her face, she took a deep breath and looked back. To her surprise, in front of the stone walls stood a line of smiling seamstresses. Madame Carré pushed forward the youngest among them, who shyly presented Grace with a bunch of delicate lilies of the valley.

'With our best wishes, Countess,' the girl said.

Grace gazed up, past the curling fronds of black wrought iron. She tried to peer through the mullioned windows but, as on the day when she'd first arrived, it was impossible to discern what lay inside.

No, there was a movement. A hand emerged; a curtain was pulled back. Grace had tears in her eyes when she saw a portly figure wearing a white smock appear on the balcony. Christian Dior was waving goodbye.

March

A modest yellow flame, having flickered briefly, now sputtered. Grace picked up more wood and tried to build up the fire.

Of late, the weather in Paris had changed from unseasonal mildness to something much wilder. Wrapping a sweater around her shoulders, she gazed distractedly at the wind-whipped Seine. As she watched the river churn beneath an onslaught of steel-coloured rain, it seemed to her that the tumult outside merely echoed her own disquiet.

Serena, who'd been playing with coloured blocks on the floor, began to pull at Grace's hand while looking longingly at the door. *It must be the Australian in her*, Grace thought. *We both hate being cooped up inside.*

She began helping Serena place one block on top of the other — the child liked nothing better than to send a stack flying — but her thoughts were far away.

It was ironic that here she was in Paris, the very place she'd always longed to be, with a life that, after so many difficulties, was more like the conclusion of a fairy tale than reality, and yet all she could think of was going back to Brookfield. In fact, right at this moment, what she most wanted was to leap onto a fast horse and go galloping down to the creek beneath a cloudless cobalt sky.

Grace bit her lip. The awful weather might be making her restless, but it wasn't the source of her turmoil. Eventually, the rain would stop, whereas she would continue to be haunted by the same question that for nearly two years she had asked herself again and again. Who was Serena's father?

Grace had sworn she would never keep such fundamental

knowledge from a child of her own, wouldn't dream of allowing her offspring to live a lie as she had been forced to do. Yet how could she tell Serena, at some time in the future, that Jack *might* be her father? And if she did go ahead, how would Philippe feel about it? Betrayed, most likely.

On the other hand, perhaps Jack had the right to know that Serena could be his daughter.

'What a mess,' Grace said under her breath. Recently, she'd heard from Charlotte that she and Jack now had a little boy. Their baby and Serena could well be brother and sister — one complication seemed to spring up after another.

Grace rubbed her temples. Her tale hadn't finished at all; one final page was yet to be written.

She gave her daughter a red ball and watched as, with a push from a gleeful Serena, it rolled away. Just for a moment, as the sphere spun round and round, it seemed to Grace that the noise of the storm outside had subsided. Instead, she thought she could hear the rustle of gum leaves and a familiar voice whispering that it was time she returned to her land.

At the sound of the front door being slammed, Grace looked up to see her bedraggled husband dripping water on the floor.

'*Il pleut des cordes!*' he said, pushing a lock of wet hair out of his eyes. 'No, you have a much better way of putting it. It is raining dogs and cats.'

'Nearly right, darling. Anyway, throw your things over the bathtub before everything gets saturated. And while you do that, I'll fetch something to warm you up.'

Philippe walked back in, rubbing a towel over his head, then drank some of the Armagnac Grace handed to him.

'That's better.' He smiled, and picked up Serena. Throwing her into the air, he caught her in his arms amid gurgles of pleasure. After a few minutes, she began yawning. '*Ah, mon petit ange*,' he said as he cuddled her. 'It's time for bed.'

'I'll take her,' Grace offered.

'No, it's special for me,' Philippe said.

When he reappeared in the sitting room, it was with a warm smile. 'I now intend to devote my full attention to my daughter's *maman*,' he said. With that, he pulled Grace onto the sofa and gave her a long, lingering kiss.

'Mmm, delicious,' Grace murmured. 'How was your day?'

'Quite good, actually. I rather like being on secondment to the detective squad of the Paris Police. It's much easier to track down jewel thieves than it is to unearth spies. They're less, ah …'

'Two-faced?' As Grace said the words, she felt jolted by a disconcerting resonance.

'Exactly. But what about you? Now that I can see you properly, you seem a little preoccupied. Are you quite well, *chérie*? That illness you had in the mornings hasn't returned?'

'No, nothing like that,' Grace reassured him.

'What then?'

She sighed. 'I miss home. Brookfield, I mean.'

'I see.'

'And I've been thinking …'

'*Oui?*'

'I've been thinking how much it would mean to Olive if I took Serena on a visit to Australia. I know Mum can't wait to show her off to her friends.'

'Is that the only reason you want to go?' he asked.

'Look out of the window!' She laughed. 'Seriously though, you're right. There is something else. I have loose ends that need tying up — you know how complicated my past has been.'

Philippe frowned. 'And when might this trip take place?'

'Well, if I left for Australia in a week, I could stay with my mother for a bit and still be in Paris in plenty of time for this next little one's birth.'

'I would miss you horribly.'

'Oh God, I'd miss you too,' she said, reaching up her hand to stroke her husband's handsome face. 'But I'm convinced it's something I have to do.'

'Then I have no time to lose.'

'What do you mean?'

'I need to show you how much I love you as often as I can before you leave.'

Philippe took the sweater from Grace's shoulders and began to undo her blouse. He kissed her over and over, as if determined to memorise her taste and the feel of her lips on his own.

'I don't want to rush you.' Grace smiled. 'But just in case we're interrupted, I think I should take off your clothes.' Soon both were naked, wrapped in each other's arms in front of the flickering flames.

'Remember the first time we made love?' Philippe said, caressing Grace's swelling breasts and the slight mound of her stomach. 'I didn't think you could be more irresistible, but the way you look now — God, I can't believe how much I want you.'

They made love with a sweet intensity, their intimate knowledge of each other's desires heightening their pleasure. Like a pair of perfectly matched dancers, they moved to the same inner rhythm until, together, they reached a passionate crescendo.

As they lay still, their entwined bodies bathed by the fire's golden light, Philippe said, 'There is only one thing I must ask you to promise.'

'Yes?'

'When these loose ends, as you call them, have been dealt with — come back to me.'

CHAPTER FIFTY-SIX

Sydney, April 1951

The Hotel Australia was exactly as Grace remembered. The same gleaming foyer replete with marble and mirrors, the same exhilaration as new guests swept in and others departed.

'Welcome back, Mrs Boyer — or do you prefer Countess these days?' the manager said, shaking hands. 'I still remember the very first time you stayed with us, although back then I worked at reception and you were a Miss Woods.'

'As time passes, I imagine it becomes increasingly difficult to keep track of who exactly is who,' Grace said breezily. 'So let's keep things simple,' she added with a smile. 'I'm more than happy to be Mrs Boyer, you know.'

Sinking into one of her suite's luxurious armchairs, Grace was struck once more by the reassuring familiarity of her surroundings: the swagged curtains, the plush upholstery, the watercolours on the wall — all still there.

A knock interrupted her musing.

'That will be room service. I hope they don't wake Serena,' Olive said, hurrying towards the door.

When they were sitting at a small table, drinking tea and eating curls of buttered brown bread wrapped around spears of tinned asparagus, Grace noticed her mother's uneasy expression. 'Is something wrong, Mum?'

Olive retrieved a handkerchief from her pocket and began twisting it in her fingers. 'I wasn't sure when I should tell you, especially considering your pregnancy,' she said, 'but I suppose now is as good a time as any.'

Grace reached across the table and touched her mother's hand. 'You're not ... not ill, are you?'

'This isn't to do with me,' her mother said.

'Who then?'

'It's Jack.' Olive folded her handkerchief into a neat square. 'Gracie, there isn't an easy way to say this. He's been killed.'

'No!' Her childhood companion, her former husband, and perhaps Serena's father — dead. Grace's stomach lurched. She thought she might be sick. 'What happened?'

'Heading back to Merindah after ... well, I gather it was after he'd had quite a few drinks in Parkes.' She frowned. 'The police said he swerved suddenly — perhaps there was a kangaroo on the road. It was getting dark, so it would have been hard to see what was ahead. He smashed into a tree. It's such a waste of a young life, and so desperately unfair. When I think of what that boy went through, being shot at in those planes he flew over the Channel ... and now he goes like this.'

Grace tried to speak but found that she couldn't.

'I think you should have more tea,' her mother said.

Still feeling stunned, Grace watched as Olive poured from a china pot. 'Jack's accident,' she said. 'When was it?'

'While you were still on the ship. The funeral took place only three days ago. It was dreadful.' Olive dabbed at her eyes. 'You can imagine the terrible state the Osbournes were in.'

All Grace could think of was Charlotte — her anguish and grief, how alone she must feel. 'Mum, we'll need to check out early tomorrow morning,' she said. 'I have to see Lottie.'

Brookfield

Late the next afternoon, after the long train journey to Parkes and then the dusty run in the car out to Brookfield, Grace was finally able to make a start for Merindah. She went to the stables in search of Bill Gleason.

'So you're back,' he said with a laconic half smile that did nothing to disguise how pleased he was to see Grace again.

'I thought it was about time,' she replied. 'Riding is out for me at the moment — I was wondering if there was a spare set of wheels I could borrow?'

'Still remember how to drive a truck?' Gleason asked, a quizzical look on his leathery face.

Grace grinned. 'More or less.'

'Well, we've just got a new sort from Holden — it's called a ute.' He threw Grace a set of keys. 'Good to see you again, Grace.'

'You too, Bill.'

Grace jolted her way towards Merindah, past the familiar wheat fields and paddocks inhabited by scattered sheep. She'd grown unused to driving, especially on gravel-strewn, unsealed country roads, yet as she wrestled with the rugged terrain, Grace couldn't help thinking about Jack's death and what it might mean.

That it was both a tragedy and an unspeakable loss for Charlotte was self-evident. But Grace was also painfully aware that now Serena would never have the opportunity to set her eyes on — let alone grow to know — the man who might have been her father.

When she arrived at Merindah it was to the familiar shrill sound of the pink and grey galahs as they began roosting in the big eucalypt for the night. After slamming shut the door of the utility, she stood for a moment and looked at the homestead. More than two years of her life had been spent living here, yet she'd never considered it her home. When Grace had left she'd told Jack she was never coming back, but here she was. She hadn't imagined it would be under these circumstances. Grace shook her head. It would have been better for everyone if Jack had married Charlotte in the first place.

There she was now, dearest Lottie, running out of the front door. Still pretty, still blonde, but looking pale and strained. The two women embraced.

'I can't tell you how glad I am that you're here.' Charlotte choked back tears. 'It's been a nightmare.'

The friends walked into the gloomy sitting room. 'I'll put on a light,' Charlotte said, 'and make us some gin and tonics.'

She brought their drinks over and sat next to Grace on the sofa. 'Since Jack …' Her voice trailed away. 'Since the accident, I seem to have done nothing but sit in the dark, thinking. Well, I do get through a few of these,' Charlotte pointed to her glass, 'and I weep.'

'Where is your baby?'

'I can't cope with Michael at the moment.' Her bottom lip trembled. 'Mum's taking care of him, back at Oakhill.'

'To lose Jack like that,' Grace said gently. 'I can't imagine how awful it's been for you. But perhaps it would be better if your mother looked after Michael here at Merindah?'

Charlotte didn't reply.

'I'm sorry, Lottie, I mean when the time is right,' Grace said. 'I just thought it might give you some comfort to have your son near, especially as he's — you know, a part of Jack.'

Charlotte walked across to the drinks tray and topped up her gin and tonic. 'There is something I left out of the letter I sent,' she said. 'It's about Michael.'

Grace looked anxiously at her friend. 'What do you mean?'

'He's not Jack's.'

'You're not telling me there's been —'

'Someone else? No, nothing like that. Jack couldn't have children.' Charlotte shrugged. 'I thought you knew.'

Grace put her untouched glass down so abruptly that its contents splashed the front of her dress, leaving a damp, haphazard pattern. 'He never uttered a word,' she said.

'Remember the crash he had in the war?' Charlotte asked.

'I do.' Grace recalled the jocular letter Jack had sent her afterwards. 'He always passed it off as a great lark.'

'It was serious.'

'He had those scars ...' Grace frowned.

'Yes, he did.' Charlotte took a gulp of her drink before adding, 'It seems that as soon as the doctors in England saw his injuries, they informed him that although everything would still be in what they quaintly termed "working order", he'd never be able to father a child.' She looked at Grace. 'Even though Jack did a test that confirmed the doctors' opinion, he still maintained it was rubbish. Deep down, though, I think all along he knew they were right.'

Grace was overcome. Finally, she had an answer; after all the anguish, the long nights spent wondering, now she knew without doubt that Philippe was Serena's father. If only poor, troubled Jack had been able to share his terrible burden, it would have saved so much torment. If only he'd never kept the truth a secret.

'For a man like Jack, it must have been devastating,' she said. 'Perhaps that's why he had so much anger inside him.'

'Very likely.' Charlotte sighed. 'I only found out because of a chance remark he made, and even then I had to drag it out of him. He said it was humiliating, that he wasn't much better than a gelded animal.'

Grace studied Charlotte's face. 'So you adopted Michael,' she said.

'Yes.'

'And ... will you tell him that?'

'I don't know,' Charlotte said slowly. 'Probably not.'

Grace squeezed her friend's hand. 'I imagine it's not an easy decision to make.'

May 1951

The two women sat next to each other on Brookfield's wide veranda in the same wicker chairs that had been there for years. Serena lay in Grace's lap; she was conscious of the gentle rise and fall of her daughter's small body as she slept.

'Here, give the poppet to me,' Olive said. 'You can't be comfortable in your condition with her sprawled all over you like that.'

The little dark-haired girl barely stirred as Grace settled her in Olive's arms. 'Serena has thrived here in the bush, Mum.'

'Of course she has,' Olive said. 'Remember how she laughed when she first heard the kookaburras? And the way she chased after that goanna!'

Already, as if by alchemy, these small incidents were

being transformed into burnished memories. *Dear Mum*. She was still careful with her appearance. Even now, with her granddaughter lying on top of her, Olive was wearing her new blue and white printed frock from Miss Louise, donned in honour of their last night together.

Grace noticed that Olive had fallen silent. She was gazing past the tendrils of jasmine at some imperceptible point far away in the distance. Grace suspected she was thinking about Alfred. Or perhaps Serena reminded her of the absence of another precious child.

As pink and gold clouds began to stream across the darkening sky, Grace reflected on the knowledge she'd gained since she'd travelled across the world to the City of Light. She was now well versed in the sublime realm of haute couture. As for international politics — she had to admit, she'd had a crash course. She'd been to the opera and fabulous balls, eaten in some of Paris's finest restaurants, met and mingled with the rich, the famous and the infamous.

She had learnt harder lessons: about the complexities of identity; the truths that hid behind secrets and lies; the challenges of making heartbreaking decisions in a world of elusive certainties and infinite grey shades.

Grace had made other discoveries too. That courage could be displayed in many different ways. What it was like to truly love a man. And, most important of all, that one's destiny need not depend on a name, whether it be Wood or Woods, Dubois, Osbourne, Boyer or even — she smiled — the Countess d'Andoise.

Grace looked at her slumbering child. She'd thought that knowing the identity of Serena's father was vital. However, almost as soon as she'd acquired this information, she had begun reconsidering its significance.

Philippe had proved wiser than she. But then he was already aware that being a parent was much more than biology. Now she knew it meant an elegant grazier riding fast with his child across dusty paddocks; a horse trader teaching that same child to play the piano; a countrywoman introducing her to the thrilling world of high fashion and, yes, even demonstrating the proper way to apply royal icing.

Grace recalled the day at Charincourt in the sunny vegetable garden when old Claude had tilted his head and remarked, 'You only have one mother, you know.' Yet that hadn't been true. She'd been luckier than most people.

I have been blessed, she thought, *blessed to be a part of the lives of four rare individuals*. One day, she vowed, when both Serena and her unborn child could understand, she would tell them the story of her life, how it was that she came to have two sets of parents and what their love for her led them to do.

Grace inhaled the sweet sharpness of the gum trees, heard the buzz of insects fade away. As the red ball of the sun began to slip below the horizon, there was just enough light to make out the brilliant colours of the rosellas, wheeling against the vast Australian sky.

AUTHOR'S NOTE

A coincidence is a small miracle

Attributed to Albert Einstein

The Paris Model was inspired by real people and events.

I was sipping tea in the fragrant garden of 'S', a dear friend, when she revealed the heartbreak that shaped the life of her beautiful and spirited mother, Grace Woods. 'S' told me that after simultaneous tragedies, the newborn Grace was given to a wealthy grazier and his wife by their unlikely friend, a rough-and-ready, piano-playing horseman. She explained that just one factor eased the passage of this very private arrangement. Due to an extraordinary coincidence, all that was required was the addition of a single letter to the child's last name.

Immediately captivated, I began to imagine the many ways that these remarkable circumstances might have impacted upon the infant who grew up to be an acclaimed, green-eyed mannequin.

I soon decided that, as Grace, Reuben, Alfred and Olive were real people, I had to use their actual names. However, *The Paris Model* remains a work of fiction. For example, although Grace married a local boy who became a World War II flying ace, he was not Jack Osbourne.

A host of other characters portrayed in the book existed. Likewise, many of the incidents recounted — including even Reuben's desperate attempt to feed his starving baby with an eyedropper — actually took place. These instances are too numerous to list, although readers may be interested to know the following details.

Christian Dior's headline-making New Look was initially shown at David Jones in Sydney on the night of 31 July 1948. Astonishingly, this was the first time the collection had been modelled outside Paris. As quoted, Dior complimented Australians on their 'cleaner, brighter outlook' compared to that of the 'tired' people of Europe. The women I've portrayed in leading roles in his atelier are all real historical characters: Mesdames Raymonde, Carré, Luling, Beguin, Bricard and Tutu (Baronne de Turckheim). The *maison* also employed a distinguished doorman named Ferdinand.

The sheer number of individuals, either already famous or destined to be so, who made their way to Paris during the early post-war period might be thought unbelievable, were it not for the fact that, after being closed to the world during the long years of Nazi Occupation, the city — and its uniquely seductive pleasures — was suddenly available to all.

Unlike London and so many other great European centres, Paris did not suffer from sustained German bombing. During the late 1940s, its undamaged beauty, the devalued franc and — once the Marshall Plan's bounty began flowing — renowned restaurants, bars and cafés created a veritable magnet for returning French citizens and hordes of eager foreign visitors. Artists, writers and philosophers; film stars, playboys and heiresses; British aristocrats and American diplomats — all flocked to Paris. The City of Light was irresistible, and nothing symbolised its extravagant glamour better than a dress from Christian Dior.

Princess Margaret first visited the atelier in 1948, but the strapless ball gown she selected was thought by her parents to be far too daring for their eighteen-year-old daughter. The spectacular white, off-the-shoulder confection Christian Dior later designed for the princess was not worn until her twenty-first birthday. Years afterwards, she described it as 'my favourite dress of all'.

In addition to Princess Margaret, the Duchess of Windsor, the Countess de Ribes, the Viscountess de Noailles, Eva Perón, Pamela Churchill (former daughter-in-law of Britain's famous wartime prime minister) and Rita Hayworth, a multitude of other celebrated women — from prima ballerina Dame Margot Fonteyn to the German-born actress Marlene Dietrich — were enthusiastic Dior clients.

Eva Perón did say, 'My biggest fear in life is to be forgotten.'

The details related by Ferdinand of Rita Hayworth's lavish wedding reception, held after she married Prince Aly Kahn in 1949, reflect contemporary accounts.

In the same year, Jacqueline Bouvier, the future Jackie Kennedy Onassis, stayed with the Countess Germaine de Renty while she studied at the Sorbonne.

Both the Countess de Renty and Christian Dior's sister, Catherine (after whom the fragrance Miss Dior was named), were interned in the notorious Ravensbrück concentration camp as a result of their Resistance activities.

Evangeline Bruce was the young and supremely elegant wife of David Bruce, US Ambassador to France from 1949 to 1952. She was tasked with fabricating personal histories for secret agents during her time in London with the OSS

(Office of Strategic Services), which, as mentioned, was the forerunner of the CIA.

Julia Child, another wartime employee of the OSS, although far better known for her ground-breaking books on French cuisine, lived in Paris with her husband, Paul, a US diplomat, in 1949. This was also the year she began a course at the famous Cordon Bleu cooking school.

Count Étienne de Beaumont was renowned for his fancy-dress balls, some of which have been mentioned. He hosted the first great post-war *fête*, the Ball of the Kings and Queens, in 1949. The identities of a number of guests and descriptions of their costumes have been included.

Coco Chanel attracted considerable opprobrium for consorting with the enemy. Nevertheless, she eventually returned to Paris and, in 1954, aged over seventy, launched a new collection in her rue Cambon premises. Just as Brigitte predicts in the pages of this book, she went on to attract widespread acclaim, her misdemeanours apparently forgotten.

Pablo Picasso was a major financial donor to the French Communist Party. *L'Humanité* reported that he donated one million francs in 1949 alone.

General Charles de Gaulle, fearing that post-war France would become a Soviet republic, stated, 'If France falls, every country in Western Europe will fall too, and all the Continent will be Communist.'

Journalist Malcolm Muggeridge, then a British spy, passed on information regarding Soviet infiltration of the French government as early as 1944. Unfortunately, these concerns were referred to his superior, Kim Philby, who was himself a double agent.

Joseph Stalin personally ordered the elimination of a number of high-profile foreign leaders and anti-communists.

The notorious 13th Department of the KGB, named the Directorate of Special Tasks, was charged with carrying out these assassinations.

The scene in which Grace receives ever-more lavish floral tributes from Giscard Orly was inspired by published rumours claiming that while the fiercely pro-Stalinist politician Maurice Thorez was conducting an affair with Marie Bell of the Comédie-Française, he regularly sent her vast bouquets of flowers at fabulous expense.

The passages concerning the Abbaye de Sainte Jeanne's missing portrait of Joan of Arc were inspired by the fact that a striking Rembrandt painting of an angel was stolen by the Nazis from a French château during World War II. Unlike the abbey's painting, however, this work of art has never been recovered.

It is estimated that immediately after World War II at least 20,000 French women (*les tondues*) suffered the terror and ignominy of having their heads shaved. In addition, they were often stripped naked, beaten, tarred, branded with swastikas and publicly humiliated. Historian Antony Beevor called it 'the equivalent of rape by the victor'.

Passports were not issued to married Australian women by the Federal Government without their husband's written permission until 1983.

Almost all the locations in *The Paris Model* existed. Maxim's, Le Tour d'Argent, Café de Flore, the Lido and the Folies Bergère continue to this day, as does 25 rue Dauphine, although the view from its windows may well be different. Le Chat Noir and La Voiture Folle are based on similar nightclubs popular in late 1940s Paris; Charincourt is an amalgam of a number of châteaux in the Loire Valley; the great sheep and wheat farms of Brookfield, Merindah and Oakhill are also amalgams of similar properties.

The RAAF air base near Parkes did not operate until 1941, a little later than I sent Jack off to undertake his training.

The epigraph at the front of *The Paris Model* quotes Simone de Beauvoir's *The Second Sex*, published in Paris in that landmark year, 1949. In it, the author exhorted women to challenge the myth that their modest and compliant 'essence' was immutable, and to instead throw themselves into lives that were not defined by gender. I don't know whether Grace ever read de Beauvoir's book, although it wouldn't surprise me.

A.J.

ACKNOWLEDGEMENTS

I would like to pay a particular tribute to Grace Woods (1 September 1922 – 27 April 2013). She not only ignited my imagination but also captured my heart.

My publisher, Anna Valdinger, bowled me over with her enthusiasm. I am incredibly grateful for her terrific expertise and unflagging support.

My thanks also go to the HarperCollins team, including all those from editing, design, promotion and sales who worked on *The Paris Model*, with a special shout-out to campaign manager Lucy Inglis and account manager Kerry Armstrong; designer Hazel Lam for creating a stunning cover that truly reflected my dreams; structural editor Nicola O'Shea and copy editor Dianne Blacklock for their scrutiny of the manuscript; and senior editor Scott Forbes for his careful attention to both the text and production.

Special thanks to Fiona Daniels, my eagle-eyed friend and inspiring mentor.

Similarly, the wise counsel of my agent, Catherine Drayton, has been greatly appreciated.

This book would never have been written without the generosity and trust of Sharyn Storrier Lyneham and her family. I am also grateful for the expert advice provided by her husband, Dr Robert Lyneham.

A big hug to my early readers and close companions Susan Williams, Jane de Teliga and Lyndel Harrison, who, together with my gorgeous daughter-in-law Anna Reoch, provided much helpful input and good cheer throughout the writing process.

While researching *The Paris Model* I was fortunate to visit three breathtaking retrospective exhibitions marking the seventieth anniversary of the establishment of the House of Dior: first in Paris in 2017 at the Musée des Arts Décoratifs; later that year at Melbourne's National Gallery of Victoria; and at London's V&A Museum in 2019. You could say that I became an international Dior exhibition groupie!

It would be impossible to list the many books I consulted, but those relied on most heavily included: *Paris After the Liberation* by Antony Beevor and Artemis Cooper; *Les Parisiennes: How the Women of Paris Lived, Loved and Died in the 1940s* by Anne Sebba; *Parisians: An Adventure History of Paris* by Graham Robb; *Dior by Dior: The Autobiography of Christian Dior* by Christian Dior; *Dior in Vogue* by Brigid Keenan; *Christian Dior: The Man Who Made the World Look New* by Marie-France Pochna; *Mes Années Dior: L'esprit d'une époque* by Suzanne Luling, *Christian Dior* by Richard Martin and Harold Koda, *Dressed to Kill: 100 Years of Fashion*, produced by the National Gallery of Australia; *The Musée Christian Dior, Granville*, published by Connaissance des Arts; *Christian Dior: The Magic of Fashion*, published by the Powerhouse Museum; *Jacqueline Kennedy Onassis: A Life Beyond Her Wildest Dreams* by Darwin Porter and Danforth Prince; *Diana Cooper* by Philip Ziegler; *Chanel* by François Baudot; *The World of Coco Chanel: Friends, Fashion, Fame* by Edmonde Charles-Roux; *Châteaux of the Loire Valley* by Alexis Averbuck, Oliver Berry, Jean-Bernard Carillet and Gregor Clark; *In Vogue: Sixty Years of*

Celebrities and Fashion from British Vogue by Georgina Howell; and *The Weekly* by Denis O'Brien.

My family, particularly my wonderful children, Arabella and Bennett, have been endlessly encouraging. Rather like Olive's tutelage of Grace, my own beautiful mother, Sybil, introduced me to the joy of high fashion. The support of my husband Philip and the delight he takes in my work mean the world to me. Believe it or not, it was only when I was well into the creation of this book that I realised I had unconsciously given my irresistible leading man the French version of his name.

Finally, to my readers: thank you for your lovely emails, messages and letters, for attending events, asking fantastic questions and, most especially, for sharing your own stories with me. *The Paris Model* came about because of one of you.

'A mesmerising
storyteller'
The Australian

She never
dreamed she
would become
the story

ALEXANDRA JOEL

When Blaise Hill, a feisty young journalist from one of Sydney's toughest neighbourhoods, is dispatched to London at the dawn of the swinging sixties to report on Princess Margaret's controversial marriage to an unconventional photographer, she is drawn into an elite realm of glamour and intrigue.

As the nation faces an explosive upheaval, Blaise must grapple with a series of shocking scandals at the pinnacle of British society. Yet, haunted by a threat from her past and torn between two very different men, who can she trust in a world of hidden motives and shifting alliances? If she makes the wrong choice, she will lose everything.

Inspired by real events, *The Royal Correspondent* is a compelling story of love and betrayal, family secrets and conspiracy that takes you from the gritty life of a daily newspaper to the opulent splendour of Buckingham Palace.